2363

KILLER DREAMS

ALSO BY IRIS JOHANSEN
available from Random House Large Print

On the Run
Countdown
Blind Alley
Firestorm
Fatal Tide
Dead Aim
No One to Trust
Body of Lies
Final Target
The Delaney Christmas Carol
(with Kay Hooper and Fayrene Preston)

IRIS JOHANSEN

—

KILLER DREAMS

RANDOM HOUSE
LARGE PRINT

Copyright © 2006 by Johansen Publishing LLLP

All rights reserved.
Published in the United States of America by Random House Large Print in association with Bantam Dell, New York.
Distributed by Random House, Inc., New York

Library of Congress Cataloging-in-Publication Data
Johansen, Iris
Killer dreams / by Iris Johansen—1st large print ed.
p. cm
ISBN-13: 978-0-7393-2595-7
ISBN-10: 0-7393-2595-7
1. Women physicians—Fiction. 2. Sleep disorders—Fiction. 3. Conspiracies—Fiction. 4. Billionaires—Fiction. 5. Large type books. 6. Psychological fiction. I. Title
PS3560.O275K497 2006b
813'.54—dc22
2006009931

www.randomlargeprint.com

FIRST LARGE PRINT EDITION

10 9 8 7 6 5 4 3 2 1

This Large Print edition published in accord with the standards of the N.A.V.H.

KILLER DREAMS

PROLOGUE

I told you this was a great place." Corbin Dunston beamed with pride as he held up the trout he'd just reeled in. "Look at this beauty. It must weigh three pounds."

"Amazing." Sophie grinned as she got to her feet. "Now may we go back to the restaurant and get some lunch, Dad? Michael and Mom are waiting for us."

"Michael should have come with us instead of hanging out in the restaurant. A boy should have his time in the sun. Besides, I wanted to show off for him. It's a grandfather's privilege."

"Next time. I told you he had a cold. I didn't want to chance him getting chilled out here on the pier."

"It wouldn't have hurt him. Michael's not a namby-pamby. He's a tough little rascal."

"He's only eight years old, Dad. Let me pamper him for a little while longer. And it gives Mom a chance to have him to herself for a while. You and he have enough man-to-man time."

"I guess you're right. And it will keep her from spending all day making client calls. She might as well be in the office." Her father threw the fish into the basket, got to his feet, and stretched before starting up the pier. "Yeah, I suppose it's better. In between playing with Michael, she'll get to chat with all the waitresses in the restaurant and make a few calls to keep her from feeling guilty." He shrugged. "I told her she should retire like me, but she said she'd go nuts." He shook his head. "You must have inherited your type-A personality from her. You'd both be better off if you just relaxed and enjoyed life."

"I do enjoy life. I just don't enjoy fishing. I wish you'd stop trying to convert me. You've been dragging me to lakes since I was six years old."

"And you've let me." Her father clapped her on the shoulder. "And most of the time you don't even complain. I know you think I wanted a boy and maybe you're right. But no one could have been a better companion to me than you've been through the years. Thanks, Sophie."

She cleared her throat to rid it of tightness. "I'm complaining now. You caught me in the middle of a megabig project." She smiled. "You should understand. If I remember correctly, you've been pretty stressed yourself on occasion."

"Past history." Corbin gazed out at the lake. "Lord, look at that sunset. Isn't that beautiful?"

"Beautiful," Sophie agreed.

"And worth coming out here and leaving your precious project behind?"

"No." She smiled. "But you're worth it."

"That's a start." Corbin chuckled. "And you're right. I am worth it. I'm witty and clever and I've found the secret of life. Why wouldn't you want to hang out with me?"

"No reason at all," Sophie said, gazing at him. Corbin's cheeks were flushed with sun and his tall, muscular frame was that of a much younger man than his sixty-eight years. And God, he looked happy, Sophie thought. No tension, no sign of tiredness. "That's why I dropped everything and came running." She paused. "I've missed you. I meant to come down last month, but time got away from me."

"It always does. That's why I got out of the rat race five years ago. People are more important than projects. Every day should be an adventure, not a treadmill." He sighed and reluctantly glanced away from the setting sun. "Your mother and I are going on a cruise to the Bahamas next month. I want you and Michael to come with us."

"I can't do—" She stopped as she met Corbin's eyes. What the hell? She could work harder and clear her desk. Her father and mother weren't getting any younger and Corbin was right. People were more important than projects, particularly these people she loved. "How long?"

"Two weeks."

"No fishing?"

"Maybe a **little** deep-sea fishing. I've never taken Michael deep-sea fishing before."

Sophie sighed. "As long as you don't mind Mom and me drinking margaritas and lazing on deck while the two of you do your thing."

"I don't mind." Corbin paused. "Bring Dave if he can make it. He needs a break too."

"I'll ask him. But he has a big civil suit going on right now and he's working around the clock. It means a big fat fee for him."

"Another workaholic." He grimaced. "I don't know how the two of you even had time to conceive Michael."

She grinned. "There are always lunch hours."

"It wouldn't surprise me." His pace quickened. "There's your mother and Michael. I can't wait to tell him about the cruise." He waved at Mary Dunston and Michael, who'd just come out of the restaurant and were waving at them. "She'll be happy as a clam you're coming with us. She bet me I wouldn't be able to persuade you." He made a face. "If I didn't get you to go, I promised I'd go to one of those spas with her. She wants to lose a few pounds."

"She doesn't need it."

"I know. She's gorgeous." Corbin's face softened as he gazed at his wife. "The older she gets the better she looks. I tell her that I don't know why I fell in love with her when she was twenty. All that smooth skin with no character lines and not even a hint of wisdom in her eyes. She tells me to quit bullshitting her. I'm not bullshitting her, Sophie."

"I know you're not." The love between her mother and father had been a fact of life to her all the years of her childhood. "She knows it too."

Michael was running toward them. "Grandpa, can we stop at the arcade on the way home?

I want to show you the new video game I found."

"I don't see why not. If there's time after dinner."

"It's about time you got here." Mary Dunston caught up with Michael. "I'm starved, Corbin. Did you catch anything?"

"Of course I did," Corbin said. "Two gigantic trout."

"Semi-gigantic," Sophie corrected.

"Okay." Corbin shrugged. "But definitely sizable. Finish up your calls, Mary?"

She nodded. "I may get that listing in Palmaire." She gave him a quick kiss. "Now let's get some food."

"Right away." He opened his fishing basket.

"I don't want to see your blasted fish," Mary said. "I'll take your word for it. Stupendous. Gigantic."

He reached into the basket. "No, I'm not showing you the fish, Mary."

He pulled out a .38 revolver and shot her in the head.

"Dad?" Sophie stared in disbelief as her mother's skull exploded. No, it had to be some kind of elaborate practical joke. It couldn't be—

It wasn't a joke. Her mother was falling to the ground.

Corbin turned, pointed the gun at Michael.

"No!" Sophie rushed between them as her father pressed the trigger.

Tearing pain in her chest.

Michael screaming.

Darkness.

1

Two years later
Fentway University Hospital
Baltimore, Maryland

Whats going on? You're not supposed to be here."

Sophie Dunston looked up from the chart to see Kathy VanBoskirk, the head night nurse, standing in the doorway. "An overnight apnea study."

"You worked all day and now you're monitoring an overnighter?" Kathy came into the room and glanced at the bed on the other side of the double glass panel. "Ah, an infant. The light dawns."

"Not so much an infant any longer. Elspeth's

fourteen months," Sophie said. "She'd stopped having incidents three months ago and now they're back. She just stops breathing in the middle of the night and her doctor can't find any reason for it. Her mother is worried sick."

"Then where is she?"

"She works nights."

"So do you. Days **and** nights." Kathy gazed at the sleeping baby. "Lord, she's beautiful. Makes my biological clock start ticking. My kid is fifteen now and there's nothing lovable about him. I'm hoping he'll turn back into a human being in another six years. Think I have a chance?"

"Don is just your typical teenager. He'll get there." Sophie rubbed her eyes. They felt as if they had sand in them. It was almost five and the sleep study would be over soon. Then she'd run the errand that was on the top of her list before getting to bed and grabbing a few hours of shut-eye before she had to get back for her first one o'clock session with the Cartwright child. "And he offered to clean my car last week when you had him at the office."

"He probably wanted a chance to swipe it." Kathy grimaced. "Or maybe he wanted the chance to score with an older woman. He thinks you're cool-looking."

"Yeah, sure." Right now, Sophie felt older than her years, frumpy, and ugly as sin. She turned back the chart and checked Elspeth's case history. She'd had an apnea episode about 1:00 A.M. and nothing since. There might be something there that would help her pin down—

"There's a message for you at the nurses' station," Kathy said.

Sophie stiffened. "Home?"

Kathy quickly shook her head. "No. God, I'm sorry. I didn't mean to panic you. I didn't think. The message came in during the shift change at seven and they forgot to give it to you." She paused. "How is Michael?"

"Sometimes terrible. Sometimes okay." She tried to smile. "But all the time wonderful."

Kathy nodded. "Yes, he is."

"But in five years I'll probably be pulling my hair out like you're doing." She changed the subject. "So who left the message?"

"It's from Gerald Kennett again. Aren't you going to call him back?"

"No." She checked Elspeth's meds. Allergies?

"Sophie, it wouldn't hurt to talk to him. He offered you a job that will pay you more in a month than you make in a year here at the university. And he might even up the salary since he keeps after you. I'd jump at it."

"Then you call him back. I like my work here and the people I work with. I don't want to have to answer to any pharmaceutical company."

"You worked for one before."

"When I first got out of medical school. It was a big mistake. I thought they'd free me up to do research full time. It didn't happen. I'm better off doing the research in my spare time." She circled one of the medications on Elspeth's chart. "And I learned more dealing with people here than I'd ever learn in a lab."

"Like Elspeth." Kathy's gaze was on the baby. "She's stirring."

"Yes, she's been in NREM for the last five minutes. She's almost there." She put down the chart and headed for the adjoining door to the test room. "I've got to get in there and remove those wires before she's fully awake. She'll be scared if she wakes up alone."

"When's her mother supposed to get here?"

"Six."

"Against the rules. Parents are to pick up their children promptly at the end of the session and this one ends at five-thirty."

"Screw the rules. At least she cares enough

about the kid to have the tests. I don't mind staying."

"I know," Kathy said. "You're the one who's going to have the night terrors if you don't stop exhausting yourself."

Sophie made the sign to ward off demons. "Don't even talk about it. Send Elspeth's mom in as soon as she gets here, will you?"

Kathy chuckled. "Scared you."

"Yes, you did. There's nothing scarier than night terrors. Believe me, I know." She went into Elspeth's room and went over to the crib. It took only a few minutes to remove the wires. The little girl had dark hair like her mother and her skin was a silky olive now flushed with sleep. Sophie felt a familiar melting as she gazed at her. "Elspeth," she called softly. "Come back to us, sweetheart. You won't be sorry. We'll talk and I'll read you a story and we'll wait for your mama. . . ."

She should get back to work, Kathy thought as she looked through the glass at Elspeth and Sophie. Sophie had picked the baby up, wrapped her in a blanket, and was sitting down in the rocking chair with the baby on her lap. She was talking and rocking the child and her expression was soft and glowing and loving.

Kathy had heard other doctors describe Sophie as brilliant and intuitive. She had a double doctorate in medicine and chemistry and was one of the best sleep therapists in the country. But Kathy liked this Sophie best. The one who effortlessly seemed to be able to reach out and touch her patients. Even Kathy's son had responded to that warmth the one time he'd met her. And Don was definitely a hard sell. Of course, the fact that Sophie was blond, tall, and slim and bore a vague resemblance to Kate Hudson probably had a lot to do with her son's admiration. He wasn't into the maternal types. Unless Madonna was the one on the album covers.

But Sophie didn't look like Madonna any more than she did the statue of the Holy Virgin. In this moment she was very human and full of love.

And strength. Sophie would have had to be strong to be able to endure the hell she had gone through in the last few years. She deserved a break. Kathy wished she'd take the Kennett job, scoop up the big bucks, and forget about responsibility.

Then she shook her head as she glanced at Sophie's expression again. Sophie couldn't shun responsibility, not with this baby, and not with Michael. It wasn't in her nature.

Hell, maybe Sophie was right. Maybe the money wasn't as important as the payback she was getting in there with that kid.

"Bye, Kathy." Sophie waved as she headed for the elevator. "See you."

"Not if you have any sense. I'm on night duty all this month. Did you find any cause for the increase in apnea?"

"I'm changing one of the meds. It's mostly trial and error at Elspeth's age." She stepped inside the elevator as the doors opened. "We just have to monitor her until she grows out of it."

She leaned back against the wall of the elevator as the doors shut and closed her eyes. She was too tired. She should go home and forget about Sanborne.

Stop being a coward. She wasn't going home yet.

A few minutes later she was unlocking the door of the van. She avoided looking at the gun case with the Springfield rifle in the back of the Toyota. She'd checked it earlier to make sure it was in order. Not that she really had to do it. Jock always took care of the weapons and he wouldn't let her go with a faulty rifle. He was too much the professional.

She wished she could say the same for herself. She'd blocked the thought of Sanborne all night but she was trembling now. She leaned her head on the steering wheel for a few minutes. Get over it. It was natural that she'd feel like this. Taking a life was a terrible thing. Even vermin like Sanborne.

She drew a deep breath, raised her head, and started the van.

Sanborne would be arriving at the facility at 7:00 A.M.

She had to be there waiting for him.

Run.

She heard a shout behind her.

She skidded down the slope of the hill, fell, picked herself up, and flew down the bank of the creek.

A bullet whistled by her head.

"Stop!"

Run. Keep on running.

She could hear a crashing in the brush at the top of the hill.

How many were there?

Duck into the bushes. The van was parked on the road a quarter of a mile from here. She had to lose them before she reached the van.

The branches were whipping her face as she tore through the shrubbery.

She couldn't hear them anymore.

Yes, she could. But they sounded farther away. Maybe they'd gone in another direction.

She'd reached the van.

She jumped in the driver's seat and threw the rifle into the back before she peeled out onto the road.

Her foot stomped on the accelerator.

Get away. It could still be okay. If they hadn't gotten a good look at her.

If they weren't close enough to put a bullet through her head. . . .

Michael was screaming when Sophie came into the house an hour later.

Shit. Shit. Shit.

She threw her bag down and raced along the hall.

"It's okay." Jock Gavin looked up when she ran into the room. "I woke him as soon as the sensor went off. He didn't get much of it."

"Enough."

Michael was sitting up, panting, his thin chest heaving. She flew over to the bed and gathered him into her arms. "It's okay, baby.

It's over," she whispered. She rocked him back and forth. "It's all gone."

Michael's arms tightened desperately around her for an instant before he pushed her away. "I know it's okay," he said gruffly. He drew a deep breath. "I wish you wouldn't treat me like a kid, Mom. It makes me feel weird."

"Sorry." Every time she swore to herself that she wouldn't act this emotional, but she'd been caught off guard. She cleared her throat. "I'll watch it." She smiled shakily. "But some people would think you were a kid. Imagine that."

"I'll go make you some breakfast, Michael," Jock said as he headed for the door. "Get a move on. It's seven-thirty."

"Yeah." Michael got out of bed. "Cripes, I've got to get ready for school. I'll be late for the bus."

"No hurry. I can drive you if you miss it."

"Nah, you're tired. I'll make it." He looked back over his shoulder. "How's that little baby?"

"One episode. I think it's one of the meds she's on. I'm going to try to substitute."

"Great." He disappeared into the bathroom.

And when he closed that door, he was probably leaning against the sink and giving himself a minute to fight the nausea the terror brought.

She had taught him how to do that but lately he was closing her out of the process. Perfectly natural reaction and there was no reason for her to feel hurt. Michael was ten and growing up. She was lucky they were still as close as they were.

"Mom." Michael had stuck his head out of the bathroom, a grin lighting his thin face. "I lied. It doesn't really make me feel weird. I just thought maybe it should."

He was gone again.

Warmth and overpowering love poured through her as she headed for the kitchen.

"Nice kid." Jock was standing at the counter. "Guts too."

She nodded. "Oh, yes. Any other episodes last night?"

"Not according to your instruments. No significant increase in heart rate until just a few minutes ago." Jock turned away. "Tell Michael that I made him toast and orange juice. I've got to go make a phone call. It's time I checked in with MacDuff."

She smiled. "The first time I heard you say that I thought MacDuff was your parole officer instead of a Scottish Laird."

"In a way he is." His eyes were twinkling. "If I didn't check in every now and then, he'd be on my tail to make sure I was doing what I was supposed to be doing. We have an agreement."

"Because you grew up in a village on his estate doesn't mean that he has any right to tell you what to do."

"He thinks it does. He grew up being very responsible and possessive about everyone in our village. He considers us all his family." He smiled. "And sometimes I still think so too. He's also my friend and it's hard to tell a friend to go to hell." His smile faded as he looked at her. "You have a scratch on your cheek."

She kept her hand from flying to her face. She'd cleaned up at a gas station but there was no way to hide the scratch. She should have known Jock would notice. He noticed everything. "It's nothing."

His eyes were narrowed on her face. "I expected you an hour ago. Where were you?"

She didn't answer directly. "You could have reached me if there had been a problem with Michael."

"Where were you?" he repeated. "The facility?"

She wouldn't lie to him. She nodded jerkily. "He didn't come. He's shown up by seven on Tuesdays for the last three weeks. I don't know why he didn't come today." Her hands clenched into fists at her sides. "Dammit, I was ready, Jock. I was going to do it."

"You'll never be ready."

"You taught me. I'm ready."

"You may kill him, but it will still tear you apart."

"Killing didn't tear you apart."

He made a face. "You should have seen me a few years ago. I was a basket case."

"All the more reason to kill Sanborne," Sophie said. "He shouldn't be allowed to live."

"I agree. But you shouldn't be the one to do it." He paused. "You have Michael. He needs you."

"I know that. And I've made arrangements with Michael's father to take care of him if necessary. He loves him but he couldn't take it during that first year. But Michael's much better now."

"He needs **you**."

"Shut up, Jock. How can I . . ." She rubbed her aching temple and whispered, "It's my fault. They're still doing it. How can I let them go on?"

"MacDuff knows a lot of important people. I could ask him to call someone with your government."

"You know I tried that. I called everyone I knew. They patted me on the head and told me that I was understandably hysterical. That Sanborne was a respected businessman and there was no proof he was the monster I said he was." Her lips twisted. "By the time I got to the fifth bureaucratic bastard of a senator, I **was** hysterical. I couldn't believe they wouldn't believe me. Yes, I could. Payoffs. All the way up the line." She wearily shook her head. "Your MacDuff would run into the same wall. No, it has to be this way." Her lips tightened. "And you're wrong, it wouldn't tear me apart. I wouldn't let Sanborne hurt me any more than he's done already."

"Then let me kill him for you. That's a much better solution."

Jock's tone was casual, almost without expression, she thought. "Because it wouldn't bother you? That's a lie. It would bother you. You're not that callous."

"Aren't I? Do you know how many kills I've done?"

"No, and you don't know either. That's why you've helped me." She pressed the start on the coffeemaker and leaned against the counter. "One of the guards saw me. Maybe more than one guard. I'm not sure."

He stiffened. "That's bad. Were you caught on the video camera?"

She shook her head. "And I was wearing a

coat and my hair was tucked under a cap. I'm sure no one saw me until I started to leave, and then only for a minute. It could still be okay."

He shook his head.

"Yes, it **will**. I'll make it work. No one's going to call the police. Sanborne doesn't want to call attention to anything out of the ordinary at the facility."

"But they'll be on the alert now."

She couldn't deny that. "I'll be careful."

Jock shook his head. "I can't allow it," he said gently. "Maybe MacDuff has infected me with his sense of responsibility. I killed my personal demon years ago, but I pointed you in the right direction to get Sanborne. You might never have found him if I hadn't led you to him."

"I'd have found him. It would have just taken me longer. Sanborne Pharmaceutical has facilities all over the world. I would have checked every one of them."

"And it had taken you eighteen months to get that far."

"I couldn't believe it. Or maybe I couldn't accept it. It was too ugly."

"Life can be ugly. People can be ugly."

But Jock wasn't ugly, she thought as she gazed at him. He was perhaps the most beautiful human being she had ever seen. He was slender, in his early twenties with fair hair and features that were completely remarkable. There was nothing effeminate about him, he was totally masculine and yet that face was . . . beautiful. There was no other way to describe it.

"Why are you looking at me?" Jock asked.

"You wouldn't want to know. It would offend that manly Scottish pride of yours." She poured herself a cup of coffee. "I had a patient last night whose name was Elspeth. That's Scottish too, isn't it?"

He nodded. "And did she do well?"

"I think so. I hope so. She's a sweet little girl."

"And you're a good woman." He paused. "Who's trying to avoid an argument by changing the subject."

"I'm not arguing. This is my battle. I pulled you into it to help me, but I'm not going to let you run any risk or accept any guilt."

"Guilt? Lord, if you'd thought it through, you'd realize how silly that is. My soul must be as black as hell's own cauldron by now."

She shook her head. "No, Jock." She bit her lower lip. Damn, she didn't want to say this. "I appreciate all you've done, but maybe it's time you left me."

"That's not going to happen. We'll talk later. Good day, Sophie." Jock was heading for the door. "I promised to pick up Michael from his soccer game this afternoon so you don't have to bother if you're tied up. Get to bed and try to sleep. You told me you had a one o'clock appointment."

"Jock."

He glanced over his shoulder and smiled. "It's too late to try to rid yourself of me. I can't have you killed. I'm being entirely self-ish. I have too few friends in this world. I seem to have lost the knack. It would hurt me to lose you."

The door slammed behind him.

Dammit, she didn't need this reaction from Jock. She should have kept her mouth shut about being seen. She knew how protective he could be. He'd kept arguing with her about letting him do the kill but when she'd refused he'd set about teaching her the safest and best way to do what had to be done. He'd stayed by her during these months to oversee and pro-tect and to be there in case she changed her mind. She should have sent him away after he'd taught her what she needed to know. He'd said he was being selfish, but she was the one who'd been selfish. Having him here to keep an eye on Michael when she had to work late had been a blessing in itself. She'd felt terribly alone and Jock had been a comfort. But she had to force him to go now.

"I've got five minutes." Michael came tearing into the kitchen. He grabbed the orange juice and downed it. "No time for breakfast." He grabbed his book bag and headed for the door. He gave her a quick peck on the cheek as he passed. "I won't be home until six. Soccer."

"I know. Jock told me." She gave him a hug. "I'll see you at the game."

His face lit up. "You can make it?"

"I'll be late, but I'll be there."

He smiled. "Great." He started to leave and then stopped. "Quit worrying, Mom. I'm okay. We've got this licked. It only happened three times this week."

Three times when his heartbeat tripled and he woke screaming. Three times when he could have died if she hadn't had a monitor on him. Yet he was trying to keep her from fretting. She forced a smile. "I know. You're right. You're on the uphill path. What can I say? I'm a worrywart. It goes with the territory." She pushed him toward the door. "Take a protein bar since you don't have time to eat your breakfast."

He grabbed the bar and was gone.

She hoped he'd remember to eat it. He was

too thin. After the terrors he had trouble keeping food down, yet he insisted on being involved in soccer and track. It was probably good for him to be busy and she wanted desperately for him to have as normal a life as possible. But there was no question the sports had helped to melt the pounds off him.

Her cell phone rang.

She stiffened as she checked the ID. Dave Edmunds. Jesus, she didn't need to deal with her ex-husband now. "Hello, Dave."

"I hoped I'd catch you before you went to work." He paused. "Jean and I are catching a flight to Detroit Saturday night, so I'll have to bring Michael back early. Is that okay?"

"No. But I guess it has to be." Her hand tightened on the phone. "Christ, it's the first time you've had Michael for a weekend in six months. Do you think he's not going to know why you won't have him overnight? He's not stupid."

"Of course not." He paused. "It's those damn wires, Sophie. I'm afraid of doing something wrong. He's better off with you."

"Yes, he is. But I showed you how to connect the monitor. It's simple. Just the index-finger pulse-ox and the backup chest band. Michael does it himself now. You just have to check the monitor to make sure it's working properly. You're his father and I won't have him cheated. For God's sake, he doesn't have the plague. He's wounded."

"I know that," Dave said. "I'm working on it. It scares the hell out of me, Sophie."

"Then get over it. He needs you." She hung up, blinking to suppress the stinging tears. She'd hoped Dave was making an adjustment at last but it didn't look promising. The safe haven she'd set up for Michael with his father was disintegrating before her eyes. She'd have to think of something else, make other plans. Before that hideous day she'd thought their marriage could make it, although they were having a few problems. She'd been wrong. It hadn't been strong enough to survive more than six months after she'd gotten out of the hospital.

But, dammit, he **had** to be there for Michael if he needed him. He had to be.

Keep calm. She couldn't do anything right now. She'd find a way to protect Michael. Go to bed. Go to sleep. Then go back to the hospital where she could keep herself busy doing what she'd been trained to do.

Help people, instead of planning to kill them.

"I'm asking you to release me from my promise," Jock Gavin said when MacDuff picked up the phone. "I may have to kill a man." He waited, listening to the Laird cursing on the other end of the line. When he stopped, Jock said, "He's a very bad man. He deserves to die."

"Not by your hand, dammit. That's all over for you."

It could never be over, Jock thought. He knew that even if the Laird did not. But Mac-Duff wanted it so badly that he was willing it so. "Sophie is going to kill Sanborne, if I don't. I can't let her do it. She's been hurt too much already. Even if she doesn't get caught, it will scar her."

"She'll probably back down. You said she didn't have the killer instinct."

"But now she has the skill. I've given it to her. And along with the skill, she has the hatred and a sense of doing the wrong thing for the right reason. That will push her over the edge."

"Then let her do it. Get out of there."

"I can't do that. I have to help her."

MacDuff was silent for a moment. "Why? What do you feel for her, Jock?"

Jock chuckled. "Don't worry. Not sex. And, God knows, not love. Well, maybe love. Friendship is love too. I like her and the boy. I feel a bond because of what she's suffered. What she's still suffering."

"That's enough for me to worry about if it's making you take up old habits. I want you to come back to MacDuff's Run."

"No. Release me from my promise."

"The hell I will. I've left you on your own to find your way for a long time. It was damn hard for me. The only thing I asked was that you keep in contact and that there would be no more killings."

"And there haven't been."

"Until now."

"It hasn't happened . . . yet."

"Jock, don't you—" MacDuff stopped and drew a deep breath. "Let me think." There were a few minutes of silence and Jock could almost hear the Laird's mind clicking, turning over the possibilities. "What would make you come back to the Run?"

"I don't want her to kill Sanborne."

"Can we get the FBI or a government agency on it?"

"She said she'd tried. She thinks there's a payoff."

"It's possible. Sanborne's got almost as much money as Bill Gates and that potential could be pretty dazzling to most politicians. What about the media?"

"Sophie was in a mental hospital for three months with a nervous breakdown after the killings. That was one of the reasons she couldn't get anyone to listen to her."

"Shit."

"Release me from my promise," he repeated patiently.

"Forget it," MacDuff said curtly. "You don't want her to kill Sanborne? Then we'll throw someone else into the mix who will do the job for her."

"If she won't let me, she won't let anyone else either. She said she feels responsible."

"Who's going to tell her? We'll just get rid of the bastard."

Jock chuckled. "So much for preventing homicide. You're beginning to sound like me, MacDuff."

"I don't mind stepping on a cockroach. I just don't want you doing it. What about pulling Royd into the picture?"

Jock went still. "Royd?"

"You told me that he was on the hunt. Is there any doubt that Royd will take over and follow through if he gets the chance?"

"No doubt at all. He's a powerhouse. I'd only have to worry about him stampeding over Sophie."

"And that would be a good thing if it kept her safe."

"Sophie wouldn't think so," Jock said dryly. "And she'd only get up and track him down like she did me."

"Call Royd, and then come home."

"No."

Silence. "Please."

"I don't want—" He sighed. A promise was a promise and he owed MacDuff more than he could pay in a millennium. "I'll think about it. It may take me a little while to locate him. For all I know Royd may be dead. The last I heard he was somewhere in Colombia. I'll try to reach him."

"If you need help, let me know. Get him there and get on that plane. I'll meet you in Aberdeen." He hung up.

Jock slowly pressed the disconnect. Mac-Duff's response was not unexpected but he was still disappointed. He wanted to end Sophie's torment in the quickest and most efficient manner and there was no one more efficient than he was at the task she'd set herself.

Except perhaps Royd.

As he'd told MacDuff, Royd was a powerhouse in every sense of the word. He'd had MacDuff investigate Royd's background when the man had contacted him a year ago. He seemed to be filled with passion and bitterness, but Jock had lived with lies and deception too long and was not going to chance being used again. Royd was smart, ruthless, and managed to pull off operations that were difficult, if not impossible.

And he had cause for the passion and bitterness he'd shown Jock. There was little doubt that he would focus single-mindedly on Sanborne and REM-4 once he knew where the facility was located.

But, dammit, Jock didn't like the idea of not being around to monitor Royd's actions. He **liked** Sophie Dunston and Michael, and gentle emotion of any kind was rare and precious in his life. He'd had to learn how to respond again and that knowledge was something to be treasured and protected.

He smiled without mirth at that last thought. It was bizarre to be dwelling on gentleness when he was fighting to commit the most horrendous of sins in the name of kindness.

And it might still come to that if Royd had lost interest in the hunt.

Not bloody likely.

2

"Could it be her?" Robert Sanborne asked as he looked up from the report on his desk.

"Sophie Dunston?" Gerald Kennett shrugged. "I suppose it could be her. You read the security guard's report. He only got a glimpse of the intruder. Sex unknown. Medium height, slim, brown jacket, tweed cap, and carrying a rifle. I guess there might be footprints. Should I pull some strings and get the police to send a forensics crew to check it out?"

"What an idiotic question. We can't have police anywhere near the facility. Send some of our men to look around."

Gerald tried to keep Sanborne from seeing

how the contempt in his voice stung. The more he came into contact with Sanborne the more the man irritated him. The son of a bitch had a God complex and was only diplomatic with the people he had to be. Well, let him think Gerald was his inferior. He would take Sanborne for everything he could and then walk away. "You actually believe she'd try to shoot you?"

"Hell, yes." Sanborne looked back down at the report. "If she can't get me any other way. I've been expecting her to make a move since Senator Tipton refused to listen to her. She's a desperate woman."

"So what are you going to do?" Gerald added quickly, "I didn't come on board to become involved in anything violent. I just agreed to bring her to you if she agreed to a meeting with me."

"Why, Gerald, it's Sophie Dunston who's becoming violent," Sanborne said silkily. "But what can you expect when you consider her unstable background. One should feel sorry for the poor woman. She has such burdens to bear that she must often feel suicidal."

Gerald gazed at him warily. "Suicidal?"

"I'm sure that her coworkers would testify that she was under a strain. Her poor son, you know."

"What are you saying?"

"I'm saying that it's time to rid myself of that bitch. I've been biding my time because it would be too suspicious since she's been so vocal among the FBI and political circles. And I thought I might be able to get some information I needed from her." He tapped the report. "But this is making me uneasy. I may have to adjust my plans. The crazy woman might get lucky if those idiot security guards aren't more efficient. I didn't get this far marketing the project to have Sophie Dunston try to blow me out of the water."

Gerald raised his brows. "I can see how it would be a serious inconvenience."

Sanborne's eyes narrowed. "Sarcasm, Gerald?"

"No, of course not," Gerald said quickly. "I just don't know how—"

"Of course you don't. You're out of your depth here. You're hoping to skim the profit off our deal and keep your hands from getting dirty," Sanborne said. "But I'd bet you wouldn't mind looking the other way while Caprio got his hands dirty."

Caprio. Gerald had only met the man once since he'd started to work for Sanborne, but the mention was enough to cause him to instinctively stiffen warily. He imagined that ripple of uneasiness was the reaction most people felt for Caprio. "Perhaps."

"Caprio doesn't mind a little dirt. He enjoys it." Sanborne added, "And you're already dirty. You embezzled over five hundred thousand dollars from your company and your ass would be in jail by now if I hadn't given you the money to replace it."

"I would have found the money."

"In your Christmas stocking?"

"I have contacts." He moistened his lips. "I wasn't afraid of being caught. I came to you because you offered me a deal I couldn't refuse."

"The deal is still on the table. I might even sweeten it if you prove your value to me by delivering Sophie Dunston in the next week. In the meantime I'll make a few moves of my own." He reached for the telephone and dialed. "Lawrence, things are heating up. We may have to move fast." He paused. "Tell Caprio I need to see him."

Chains cutting into his shoulders.
   Had to move. Had to get free.
   Oh, God.
   Blood!
   Royd jerked upright in bed, his eyes flying

open. His heart was pounding and he was coated with sweat.

He shook his head to clear it and swung his feet to the floor. Just another bitchin' nightmare. Block it out. It wouldn't bring Todd back it only filled him with anger and frustration.

He stood up, grabbed his canteen, and left his tent. He dumped the water on his face and took a deep breath. It was almost morning and time to go after Fredericks. If the rebels hadn't decided to make an example of him and already blown his head off.

He hoped to God they hadn't. From what he'd heard from Soldono, his contact with the CIA, Fredericks was a pretty decent guy for a CEO. Which didn't mean shit in this world. Power was the name of the game and nice guys did finish last if they didn't have the muscle to protect themselves. Fredericks did have the muscle, and his bodyguards had to have either been inefficient or bribed by—

His cell phone rang. Soldono telling him the rescue was scratched?

"Royd."

"Nate Kelly. Sorry to call you this early but I've just gotten back from the facility. I think I've got it. Do you have time for me?"

He stiffened. "Talk and talk fast. I have to get moving in a few minutes."

"This won't take more than a few minutes. I located the initial experimental REM-4 records. No formulas. They must keep them somewhere else. But three names. Sanborne, your favorite, General Boch, and one more."

"Who?"

"Dr. Sophie Dunston."

"A woman? Who the hell is she?"

"I don't know yet. I haven't had time to investigate. I called you right away. But her file was cross-referenced to a current file. I was going to go through it but I had to get out of the file room quick."

"Then she's still involved."

"It would seem that's an affirmative."

"I want to know everything about her."

"I'll do my best. But they're moving everything at the facility out within the next week. I don't know how long I'll have access to the record room."

Shit. "A week?"

"That's the scuttlebutt."

"I've got to have that information. I can't touch Boch or Sanborne unless I get those REM-4 research records too. It has to be a package deal. But the woman might be a lead if I can get my hands on her."

"And what will you do with her?"

"Find out everything she knows."

"And then?"

"What do you think? Do you actually believe because she's a woman that I'd let her out from under?"

Kelly was silent a moment. "No, I guess not."

"That's because you're not a fool. Can you get the information about her before they jerk the files?"

"If I work fast and they don't nail me."

"Do it." He spoke slowly, enunciating every word clearly. "I haven't searched for REM-4 for years to be put off now. I want to know everything about Sophie Dunston. I need her. And I'm going to have her."

"I'll go back tonight. I'll meet you at Washington National Airport tomorrow with whatever I can gather."

"I can't be there tomorrow." He thought about it. He was tempted to blow this job and toss it back to the CIA, but it was too late. By the time they got through hemming and hawing, Fredericks would be dead. "Give me a week."

"I can't promise she'll still be around by then. If Boch and Sanborne are moving out, she may be meeting them."

Royd muttered a curse. "Two days. I have to have at least two days. Find her and call me if it looks like she's taking off. Keep her on ice until I get there."

"Are you suggesting I kidnap her?"

"Whatever it takes."

"I'll consider it. Two days. Phone me when you board your flight to Washington." He hung up.

REM-4.

Royd pressed the disconnect, frustration searing through him. Jesus. He was coming so close but this was the first real break he'd gotten in the last three years. And it came at a time when he had to be tied up with Fredericks.

Two days.

He started to throw on his clothes. Get Fredericks out of here and get on that plane. No time for mistakes. No time for games. He'd get Fredericks away from the rebels today if he had to napalm a path through the whole jungle between here and Bogotá.

And he'd damn well be in Washington sooner than the two days for which he'd bargained.

Just don't let her get away, Kelly.

Michael's scream tore through the house at the same time the monitor went off on Sophie's bedside table.

In seconds Sophie was on her feet and running toward his bedroom.

He screamed again before she reached his bed.

"Michael, it's all right." She sat down on the bed and shook him. His eyes opened dazedly and she gathered him close. "It's all right, you're safe." It wasn't all right. It was never all right. She could feel his heart, throbbing, jumping erratically. He was shaking as if he had malaria. "It's over."

"Mom?"

"Yes." Her arms tightened around him. "You okay?"

He didn't answer for a moment. It always took a few minutes for him to recover even when they caught the terror before he sank all the way into it. "Sure." His voice was uneven. "I'm sorry that you— I should be stronger, shouldn't I?"

"No, you're very, very strong. I know grown men who have these terrors and you do much better than they do." She drew a little away and brushed the hair back from his face. Tears were running down his cheeks, but she didn't try to wipe them away. She'd learned to ignore them to avoid embarrassing him. It was a small thing, but all she could do to save his pride when he was so dependent on her. "I keep telling you it's not a question of weakness. It's an illness that has to be cured. I know your pain and I'm very proud of you." She paused. "There's only one thing that would make me prouder. If you'd talk to me about them . . ."

He looked away from her. "I don't remember."

It was a lie and they both knew it. It was true that night-terror victims often didn't remember the content of their dreams, but Michael's had to be connected to that day on the pier. Just the way he behaved when she asked him about it was a sign that he did recall them. "It would help you, Michael."

He shook his head.

"Okay, maybe next time." She stood up. "How about a cup of hot chocolate?"

"It's four-thirty. You have to work today, don't you?"

"I've had enough sleep." She headed for the door. "You go wash your face and I'll make the chocolate." He was pale and this had been a bad one. Jesus, she hoped he didn't throw up. "Kitchen. Ten minutes, okay?"

"Okay."

He had a little color back in his cheeks when he sat down at the table five minutes later. "Dad called me yesterday afternoon."

"That's nice." She poured the hot chocolate into the two mugs and added marshmallows on the top. "How is he?"

"Pretty good, I guess." He took a drink. "I'm coming home Saturday night. He and Jean are going out of town. I told him that it was okay with me. I'd rather come home and be with you anyway."

"I'm glad. I miss you." She sat down and cradled the cup in her cold hands. "But why? You like Jean, don't you?"

"Sure. She's neat. But I think she and Dad like to be alone. Newlyweds do, don't they?"

"Sometimes. But they've been married almost six months and I'm sure there's room for you in their lives."

"Maybe." He took another drink and looked down at his chocolate. "Is it my fault, Mom?"

"Is what your fault?"

"You and Dad."

She had been waiting for him to ask that question since Dave and she had separated. She was glad that he had finally let it come out. "The divorce? No way. We were just different people. We got married in college when we were kids and we changed when we got older. It happens to lots of couples."

"But you guys argued a lot about me. I heard you."

"Yes, we did. But we argued a lot about most things. And that doesn't mean we wouldn't have gotten a divorce anyway."

"Honest?"

She reached out and covered his hand with hers. "Honest."

"And it's all right if I like Jean?"

"It's great that you like Jean. She makes your dad very happy. That's important." She took a paper napkin and wiped the melted marshmallow from his mouth. "And she's nice to you. That's even more important."

He was silent a moment. "Dad says Jean's a little nervous about my nightmares. I think that's why they don't want me to stay overnight."

That bastard. He'd passed the buck to Jean so that he'd come out smelling like a rose. She forced a smile. "She'll get used to them. Heck, she may not have to get used to them. Like you said, they don't come every night any longer. You're getting better and better."

He nodded and was silent a moment. "He asked me about Jock."

She sipped her drink. "Really? You told him about Jock?"

"Sure. I mentioned him a couple times the last time Dad and I went to the movies."

"What did he want to know?"

He grinned. "He asked what he was doing here at the house all the time. I think he thought there was something mushy going on."

"And what did you tell him?"

"I told him the truth. That Jock was your cousin and he was only in town looking for a job."

It was the truth as far as Michael knew. She'd had to concoct a logical story when Jock had shown up. "Lucky for us," she said. "Jock's been a great help, hasn't he? You like him, don't you?"

His smile faded as he nodded. "You know, it kind of embarrasses me to have strangers around when I have bad dreams. But I don't feel like that with Jock. It's like . . . he knows."

Jock did know. No one could know that torment better. "Maybe he does. Jock is a pretty sensitive guy." She stood up. "You finished? I'll wash your cup."

"I'll do it." He got to his feet and took his cup and her own to the sink. "You made the chocolate. Fair's fair."

But there wasn't anything fair about what Michael was going through, she thought bitterly. "That's right. Thanks. Are you ready to go back to bed?"

"I guess so."

She searched his face. "No guessing about it. If you're not ready, we'll sit around and talk. Maybe watch a DVD."

"I'm ready." He smiled at her. "You go back to bed. I'll fasten myself up to the monitor." He grimaced. "I'll be glad when I can do without it. I feel like something from a science-fiction movie."

She tensed. "It's necessary, Michael. You can't do without it. Maybe in a few weeks, we'll be able to do without the thumb pulse-ox."

He nodded and looked away from her as he headed for the door. "I know. I was just talking. I don't want to do without it yet. It gets pretty scary. 'Night, Mom."

"Good night."

She watched him walk down the hall. He looked so small and vulnerable in those blue flannel pajamas.

He was vulnerable.

Vulnerable to pain and terror and even death.

Pretty scary?

Terrifying.

And he was managing to deal with it and survive. She had told him she was proud of him, but that was an understatement. He fought the confusion, threat of death, and ugliness with a courage that amazed her. Any other boy would have been beaten down, crushed, and completely destroyed by the punishment Michael took.

Jesus, she hoped the terror didn't come back tonight.

"You look tired," Kelly said as he watched Royd stride out of customs at Washington National. "Did I push you a bit?"

"I pushed myself," he said curtly. "And, hell yes, I'm tired. I've gotten maybe three hours' sleep in the last two days."

He looked it, Kelly thought. Royd's broad, high-cheekboned face always had an expression of tenseness and alertness, but his dark eyes were strained and glittering restlessly and his mouth was tense. In the worn jeans and khaki shirt he wore, his big, powerful body looked as if it should belong to a lumberjack. "As it played out, they're not moving as fast as I thought they would," Kelly said. "You could have taken a little more time."

"No, I couldn't. It was driving me crazy." Royd asked, "What did you find out about her?"

"Not much. Everyone at the facility is pulling twelve-hour shifts to get ready for the move and I was only able to get to the current file room once. She's a sleep therapist and practices at Fentway University Hospital."

"Sleep therapist." His lips tightened. "Oh, yes, that would fit. Do you have an address?"

Kelly nodded. "She has a house in a suburb of Baltimore. Close to the hospital."

"And close to the facility?"

"Right." He paused. "You're definitely going after her?"

"I told you I was. Did you find out anything else?"

"Not really. She's divorced and has a ten-year-old son."

"Is there anyone else in the house?"

Kelly shrugged. "I told you my info was scanty. I've been too busy to stake her out. It would be better if you wait until I can find out—"

"And risk her flying the coop?" He shook his head. "I'm moving now. Do you have a photo?"

"An old one from the personnel records." Kelly reached into his pocket and handed him a photocopy. "Nice-looking."

Royd glanced at the photo. "Yes, do you know if she sleeps with Sanborne?"

"I told you that I haven't had a chance to—"

"I know. I know. Just a thought. When you're checking, look into it." Kelly had paused beside a car and Royd gazed at the photo as Kelly unlocked it. "Maybe not. She looks like she'd be hard to push around and he's into sexual power games. He killed a prostitute in Tokyo a few years ago."

"Charming. You're sure?"

"I'm sure. There's not much I don't know about Sanborne. Check it anyway." Royd got into the car. "Are you going back to the facility?"

Kelly nodded. "That's what you're paying me for. Things are in a bit of a turmoil with the move. I might get a break."

"And you might get your neck chopped."

"I'm touched by your concern."

Royd was silent a moment. "I am concerned. I don't want to serve up any more lives to Sanborne than he's already taken."

Kelly grinned. "Besides, you like me."

"Sometimes."

"That's a concession from you." Kelly added, "And after I've only been laying my ass on the line for you for almost a year." He grimaced. "I'll be okay. I've been careful. And this might be my last chance to get my hands on those formulas. Are we sure that there aren't other copies?"

"Sanborne wouldn't chance copies floating around. The value of REM-4 lies in exclusivity. He was almost fanatical about his secrecy and control over the process when I was under his thumb. But we may be able to get hold of them through the Dunston woman." Royd's lips tightened. "I'll know tonight."

"You're going straight there?"

"I'm not going to chance letting her slip through my fingers."

"You could wait at least until I find out more about her."

"I've waited too long already. You've told me that she was a key figure in the initial experiments. There's a good chance she knows where in the facility those files are located. That's all I need to know to go forward."

"Do you want me to come with you?"

"You do what you're good at. I'll do what I'm good at." His lips twisted. "Thanks to Sanborne."

"And maybe Sophie Dunston."

"Like I said, she fits. I'll call you if I find you can opt out of the search for the files."

"If you can force her to talk."

Royd's answer was only a cool glance but it

was enough. That had been stupid, Kelly thought. Besides being one of the most lethal sons of bitches he'd ever run across, Royd was a driven man. There was no question he'd do whatever he had to do.

And heaven help Sophie Dunston.

3

I've talked to MacDuff twice in the last two days," Jock said, when Sophie picked up the phone. "He wants me to come home."

Sophie tried to smother the surge of disappointment. After all, this was what she had wanted, wasn't it? "Then go. I don't need you. I was hoping when you didn't show up for the last few days that you'd taken me at my word."

"Stop trying to get rid of me. I told Mac-Duff I'd come if I could work things out. That hasn't happened yet. You're being very stubborn. How is Michael?"

"He had an episode last night, but I woke him up pretty quickly."

"Damn. It doesn't get any easier. Tell him I'll be by tomorrow to take him to the new sci-fi flick he wanted to see, or we could just go to Chuck E. Cheese's if he wants."

"Jock, I'll take him. He doesn't need a big brother. Go home." She paused. "His father asked about you."

"Fine. A little competition for the boy's affection may stir him up. I'm not admiring your choice in husbands. It's a wonder Michael turned out so well."

"Dave has many fine qualities."

"But I've noticed he appears to care more about going for the big bucks than he does Michael."

"Money is important to Dave but so is Michael."

"We won't argue about it." He paused. "I've been out to the facility. They're in a big hurry to pack up those moving trucks with everything that's not nailed down. Maybe you made Sanborne a little nervous. Nervous men are unpredictable. We need to talk again. Invite me in for a cup of tea after I bring Michael home."

"The hell I will."

"On second thought, I think I'll come over right away. I need to start to work on you. You're getting more stubborn as time passes."

"I'll lock the damn door on you. Go back to Scotland."

She heard him chuckle before he hung up.

She shook her head as she hung up the phone and stood. She shouldn't be feeling this sense of relief. It wasn't fair to Jock to keep him here and she wouldn't do it. She'd call MacDuff and tell him to put more pressure on Jock. He certainly wasn't listening to her.

Tomorrow.

It was late and she had an eight o'clock appointment in the morning.

She went down the hall and checked Michael.

Please, sleep deep and well, baby. Every night is a gift.

She carefully closed the door and went back down the hall and got the automatic coffeemaker ready for the morning. She needed all the caffeine she could get just to keep going these days.

She went into her bedroom and reached out to flip on the light.

An arm snaked around her neck!

"Scream and I'll break your neck, bitch."

Christ.

She didn't scream. She lashed her elbow back into his stomach and kicked his shin at the same time.

He grunted and his grip loosened.

She tore away and ran toward the night-stand where she kept the gun Jock had given her.

She fell to her knees as he tackled her before she was halfway there. He was on top of her, his hands encircling her throat.

Pain.

She couldn't breathe.

Her hands tore at his fingers.

Jesus, she couldn't die.

Michael . . .

She spat in his face.

"Bitch!" He released one hand to slap her face.

She twisted her head and sank her teeth into his hand.

The coppery taste of blood. His scream of outrage and pain.

She rolled out from under him. His hand caught her hair before she could get to her knees.

A glint of metal shone in his hand.

Knife.

Death.

No!

She stared up at his twisted, contorted face as she fought to get away. Ugly. So ugly.

"Scared?" He panted. "You should be. It would have been easier for you if—" His eyes widened, his body arched. "What is—"

Then she saw the tip of the dagger protruding from his chest.

His eyes were glazing as he started to slump forward toward her. He was pushed to one side by the man standing behind him. Jock? she wondered dazedly.

"Did he stab you?"

Not Jock, she realized. Tall, muscular, close-cut dark hair and his tone was as totally without expression as his high-planed face.

"Did he stab you?" he repeated. "You're covered with blood."

She looked down at her blood-spattered blouse. "No, it must be his blood."

He glanced at the man slumped on the floor. "I guess so. Who is he?"

She forced herself to look at her attacker's face. Thinning brown hair, gray eyes staring wide open from a triangular face. "I don't know," she whispered. "I've never seen him before."

"Oh, just dropped in to slit your throat?" he asked skeptically.

She was shaking, she realized. She felt weak and vulnerable and angry. "Who the hell are you?"

"Matt Royd. You might recognize the name."

"No."

He shrugged. "But then there were so many, weren't there?"

"I don't know what you're talking about."

"Your son's room is down the hall, right?" He was turning toward the door.

She jumped to her feet. "How do you know that? Don't you go near him."

"I did a little reconnoitering before I saw your friend jimmying the window open. But whoever you pissed off might have decided to—"

"I just left Michael." But someone else could have gotten into his room while she was struggling, she thought in panic. She pushed past Royd as she raced down the hall. She threw open Michael's door. It was dimly lit by a night-light but she could see him lying safely in bed.

Maybe.

She had to be sure. She glided quietly across the room. He was breathing deeply, evenly. Not that deeply. He drowsily opened his eyes. "Mom? Anything wrong?"

"Hi," she said softly. "You're fine. I was just checking. Go back to sleep."

"Okay . . ." His eyes closed. "You been cooking? You've got ketchup on your blouse."

She'd forgotten the blood. "Pasta sauce.

Spaghetti for tomorrow night. I made a mess. Good night, Michael."

" 'Night, Mom . . ."

She turned and left the room.

Royd was standing in the hall. "He seems okay."

She nodded jerkily as she closed the door. "How did you get into my house?"

"The back door."

"It was locked."

"A pretty good lock. It took me a few minutes to spring it."

"Are you a thief?"

His lips twisted. "When ordered. I did a little of everything and a lot of the activities practiced by the man who wanted to slit your throat. That came easiest to me. I had training and experience before REM-4."

She stiffened. "What?"

"REM-4." His gaze was narrowed on her face. "Don't pretend you don't know what I'm talking about. I'm on a short fuse right now. It wouldn't take much to push me over the edge."

"Get out of my home," she said unevenly.

"No thanks for saving your life? How rude." His lips tightened. "If you start cooperating, I might rid you of that body in your bedroom. I'm good at things like that."

"How do you know I won't call the police? He invaded my home." She stared him in the eye. "Like you."

"A threat?" he asked softly. "I don't like threats."

Fear iced through her. Jesus, he frightened her more than that maniac in the bedroom. She moistened her lips. "You're the one threatening me. You broke into my home. How do I know that if that man in the bedroom hadn't attacked me you wouldn't have done it?"

"You don't. I may still do it. It's very tempting. But I'm trying to control myself. If you give me what I want, you have a chance of surviving."

Her heart was beating so hard she could scarcely breathe. She backed against the wall. "Get out."

"You're frightened." He took a step nearer and put his hands on either side of her shoulders on the wall. "You have a right to be. It would be a shame if your son lost his mother because she was stupid."

He was only inches away and she felt trapped. His blue eyes were glittering down at her. Hard, cold, ice-cold. "Who sent you?"

He smiled. "Why, you did."

"The hell I did." She kneed him in the nuts

and ducked under his arm as he bent double
with pain. She ran toward the front door. Get
away. Get help. No time to think.

He was right behind her as she flung open
the front door.

And ran straight into Jock's arms.

She tried to push him back. "Jock, be careful. He's—"

"Shh, I know." He was looking beyond her
and put her gently aside. "What's happening, Royd?"

Royd stopped, his gaze wary. "You tell me,
Jock. I wasn't expecting to see you here. Are
you saying you have first dibs on her? No way."

Sophie's eyes widened in shock. "You know
each other, Jock?"

"You could say that. We attended the same
school." He met Royd's gaze. "You're on the
wrong track. She's not your target."

"The hell she's not," Royd said harshly. "Her
name was in Sanborne's files, both past and
current."

"How do you know?"

"Nate Kelly. He's a good man. He doesn't
make mistakes."

"That doesn't mean he might not interpret
what he finds incorrectly." He turned to Sophie. "Is Michael okay?"

She nodded jerkily. "But there's a dead man in my bedroom."

Jock looked at Royd. "One of your men?"

"I don't kill my own men," he said sarcastically. "He got here ahead of me. He was going to take her out. I couldn't have that. I needed her."

Jock's gaze shifted to her. "Sophie?"

"He killed him."

"Who's the man he killed?"

She shook her head. "I don't know."

"Then I think I'd better take a look." He took Sophie's arm. "Come on. Let's get off the porch. You don't want the neighbors curious."

She didn't move, her gaze on Royd.

"He's not going to hurt you," Jock said. "It's a misunderstanding."

"Misunderstanding? He killed a man five minutes ago."

"And saved your neck," Royd said coldly.

"Obviously for your own purposes."

"Absolutely."

"Royd, she's not the target," Jock repeated. "When I get the chance, I'll explain it to you. In the meantime, back off."

Royd stiffened. "Are you threatening me?"

"Only if you don't back down. But it would be stupid for us to pit ourselves against each other. We're on the same side. In fact, I've been trying to track you down for the last few days." He made a face. "And I'm not sure I could take you. MacDuff has seen that I haven't had any practical experience for a good while. And you've lived a life that definitely keeps you sharp."

"Don't bullshit me. You were the best and you don't forget."

"We're on the same side," Jock repeated. "Give me some time and I'll prove it."

Royd didn't want to give in to Jock, Sophie thought. She could see the tenseness, the violence brimming beneath the surface. For a moment she thought that violence would erupt and then he turned abruptly and started back down the hall. "Take a look at the body. If he was professional, he let emotion get in the way. He was so angry with her that he didn't hear me behind him."

"I don't want this Royd in my house, Jock," Sophie said. "I don't care what's between the two of you. It's not going to affect me or my son."

"The devil it's not." Royd whirled, eyes glittering. "You're in this up to your neck and everything I do from now on is going to affect you. You'd better hope that Jock can make me believe what he's telling me. It's not likely."

"Easy." Jock pushed Sophie into the house and closed the front door. "Sophie, go make a pot of coffee while we go check out your intruder. You look like you could use it."

"I want to go with—" It was a lie. She didn't want to see that murderer with the bloody knife sticking out of his chest again. And it would be of no purpose. "I'll go do another check on Michael and meet you in the kitchen."

Ten minutes later she was putting the coffee on and trying to regain her composure. Lord, she was shaking so badly she wouldn't be able to hold a cup without spilling it. Reaction must be setting in. She'd be fine in a minute. She closed her eyes and took a deep breath. After her parents' deaths she'd had months of periods when she'd lost control. But she was strong now and that man meant nothing to her but a threat.

Blood gushing from that bloody wound. Senseless. Senseless. Senseless.

No, she wouldn't lose control. She was fine now.

"Sophie?" Jock was coming into the kitchen.

She opened her eyes and nodded. "I'm okay. I guess it brought back a few memories."

"What memories?" Royd asked as he came into the room after Jock.

She gave him a cool glance. "None of your business."

"Go to the bathroom and get cleaned up." Jock handed her a white blouse he was carrying. "I didn't think you'd want to go back into your bedroom right away."

"Thanks." She took the blouse and went past him and Royd as she left the kitchen. Royd was leaning on the doorjamb and she was careful not to touch him. But she could still feel his tension, sense the passion of emotion that was electrifying him. She didn't want to deal with that passion until she could get herself together. Let Jock handle him. Let Jock get him out of her house.

She washed up, changed her blouse, and ran a comb through her hair. Then she took a moment to try to block out the thought of that body in her bedroom. It didn't work. It shouldn't work. She had to deal with what had happened and she had to deal with Matt Royd. So stop whining and face it.

Jock and Royd were sitting at the kitchen table when she entered the room. Royd looked as comfortable as a tiger forced to balance on a stool. Tiger. Yes, that description was very apt.

"I poured your coffee." Jock gestured to the chair beside him. "Sit down. We have to talk to Royd."

She shook her head.

"Sit down," Jock repeated. "You have enough trouble on your plate. You don't need Royd to come down on you."

She hesitated and then slowly sat down. "Did you recognize the man in the bedroom?"

He shook his head. "And neither did Royd. But we may hear soon. He used his phone to take a photo of him and sent it to his man at Sanborne's facility."

She stiffened. "His man?"

"He hired a man to go undercover and get information from Sanborne's files. He works with the video monitors in the security center at the plant."

"Why did he do that?"

"He doesn't like Sanborne," Jock said. "I'd say on the same scale that you don't."

"Why?" Her gaze searched Jock's face as she recalled everything Royd had said to her in those moments in her bedroom. And then Jock had said they'd gone to the same school. She felt sickness churn through her. "Another one? Like you, Jock?"

Jock nodded. "A little different circumstances but the result was much the same."

"Oh, God."

"We're not talking about me," Royd said. "I'm not hearing anything that convinces me she's not in Sanborne's pocket, Jock."

Jock was silent a moment. "Two years ago her father shot her mother, tried to kill her son, and ended up shooting Sophie before he killed himself. No apparent reason. The attack came out of the blue."

Royd's cool glance shifted to Sophie. "One of your experiments that backfired?"

"No." Her stomach twisted. "God, no."

"Rough," Jock said quietly. "Too rough, Royd."

Royd's gaze never left Sophie's face. "It's possible. How do we know?"

She shook her head. "I would never— I loved him. I loved both of them."

"And you weren't to blame for anything. Your name figured prominently in Sanborne's file on the initial experiments on REM-4 but it didn't mean a thing."

"I didn't say that." She reached blindly for the coffee in front of her. "It meant something. It meant everything."

"Why? How?"

She felt as if he were battering her, ripping at her. "I was to blame. It was my fault. All of it was—"

"Easy, Sophie." Jock reached out and covered her hand. "I can tell him later. You don't have to go through this."

"You can't protect me." She moistened her lips. "And I can't hide from what I did. I have to face it every day. Every time I look at Michael and know I—" She stopped and then her eyes lifted to Royd's face. "And nothing you can say can make me feel any worse than I do now. You can tear open the wound but it can't go any deeper. You want to know what happened? I was young and smart and thought I could change the world. I was fresh out of medical school and went to work for Sanborne Pharmaceutical because they promised me I could devote my time to working on research I'd been doing on the side all through med school. I'd gotten a doctorate in chemistry as well as medicine and I was specializing in sleep disorders because my father had been plagued by insomnia and night terrors most of the years of my childhood. I thought I could help him and other people like him."

"How?"

"I'd developed a process to chemically induce the subject to immediately go to REM-4, the most psychologically active level of sleep. While in that state, it was also possible to give suggestions to encourage pleasant dreams instead of night terrors, even to rid the subject of insomnia. Sanborne was very excited and enthusiastic. He coaxed me to bypass the FDA and go to Amsterdam for tests. He wanted it kept top secret until we were sure they were as promising as we thought they'd be. He didn't have to work very hard to persuade me into getting on the fast track. I knew the FDA took forever to approve anything and I had complete faith in the safety of the process. The tests were amazingly successful. People who'd been victims of terrors all their lives were free of them. They became happier, more productive people with no obvious side effects. I was over the moon."

"And?"

"Sanborne said we had to slow down. He took the tests out of my hands and tried to persuade me to turn over the research I'd done for all the enhancements for REM-4. When I refused, he shut me out. I was angry and frustrated but I didn't suspect anything criminal."

She paused. "But I wanted to know how the tests were going so I went to the lab and rifled through the files one night." She drew a ragged breath. "You can guess what I found. They were using the vulnerability that the drug induced to develop mind control. There was correspondence between Sanborne and a General Boch about the advantage that such control could offer during wartime. I went to Sanborne and told him I was quitting, taking my research, and opting out. I could tell he was angry, but then he seemed to simmer down.

"The next day I had two lawyers knocking on the door. They claimed since I was employed by Sanborne at the time, the research was legally his. I could either sign a release or go to court." Her lips twisted. "You know what chance I would have had against Sanborne's legal eagles. I didn't want to pursue the research any further. It was clearly too potentially dangerous. But I didn't want Sanborne to go forward with it in his direction either. I told him I'd go to the media and tell them what he was doing if he continued the mind-control experiments. He agreed. I thought I'd won. I got another job with a university hospital in Atlanta and tried to put it all behind me."

"Without proof Sanborne was complying?"

"I had friends in the lab. There was an excellent chance that I'd be told if he wasn't."

"A chance?"

"All right, I was naive. I should have gone to the media right away. But I'd spent most of my adult life studying medicine and I didn't want to blow it. Those lawyers would have made mincemeat of my career and my life." She drew a deep breath. "And the experiments stopped. I checked periodically during the next six months and the project was shut down."

"And after the six months?"

Her hands tightened on her cup. "After that, I didn't have to worry about my life exploding in my face. It already had. I went fishing one day with my father and mother. Jock told you what happened. My father went crazy. One moment he was perfectly loving and sane and the next he'd killed the woman he'd loved for most of his life. He would have killed my son if I hadn't gotten between them. The bullet still struck him but it went through me and was deflected. I woke up a day later in the hospital. I fell apart when I realized what had happened. It made no sense. Things like that couldn't happen. I ended up in a mental hospital for a couple months." She clenched her fists. "I was weak. I should have been there for Michael but Dave never told me that he was having problems. I should have been there."

"It was two months, Sophie," Jock said quietly. "And you were having a few problems yourself."

"I'm not a child," she said harshly. "I'm a mother and I should have been there for him."

"Very touching," Royd said. "But I'd like to get back to Sanborne."

Christ, he was a tough bastard. "Sorry to waste your time. I wasn't trying to play on your sympathies. I doubt if you have any. Actually, we never got away from Sanborne." She lifted her cup to her lips. "When I was in that mental hospital, the only way I could survive was to try to understand what had happened. I couldn't believe my father had just gone insane. He was . . . wonderful. Kind and normal in every way." She paused. "Except for the sleep disorders he'd suffered since he was a child. But even those were dwindling in the past few months. He was going to a new specialist, Dr. Paul Dwight. I checked him out and he was very well respected. He was seeing him much more frequently than he had his last therapist and it seemed to work. He was sleeping through the night and the night terrors were coming less frequently. My mother was very happy for him. That last day he looked more rested than I can remember seeing him. And then I remembered how rested and happy those volunteers in Amsterdam looked when they woke after the REM-4 therapy." She shook her head. "I thought I was reaching, imagining, making connections where none existed. But I had to make sure. After all, wouldn't it be the perfect way to get rid of me? I haven't the slightest doubt my father would have turned the pistol on me if I hadn't already taken the bullet meant for Michael. You hear about madmen who kill their entire families and then themselves. A family tragedy. No mysterious assassin that might spark an investigation. I'd be gone and then Sanborne would be free to go on with his plans for REM-4."

"And what did you do about it?"

"When I got out of the hospital, I went through my father's records and got the name and address of his therapist. I called to make an appointment. The phone had been disconnected. The doctor had been killed in an automobile accident three weeks before."

"Convenient," Jock murmured.

"That was what I thought. I hired a private detective to try to trace a connection between

Dr. Dwight and Sanborne. The only thing he could come up with was a meeting at a convention in Chicago that same year. And bank deposits of close to half a million dollars Dwight made in regular intervals during the last few months."

"Not conclusive."

"Not for a court of law, but it was enough for me. It gave me a lead, a rope to pull me out of the quicksand. But I had to know more. I still had friends at Sanborne's company and I started asking questions. I was assured no more experiments had been done on the premises. The department had been completely closed down and the personnel had all been transferred to other projects. I didn't believe it. I asked my friend Dr. Cindy Hodge to snoop around and see what she could come up with." She paused. "She came up with a list of names. And she came up with a place. Garwood, North Dakota." She stopped as she sensed a change in Royd's demeanor. "You recognize the name?"

"Oh, yes. I'm very familiar with Garwood." He glanced at Jock. "And you?"

"My training was different from yours. I didn't even remember Garwood until last year when my mind was drifting back to me." He nodded at Sophie. "And Sophie nudged that memory when she came looking for me."

"She was looking for you?" Royd asked.

"Did you think I was tracking her down? I was trying to come to terms with what I was and am. I didn't break free as quickly as you did."

"I was at Garwood a long time before you were brought there. And it didn't seem quick," Royd said. "Any more than fighting your way through hell is quick."

"You weren't together at Garwood?" Sophie asked. "I don't understand."

"Jock was brought to Garwood at the request of Thomas Reilly, who was training his own mind-control zombies," Royd said. "He paid Sanborne to use REM-4 to help manipulate Jock's and some of his other victims' wills. But he had other methods he was experimenting with too, and Sanborne was only a tool."

"And you?"

"Oh, I was a present from General Boch to Sanborne when they opened the lab at Garwood." He smiled mirthlessly. "The General wanted to get rid of me and he couldn't think of a more advantageous demise than to send me to Garwood to his partner in crime. He liked the idea of breaking my will and, if it didn't work, there was always the chance of my going insane. It happened to two men while I was at Garwood."

Horror surged through her. "No," she whispered.

He gazed at her skeptically. "You had to know about it if you knew about Garwood."

She shook her head. "It wasn't in the records at Sanborne's."

"From what I hear, the villagers living near Auschwitz claimed they didn't know either."

"I tell you, I didn't—"

"If she says she didn't know, she's telling the truth," Jock said. "Sanborne wouldn't have kept records of a failure. He'd eliminate the subject and wipe the slate clean."

"You're sure?" Sophie asked. "The REM-4 I created was physically and mentally safe. I swear it was safe."

"Not when they got through with altering it," Royd said. "They increased the suggestibility factor enormously. Some minds couldn't accept that degree of submission without breaking. Oh, yes, it was definitely changed. There were fifty-two men at Garwood who'll testify to that."

"There were only records on thirty-four," Sophie said.

Royd just looked at her.

"He . . . killed them?"

He shrugged. "I counted fifty-two before I took off. I don't know what happened to them. I can guess. I was in hiding for over three months and it was during that time that the CIA uncovered Thomas Reilly's installation. Sanborne was scared that Reilly's records might lead the CIA to Garwood so he cleaned it up so well that no one could possibly know what it was used for. Then he closed it down and moved the operation."

"To his plant in Maryland," Sophie said. "Why didn't you go to the police?"

"The police aren't inclined to listen to assassins. And I'm sure the General would have made sure that at least one of the kills I was sent on was documented." His lips tightened. "After all, it was perfectly reasonable I'd go off on a killing tangent. I was a SEAL for four years and everyone knows that we're trained in violence and death. I had to find another way to get them."

"What way?"

"I had to make enough money to buy information. It took me a while but I managed to find the REM-4 facility and put a mole into Sanborne's company." He met her eyes. "And that led me to you."

"I didn't—I wouldn't ever—" She stopped and wearily shook her head. "But I did do it. I started it. It was my fault. I can't blame you for—"

Michael's monitor was going off.

"Jesus!" She jumped to her feet. "Michael . . ."

She ran out of the room.

4

Royd muttered an oath and started to get to his feet.

"She's not trying to get away," Jock said. "Sit down and finish your coffee. She's just going to take care of her son. She'll be back."

Royd slowly sat back down. "What's wrong with him?"

"Night terrors. Occasionally he has an apnea episode when he stops breathing."

"Christ."

"And, before you ask, she didn't experiment on him either. He started having the episodes after his grandfather tried to kill him and he saw his grandmother and mother shot. She tells me he used to be much worse and he may be on the way to recovery." He grimaced. "It's still pretty rough watching him. He's only a kid."

"You said she found you. How?"

"The Garwood records she'd gotten from her friend had cross-references to Thomas Reilly's cases that were brought there. The Garwood subjects had 'disappeared' but there were still leads to some of Reilly's. He had an entire compound of men to tap for service to the highest bidder. They dispersed when the CIA was closing in on Reilly. Most of them were picked up but some of us stayed free." He paused. "But you knew all this. You tracked me down yourself almost a year ago."

"And you told me you knew nothing about where Sanborne had moved his REM-4 experiments. Lies?"

Jock shook his head. "I didn't remember much of anything at that time. It took a hell of a long time for me to heal enough to be able to put any kind of facts together. I was pretty much of a vegetable when MacDuff found me in that asylum in Denver after I'd broken free of Reilly. You were too early in my recovery. If you'd come a few months later you'd have gotten more out of me. Sophie came at just the right time. I was ready to remember. She prodded me and it came flowing back to me."

Royd studied him. He was probably telling the truth. Jock was different from the man he'd first met. At that time he'd been a little vague and remote. There was nothing vague or remote about this man across the table from him. That Scottish brogue was soft but everything else about him was decisive and unyielding. "And what did you remember?"

"That Reilly was going to send a few of his newer subjects to another Sanborne location for training even before the CIA raid. Somewhere in Maryland."

"And why didn't you contact me? Dammit, you knew I had to know. It took me months to find out that information for myself."

"I was a little busy with Sophie. I didn't want interference."

"Busy?"

"She didn't really know the scope of what Sanborne had done until she met me. She was pretty devastated. She was going to go after Sanborne on her own." He shook his head. "I couldn't allow her to do it."

"Why not?"

"She touched me," he said simply. "She was full of guilt and pain and was no match for Sanborne and his goons. At first, she wanted to try to get into the facility and destroy the research that had created REM-4. But they had changed all the security codes and she couldn't do it. So that left her with only cutting off the head of the snake and hoping that would destroy the poison."

"So she asked you to do it?"

He shook his head again. "She's so burdened by guilt at what she'd helped to do to me that there's no way she'd let me kill him. The only thing she asked was for me to teach her how to kill a man."

"And you did it?"

"Yes, she's technically very good. She's almost as fine a shot as I am. Can she do it? She thinks she can. It depends how much hate she has stored up. Hate can make the difference." He stared Royd in the eye. "Can't it?"

Royd ignored the question. "She **is** guilty. How do you know that she wasn't involved with Sanborne's scheme from the beginning and then had a falling-out?"

"I trust her."

"And I don't."

"I'm not a fool, Royd. She told me the truth." He studied him. "You look frustrated as hell. Why do you want her to still be in Sanborne's pocket?"

"Because it was my chance to squeeze

enough information out of her to locate the REM-4 formulas and bring down Sanborne and Boch. Now you tell me she's practically an innocent bystander." His hand clenched into a fist. "No, I won't buy it."

"You'll buy it. You're too smart to be blinded by the way you want things to be. You just have to get used to the idea."

"Maybe."

Jock's gaze narrowed on his face. "What are you thinking?"

"Ever since I escaped Garwood I've had to manipulate every situation to make sure I survived and stayed on the road to Sanborne. I have to do the same with this one." His lips clenched. "I'm too close, Jock. If I can't use her, I'm not going to let Sophie Dunston get in my way. I'd have no compunction about—"

His cell phone rang and he glanced at the ID.

Nate Kelly.

"Cross your fingers he's found out who that son of a bitch in the bedroom is," he murmured as he pressed the button.

Sophie took a moment outside Michael's bedroom door to take a deep breath and prepare to go back into the kitchen and face Matt Royd again.

Michael's episode hadn't been terrible tonight and she thanked God for it. The entire night had been a horror, and a bad night terror for Michael would have been the crowning blow. She wouldn't have been able to bear it.

Yes, she would. What a wimp. She could bear anything life threw at her.

Including Royd, who stared at her with that icy coldness and accusing animosity.

She squared her shoulders and walked down the hall and into the kitchen.

Jock looked up. "Michael back to sleep?"

She nodded. "It wasn't too bad. I just sat and talked to him for a while and he drifted off."

"Good," Jock said. "Let's hope he stays asleep. We have some business to take care of. Royd just got an E-mail from his man at the facility."

Her gaze flew to Royd's face. "You found who that killer was?"

"One of Sanborne's bodyguards," Royd said. "At least that's how he's listed on the personnel records. Arnold Caprio."

"Caprio," Sophie repeated.

"You've heard of him?"

She shook her head. "I don't think so. But the name sounds familiar. . . ."

"Think."

"I told you, I don't think I've—" She broke off. "Yes, I have. I know who—" She strode out of the kitchen to the living room and opened the top desk drawer. The list was tucked in a leather ledger. She flipped it open and her index finger ran down the list.

Arnold Caprio's name was in the middle of the list.

She closed her eyes. "God."

"Who is he?"

She opened her eyes and turned to face Jock and Royd. "Caprio was one of the names on the list Cindy gave me of the men who'd undergone the Garwood experiments. Sanborne must have kept him close to act as his bodyguard. Only it seems he wasn't just a bodyguard. He evidently used him to rid himself of threats like me." She had to stop shaking. "It's rather ironic, isn't it? Sanborne sent me one of the victims I'm responsible for to take my life."

"You're not responsible," Jock said. "You never meant this to happen. You tried to stop it."

"Tell that to Caprio." She looked at Royd.

"Tell that to Royd. You think I'm responsible, don't you?"

He stared at her for a moment and then shrugged. "It doesn't matter what I think right now. I should tell you that Sanborne didn't always pick up young kids to train as assassins like Reilly did. He liked a head start. He thought the experiments worked best on men with an ingrained streak of violence. Boch often sent him military snipers and ex-SEALs like me. He'd trump up so-called sensitive missions to get them to the area and then have Sanborne send his goons to collect them. And I know of two drug runners and at least three hit men at Garwood."

She stared at him in surprise. "Jesus, are you trying to make me feel better?"

"No. You asked me a question. Now I'll ask you one. You didn't recognize my name. Wasn't it on the list?"

She thought about it. "No, but Jock's name was there."

Royd shrugged. "Maybe the list only covered Sanborne's recruits and the subjects he personally acquired. I was a gift from his partner." He turned to Jock. "We'd better get rid of Caprio. Do you know a place?"

"The marshes west of here," Jock said. "He won't be found for months, maybe years."

"Write down the directions. I'll get some garbage bags from the kitchen and bundle him up. You go scout around and make sure this neighborhood is as sleepy as it looks before I take him to the car."

"Do you have to—" Sophie started again. "Isn't there some way we can get him out of my house without throwing him into a swamp to rot?"

"Yes," Royd said. "Would you like me to just toss him on Sanborne's front lawn? It would be my pleasure."

He'd do it, Sophie realized, and with every bit of the savage enjoyment she saw in his expression. "I can see that."

"But it wouldn't be smart," Royd said. "A slap in the face is a warning and I don't want to give Sanborne and Boch any warning. I'm the one who killed Caprio and I don't need anything in my way. So we'll get rid of Caprio because not to do it might give Sanborne an edge. He might find a way to twist the attempt and incriminate you. With his money and influence it's possible." He started to turn away. "And before you start feeling sorry about getting rid of that scum I believe I should show you something I found on the floor of your bedroom." He was gone for only a minute and when he returned he threw two objects on the coffee table. "He came prepared."

She stared down at the rope. "Nooses?"

"The knife was an afterthought. Caprio obviously wasn't nearly as well trained as Jock and me. He lost his temper and his focus. He was sent to hang you and make it look like an accident. But there were two nooses. What does that tell you?"

"Michael?" she whispered.

"An unstable woman who kills her only child and then herself. You'd think it would be more likely for you to poison your son but Sanborne isn't very clever about emotional reactions. I suppose considering your background the nooses aren't entirely unreasonable." He said over his shoulder to Jock, "I'll finish the cleanup and be ready in ten minutes. Make sure it's safe for me." He gave Sophie a glance. "We'll talk when I get back."

She watched him go down the hall before she turned to Jock. "I should help if it has to be done."

"And leave Michael alone?" Jock looked down at the nooses. "Royd could have spared you those ugly little objects." He picked up the nooses and threw them in the wastebasket in the corner.

"He doesn't want to spare me anything," Sophie said wearily. "I can't blame him. What can I do to help, Jock?"

"Stay here and take care of your son." Jock shook his head as he headed for the front door. "We know what we're doing. You'd get in our way."

She watched in helpless frustration as the door shut behind him.

No, she couldn't leave Michael, but she was letting Jock incriminate himself by helping her, and she'd never wanted that to happen.

And Royd. She should feel just as bad about letting Matt Royd run a risk. After all, he had saved her life when he'd killed Caprio. Yet it was difficult to feel either guilt or gratitude where Royd was concerned. He was too hard, too sharp, and his attitude toward her was antagonistic in the extreme.

And who could blame him? she thought. She was lucky Jock didn't feel the same way. From the moment she had heard about Garwood she had been in an agony of self-recrimination. She had hurt those men, all of them, in ways too terrible to imagine.

But she did think and imagine and wonder.

She couldn't stop. She didn't think she could ever stop.

Until she stopped Robert Sanborne.

Jock came back into the house almost immediately after they'd carried Caprio to Royd's car.

"I thought you were going with him," Sophie said.

"So did I. Royd said there was no use both of us being at risk when he could take care of it by himself. He didn't like leaving you alone."

"It's hard to believe that would bother him. He's not like you."

"Yes and no. We have a good deal in common. When he came to see me a year ago, I felt a kind of bonding. We belong to a very exclusive club."

She had sensed that tie when she had sat at the table with them. They were both so different and yet they had seemed to have a perfect understanding of each other. "He's angry and bitter. The way you should be."

"He's frustrated. As I told you, I killed my demon when I killed Thomas Reilly. He's still fighting his demons. He won't rest until he puts down Boch and Sanborne."

"And me?"

He shrugged. "Not if I can convince him you were telling the truth. He doesn't want to believe it. He thought at last he had his hands on someone who could bring him close enough to Boch and Sanborne for him to do the job. He doesn't want you to be another victim, he wants a key. It will take a little while for him to adjust but he'll do it. But even when he accepts the truth he's still not above using you if he can. He's been searching for revenge for a long time."

"I can understand that."

"Not only because of REM-4. He lost his brother at Garwood."

"What?"

"Boch needed to lure Royd to Garwood so he had Sanborne hire his younger brother to work there. Todd called him from the facility asking for help. Royd went after him."

"How did his brother die?"

"Royd didn't tell me. Whatever happened wasn't pretty."

"REM-4?"

"Sophie, all the ugliness that went on at Garwood wasn't directly attributed to REM-4. Sanborne and Boch are complete bastards and they have very nasty agendas. Royd told me that the reason Boch wanted to take him out was that he'd witnessed a meeting between Boch and a Japanese narcotics kingpin in Tokyo. Boch needed to get rid of him. So he called his partner Sanborne and told him to find a way to get Royd to Garwood. But if it hadn't been Garwood, they would have found another way to gather him in."

Sophie wearily shook her head. "But there was Garwood. What was Royd doing in Japan?"

"He'd just gotten out of the SEALs and was kicking around the Orient before he went back to the U.S. He was thinking about starting an import company if he could get the funding. He told me he'd grown up in the slums of Chicago before he joined the service. A background like that usually sparks the desire for the security money brings."

"But he didn't get the chance. Garwood ruined it for him."

"He'll get what he wants. I've never met anyone as determined as Royd. He's just put it on hold for a while."

She remembered the total concentration and focus Royd had shown as he'd watched her face at the kitchen table. Yes, she could believe he'd be completely relentless about any goal he set himself. She turned away.

"How long do you think it will be before he gets back?"

"An hour or so."

"And then what?"

"We'll have to make plans."

"I have a plan and it happens next Tuesday."

"If Sanborne sent his pet tarantula to sting you, there's a good chance you may not get your opportunity. His routine will be altered."

He was right. She had thought of that possibility but she hadn't wanted to admit it to herself. "We'll have to see, won't we?"

"I don't believe Royd is going to be willing to wait around for you to get your chance. You'll have to accept that there's a new element to deal with."

"I don't have to accept anything." She sat down on the couch. "Go away, Jock. This is becoming more of a horror story every minute. Let me handle it."

"Would you like a drink?" He sat down in the chair opposite her. "We may have a long time to wait."

"It's going to seem like forever." She leaned back and closed her eyes. She couldn't forget the sight of those two nooses Royd had thrown down. One for her. One for Michael. She'd worried about the consequences to Michael if she killed Sanborne, but she'd never believed his life would be in danger. She'd thought she'd be the only target. Why would anyone kill a child? True, her father had tried to kill Michael, but that had been only a ploy to make everyone believe he'd gone insane. Yet here was another threat to Michael. Damn Sanborne. "And I don't want a drink. I want this night to be over."

"Has Caprio checked in yet?" Boch asked when Sanborne picked up the phone.

"Not yet."

Boch muttered a curse. "I told you that you had to be careful with him. He was a sniveling two-bit hit man when we took him on, and REM-4 didn't make him any smarter."

"But it made him loyal to me. I told him exactly what to do and he'll do it. The experiments demonstrated that intelligence doesn't always make the best subjects. Look at Royd."

"He was the best subject we ever had."

"Until he shrugged off the training as if it didn't exist."

"It wasn't that easy for him. But we're not talking about Royd. I want to know why Caprio hasn't contacted you. Send someone else to Sophie Dunston's house."

"And chance them being seen when the bodies are discovered? No way. We'll wait."

"You'll wait. I'm not that patient. I have my own men and they're not zombies like your choices. I'll give you another two hours to take care of her."

"Why are you frothing at the mouth? She doesn't even know about you. She's after me."

"And how did she know that REM-4 was at this facility? If she knew about that, then she might have found out about our connection. You should have gotten rid of her when she set up shop on our doorstep."

"There was a possibility she could have helped us if I could have gotten my hands on her. REM-4 isn't perfect and she jerked the follow-up research she was working on that could have increased the effect tenfold and made it safer."

"Nothing is perfect. We didn't need her. She wasn't the only fish in the sea. What we've got now is good enough."

"Your clients might not think so. Three out of ten end up dead or insane."

"That's an acceptable casualty percentage. I can't afford to have her snooping around. In three months my retirement goes into effect and I have to be clean if I'm going to keep my contacts."

Boch's precious connections, Sanborne thought impatiently. But those connections would prove important to both of them. The bastard knew every crooked military man in the service and he had overseas links that would be invaluable once REM-4 was set up. He struggled to regain his temper. "You'll keep them. For God's sake, Caprio's only an hour late checking in. Why are you so nervous?"

Boch was silent a moment. "My informant with the CIA phoned me and told me that Royd's left Colombia."

"What?"

"It could mean nothing. He could have taken on another job. He's in demand."

"You told me you were going to send someone to take him down."

"I did. Three times. He's good. We made him good."

"And you're a fool."

"You can't talk to me that way. I won't have it."

I've hurt the idiot's giant ego, Sanborne thought bitterly. "He was out of the country and it was your best chance to bring him down."

"I kept an eye on him."

"So well that you let him slip away. Jesus, I remember him at Garwood. Good? He was a damn expert. No one was better than Royd."

"I'll find him." Boch paused. "But don't you ever talk to me like that again."

Sanborne hesitated. Shit. Pacify the son of a bitch. "Sorry."

"And mind your own concerns. Sophie Dunston may only be a woman but she has to be eliminated. I want to be free and clear before we set up on the island." He hung up.

Did Boch believe he didn't know that? Sophie Dunston had been a thorn in his side since the moment she had found out he was continuing the Amsterdam experiments. He had been able to block her but she wasn't going to give up. She just kept on searching, digging, trying to find someone who would listen.

But he could be worrying about a problem that had already been solved.

If Caprio had strung up the bitch.

"Taken care of?" Jock asked Royd when he came into the house an hour and thirty minutes later.

Royd nodded. "There was more traffic than I thought at this hour." He glanced at Sophie. "You look like shit. Go to bed. We'll talk later."

She shook her head. "You weren't seen?"

"I wasn't seen." He turned to Jock. "You can leave. I'll stay here and make sure she's all right."

"My job."

"Oh, for goodness sake, I'll watch out for myself," she said in exasperation. "Both of you get—"

Michael.

"Okay, one of you stays. Flip a coin." She turned and headed for the door. "I'll be in the guest room down the hall. I don't want to go back in my bedroom yet."

"I'll set up the monitor while you're in the shower," Jock said. "And I'll listen for the alarm until you're out of the bathroom."

"Thanks." She shivered as she went down the hall past her bedroom. A haven of comfort and security had been transformed into something ugly in the space of a few violent moments. She didn't know if she'd ever be able to go in that room again with any degree of comfort.

Don't think about it. Go to sleep. Maybe then she'd be able to cope when she woke.

She didn't go to sleep for another hour. She lay there thinking, trying to get a plan together. She could hear nothing from the other room. Maybe they had both left the house. No, Jock would not have left her. . . .

5

"Wake up."

Michael!

She jerked upright in the bed and swung her feet to the floor. She was half out of the bed when she was pushed back on the pillows.

"Easy. Nothing's wrong. I just had to wake you," Royd said. "I gave you a few hours' sleep but your son's due to wake up soon and I didn't want to scare him by having him face a stranger in the house. You wouldn't want that."

"Oh, no," she said vaguely as she brushed the hair back from her face. She glanced at the clock on the nightstand. Five-thirty A.M. "No, I wouldn't want Michael to—" She shook her head to rid it of sleep. "But Michael doesn't get up until seven."

"Good." He poured a cup of coffee from the carafe on the nightstand and handed it to her. "Then we have a little time to talk." He sat down in the armchair near the bed. "Get back in bed and cover up. It's chilly in here."

"I'm not cold." It was a lie. The jersey night-shirt she was wearing offered little protection and the fact that she was emotionally and physically drained had probably affected her body temperature. "I gather you won the toss."

"Jock would never depend on chance. Actually, he wanted to stay with me. But I persuaded him that I was going to talk to you anyway and I needed some time alone." He grimaced. "Of course I had to assure him I wouldn't lose my temper and cut your throat."

"I can see how he'd worry about that," she said dryly. "Jock and I have become good friends and you're a very angry man." She shrugged wearily. "And that anger is aimed at me. I can understand that."

"Excellent. Then we're on our way to an understanding." He leaned forward, grabbed a blanket, and threw it over her bare legs. "For God's sake, cover up. You've got goose bumps."

"I hoped our discussion wouldn't last long. What is there to say? I hurt you. I'm sorry. If there were anything I could do to make it up to you, I'd do it." Her lips lifted in a sardonic smile. "But I can't let you kill me. I have to think of Michael."

He didn't speak for a moment, studying her face. "My God. And, if there wasn't Michael, I believe you'd let me do it."

"Don't be ridiculous." She looked away from him. "But I did a terrible thing. There has to be some form of restitution I can make."

"If you're telling me the truth, you didn't know what Sanborne was doing with REM-4."

"Did that stop you and Jock and all those other men from being twisted and hurt? Did it save my mother and father? It was my fault." She met his eyes. "And unless I stop Sanborne, it's going to keep on happening. I can't stand that, Royd."

"Killing Sanborne won't get rid of REM-4. If that would have done it, I'd have targeted Sanborne as soon as I escaped Garwood. There's still Boch. Kill one and the other one would snatch the REM-4 disk and go under-cover. I have to get rid of both and the facility and every record and formula they used at Gar-wood. I'm going to wipe REM-4 from the face of the earth. No one is ever going to be able to do what they did to me again." His tone roughened. "And you're not going to ruin my chances of doing that by killing Sanborne. I want it all."

There was such passion and intensity in his voice that it stunned her for an instant. "And what would you do if I did?"

"You don't want to know. You think I'm angry now?"

Yes, she could imagine the lethal rage that would burn through Royd if he was thwarted. "You may have to deal with it."

"The hell I will. If you want Sanborne, you'll have to come over to my camp."

She stiffened. "I don't want to—"

"Do you think I want you? But I may need you. When I came here, I thought there was a chance that I could squeeze information out of you that would make it easier for me to take down Sanborne and Boch. You were listed on the Amsterdam experiment list. I thought you were working with them."

"I'm sorry to disappoint you."

"You did disappoint me. I didn't want to have to take out Caprio. I wanted to zero in on you."

She smiled without mirth. "And instead you were forced to save my worthless life."

"It's not worthless to me. I won't let it be worthless."

"I was joking. My life has meaning. I'm a doctor and I help people. I'm a mother and I believe I'm a good one. And I don't give a damn about whether I'm of worth to you."

"Yes, you do. You feel you owe me something and I'll use that to the max." He leaned back in the chair and stretched his legs out before him. "So get used to the idea that you're not killing Sanborne until I give you the go-ahead. Now relax and let me talk."

"Stop giving me orders. I'll do what I wish, Royd."

"And do you wish REM-4 to survive Sanborne? It will, you know. Mind control is just too tempting not to attract the scumbags of the world. The military of half a dozen countries have been experimenting with it for decades. But everyone struck out until you came along. You handed the answer to Sanborne on a silver platter. You have to help me take it back."

"I don't have to do anything I don't want to do."

"But you want to do this. You may not like me taking over the action, but this is something you want to do. Jock told me you'd have gone into the facility and destroyed every bit of your research connected with REM-4 if you could have done it. Instead, you opted to kill the snake by chopping off the head. You can't kill REM-4 by cutting off Sanborne's head. You have to blow the entire beast to kingdom come."

She drew a deep breath and tried to rid herself of the resentment his bluntness had stirred. He was right. She hadn't thought past getting rid of Sanborne when she'd found she couldn't get into the facility. Hell, she hadn't even known about Boch.

His gaze was narrowed on her face. "If you regret what you did, then do something about it. Get rid of REM-4, dammit."

She didn't speak for a moment. "How?"

"Good, a breakthrough." He leaned forward. "My man at the facility, Nate Kelly, says that during the last six months Sanborne seemed to be trying to arrange a complete break from everything and everyone connected with the REM-4 facility here. A total cleanup. He said that there were rumors of a move out even before they started shipping out equipment and records. Sanborne's either fired or transferred the twelve key personnel who had ever been connected with the experiments. Kelly tried to contact two of them whose records he managed to locate. One of them had been killed in an automobile accident, the other had gone on an extended vacation and wasn't expected back anytime soon."

"More murders?"

"Probably. As I said, a total cleanup. I imagine we'll find— What's wrong?"

She moistened her lips. "My friend Cindy, who gave me the information about Garwood."

"Have you heard from her lately?"

She shook her head. "She resigned from Sanborne's over a year ago. But she was involved in the early experiments."

"She might be safe. Call her." He paused. "And you would have been very close to the top of the list to be eliminated."

"Sanborne hasn't made a move on me since right after I got out of the hospital. He called me just once and offered me big money to come back to work for him. I told him to go to hell. But I've been very vocal to the FBI and several congressmen. It didn't do me any good, but Sanborne wouldn't want me to die suspiciously."

"He made a move last night."

It was true. "I was seen at the facility. He might have decided he had to get rid of me in self-defense."

"You'll pardon me if I doubt that he'd be intimidated enough by you to spur him to move this quickly. I believe he'd probably set you up already and just moved the action up a little."

"Why is he getting rid of all these people now?"

"I can make a guess. He's going international."

"What?"

"He thinks he's got REM-4 down to the point that they can start taking on foreign customers. But they need a base that's not on U.S. soil where they can operate freely and their customers won't come under scrutiny."

"He's going overseas?"

"Kelly says that's his take on it. Overseas or an island close to the mainland. The foreign market is where the real money would be." He grimaced. "And that's why he wants to make sure his boat isn't rocked. He wants any story you told the FBI to fade away into the sunset, and you with it."

"A noose isn't likely to make me fade away." Of course it would, she realized. If everyone thought it was suicide. "Where overseas?"

Royd shook his head. "Kelly wasn't able to find out. He does know that the trucks leaving the facility are going to a dock outside Baltimore."

Her hand clenched on the sheet. "We have to find out."

"I have every intention of finding out. That's why I'm here."

"You thought I might know."

"I was hoping. But it's not a wasted trip. I can still use you."

"I beg your pardon."

"Isn't that what you want? It's clear you're eaten up with guilt and looking for some way to make things right. Well, if I can use you, then you'll have what you want."

"I don't like that word."

"I'm calling it what it is. I'll use you however I can. In ways that Jock would probably disapprove of."

"What ways?"

"Sanborne turned his dogs loose on you for a reason."

"You told me that he wanted to make sure that no one in the FBI paid attention to me."

"He also didn't want his foreign customers paying attention to you. You're the only one who knows the basic formula for REM-4. He wouldn't have an exclusive product if you were around."

Her eyes widened. "He couldn't believe I'd actually sell it. I've been fighting him for years."

"Sanborne and Boch believe in the ultimate power of corruption. Garwood was based on that premise. They'd assume there was a chance you'd succumb in the end. You're too big a threat to assume anything else. Also, you said you were working on an enhancement that could make REM-4 more effective. They'd love to get their hands on it. That means you're going to be a prime target from now on."

"So?"

"That's good for me," he said simply. "If they want you bad enough, then they'll go after you. They could make mistakes. They might send someone who has information I can use." He looked her directly in the eye. "Or I can use you as bait."

"You think I'd let you?"

"Yes, I'm beginning to know you. You'd let me do almost anything to you if it meant making up for what you deem past sins."

"That would be foolish."

"You'd do it. Wouldn't you?"

She didn't answer. "Why do you think that?"

"Because we're more alike than you'd believe. I'd be willing to be crucified if I could turn back the clock."

The words were said quietly but that passion was there again in his face. "Why?"

"I had a choice and made the wrong one. You did the same thing."

She wanted to ask him what choice but she didn't want any confidences that would bring closer intimacy. It would be like being intimate with a tiger.

It wasn't the first time that similarity had occurred to her, she remembered. Sitting there, big, powerful, with that tension only slightly disguised, it hit home again.

Tiger, tiger, burning bright . . .

She looked away from him. "I wouldn't be that self-sacrificing."

"The hell you wouldn't. REM-4 has been monopolizing your life for years." He held up his hand as she started to speak. "Come with me and see REM-4 die or go after Sanborne by yourself and risk REM-4 going on. I don't care."

"Don't give me that bullshit. You do care."

He smiled faintly. "Okay, I do care. You could make it easier for me. Maybe."

She was silent a moment. "What does Jock say about this?"

"Jock is being pulled in a couple directions. He needs to return to Scotland. He knows I'm capable of taking care of you. He knows I might not do it if it suits me. He's right on both counts."

No, Royd would do exactly as he pleased. But the path that was his goal was the one she'd wanted to follow desperately for years. "I'll think about it."

"Not long. I want you out of here. I figure we've probably got a few more hours before Sanborne sends someone else to check on Caprio. Maybe he already knows Caprio slipped up and is giving his assignment to someone else."

"I have a career. I can't just vanish."

"Call in sick. You're a doctor. Reel off some convincing symptoms."

"I don't lie."

"I do. When it saves my ass." He got to his feet. "I'll take a look around outside and check it out. Keep your phone handy." He gave her a card with his cell phone number. "I'll stay within shouting distance. If I don't hear from you, I'll come back in an hour. You can introduce me to your son so he'll be familiar with me. I wouldn't let him go to school if I were you. It might not be safe."

A chill went through her. "I'll consider it. But he wouldn't understand."

"You don't want him to understand. He's got enough on his plate." He frowned. "He may be a problem. I'll have to work something out."

"You'll have nothing to do with my son. You're not going to use **him**."

He smiled faintly. "You see, you're already accepting that you're going to let me use you. The supreme power of guilt."

She gazed at him in wonder. "I believe you may be a terrible, terrible man, Royd."

"I believe you may be right." He moved toward the door. "And who would you rather have to rid you of an even more terrible man? You won't even have to care which one of us bites it." He glanced over his shoulder. "I'll start more coffee going. Then I'll call Jock and get him back here. He's going to want you to tell him that it's all right with you for him to go back to MacDuff's Run."

"I've already told him that."

"But now you have a more convincing argument."

"I haven't made a decision yet, Royd."

"Then make it. I'm your best bet. I'll even make you a promise that neither your son nor you will be killed if you do what I say."

She heard his footsteps in the hall and then the front door closing behind him.

Christ.

She lay back against the pillows, thinking about Royd's words. Before he'd come on the scene, she'd thought that by killing Sanborne she had a chance of destroying all the misery she'd started. No longer. It was going to be much more complicated and involved than she'd dreamed.

But she wouldn't be alone.

Royd would be going after Sanborne whether she did or not. She was the one being railroaded into doing what Royd wanted. No, that wasn't true. Perhaps he was going to try to force her and use her, as he'd told her, but there would be no guilt about her using him.

She couldn't rest any longer. She was too wired. She got out of bed and moved toward the bathroom. Fifteen minutes later she was dressed and heading to the kitchen.

She stopped short as she reached the door.

That manipulative son of a bitch. Damn him to hell.

On the counter, beside the coffeepot, where Royd had known she'd see them, were the two nooses Jock had thrown in the wastebasket.

"Okay, you're not needed there any longer," MacDuff said. "Come home, Jock."

"Sanborne's stirring. He tried to kill her."

"And Royd stopped him. You told me that

Royd had guaranteed her safety. Don't you trust him?"

"I trust the man I met a year ago. I think I trust the man he is now but I'm not the one whose life is going to be on the line. Will you call Venable with the CIA and see if you can get a recent report on him?"

"He doesn't work in South America. And he's been promoted since he helped get rid of Reilly. He may not want to risk his job by revealing classified information."

"Persuade him. He has to have contacts in Colombia. I need to know."

"And if the report is good, you'll come home?"

Jock was silent a moment. "For a while. I'll have to see how it goes."

MacDuff muttered a curse. "Jock, it's not—" He stopped. "I'll call you right back." He hung up.

Jock pressed the disconnect and rose to his feet. He'd take a shower and get back to Sophie's house. Royd had said that he'd told her to stay home and keep Michael with her but Royd didn't know Sophie. She'd do what she thought best regardless of any orders from Royd.

With any luck MacDuff would have the information he needed shortly. When the Laird

focused on any objective, it was with decisive-
ness and ruthless efficiency. He wanted Jock
home and he'd do anything he could to ensure
that goal.

And Jock knew that if he didn't get his way,
MacDuff would probably be on a plane to
Washington. Jesus, Jock didn't want him involved in this mess. MacDuff had already
saved his neck and sanity, and just the knowledge that the Laird was there in the background kept Jock steady these days. But his
dependence on his friend had to stop sometime.

His phone rang.

"She just got in her car with the kid," Royd
said. "Where the hell is she going?"

"Did she have any luggage?"

"No."

"Then she's taking Michael to school.
She'll probably stay outside and make sure
he's okay."

"I told her to keep him home, dammit."

"Are you following her?"

"Of course I am."

"If you lose her, Michael goes to Thomas
Jefferson Middle School. And I wouldn't at-
tempt to confront her in your present mood.
Not if you want to get any cooperation from

her. You must have done something to upset her. Did you?"

"Maybe. I took a calculated risk. It could have either frightened her into coming into my camp or made her defiant."

"It seems you lost."

"She may have been the one who's lost. Boch and Sanborne must know by now that Caprio didn't complete his mission. They'll send someone else."

"But they'll scout around and make sure it's safe."

"She's not safe in that house. She may not be safe anywhere in the city. Convince her."

Jock paused. "But she'll be safe with you?"

"I promised her. I keep my promises, Jock. Talk to her."

"I'll think about it."

Royd was silent a moment. "I'm not like you. I won't be kind to her or forgiving if she screws up. I'll manipulate and use her to get what I want. But in the end REM-4 will be dead as a doornail and she'll be alive. Isn't that what we both want?"

"And the end justifies the means?"

"Hell, yes. Don't pretend that you don't feel the same way."

"I try not to. That's part of the training we

both went through at Garwood. I don't want to give those bastards anything."

"But it's not working, is it?"

No, it wasn't entirely working, Jock thought wearily. That mind-twisting they had gone through had been aimed at appealing to the most savage of instincts that drove man. "Sometimes."

"Yeah, sometimes. But not when it concerns Boch and Sanborne." He paused. "I'm driving through a school zone."

"What street?"

"Sycamore."

"Like I said, she's taking him to school. She'll park and watch the school. She won't risk him. Do you want me to take over surveillance?"

Silence. "Yes, I have to contact Kelly and make plans. I'll call you when I can take my turn."

"I'll be there in thirty minutes."

Blast Jock.

MacDuff stood up and went to the window of his study to look down at the sea crashing against the cliff. He didn't need this problem Jock had dumped in his lap. Why couldn't the boy just do what he said and come home?

Because Jock wasn't a boy any longer and he did what he wanted, not what MacDuff ordered these days. In some ways it had been easier when Jock was that sick robot he'd been when he'd found him all those months ago.

Easier, not better. Jock was gradually coming around to be the man he might have become if he'd not been victimized by Thomas Reilly. No, that wasn't true. His experiences had changed him and he'd never be the lively, cheerful boy who had run in and out of the castle all through his childhood. But he had a chance to come out of the darkness into the light, and by damn, MacDuff would see that he did it.

Okay, get him home. Involve him in the search and make him forget about Sophie Dunston and her problems. God knows, Jock had problems enough of his own.

He reached for his phone and dialed Venable. "MacDuff. I have a favor to ask."

"Again? I did you a big favor when I let you take jurisdiction over Jock. I'm not about to put my ass on the line a second time."

"It's no big deal. I just need some information."

Venable was silent a moment. "I told you I couldn't do anything about Sanborne. He has too much clout. No one can make a move on him without a truckful of proof. I assigned someone to check on Garwood and there was absolutely no connection with Sanborne. It was a plastic factory that failed after only a year in business. The CIA's position on Sophie Dunston is that she's a wacko and out to get revenge on the company that fired her."

"Jock believes her."

"And do you think that the Company would think him any more stable? For God's sake, he was in a mental hospital too. And he tried to commit suicide three times."

Better to get away from Jock's past, Mac-Duff thought. Venable hadn't wanted to trust him with Jock's custody and didn't need any reminders of how volatile Jock had been. "I'm not asking you to go after Sanborne."

"Good, because it's not going to happen."

"I want you to run a check on a man who works with one of your operatives in Colombia. I need it right away. A few hours max."

"Tough. I'm a busy man."

"I know. But it will help me bring Jock under my wing here. You've never approved of him running around on his own."

"You've got that right," Venable said sourly. He sighed. "Okay, give me the damn name."

"Hi, Sophie."

She stiffened and then relaxed as she saw Jock walking toward her car.

He held up a McDonald's bag. "I brought you a cheeseburger and fries. I'd bet you haven't had any breakfast and I thought you might need some fuel. You've been sitting there for four hours."

"How do you know?" She unlocked the passenger door, took the cheeseburger, and unwrapped it. "Did you follow me?"

"No, Royd followed you. He turned you over to me. He said he had things to do but I think he wanted me to smooth over ruffled feathers. He said he made a calculated move and it could have backfired."

"Bastard." She bit into the cheeseburger. "Christ, he's an iceberg."

"Not really. Actually, the opposite is probably closer to the truth. He's on fire. French fry?"

She took one. "You're defending him?"

"No, I'm explaining him. I wouldn't waste my breath if I didn't believe you may have to understand Royd."

"Why?"

"I think you know. You're angry but you already realize that Royd could help you."

"And I'm supposed to trust him?"

He nodded. "MacDuff thinks you can."

"What?"

"I asked him to check on Royd's current operations in Colombia."

"And?"

"A friend in the CIA contacted Ralph Soldono, the operative who deals with Royd in Colombia. Soldono is very impressed with Royd. He thinks he's some kind of military superman. He goes in either by himself or with a few of his men and he does the job."

"What kind of job?"

"Everything from rescuing kidnapped executives held by the rebels to eliminating a particularly vicious band of bandits. He's fast, smart, and he doesn't quit."

She remembered the air of confidence that surrounded Royd. "I could guess all that."

"Soldono also said that he'd never taken on a job and then backed out, no matter how tough or dirty it became." He paused. "And that he kept his word. That's what you really want to know, isn't it?"

"Yes, that's what I want to know." Her

hands clenched on the burger. "He promised me he'd keep Michael alive and that REM-4 would be destroyed. Should I believe him?"

He smiled. "I know better than to interfere with your decisions. I can only give you the best information I have and leave it to your judgment. He's evidently fairly incredible and Soldono finds him reliable. That being said, he's not subtle or polite and he'll probably risk your life. You've got to decide whether he'll be able to keep you alive and make the risk worth your while. And he'll probably rub you the wrong way a dozen times a day."

Her lips tightened as she remembered the two nooses on the counter. "Oh, yes."

Jock was studying her expression. "But you're leaning in his direction."

"You know I've wanted to get into the facility and destroy all the REM-4 records. I just couldn't get in to do it. Royd has a man on the inside at the facility and he knows more than I do. Probably a lot more. He says he's going to use me. Let him try." She tossed the rest of the sandwich into the bag. "I might end up using him." She looked at him. "But I want you out of this, Jock. Go home."

"I keep hearing that." He made a face. "And if I like Royd's plan of attack I may go back to MacDuff's Run for a while. I'll have to see. Have you told Michael anything?"

"No, I woke him up late and used that as an excuse to drive him to school."

"That can't go on. He'll—"

"I know that," she interrupted. "But I'm not going to tell him anything until I have to do it. I have enough trouble keeping him calm. I don't want to give him any more reason for bad dreams."

He nodded. "Just be prepared." He opened the car door. "I'll go back to my own car. I have some phone calls to make. I'll stay here and pick up Michael when he gets out of school, if you like."

She shook her head. "He has soccer practice again. I'll take him by Chuck E. Cheese's before I bring him home."

"Do you want company?"

"No, I've cleared my schedule for today and I have some thinking to do."

"I'll still stick around for a while. And either Royd or I will be shadowing you for the rest of the day. Call me if you change your mind."

She watched him walk away. She'd much

rather Jock stick around than Royd, and she wished she could change her mind. But Royd was driven and Jock needed to go home. It was much better she deal with that damn bastard until she could see her way clear.

6

"What's going on, Mom?" Michael wasn't looking at her, his gaze fixed out the car window. "What's wrong?"

Her hands tightened on the steering wheel. Michael had been very quiet during dinner and she'd half expected this question. "What do you mean?"

"You're worried. At first, I thought it was about me, but it's more. Isn't it?"

She should have known Michael would sense her inner disturbance. After all he'd gone through, his awareness had been honed to razor sharpness. Sometimes she wondered how he managed to be as normal as he was. "It's nothing for you to worry about. It's work stuff."

His gaze swung to her face. "Honest?"

She hesitated. She wanted to protect him, but was protecting him from the truth best? The situation was becoming ugly and there might come a time when he might be faced with that ugliness. "Yes, it's nothing for you to worry about right now. And no, it's not about work."

He was silent a moment. "Grandpa?"

She bit her lip. It was the first time he'd mentioned his grandfather since that day on the pier. "Partly. I may have to send you away to your father for a while."

He shook his head. "He won't want me."

"He **will** want you. He loves you."

"He acts funny around me. I think he's glad when I go home."

"Maybe he thinks you don't want to be with him. You should talk."

He shook his head again. "He won't want me. And I wouldn't go anyway. If you're in trouble, I'm going to stay with you."

So much for honesty. She drew a deep, frustrated breath. "We'll talk about it when we get home. I'm not really in trouble and there's nothing—"

"Look at those trucks." Michael was rolling down the window. "What's happening?"

Three blue and white trucks with Baltimore Light and Gas emblazoned on the sides were parked at the side of the street with lights flashing. Her own headlights illuminated the figure of a policeman in the middle of the street talking to the motorist in the sedan in front of her.

She slowed down and then stopped. "I don't know. We'll have to see." The policeman was waving the motorist to go on and was walking toward her. "What's the problem, Officer?"

"Gas leak. Do you live in this block?"

"No, four blocks down." She glanced at the gray-uniformed utility employees who were going from house to house. "Are they evacuating?"

"Nah, they're just checking out the houses for leaks and they want us to keep anyone from entering until they finish." He smiled. "They've only found two minor ones so far. But we have to be careful. We're advising everyone on the street to not turn on any power sources until we give the okay."

"I'm on High Tower Street. Does that go for us?"

He checked his clipboard. "No reports of leaks past Northrup. You should be okay. Might be a good idea to take a few extra precautions." He waved her ahead. "Call the gas company if you have any questions."

"Don't worry, I will."

"Will we be able to smell the gas if we've got a leak?" Michael asked as she drove past the roadblock.

"I'm sure we can. They put in scent as a safety measure so that we can detect it. That's how people can tell to call the gas company." There were no utility trucks in the next block, or in the next one. Her own block was equally quiet. "I think we'll call the gas company anyway." She pulled into the driveway and pressed the garage opener. "In fact, we probably should do it before we go into—"

"Stop." Royd was at her window. "Now!"

She instinctively hit the brakes.

"Get out! Both of you."

His tone was so urgent she didn't hesitate. She opened the door. "Michael, get out."

"Mom, what . . ." But he was scrambling out of the car as he spoke.

"Good." Royd was getting into the driver's seat. "Now take him to my car, the tan Toyota parked on the street. The keys are in the ignition. Get him out of here. I'll call you when it's safe to come back."

She hesitated.

"Get the hell out of here."

She grabbed Michael and ran toward the Toyota.

A moment later they were halfway down the block.

"Mom, who was—"

"Hush." Her gaze was on the rearview mirror. What the devil . . . Her van was rolling toward the open garage. As she watched, the van suddenly lurched forward.

Royd jumped from the vehicle and rolled over and over on the front lawn as the van entered the garage.

What on earth?

Michael was peering over his shoulder. "What's he doing? Why did he tell us—"

The house exploded!

The windows of the Toyota rattled with the force of the blast.

Flames.

Wood, doors, and glass were shattered all over the lawn.

Royd!

Where was Royd?

The last she had seen of him, he was on the lawn, but black smoke was curling out of the wreck of the house and the grass was covered with burning beams.

Her phone rang.

"Go around the corner and drive to the end

of the street," Royd said. "Don't stop until then. I'll meet you."

"What happened? What did you do?"

He was gone.

She dropped the phone and made the turn at the end of the block. She caught a glimpse of people running out of their houses and up the street toward the inferno that had been her home.

Her home. Michael's home.

She looked down at him. His face was pale and his hands were clenched on his book bag. "Hold on, Michael. We're safe."

He shook his head as he turned around to stare straight ahead. He was probably in shock.

Who could blame him? She was in shock too.

Royd was standing on the corner. She pulled over to the curb.

He jumped into the backseat. "Drive. Get out of here. I don't want you seen."

She could hear the wail of a siren as she pressed the accelerator. "Why not?"

"Later. Get out of the subdivision and turn left at the cross-street." He flipped open his phone and dialed a number. "All hell's broken loose, Jock. Meet us at the La Quinta Inn on Highway Forty." He hung up. "Pull over and you and the boy get in the backseat. I'll drive."

"Stop ordering me around, Royd." She tried

to steady her voice. "All I need from you are answers."

"That may not be all the boy needs," he said quietly. "And I can't help him right now."

He was right. Michael had just seen his home blown to bits and she had already decided he was dazed and in shock. He did need her. She pulled to the curb. "Come on, Michael. We need to get in the backseat."

He didn't argue, but his movements were stiff and uncoordinated as he obeyed her.

"It's okay, Michael." That was a lie. "No, it's not okay." She slipped her arm around his shoulders. "It's terrible, but we'll find a way to make it okay."

He didn't look at her. His gaze was fixed on Royd as he got into the driver's seat. "Who is he?"

"His name is Matt Royd."

"He blew up our house."

"No, he didn't. He doesn't want to hurt us."

"Then why did—"

"I'll explain when I know myself. Can you wait until we get to this motel and we have a chance to find out? Jock is going to meet us there."

He nodded slowly.

"Good." She leaned back and drew him closer. "I won't let anything hurt you, Michael."

He lifted his head to stare into her eyes. "What kind of schmuck do you think I am? I'm not scared something will happen to me. It's you, Mom."

Her arm tightened. "Sorry." She cleared her throat. "Well, I won't let anything happen to me either." She lifted her gaze to meet Royd's in the rearview mirror. "Get us to that motel, Royd. My son and I want answers."

"Wait here." Royd jumped out of the car and strode toward the motel office. Five minutes later he came out and got into the car. "Room Fifty-two. First floor. It's at the end of the building. No one's occupying the rooms on either side of you. I paid to keep it that way."

He parked the car in the parking spot in front of the room and handed her the key. "Lock the door behind you. Go in and get the boy settled. I'll wait for Jock."

"I'm not 'the boy,'" Michael said. "My name is Michael Edmunds."

Royd nodded. "I apologize. I'm Matt Royd." He held out his hand. "Things are a little confused right now but that's no reason for me to treat you as if you weren't present. Will you take your mother into the room and get her a glass of water? She looks a bit shaken."

Michael gazed at Royd's outstretched hand and then slowly reached out and shook it. "It's no wonder," he said gruffly. "But she'll be okay. She's tough."

"I can tell." Royd's gaze shifted to Sophie. "And I think your Michael's pretty tough too. It would be a good idea to be upfront with him."

She got out of the car. "I don't need advice on how to communicate with my son. Come on, Michael."

"Wait." Michael was staring at Royd. "If you didn't blow up our house, then it was someone else. Right? It wasn't an accident?"

Royd didn't hesitate. "Right. It wasn't an accident. It was just someone trying to make it look like an accident."

"That's enough," Sophie said.

Royd shrugged. "This seems to be my time for making blunders."

"It will be a big blunder if you don't come in soon and tell me exactly what's happening." She glanced at Michael. "I mean, tell us."

He smiled faintly. "I thought that was what you meant. I'll be in as soon as Jock gets here."

"You'd better." She strode to the door and unlocked it. "I'm tired of being put off, Royd."

"He said to lock the door," Michael said as she slammed the door behind them.

She turned the dead bolt. "I was going to do it."

"You're mad at him." Michael was studying her face. "Why?"

"He rubs me the wrong way."

"Didn't he sort of save us?"

"Yes. Sort of."

"But you don't like him."

"I don't know him well. But he's one of those people who run over you if you don't get out of their way."

"I didn't like him much either at first but maybe he's not so bad."

"What?"

"Oh, not like Jock," Michael said quickly. "But he kind of makes me feel safe. Like Schwarzenegger in the **Terminator** movie I saw at Dad's."

Trust Dave to show Michael movies on the taboo list for him. "Royd's not some futuristic Terminator." It was odd that he'd picked up on the lethal violence inherent in Royd, but perhaps it wasn't a bad thing that anything or anyone could give him a sense of security at this time. "But you can feel safe with him. He used to be a SEAL and he knows what he's doing."

"A SEAL?"

She could see that had impressed him.

Maybe too much. "Sit down and try to rest. We've had quite an evening."

Michael shook his head. "You sit down." He went toward the bathroom. "Mr. Royd said you should have some water."

"Mr. Royd is an—" She stopped. Keeping Michael busy and in a protective mode was healthy. It would stop him from thinking of the past few hours. She dropped down in the occasional chair by the bed. "Thanks. That would be good."

He handed her the glass of water and sat down on the bed. "You're welcome." His expression was grave. "And Mr. Royd was right. I need to know what's going on so I can help, Mom."

Jesus, he didn't sound like a child at all.

But that didn't mean she should burden him with this horror.

But the horror had come knocking on his door again. If she didn't tell him at least part of the story, she risked him withdrawing even farther into night terrors. The unknown was usually worse than facing reality. It was a toss-up what would be best for him.

"Mom." His face was strained and his eyes were pleading. "Don't close me out. I have to help you."

"Michael . . ." She reached out to touch his

cheek. Lord, she loved him. What was she supposed to tell him? That his mother had been prepared to kill a man? That last night a man had been trying to kill them both only yards from where he slept? Okay, skip that part of the story and just give him the background. That was bad enough. "Years ago I was very worried about your grandfather. You probably don't remember, but he had terrible dreams. Sort of like you. And he didn't sleep much. I wanted very much to help him. So I started working on . . ."

"It was that man, Sanborne, who blew up our house?" Michael said.

Sophie nodded. "Probably. At least he gave the order."

"Because he wanted to kill you. He hates you?"

"I don't think he even hates me. I'm in his way. He just wants to wipe out everyone who knows about REM-4."

"Well, I hate him." Michael's eyes were blazing. "I want to kill him."

"Michael, I understand. But I have to shoulder some of the blame. It's not—"

"He hurt Grandpa and Grandma and all

those people. He hurt you." He threw himself into her arms. "It's not your fault. It's not your fault. He did it. He did it all."

She could feel his tears against her cheek as she held him close. "He'll be punished, Michael. As I told you, it's just difficult to find a way to do it."

"Why? The good guys are supposed to help. The good guys are supposed to win."

"We will win." She pushed him away to look down into his face. "I promise you, Michael." She had to make him believe. "We **will** win."

"He blew up our house," he said fiercely. "Why don't we go blow up his?"

Good heavens. "An eye for an eye?"

"I bet Mr. Royd would do it. Why don't we ask him?"

"We have a lot of questions to ask him. I don't believe that should be one of them." She kissed his forehead. Time to get back to normal, everyday things if he was going to have a chance for an undisturbed night. "Now go wash your face. Neither of us ate much for dinner. I'll call Domino's for some pizza."

"I'm not hungry." He frowned. "But you should eat. Go ahead."

"Thank you. I imagine you'll be able to choke down a few bites. I'll just step outside and ask Royd if he wants to join us." She headed for the door. "And Jock should be here soon. He likes pepperoni, doesn't he?"

"With mushrooms." Michael was heading for the bathroom. "I'll be right back."

Michael was reacting more normally than she had hoped, she realized with relief as she opened the door. She had thought fear would be the primary response, but she had underestimated him. It had been shock and then anger and protectiveness that had dominated.

Royd and Jock were sitting in Royd's Toyota and both men got out when they saw her.

"I'm sorry, Sophie," Jock said quietly. "It must have been a hell of a shock for you and Michael."

"How's he doing?" Royd asked.

"Fine." She took a deep breath. "No, not fine. You'll be glad to know I had a talk with him."

"You told him everything?"

"Almost everything. He didn't need to know about Caprio." She looked at Jock. "Or precisely what Sanborne did to you and Royd. I generalized."

"Smart," Royd said. "He might have confused us with the bad guys. I'm sure he's mixed up enough."

She nodded grimly. "Mixed up enough to think you're like the Terminator. I set him straight and told him you were definitely flesh and blood."

Jock chuckled. "Not a bad simile. The Terminator protected the kid in the last two movies."

"And was a prime villain in the first. I'm sure he prefers you, Jock," Royd said. "You're the iron hand in the velvet glove."

"I'm sure he likes me best too," Jock said. "What's not to like?"

Sophie gave him a cool glance. "The fact that the two of you were sitting out here probably making plans before coming in to face me."

"True," Jock said. "But we also thought you might need some time with Michael."

She turned to Royd. "How did you know that the house was going to blow?"

"I didn't. I thought it was a good possibility. It was a little too coincidental that there would be a gas leak the night after a failed attempt on your life."

"The leak was four blocks away."

"And therefore you would feel safer about it. But when the house blew, it would make it much less suspect to the authorities." He tilted his head. "Weren't you a little suspicious?"

"Yes, I was going to call the gas company as soon as I got into the garage."

"You wouldn't have gotten into the house. The garage was full of fumes. There was a device on the floor that would cause a spark when you rolled over it. One spark would have been enough."

"How did you know?"

He was silent a moment. "It's what I would have done. What I was trained to do."

Shock rippled through her. She shouldn't be this stunned. She glanced away from him. "Of course."

"Don't look away from me." Royd's voice was suddenly rough. "You'd better be damned glad I knew what was happening or you and your son would be dead."

She forced herself to look back at him. "I'm glad of anything that keeps Michael alive. And I don't have any right to condemn what I was instrumental in teaching you."

"Dammit, I didn't mean— That's not what I—"

She interrupted. "That doesn't mean I'm not mad as hell that you let my house be blown up. If you guessed what was going to happen you could have just told Michael and me to get out of the car. You didn't have to release the brakes and let it roll into the garage. You wanted the house to blow."

"That's right, I did."

"Why? And why did you tell me to take Michael and go? Why didn't you want us to be seen?"

"I thought we might gain an advantage if everyone thought you were dead."

"What kind of advantage?"

"Time."

She thought about it. "But when they search the ruins, they'll know we weren't in there."

"It will take a little while. That fire will burn for a while because it was fed by the gas. And then it will be too hot to explore the ashes until they're sure it's safe and there are no pockets of gas that could ignite and injure the firemen. There was a terrific explosion and they'll realize if you were inside that you couldn't survive. Any search would be for body parts and that would take a hell of a long time to be absolutely certain. If we're lucky and you weren't seen leaving the area, we'll have a chance."

"A chance to do what?"

"Get Michael away from here." Jock paused. "Get Michael away from you, Sophie."

She stiffened. "What are you talking about?"

"Michael's almost died twice in the past twenty-four hours and he wasn't even the target. As long as he's anywhere near you, he's going to be in danger."

"You want me to send him away?" Her hands clenched into fists. "I can't do that. He needs me."

"He needs to stay alive," Royd said. "And you need to be free to move without worrying about him."

"Shut up. This isn't any of your concern. You don't know what—" She stopped. It was his concern. She had made it his concern when she'd destroyed his life by creating REM-4. "You haven't been with him when he's had one of his night terrors."

"I have been," Jock said. "You trust me, don't you?"

"What are you saying?"

"I want to take Michael back to MacDuff's Run with me."

"Scotland? No way."

"He'll be safe there. MacDuff will make sure of that." He smiled. "I'll make sure of that. And I've taken care of Michael when he's had a night terror while you were working. We got along."

Michael thousands of miles away . . .

"I'd be scared to death."

"Then you'd better decide what's more important to you," Royd said. "I promised to keep both of you safe, but this would make it a hell of a lot easier for me."

She closed her eyes as waves of sick fear surged over her. She had rarely been more than five miles away from Michael since she'd gotten out of the hospital after her parents' deaths. "He's my son. I can take care of him."

Neither man answered her.

Of course they didn't. It had all been said. She was being a selfish bitch in the name of maternal love. She couldn't do that to Michael. She opened her eyes. "Have you talked to MacDuff about this?"

"Yes," Jock said. "The minute Royd called me and told me what happened. MacDuff didn't give me any arguments."

"That's not good enough. I don't want Michael to be grudgingly accepted."

Jock shook his head. "Once the Laird is committed it won't be like that. He'll take Michael as one of his own." He grimaced. "And, believe me, MacDuff has a very strong sense of family."

"I need to talk to him."

"I thought you would. Will tomorrow morning do? MacDuff arranged for Michael and me to leave on a private plane at nine tomorrow."

Good God, everything was moving too fast. "Michael doesn't even have a passport."

"MacDuff is overnighting a British passport for him."

"What?"

"Under the name of Michael Gavin." He smiled. "My young cousin."

"A phony passport?"

Jock nodded. "MacDuff was in the Marines and lived a rough-and-tumble life on occasion. He's acquired a few contacts that have proved useful."

"Crooks," she said flatly.

"Well, yes. Extremely skilled crooks. In this life it's often necessary to bypass red tape and bureaucracy."

She was silent a moment. "I'll talk to him. I'm not promising that I'll let Michael go."

"You'll let him go," Jock said. "You can talk to him every day and you'll know that I'll guard and care for him." He shot a sly glance at Royd. "Though I'm no Terminator."

"The hell you're not." Royd said to Sophie, "Do you want me to make myself scarce while the two of you break it to the kid?"

She thought about it. "No, Michael isn't going to want to leave. He's worried about me. He mustn't see me as being alone."

He smiled faintly. "You've already made up

your mind. You're only working on finding the best way to implement it."

She turned and opened the door. "The best way is to call Domino's for pizza and then have Jock talk to Michael while we're eating it. He'll listen to him."

"And what do I do?" Royd asked.

"You sit and look stern and responsible." She gave him a cool look. "And if you have to talk, you curb that damn bluntness and try not to say anything that will start him worrying."

"Why don't you go to bed?" Michael asked as he turned over to look at her sitting in the easy chair. "I'll be okay."

His eyes were glistening in the darkness and his body appeared stiff beneath the blanket. Christ, it would be a miracle if he didn't have a night terror tonight after all he'd been through, she thought. First the explosion and then the emotional hours of having Jock try to persuade him into going to Scotland with him. It was incredible to Sophie that he'd finally given in and agreed. "I'm not tired. Go to sleep, baby."

He didn't speak for a moment. "You're

afraid because I don't have the monitor. You'll stay up all night because you're scared not to do it."

"It's only one night. Jock promised that MacDuff would have one at the castle by the time you got there."

"That's not going to help you tonight. I should be the one to stay awake. I'm always causing you trouble."

"You don't— Yes, you have problems, but so does everybody."

"Not like me." He paused. "Am I crazy, Mom?"

"No, you're **not** crazy. Why would you think that?"

"I can't stop. I try and try but I can't stop the dreams."

"If you talked about them, it could help." She reached forward and took his hands. "Don't close me out, Michael. Let me help you fight."

He shook his head and she could feel his withdrawal. "I'll be okay. I feel better now that I know that Grandpa wasn't crazy. Or that he was crazy, but it wasn't his fault. I used to worry about— I didn't understand. Grandpa loved me. I know he did."

"I know he did too."

"But I didn't understand how it could happen."

"You'd have had to be an Einstein to understand. It took me months to work it out and I knew more than you did."

He was silent a moment. "I know Sanborne has to be punished but I don't want you here. I don't want you to do it. He'll hurt you."

"Michael, we discussed this."

"He'll hurt you."

"I won't let him. He won't hurt either of us. But yes, he has to be punished. And it's not safe for either of us as long as he's free." As long as he was alive, she amended silently. "You trust Jock, don't you?"

"Yes."

"And he told you I'd be safe. He said that Royd was very good at taking care of people."

He nodded. "And he's a SEAL."

Thank heaven for that, she thought. Michael had latched on to that part of Royd's past with alacrity. "So everything's going to be fine."

"Yeah." His grasp was nervously opening and closing on her hands. "Do you suppose God forgave Grandpa for what he did?"

"I know Grandma would have forgiven him. I'm sure she would intercede. It wasn't his fault."

"I guess so." His grasp tightened, hard. "It wasn't your fault either. Stop thinking that."

"Go to sleep, Michael. You have a long flight tomorrow."

"How long will I have to stay there?"

"I don't know. Not long." Lord, she was going to miss him. "But we'll talk every day."

"What time?"

"Six o'clock Scotland time."

"You promise?"

"I promise."

Michael didn't speak again but she knew he wasn't asleep. Every now and then his hand would flex in hers.

Go to sleep, Michael. I'll be here for you.

But he knew that was true, that she'd be there for him no matter what happened. She hadn't realized until tonight that he'd been afraid he was going insane. Yet she should have known. What was more reasonable to a boy who thought his grandfather was a madman?

His hand was relaxing, going limp. Sleep, at last?

She leaned back in the chair. She was tired but she couldn't close her eyes. She could sleep after she put Michael on that plane. She should call and make sure MacDuff had the right monitor. She needed to talk to him anyway.

She trusted Jock but she had to be sure that MacDuff seemed to be everything Jock had told her.

"Mom?" Michael said drowsily. "Stop hurting. . . ."

"I'm okay, Michael," she said softly.

"You're not. I can feel it. Don't hurt. It's not your fault. . . ."

He was asleep.

She bent forward and gently kissed his forehead before leaning back in the chair.

7

Royd watched Michael jerkily climb the steps to the private jet with Jock. "He's going to blow," he said quietly. "It's beginning to hit home."

Dear God, she hoped not. Michael had been silent all the way to the airport, but it was normal for him to be unhappy. "Maybe not. Jock was very persuasive."

"He's going to blow," Royd repeated. "Be prepared for it."

How could she be prepared for—

Michael was turning, lurching down the steps and tearing across the tarmac. He hurled himself into her arms. "I don't want to go," he whispered. "It's no good. No good."

Her arms tightened around him. "It is good," she said unevenly. "I'd never ask you to go if it weren't for the best."

He was silent for a moment and then pushed away from her. His eyes were glistening with tears. "You promise you'll be okay? You promise nothing will happen to you?"

"I promise. We've gone through all this." She tried to smile. "And Royd has promised you that too. Do you want us to sign a contract?"

He shook his head. "But things happen. Sometimes crazy things."

"Not to me." She stared him in the eye. "Are you backing out of going?"

He shook his head again. "I wouldn't do that. I want to stay with you but Jock says you'll be safer without me."

"Yes, I will."

"Then I'll go." His arms tightened around her in a desperate bear hug before he turned to Royd and said fiercely, "You take care of her. Do you hear me? If you let anything happen to her, I'm coming after you."

Before Royd could reply he'd whirled and was running toward the plane, where Jock was waiting. A moment later the door closed behind them.

Royd chuckled. "I'll be damned. I think he would. I believe I'm beginning to feel very close to your son."

"Oh, shut up." She wiped her eyes, watching as the plane taxied down the runway. She felt as if she were being torn apart. It was for the best, she had told Michael. And she'd talked to MacDuff earlier this morning and he'd promised to keep her son safe. But that didn't make it any easier. She waited until the plane was no longer in sight before she turned away. "Let's get out of here." She headed for the parking lot. "Have you talked to your friend Kelly?"

"I couldn't reach him last night. He told me that he wouldn't contact me unless it was safe for him." He fell into step with her. "If Sanborne's busily eliminating everyone connected with REM-4, getting near those files must be becoming increasingly difficult."

"Does that mean you're not going to make the attempt?"

"Don't be stupid," he said coldly. "It means that I'm going to wait until I have a sure thing."

"And what if you don't have a sure thing? What if he gets away with those records and sets up his little foreign stronghold?"

He opened the car door for her. "Why, then I'll find him and blow his hideaway to hell and back."

His tone was uninflected and his face without expression, yet she felt the force that was driving him as if it were tangible. She drew a deep breath and changed the subject. "Where are we going? Back to the motel?"

He shook his head. "We're leaving the city. I've made a reservation at a motel about forty miles from here. I don't want to risk a chance of someone seeing you and recognizing you. According to the news last night, you and Michael are presumed dead. I want you to stay that way as long as possible."

"I suppose I can't let my ex-husband know that Michael's alive?"

"Hell, no."

She hadn't thought so. "It's going to be hard for him. He does love Michael."

"Tough." He backed out of the parking space. "What about you? Does he still love you?"

"He's married again."

"That isn't what I asked."

She shrugged. "I had a child with him. How do I know how much feeling he has left?"

"How about you?"

She glanced at him but he wasn't looking at her. "What?"

"How do you feel about him?"

"That's none of your business. Why would you want to know?"

He didn't speak for a moment. "Maybe I'm probing for possible weaknesses. It would be the smart thing to do."

"Are you?"

"No."

"Curiosity?"

He shrugged. "Maybe. I don't know."

"Then screw your damn curiosity. All you have to know is that I'm not going to run to Dave and let him know that Michael and I are alive." She leaned back against the seat and closed her eyes. "And I'm tired of talking to you. It's like hacking my way through a field of briars. Wake me when we get to the motel."

The room at the Holiday Inn Express was clean and spare, but it had a few more amenities than the motel where they had stayed the night before.

Royd handed her the key after he'd glanced

around her room. "I booked an adjoining room." He smiled faintly. "Michael would be upset if I wasn't within calling distance."

She tossed her purse on the bed. "I need some clothes. Everything I had to wear was in that house."

"I'll go out and buy you something." He studied her. "Six?"

"Eight. Size seven shoes. And I'll need a laptop. I'm going to take a shower and then nap." She headed for the bathroom. "Will you see if there's any news about our recent demise?"

"Anything you say."

"How accommodating. One would never associate you with the man who destroyed almost everything I had in the world."

"I promise I'll replace everything of value."

"You can't do that. I don't care about furniture and appliances, but what about my photo albums? And my son's souvenirs and toys he cherished?"

"No, I can't replace those," he said quietly. "I guess I didn't think about them. I grew up in eight different foster homes and no one was interested in taking any family pictures. But I'll try to make it up to Michael. Only you can decide if the time we bought was worth what I took from you."

Of course it was worth it. Michael was flying away to safety. "You did what you thought best."

"Yes, I did. But that doesn't mean I did it in the best way. I'm not perfect." He nodded. "I'll pick up some Chinese on the way back. I'll lock the door. Don't open it to anyone but me."

The door shut behind him.

Don't open it to anyone but me.

His words had been said in an almost casual tone but the meaning wasn't casual. She was still a target and that no doubt pleased Royd. Why wasn't she more afraid? She felt tired and on edge but there was no fear. It was probably because Michael was no longer in danger. She could cope with anything as long as she didn't have to worry about her son.

She stepped beneath the shower and let the warm water rush over her body. Michael would be fine. No one could take better care of him than Jock.

Unless it was Royd.

Why had that thought popped into her mind? Royd was everything that was barbed and deadly. He had none of the gentleness that masked the threat that Jock presented to the world. He was blunt and single-minded and had as much sensitivity as a charging rhino.

Yet he had known that Michael would erupt in that last moment.

Judgment, not sensitivity. She had never doubted he was intelligent.

Don't think about him. She'd take these few moments to relax and gather herself together. She was upset and angry and was beginning to feel the first pangs of loneliness. Michael was always with her, either in person or in her thoughts. Every day ended and began with her son. Now she was cut off from him and it hurt.

Then stop whining and do what you have to do. It was the only way they could be together again. She wasn't only a mother. She was a woman with a brain and a will.

And that will had to be directed squarely at Sanborne.

Royd was sitting in a chair across the room, one leg slung over the arm and his head leaning against the back.

Tiger, tiger, burning bright.

"Awake?" Royd sat up straight and smiled.

"You were out cold. I wonder how much sleep you've missed over the last couple years."

She shook her head to clear it before she sat up and wrapped the sheet more firmly about her naked body. "How long have you been here?"

He checked his watch. "Three hours. And it took me a couple hours to gather you a wardrobe and a duffel bag."

Five hours. "You should have woken me." She swung her feet to the floor. "Or gone to bed yourself."

"I wasn't in a hurry. Though I seem to be making a habit of being the one to wake you, don't I? But this time I was enjoying it."

"That's a bunch of—" She broke off as she met his eyes. Sensual. As sensual as the way he was lounging. Lazy, catlike, totally sensual. She tore her gaze away. "Then you'd better find something else to amuse you. I don't like any intrusions on my space, Royd."

"I'm not intruding. I haven't moved from this chair since I came in here. I've just been watching you." He smiled. "Sorry. I've been in the jungle for too long." He stood up. "I'll go back to my room and heat up the Chinese in my microwave. Your clothes are in those two shopping bags across the room. I hope they fit.

I tried to choose something with a little style."
He said over his shoulder, "But you'll never
find anything that you looked better in than
that sheet."

She stared after him. Jesus, her cheeks were
warm and her breasts beneath the sheet were
suddenly full and sensitive. She felt— She
didn't want to think about how she felt. And
she didn't want to think about the man who
had made her feel like that. It was crazy as hell
anyway. She'd always been drawn to men who
were intelligent and civilized, like Dave. Royd
might be intelligent, but there was nothing civilized about him. He made up his own rules
and ignored everything else.

It was okay to feel like this. That uncon-
trolled response was purely biological and normal, considering that she'd not had sex since
months before her breakup with Dave. She'd
been caught off guard and probably would
have had the same reaction to anyone under
the same circumstances.

Maybe not anyone. Royd had a bold sexuality that—

Forget it. That moment wouldn't be repeated. She stood up and headed across the
room to the shopping bags. Get dressed, pack
the rest of the clothes in the duffel, and go into

Royd's room and eat dinner. By the time they finished it might be time to call Jock and talk to Michael.

"I've just seen the evening news," Boch said when Sanborne picked up the phone. "For God's sake, the police still don't know whether they were in that house when it exploded. Or if they do, they're keeping it under their hats."

"They had to be in it. The cop who stopped the car recognized their photos. Remnants of that same car were found in the ruins and on the lawn."

"No bodies, dammit."

"The force of the explosion. We're looking at body parts and they're not going to announce a death until they're certain. It could trigger a flurry of lawsuits against the gas company and cause a panic in the neighborhoods where the leak existed. It will take time."

"Excuses, Sanborne? Your Caprio must have fouled up and now you don't have proof that your men followed through to correct the blunder."

Sanborne kept hold of his temper. "I can't phone any of my contacts with the police. I can't be associated with her in any way. Can't you see that? I've had Gerald Kennett call the hospital and she hasn't phoned in. She usually checks up on her patients at weekends. The staff is shocked and worried."

"That's not enough. She's not stupid. She could be hiding out. She must have close friends she'd contact. Pump them."

"I have to be careful. I can't have them call the police claiming harassment." He didn't wait for an answer. "I'm way ahead of you. I sent one of my men, Larry Simpson, to interview the neighbors and the kid's soccer coach, posing as a newspaper reporter. None of them have heard from her."

"The ex-husband?"

"I have someone on the way to Edmunds's house now. Satisfied?"

"No, I'll be satisfied when the police announce that Sophie Dunston was blown to hell." Boch paused. "Ben Kaffir has been in touch with me. He's interested in REM-4 but he's playing footsie with Washington and he won't commit until we prove that he's not going to be named in any investigation. The Dunston woman has already caused too many problems."

"She won't cause any more," Sanborne said. "Be patient. Give me another day and you'll see that you're worrying needlessly."

"I'm not worrying. I'm heading for Caracas to make final arrangements. If I find out that you've screwed up again, I'll come back and take care of her myself." Boch hung up.

Sanborne leaned back in his chair. Much as he'd like to let his anger have free rein, Boch was not too far out of line. He'd been truthful about the death reports taking a long time, but he was uneasy after Caprio's disappearance. The delay in announcing the deaths might indicate that they were trying to identify body parts, but it might mean a slip-up. Things weren't going as smoothly as he'd planned and he didn't like it.

Royd?

Christ, he hoped not. He didn't need to have to contend with that bastard at this crucial time.

Okay, assume Royd wasn't on the scene and muddying the waters. Assume the woman and her son were dead, as he'd told Boch.

Try to get confirmation.

He looked down at his notebook, underlined the last name on the list.

Dave Edmunds.

Royd had put the Hunan chicken on two paper plates on the small table by the window and he was pouring wine into a second glass when Sophie came into the room. "I bought red wine. Is that okay with you?"

She nodded. "But I'd rather have coffee."

"I'll make a pot later." He gestured to a chair. "It's supermarket vino and you won't be able to tolerate more than two glasses anyway. I assure you I'm not trying to make you drunk."

"I didn't think you were."

"No?" His lips twisted. "I believe everything I do or say may be suspect. I detect a certain wariness. Sometimes I act on impulse, but I'm not going to jump you."

"Because I'm too important to you to draw Sanborne and Boch."

"That's right." He smiled. "Otherwise you wouldn't have a chance."

She sat down and picked up her fork. "I'd have a chance. Jock was a very good instructor."

He chuckled. "Then I'll definitely keep my distance." He sipped his wine. "I've heard Jock is a veritable wonder."

She glanced up and frowned. "You're acting—I don't remember you laughing before."

"Maybe I'm trying to put you at your ease so that I can pounce."

She studied him. "Are you?"

He shrugged. "Or it could be that Kelly finally called me and I know that he's not dead meat. I realize you think I'm a callous son of a bitch, but I don't like the idea of anyone I send into the fray biting it."

"But you sent him anyway."

"Yes." He looked at her over the rim of his glass. "Just as I'd send you."

"Good." She took another bite. "What did Kelly say?"

"That he hadn't found the records but he was still trying. He's going to call me later tonight."

"It may not be in the file room. Sanborne could have it in his safe at home."

"Perhaps. But I'd bet he'd want it where the security is top notch, and that's the facility."

"It will probably still be kept in a safe."

"Kelly can get into most safes, given enough time."

She remembered how easily Royd had gotten past the locks in her house. "How convenient. Even if Kelly finds it, he may not recognize the disk," she said quietly. "Unless he's a chemistry major. Sanborne labeled all his sensitive disks with code numbers. And that formula is very complicated and involved. He'll need help."

"What are you saying?"

"Can Kelly get me into the facility?"

He went still. "No way," he said flatly.

"No way, he can't get me in? Or no way, you don't want me to do it."

"Both."

"Ask him if he can do it."

He muttered an oath. "You're going to walk into the lion's mouth when we're trying to keep you away from Sanborne so that he won't cut your throat?"

"We need that disk. It's one of the prime objectives. You know that."

"And I'll get it."

"But you may be running out of time. You said it would be harder if he gets the entire facility moved offshore."

"No," he said firmly. "We'll let Kelly do his job."

"Ask him how I can get in. He must know where every security camera in the facility is located, since he works in the video-surveillance room. He could never have gotten near any sensitive files if he hadn't known how to temporarily take out those cameras."

"But once you're in the areas they can only be accessed by thumbprint."

"I know that. But Kelly managed to bypass it, if he got you information about me."

"He switched his print record in the computer with that of one of the scientists who was on vacation for a few days. He had to replace it almost immediately."

"If he did it once, he can do it again. Or manage some other way. Ask him."

"We don't need you there. Describe Sanborne's encoding marks on the label."

She was silent.

"We have to work together, Sophie."

"Unless you're the one who wants to work alone," she said dryly. "You wouldn't think twice about leaving me out in the cold."

He was silent a moment. "Maybe. What does it matter if I can get the job done?"

"It matters. You said 'if,' and that's the key word. I've given up too much to throw everything in your court." She finished her meal and lifted the glass to her lips. "I want to move. I want my son back."

He gazed at her for a long moment and then shrugged. "I'll ask Kelly. You're right, why should I stop you? You seem to want to get yourself killed."

"When will you call him?"

"I'll phone him now." He stood up and took out his phone. "Have another glass of wine. I'm going to walk around outside for a while. I need some air."

"What are you going to say to him that I can't hear?"

"I'm going to ask him how good a chance you're going to have if he does get you in. And if I don't like the odds, you're not going anywhere." The door shut behind him.

She sat there for a few minutes and then went to stand at the window. Royd was pacing back and forth in the parking lot, talking on his cell phone. She hadn't expected that reaction from him. She had thought he'd keep his promise to protect her but his response to her going into the facility had been both negative and violent. Perhaps she didn't know Royd as well as she'd thought. She'd thought his single-minded passion to get Sanborne and Boch would overshadow and choke every other facet of his personality. But the more she was with him, the more sides to his character he revealed.

Like lust, she thought. Not that that should have surprised her. He was an obviously virile man and sex ruled the world. She should have been more amazed at the fact that he cared about the safety of Kelly, an employee. He'd told her that Kelly had to take his chances, but his attitude was clearly not as callous as it seemed on the surface.

Royd was still talking and she was becoming

impatient. She hated standing here waiting for him to come back. She hated not being in control. Well, there was one area where she was in control. She turned and strode across the room to the desk where she'd left her cell phone in her handbag.

The cell phone rang as she took it out of the bag.

"I love you, too. Be careful." She hung up the cell phone and turned toward the door as she realized Royd had come into the room. "Dave called again. I wondered—" She stopped as she saw Royd's expression as he slammed the door behind him and marched across the room. "What on earth is—"

He was cursing as his hands grasped her shoulders. "You're an idiot. I told you to—"

"Take your hands off me."

"Better mine than Sanborne's. Dammit, he'll squeeze the life out of you. Why the devil take a chance just because you have a softness for an old lover? Or maybe not an old lover. Couldn't you have just done what I told—"

"Take your hands off me," she said through her teeth. "Or so help me I'll make a eunuch of you."

"Try it." His hands tightened. "Fight me. I want to hurt you."

"Then you're succeeding. I'll have bruises. Are you happy?"

"Why shouldn't I be—" He broke off and the anger left his expression. "No." His hand released her shoulders and then fell away. "No, I'm not happy." He took a step back. "I didn't mean to— Shit. But you shouldn't have answered Edmunds's call."

"I didn't." She jammed her phone in her handbag. "I never said I answered it. I said he called. You didn't give me a chance to tell you anything else. He called last night and the call went to voice mail. Then he called again tonight. I thought it was odd that he'd persist when it's logical for him to think I'm dead."

"Then who were you talking to?"

"Who do you think? Michael called. They just got to MacDuff's Run."

"Oh." He was silent a moment. "Egg on my face?"

"A whole omelet, you son of a bitch. I didn't ignore Dave's call because you told me not to take it. I did it because I agree it's the smartest thing to do." She glared at him. "And don't you put a hand on me again."

"I won't." He smiled crookedly. "Your threat hit me where I'm the most vulnerable."

"Good."

"And I'm sorry I lost it for a minute."

"More than a minute, and your apology is not accepted."

"Then I'll have to work on making amends. Will it help to distract you if I tell you that Kelly thinks he may be able to knock out the security cameras for a period of twelve minutes?"

She frowned. "Only twelve minutes?"

"Not enough time to locate the safe, get the disk, and then get out."

"It would be close."

"Close, hell. We cancel it."

"The hell we do. Let me think about it."

He was silent and then nodded. "We have until tomorrow, but we have to give Kelly time to set up the power outage."

"If Kelly is as good at safecracking as you tell me, then we might be able to do it. It won't take me that long to go through the safe. I'd recognize any of Sanborne's disks in a heartbeat. But twelve minutes is— I'll think about it." She started for the adjoining door. "Good night, Royd."

"Good night. Leave the adjoining door

cracked and lock the outside door." He added, "And don't be so pissed at me that you argue about it."

"I'd love to argue, but I'm not the stupid woman you called me. I'll let you stay up all night to protect me if you like. It would serve you right."

"Yes, it would," he said gravely. "How is Michael doing?"

"Better than I hoped. He thinks MacDuff's Run is neat. What boy wouldn't?" She shrugged. "A Scottish castle and a Laird catering to his every wish."

"I don't think MacDuff caters to anyone, from what Jock tells me. But I'm sure he'll take good care of Michael."

"Jock promised me that they'd both do that. I just hope that they keep him safe," she said wearily. "I'll see you in the morning, Royd." She didn't wait for an answer. A moment later she was stripping off her jeans and shirt and pulling a bright yellow cotton nightshirt over her head. Yellow? It was a weird color for Royd to choose. She would have thought navy or hunter green. . . .

It would be a miracle if she could sleep after the long nap she'd had earlier in the day. Maybe that would be for the best. She could lie here and come to some decision about whether she wanted to risk her neck trying to make that blasted twelve-minute deadline.

"She didn't answer." Dave Edmunds pressed the disconnect on the phone. "It went straight to her voice mail again. I told you she wouldn't answer. Her phone's probably somewhere in the wreckage or blown into someone's backyard. The police told me that calling her cell phone was one of the first things they did after the explosion."

"It was worth a try." Larry Simpson shrugged. "As I told you, sometimes the police don't dig deep enough. They have too many cases for their manpower. But I'm a freelance journalist and that means I have all the time in the world. I was hoping to get a feel-good story to sell to the papers."

"There's nothing feel-good about any of this," Edmunds said bitterly. "My son is dead. My ex-wife is dead. It shouldn't have happened. Someone's going to pay for what they did to me. And I'm going to sue the pants off the power company. They can't get away with this."

"Good move." Simpson stood up. "You have my card. If I can help, give me a call."

"I may do that." His lips twisted. "Anyone who thinks a case is tried solely in a courtroom is nuts."

"You're a lawyer. You should know." He paused, glancing down at his notes. "Did your son mention anyone else your wife might be visiting besides this Jock Gavin?"

"No."

"And he didn't say anything else about him except that he was your ex-wife's cousin?"

"I told you he didn't." His gaze narrowed on Simpson's face. "And I'm beginning to wonder about you, Simpson. I let you into my home and I've been cooperating with you because I may need public support. But you're pushy, very pushy. I wonder if perhaps the power company decided to send someone to gauge my intentions and feel me out."

"You saw my credentials."

"And I'll definitely check them out tomorrow."

"I'm sorry you're suspicious of me," Simpson said earnestly. "Although it's perfectly understandable. Perhaps we can talk more tomorrow after you've made your investigation."

"Perhaps." Edmunds strode across the room and opened the front door. "But right now I wish to be alone with my grief. Good night."

Simpson nodded sympathetically. "Of course. Thank you for your help."

Edmunds followed him onto the porch and watched him walk to his car parked at the curb.

Simpson glanced in the rearview mirror as he pulled away from the curb.

Shit.

He flipped open his phone when he was around the corner.

"He got my license number, Sanborne," he said when Sanborne answered. "And he may be checking me out tomorrow."

"Then you must not have done a good job of convincing him how upright and honorable you are."

"I did the best I could. What do you expect? He's suspicious of everyone. He's a lawyer, for God's sake."

"Okay, calm down. How can we smooth him out?"

Simpson was silent a moment. "He's going to sue the power company. He thought maybe I was hired by them. I'm not sure if he wants revenge or a fat check."

"Then we'll explore that avenue. Lawyers are always ready to plea-bargain. It shouldn't— Wait a minute." Sanborne went off the line for a moment. "Dammit, the fire department has just announced there were no bodies found in the ruins of the house."

"Then we won't have to worry about Edmunds now."

"Maybe, maybe not." Sanborne was silent a moment. "Call him tomorrow and arrange for a meeting to discuss terms on behalf of the power company. Since he has no evidence that he's a bereaved father, he should be willing to negotiate on our terms. Did you get anything else?"

"She didn't answer her cell phone. And according to the kid, the Dunston woman was hanging around with her cousin, Jock Gavin, for the last few months."

Silence. "Jock Gavin?"

"That's the name he gave me."

"I'll be damned."

"You know him?"

"I did at one time. And I heard some impressive things after he was off my radar scope."

"What kind of—"

"Get back here as soon as you can. I need to

brief you on how you're to set up Edmunds to-morrow."

"Why don't I wait and let him stew awhile?"

"Because I don't want to wait. Don't argue with me." He hung up.

8

Three A.M.

Sophie turned over in bed again, searching for a cool place on the pillow. Relax, dammit. She'd been right, that nap earlier in the day had destroyed any chance she might have had to go back to sleep. She'd been tossing and turning for the last four hours. She would have turned the TV set on and tried to find a boring movie to lull her if it hadn't been for the cracked adjoining door. She'd heard no sound from Royd since his light had gone out a few hours ago. She didn't need to wake him just because she had—

But she was hearing a sound from his room now.

Harsh, ragged breathing. Not a groan or a scream. Just that sharp, rasping breathing.

She tensed and lay there, listening.

If it was Royd, he sounded as if he was in pain.

And it had to be Royd. She would have heard a door opening.

So maybe he was having indigestion from that Chinese food. Not her business.

The hell it wasn't. She was a doctor. She'd given up the right to close her eyes to pain when she'd taken the oath. At times she wished she could, and this was one of them.

Dammit, it could be just a nightmare.

Perhaps it wasn't. She was inclined to think of every ailment in connection with her experience. Even if it was only a nightmare, she couldn't withhold the mercy of waking him.

Stop arguing with yourself. Just do it.

She jumped out of bed and was across the room in seconds. She threw open the door. Royd was lying on his stomach, the sheet half covering him.

She turned on the light on the bedside table. "I heard you. What's the—"

He knocked her to the floor and jumped astride her!

His hands tightened on her throat.

She turned her head and her teeth sank into his wrist.

His grip didn't slacken. He was gazing down at her but she wasn't sure he was seeing her. His face was convulsed with rage.

Her fist punched downward to his genitals with all her force.

He grunted in pain and his grip loosened.

She tried to roll away but his legs tightened around her. Her nails dug into his thigh.

"Shit!" The anger was fading from his expression. He shook his head as if to clear it. "Sophie? What the hell are you trying to do? Kill me?"

"Survive, you bastard. What do you think I'm doing? Let me up."

He slowly got to his feet. "Are you okay?"

"No, I'm not okay. This is the second time today you put your damn hands on me." She jerked down her nightshirt as he pulled her to her feet. "Next time I come near you, I'll bring a gun."

"You did considerable damage without a weapon." He made a face. "I remember you threatened that you'd make a eunuch of me."

"If I'd had a knife, I would have done it," she said through her teeth. "I thought you were going to kill me."

"You shouldn't have surprised me."

"I wasn't trying to startle you. I turned on the light. I didn't even touch you. There was no reason for you to—"

"Why?" He interrupted. "What happened? Why did you come in here?"

"Because you were— It didn't sound like you were dreaming. I didn't want to take the chance. I don't know your medical history. I thought you might be ill. Or having a stroke. You sounded as if— I was stupid." She turned away. "I'll know better next time."

"And you'll leave me to my heart attack or stroke?" He shook his head. "I don't think so, Sophie."

"It obviously wasn't either or you wouldn't have had the strength to half kill me."

"Did I hurt you?"

"Yes."

"I'm sorry." He paused. "How can I make it up? What do you want me to do?"

"Nothing."

He reached out and put his hand on her arm. "I hurt you. I didn't mean to do it, but words are cheap. There's nothing I won't do to make amends. Name it."

He meant it. His expression was so intense that she couldn't look away from him. She felt oddly shaken. "I don't want you to do any-thing. Let me go. I'm going back to bed."

He slowly released her arm. "Thanks for try-ing to help. But don't do it again." He smiled faintly. "If you want to wake me from one of my nightmares, throw a pillow at me or shout at me from across the room. It's safer."

She stiffened. "It was a nightmare? I won-dered, but I couldn't take the chance. You seemed in profound distress. I wasn't sure that was what was happening."

He nodded. "Oh, yes. It was definitely a nightmare."

"What about?"

"Hunt, chase, death. You don't want to hear the details."

Yes, she did. But it was clear he didn't intend to tell her. "Did you ever sleepwalk in conjunc-tion with one of them?"

"No. You're thinking that I've mistaken night terrors for nightmares?" He shook his head. "It's a nightmare. As you know, they usu-ally take place during REM, rapid eye move-ment sleep, rather than NREM, deep sleep. So they come at the end of my sleep cycle instead of closer to the beginning. My body appears to be paralyzed so that I only twitch, not flail around, and I don't scream out. I have an elevated heart rate but nothing like the ones accompanying night terror. I remember my nightmare perfectly, and that's not common with night terror."

She gazed at him in surprise. "You appear very knowledgeable. Have you been in therapy?"

"Hell, no. But when this started I knew I had to get a handle on it. So I did some research."

"In my opinion you haven't really succeeded in getting a handle on the problem. Only identifying it. You may need therapy."

"Really?" He tilted his head. "And have I aroused your professional curiosity?"

She moistened her lips. "Do the dreams have anything to do with Garwood?"

He was silent a moment. "Yes. What do you expect?"

"Exactly what's happening." She started to turn away. "Sit down and take a few deep breaths. You need to relax. I'll get you a glass of water."

"Why?"

"Just do it."

He frowned. "I don't want you waiting on me. I can get my own damn water."

"Sit down and shut up. I'll be right back."

His brows lifted. "May I put some clothes on?"

"Why? Nudity doesn't bother me and you'll be going back to bed as soon as you relax."

He looked down at himself. "Being nude in the same room with you isn't relaxing."

"Suit yourself." She went into the bathroom. Seeing Royd naked wasn't relaxing for her either. He was too male, his body too muscular and tough. He made her feel weak and womanly and not at all professional. There was no way she wanted to feel that way. But to admit that to him would be a defeat in itself.

She filled the water glass and took it back into the bedroom. He was sitting in the easy chair with his legs stretched out before him. He had taken her at her word and not gotten dressed.

Damn him.

She handed him the water and sat down on one of the upright chairs at the small table where they'd eaten earlier in the evening. "You're perspiring. Do you always do that during the dream cycle?"

He nodded.

"How often do you have the nightmare?"

"Two or three times during the week." He took a drink. "Sometimes more. It depends."

"It depends on what?"

"How tired I am. Surplus energy seems to trigger it." He shrugged. "Exhaustion must short-circuit it."

"Maybe. Or it releases the tension you build up during your waking hours instead of the nightmare doing it after you go to sleep."

"There isn't any release about them. It's an ambush." He tilted his head, studying her. "Why all the questions? What are you doing?"

"I'm a doctor. Sleep disorders are my specialty. I want to help you. Is that so hard to understand?"

"Seeing that I nearly choked you only five minutes ago, I'd say it's very hard to understand."

"You weren't in your right mind. You didn't know what you were doing."

"Now you're making excuses for me?"

"No, but it's part of my job to comprehend cause and effect. I had a patient when I first got out of med school who socked me so hard he broke my nose." She grimaced. "He didn't mean to do it. It was pure automatic reflex. But after that I was more careful."

"You weren't careful tonight."

"I didn't know I had to be. You seemed—"

"Sane?"

"In control," she substituted.

"I am in control." He made a face as he met her skeptical gaze. "Okay, except when I'm not."

"Have you tried drugs?"

"No drugs. Not ever," he said flatly. "I don't believe the adage of taking a little of the hair of the dog that bit you."

She flinched. "I wasn't suggesting— In some cases it's beneficial to find a way to relax before you enter the sleep cycle."

"I agree. I discovered that the first month I started having the dreams. I tried all kinds of remedies. Poker, crossword puzzles, chess. But mental stimulation didn't do it. I had to go for the physical. Anything that would exhaust me. I started to run seven miles every evening."

"That should definitely exhaust you."

"Sometimes." He paused. "Sex does the job better."

"I'm sure it does." She stared at him in sudden suspicion. "Were you trying to embarrass me?"

"Just clarifying. You were asking what helped me."

"And you were only supplying me with facts."

He smiled. "No, I was actually making an

opening move toward trying to seduce you. It's the truth, though. There's no release like sex. Don't you agree?"

"If I agreed, it would keep this discussion going and that's not what I want. Are you going to tell me what this dream is about?"

"No. Not right now. Maybe when we know each other better."

It was obvious from his smile that the bastard meant "know" in the biblical sense. She stood up. "Go to hell. I was trying to help you. I should have known better."

His smile faded. "I don't want to be your patient, Sophie. I'm not your son. The last thing I need is for you to hold my hand and soothe me. And I've no desire to be entirely cured of my nightmares."

"Then you're crazy."

"What a term. How very unprofessional of you."

"I've lived with Michael's pain and I know the hell those nightmares bring. The word **nightmare** comes from the Old Saxon **mara,** which means 'demon.' And nightmares can roast you alive like the demons they're called. They may not be as dangerous as the night terrors, but they're bad enough. Why the hell wouldn't you want to be rid of them?"

He was silent a moment. "They keep the memory fresh. They keep the rage bonfire high. They keep the focus sharp on what I have to do."

Bonfire high.

She was glimpsing the inferno of rage now behind that hard-edged exterior. "My God, you'd do that to yourself? I know what torture those dreams bring."

"Sanborne and Boch did it. That was their gift to me. I might as well keep it around to use against them. So don't waste your pity on me."

"I won't."

"Yes, you will. You can't help yourself. You're a do-gooder who carries the world on your shoulders." He got up and went to the bed. "You wouldn't have sunk neck deep into this mess if you hadn't wanted to help your father. You're bleeding because you can't heal your son. Now you think I need you, and I could play you like a fiddle if I chose." He got into bed and pulled up the sheet. "But I don't choose. So go to bed and let me get to sleep."

"I will, you son of a bitch." She strode toward the door. "And I hope your nightmares turn to night terrors and you have a lifetime of—" She stopped. "No, I don't. Not that."

"See?" Royd asked softly from the bed behind her. "You're even afraid of laying a curse on me."

"Night terrors are too personal to me. But there are all kinds of terrors. I can think of several I could wish on you that would make a man like you turn pale."

"Such as?"

She gave him a cool glance over her shoulder. "May your balls wither away and you develop an allergy to Viagra and all its counterparts."

He looked at her, stunned. And then he suddenly exploded into laughter. "God, you're a formidable woman."

"No, I'm not. I'm soft, remember?"

She slammed the door behind her.

"Is the boy still sleeping?" MacDuff asked as Jock came down the stairs.

"He should be for a while yet. He was exhausted but so wired he didn't manage to fall asleep until almost three A.M."

"Can you come for a walk with me? We need to talk."

Jock shook his head. "I can't leave Michael even for a few moments. I promised Sophie."

"I rigged you with that wireless wristband."

"And if he has a terror and falls into apnea when I'm ten minutes away we have a dead boy."

"Point taken," MacDuff said. "Come out into the courtyard. That's only three minutes away from any room in the castle." He smiled. "You should know. You were all over the place as a child."

"And you never made me feel inferior because my mother was the housekeeper here," Jock said as he followed the Laird out into the courtyard. "It never occurred to me that you could have been a real bastard until I got out into the real world."

"This is the real world, Jock."

Jock looked up at the turrets of the castle. "For you. It's part of your blood and bones. You live for the place. To me it's a pleasant memory and the home of my friend."

"It should be home to you, too."

Jock shook his head.

MacDuff was silent a moment, gazing out toward the Run. "I want you to stay. I let you go before because I knew you needed to distance yourself from me. You felt I was smothering you with care because you . . . weren't yourself."

Jock chuckled. "You mean, I was nuts."

He smiled. "Let's just say, you had periods of disorientation and loss of control."

"Nuts," Jock repeated. "You're not going to hurt my feelings. I still have times when I'm not totally in control." He met MacDuff's gaze. "But the times are coming less and less frequently. And I don't need to be here under your eagle eye. You've invested too much effort and worry in me already."

"Bullshit. It's not too much effort until you're totally healed and healthy again." He paused. "And what if I said that it was me who needed you. Not the other way around."

"I wouldn't believe you. As you said, you step on your own cockroaches."

"For God's sake, you have more value to me than a damn exterminator. You have a brain."

"You think it doesn't take a brain to be an exterminator?"

"Jock."

"Very well, tell me how you want me to use my fine brain."

"I haven't found Cira's gold yet."

"Cira's gold?" Jock chuckled. "You've started to search for that long-lost family treasure again?"

"I never stopped. I've been searching off and

on for the past year. I won't lose MacDuff's Run to the National Trust. It's **mine.**"

"And Cira's gold could be a myth."

"Then stay around and we'll find out if it is together. What an adventure, Jock." Mac-Duff's voice lowered coaxingly. "I've searched almost the entire property here at the Run. I need a fresh mind and viewpoint to help me find a new path."

Jock found himself tempted. MacDuff really knew how to push people's buttons. "You want to distract me from Sophie and the boy."

"Partly. But I do need you. You're like family, and I'd only trust family to find that chest of gold. It's priceless, and I'm not a trusting man. Help me, Jock."

"I'll think about it."

"Do that." MacDuff clapped him on the shoulder. "You've no need to go back to America. We'll take care of the lad until it's safe for him to go back, and then I'll deliver him back to his mother myself." He saw Jock's expression change and he shrugged. "Okay, you can take him home. Just turn around and come back here on the next plane."

"I believe you're pushing a wee bit."

"More than a wee bit. Have you ever known me to take small measures?"

"Never." His smile faded. "But we may have to do more than wait it out with Michael. I may have brought Sanborne down on you. I was thinking on the plane here that Sophie's ex-husband knew I was on the scene. Michael told him I was a relation, but Edmunds knows my name now. What Edmunds knows, Sanborne may find out."

"We'll face that when it happens."

"Sanborne's a very powerful man."

"Not here, not on my property. Not with my people. Let him come."

Jock laughed. The answer was so characteristic of MacDuff that it gave him a warm feeling of homecoming. "Then I take it you don't want me to take the lad away and hide him elsewhere?"

"What are you talking about? I took responsibility for the boy. Try to take him from me and I'd have to fight you for him."

"Then I'd better not try to do that." He started up the steps. "I've got to check in on Michael and see if he's okay. Even if he's not having one of his night terrors, he's a child a long way from home."

"He's ten. You were only fifteen when you ran away from home and decided to explore the world."

"But that was my choice. Not a smart one,

but Michael had little choice in coming here."
He looked back over his shoulder. "And I had
you to come after me and save my neck.
Michael has only me."

"Then he couldn't be luckier," MacDuff
said quietly. "I'd choose you to be in my corner
anytime, Jock."

For a moment Jock didn't know what to say.
He had always been the charge, not the
guardian. He had known with his mind that he
and MacDuff were now on equal footing, but
his emotions were another matter. Jesus, he
was touched. He smiled with an effort. "That's
good to know. Does that mean you're not going to try to tuck me and Michael away in the
dungeon for safekeeping?"

"Hell, no. It doesn't mean any such thing. I
always do what's necessary." He grinned as he
followed him up the steps. "But it happens that
the dungeon is flooded from the spring rains at
present. So you might be fortunate enough to
escape that fate."

"They've found out you and Michael weren't in
the house," Royd said when Sophie walked
into his room the next morning. "The fire department announced it last night."

"It was bound to happen soon."

He nodded. "We were lucky to buy as much time as we have. It just means that we have to be extra careful not to have you running around and being identified. Not only will Sanborne and Boch be after you, but the police may also have a few questions about why you haven't come forward."

"I'm not planning on running around anywhere unless you have something productive for me to do." Her eyes narrowed on his face. "Do you?"

He shrugged. "I heard from Kelly. He said that the best time to short-circuit the power is at nine tonight. They're picking up some more equipment from the labs about that time and they'll be stumbling over each other in the dark. The more confusion the better."

"And can he arrange it for that time?"

"He said he could," he said shortly. "He wants my okay to set it up."

"Then give it to him."

"Not unless I can work out a way to get you out of there."

"If Kelly can get me in, then he should be able to get me out."

"That may not follow. Particularly if the power comes on too soon."

"Then you work it out. I'm going in."

He was silent. "I'll tell Kelly to meet us outside the facility at eight-forty-five to get our ducks in a row."

"That will be nice. Since I don't even know what he looks like. Do you have a photo?"

"No. Kelly looks like a red-haired Fred Astaire."

"Well, that's certainly descriptive enough."

"And he manages to tap-dance his way out of a good many tight spots, but I don't want him to have to do that tonight." He nodded at the table. "I picked up orange juice and a breakfast sandwich at Hardee's. Sit down and eat."

"I'm not hungry."

"Eat anyway. It's good for you. It will give you the energy to lambaste me when you take the notion." He paused. "Unless you're too pissed to sit down at the same table with me."

"I'd be stupid to let my personal feelings get in the way. Jock warned me I'd probably be annoyed with you at least once every day." She sat down and unwrapped the sandwich. "He underestimated. He must not know you as well as he thinks he does."

"He knows one part of my personality very well indeed. The rest he's basing on judgment."

"Which part does he know?"

"The part that chafed beneath the chains, the part that he went through too."

"Chains?"

"Mental, sometimes physical. Suppression of free will, the knowledge that you have no choice but to obey." His lips lifted in a sardonic smile. "You're so eaten by guilt that I'm sure you think Jock and I are too. I can't speak for Jock, but I'm too selfish to worry about the sin of committing crimes when I had no control. I hated being made a slave to those bastards. Of being too weak and not being able to fight off that damn drug and its side effects and not being able to kill those sons of bitches who gave it to me."

"I gave it to you," she whispered. "Or I might just as well have done it."

"Bullshit, if I thought that, you'd be a dead woman." He dropped down in a chair and pulled the tab on the orange-juice carton. "So stop moaning and take the healthy, selfish view I do." He poured the orange juice into her glass and then his own. "If you want me to shut up about Garwood, I'll do it. But I've always thought air and sunlight are good for a wound."

"And a little hate thrown into the mix?"

He nodded and lifted his glass in a mock toast. "Now you've got it."

"I do hate Sanborne. How could you doubt it?"

"I don't doubt it. We just approach it differently. Perhaps it's because your job is full of mercy and mine is basically the job I was trained to do at Garwood."

"And you have to keep the bonfire high."

"Oh, yes."

She changed the subject. "Where are we going to meet Kelly?"

"There's a creek about two miles from the facility. No security cameras are near there."

She remembered the creek from the day she'd had to run from the security guards. "Has he located the safe?"

"He's located **a** safe. It's in an office near the lab but it's not an executive office. It's in the human resources department."

"It could still be Sanborne's safe. A little sleight of hand."

He nodded. "It's worth Kelly checking out. I'm not sure it's worthwhile to have you go in with him."

"I'm sure." She finished her orange juice. "If he blows the power, then everyone in the facility is going to be under suspicion. He may not get another chance." She stood up. "I'm going, Royd."

He shrugged. "Suit yourself. Why should I care?"

"Because if you lose me, you lose your bait."

"I never said I'd use you for bait." He frowned. "Well, maybe I did, but it would be a last resort."

She shook her head. "By God, I believe I see a sign of softening."

"No way." He leaned back in his chair. "I'm probably trying to deceive you into thinking that a nice guy like me wouldn't be too bad to go to bed with."

"Nice guy?" She gazed at him in astonishment. "You have a long way to go, Royd."

" 'The longest journey begins with a single step,' " he quoted. "Maybe you're reforming me. What do you think?"

"I think you're being ridiculous."

He smiled. "Well, you're into therapy and we have all day with time on our hands. You have to hole up and keep a very low profile. Want to come to bed and we'll get all loose and relaxed for the job tonight?"

"No, I do not. You're disgusting."

"Not in bed. In many other phases of behavior, but not between the sheets. You'd like me."

"Arrogant bastard." She started for the door to her room. "I'm not interested in sex with you."

"I believe I detected a trace of interest and I'm such a horny son of a bitch I have to take what I can get."

He was outrageous. She gazed at him lolling lazily in that chair, positively radiating sexuality. Yet suddenly she was aware of something else. A puckish twinkle behind that bold stare. Her annoyance ebbed. "That's not why either of us is here."

"But I might not get another chance to lay you if you get yourself killed tonight." His smile was sly. "And you could miss the experience of a lifetime."

"If I get killed tonight, I won't have a lifetime to regret you."

"When you're as good as I am, every minute you spend with me is a lifetime."

In spite of herself she couldn't keep her lips from twitching. "I believe I'm getting ill."

"Okay, I'll knock it off." His smile faded. "But if you're not going to let me pleasantly distract you then I suggest you find something else. If you don't, you'll be nervous as hell by tonight."

"I can always find something to do. I don't have my files but there's nothing wrong with my memory. I'll do some thinking about the patients I'm having problems with and make some notes." She paused. "But there's something I want you to do."

"I'm at your service . . . maybe."

"I can't call my friend Cindy Hodge, but you could do it for me. Tell her you're phoning for me. You'll need some sort of proof. . . ." She thought about it. "Remind her that we always had a date to see the **Star Wars** movies the first afternoon they came out. I want to know if she's alive, and if she is, then I need to warn her to run."

He nodded. "Give me her telephone number. I'll phone her from the convenience store down the street."

"I'll get it from my cell directory. When will you do it?"

"When do you think?" he asked roughly. "You asked me for a favor. You're worried. Am I supposed to keep you on pins and needles? It'll be done within the hour."

"Thank you." She closed the door behind her.

Christ, he was an enigma. Rough and hard-edged, sensual and raw, passionate and cold. And yet that sliver of humor that she had been surprised by only moments ago had touched a response in her. There hadn't been many moments of humor or repartee in her life in the past years. Even when she was married to Dave, they had been too busy concentrating on their careers to have much time for anything else.

Not that the sex hadn't been good. Sex was always good if two people were considerate of each other. God, that sounded boring and cerebral.

How would sex be with Royd? There was no guarantee he'd be considerate. And he probably wouldn't be gentle. Every time she was with him she could sense that leashed animalistic explosiveness. The physical signals that he sent out were almost tangible.

What was she thinking? **Every** time? She hadn't even been conscious of being that aware of Royd. Just that one time when—

She drew a deep breath. All right, admit it. She was physically drawn to Royd. That didn't mean that she'd jump into bed with him. That didn't mean that attraction wouldn't pass when this was over. It just meant that she needed sex and he was available.

Her cell phone rang. Royd.

"Hello."

"Cindy Hodge is with her mother in the Catskills. I spoke to her. I told her to lay low."

Relief poured through her. "Thank heavens."

"I'll see you later." He hung up.

He'd kept his word and now she could concentrate on what was important. She went to the desk and drew out stationery and pen and dropped down in the easy chair by the window.

Think about her patient Elspeth.

Think about Randy Lourdes, who had severe insomnia.

Don't think about Royd naked in that room last night.

Don't think of Royd lolling in that chair saying words that were provocative and faintly amusing.

Don't think of Royd, period.

9

S impson was late.

Dave Edmunds glanced at his watch again. Where the hell was he? It was bad enough that he'd been persuaded to meet Simpson on this country road in the middle of nowhere. At first, he'd turned them down, but he could understand why they wanted to make sure any negotiations would be completely secret. He had no desire for publicity either. It would blow the little leverage he had left after the announcement that Sophie and Michael had not been in that house. Naturally, he was happy that there was a chance they were alive and he'd do everything he could to find them. But until there was absolute proof, he still had an opportunity to come to terms and get a settlement before they showed up. Someone had to pay and it might as well be to him. Hell, he could squeeze enough money out of them to take a nice percentage for himself and still send Michael to college.

And those utility executives must realize what a stink he could raise if they didn't negotiate. Otherwise Simpson wouldn't have called to admit he worked for the power company and set up this meeting.

Yet now that bastard Simpson was keeping him waiting. A psychological ploy?

No, there he was coming around the turn. He recognized the car. He went to meet him as the car pulled to the side of the road and Simpson rolled down the window.

"You're late." He glanced impatiently at his wristwatch. "Twenty minutes. I hate tardiness. Do you realize how many cases I would have jeopardized if I were late in court?"

"Sorry," Simpson said. "I was delayed at the office. It's the weekend, but this is a big deal. When I spoke to you on the phone, you told me that you wouldn't accept less than the figure you mentioned and my superiors were balking."

"Don't bullshit me. I have them over a barrel. They can settle or have me sitting on that stand in court pale and trembling telling a jury how the power company threatened the life of my son."

"You actually think you could squeeze us when there was no physical harm done?"

"We don't know that. Maybe my ex-wife suffered a concussion and is wandering around lost and in pain. After all, she hasn't surfaced yet. I may need to hire private investigators. They cost money." Go for the jugular. "You have no idea of the trouble I can make for you. By the end of the week every house owner in that subdivision will be filing suit against the power company for mental and physical endangerment. You'd do much better to settle now and keep me quiet."

"My superiors agreed with you." Simpson smiled. "They just wanted me to bargain a bit. I told them you wouldn't go for it." He paused. "But I don't have the authority to negotiate for the kind of settlement you're asking. If it's okay with you, there's someone on his way who can do that for the company."

"Who?"

"George Londrum."

"The public works commissioner?" Edmunds gave a low whistle. "I heard that he'd divested all his stock when he took over the commission."

"That doesn't mean he's not interested in keeping the utility company healthy and prospering. He'll only be doing public service another two years and then he'll want a cozy berth to return to."

"The company won't be healthy if I have to bleed them dry."

"Then may I phone him and tell him to come ahead? He's waiting at the service station a few miles from here."

Edmunds thought about it. Why not? Londrum was a politician, and he knew how to handle politicians. And the fact that Edmunds now knew he was still in the power company's pocket would be a prime negotiating weapon. "By all means, tell him to come. I'll gut the crooked bastard."

Simpson smiled. "Very colorfully put." He dialed his phone. "Mr. Edmunds says he'll be delighted to deal with you." He started to roll up the window. "Now, if you don't mind, I'll get out of here. I'm sure neither one of you wants to have a witness to your meeting. Mr. Londrum will be here in a few minutes. You do know what he looks like?"

"Of course I do." He watched Simpson drive away. Simpson was right, he wanted no witnesses. But damn, he wished he hadn't been afraid to wear a wire to record this meeting.

He'd had no idea that the commissioner was involved with the power company.

Simpson was slowing as he passed a sleek Lincoln Town Car at the turn. He lifted his hand and then continued down the road.

A Lincoln Town Car. Wouldn't you know Londrum would be driving a big, luxurious vehicle? He probably wanted to impress and intimidate him. Guess again.

Edmunds braced himself as he watched the car drive toward him.

"Christ." Jock threw down his cards as the alarm on the library monitor went off. "Michael." He jumped to his feet. "I suppose I should have expected this. We were lucky that it didn't happen last night."

"Sit down." MacDuff stood up and strode toward the door. "I'll take care of it."

"He's my responsibility. I promised Sophie that— He doesn't even know you."

"Then he'd better begin now." He smiled over his shoulder at Jock. "Trust me. I took care of you when you were a raving maniac. I can take care of the boy."

"But why do you want to do it?" Jock had followed him out into the hall. "It's my—"

"I accepted him here." MacDuff was taking the stairs two at a time. "It's time I got to know him."

"Because he's one of yours," Jock said softly.

"Not yet. I'm not that easy. But you're fond of him and that makes it difficult for me." He started down the upper hall. "Stay down there unless I call you. I can handle this, Jock." He threw open the door of Michael's room as a scream shattered the night. The boy was sitting bolt upright, his chest heaving with the effort to breathe.

MacDuff was across the room in seconds, shaking Michael gently. "Wake up, boy. Nothing's going to harm you."

Tears were running down Michael's face and he opened his eyes.

And screamed again as he saw MacDuff's face. He tore away from him and rolled over to the other side of the bed. He reached for the lamp on the bedside table, tore the cord from the wall, and hurled the lamp at MacDuff.

MacDuff barely managed to ward it off with an upraised arm. "Dammit, boy. I've no desire to—" He dove across the bed and grabbed Michael in a bear hug. "Will you stop trying to mangle me? Jock will laugh himself silly if you manage to bruise me."

"Jock?" Michael suddenly went limp in his arms. "Jock? Where is he?"

"Downstairs. Reluctantly waiting for me to come back." MacDuff pushed the boy away. "Do you know who I am now?"

"The Laird." He moistened his lips. "I'm sorry, sir. I didn't mean—"

"Stop apologizing. I startled you. I was half-expecting it." He made a face. "But I wasn't expecting a lamp thrown at my head."

"I didn't realize who—"

"I know that." The boy was still shaking and trying to hide it. Give the lad a chance to save his pride. He got up and went to the window. "It's stuffy in here." He threw open the casement. "No air. I'd be having nightmares too."

Michael didn't speak for a moment. "That's not why I have nightmares. I think you know that, sir."

MacDuff glanced over his shoulder. He could see the pulse still leaping in Michael's temple but he seemed to be calming. "Yes, I do. But it seemed the thing to say at the time."

"Are you going to ask me about them?"

"Why should I? It's none of my business."

"Then why are you here?"

"I invited you to the Run. If you have a problem, it's my responsibility to help deal with it. I can't do that if I don't know you, Michael."

"Jock brought me," he said haltingly. "I don't want to bother you."

"If it were bother, I wouldn't have told Jock to let you come." He paused. "Let's get this clear. I'm not asking you questions and I'm not your mother."

"Yeah." The faintest smile touched his lips. "I wouldn't have hit Mom with a lamp."

"I hope not." MacDuff's brows lifted. "Woman-beating is definitely not allowed here at the Run."

"You can leave now. I'm okay."

"Stop trying to get rid of me. I've an idea that I'm not fully doing my duty as substitute. What does your mother do after you wake from one of these nightmares?"

"But you're not my mother," Michael said gravely.

"Smartass."

Michael's eyes widened. "I'm sorry, sir. It just came out. I know it wasn't polite or even—"

"Stop treating me as if I were an ogre. I'm not going to behead you."

"But you're old and some kind of Lord and Mom would say I'm supposed to be polite to you."

He bristled. "I'm not old."

"Older than Jock."

"Half the population is older than Jock. I'm

in my thirties and they were rich, well-spent years that made me the exceptional human being I am." But MacDuff could see the faintest gleam of humor in Michael's eyes as he looked down at the floor. "And you're having me on. You Americans have no respect."

"Do you know a lot of Americans?"

"A few. Now tell me what your mother does after one of these sessions."

"She makes me hot chocolate and talks to me."

"I'm not about to go down to the kitchen and brew up chocolate, and we don't know each other well enough for involved conversation."

"I can go back to sleep. You don't have to do anything."

"Nonsense. It's a strange place and it would take you a long time to get rid of that tension. I think I'd better beat it out of you."

Michael tensed. "Sir?"

"Not literally. Jock says you play soccer."

"Yes."

"I played when I was a boy in school. Only we call it football. Let's go down to the Run and practice a little. I guarantee you'll be limp as a noodle by the time we finish."

"Now? In the middle of the night?"

"Why not? Do you have anything better to do? Put on your shoes and come hopping."

Michael threw his blanket aside. His face was lit with excitement. "Run? Where's this Run?"

"It's a stretch of land on the cliff at the back of the castle overlooking the sea. My ancestors are from the Highlands and used to test themselves with games of strength and skill. The ground is flat and I can dig up a ball somewhere."

"What if I kick the ball off the cliff into the sea?"

MacDuff headed for the door. "Why, I pitch you over after it. What else?"

Nate Kelly did look a little like Fred Astaire, Sophie thought as she watched him walk toward them. But his stride was less rhythmic and more purposeful.

"We have to move fast," he told Royd from a few yards away. "We have to be inside by the time the power goes off and near the human resources office." He glanced at her. "Sophie Dunston?"

"Yes."

"Glad to meet you. Follow close and do what I say and we may come out of this alive." He turned and headed for the facility. "Are you going in with us, Royd?"

"No, I'm staying outside in the shipping yard in case you need someone to get you out of a mess."

"We'll be okay as long as the power stays off. No one is in the human resources department at this time of the night."

"Famous last words. I've always found that you can't count on anything in situations like this." Royd said to Sophie, "Last chance. Let Kelly do his job."

"And miss the opportunity of getting my hands on the disk? If he has to go through every disk and piece of paper in the safe, then the lights will go on before he gets out of the office. I'll be able to tell right away if the disk is there."

"True," Kelly said. "But you may not be able to get out of the facility to the shipping yard by that time. You'll be on your own once you've searched the safe. I've got to get back to the video room and look like I've been there all the time before those lights go back on." He looked over his shoulder at Royd. "Unless you want me to risk it and deliver her to you?"

"No," Royd said curtly. "It's her choice. I'm not risking you or running the chance of losing you here at the facility. If I see a problem, I'll go in and get her myself."

"The hell you will," Sophie said. "No one runs any extra risk for me. You both do your jobs and let me do mine. I'll get out without you—" She stopped. They had crested the hill and the facility lay before them. The three-story factory was enclosed by a chain-link fence and light poured out of every window. She could see three large trucks parked in the shipping yard and men moving back and forth loading them. She tried not to show the chill that went through her. "How are we going to get past those men?"

"We go through the basement on the other side of the facility. It's a hell of a lot less busy. One guard and he's usually at the corner watching them load the trucks," Kelly said. "I left the basement door and south gate un-locked when I came out." He was skidding down the side of the hill. "The basement stor-age has already been loaded and shipped so the chances of us running into a guard aren't too bad. We go straight left to the emergency stairs and up to the second floor. Then we go left for a hundred yards and then turn right and go an-other twenty. Have you got that?"

"Left to the emergency stairs. Second floor, go left for a hundred yards, right, and go an-other twenty."

"Good. Don't forget. Memorize every step of the way. You'll be going back by yourself. I've got infrared glasses for you, but things sometimes appear different."

"No flashlights?"

"We'll use one in the human resources room because we have to do it to accurately see the safe lock and the contents. But those offices on the second floor are glass enclosed and we don't want anyone who might be checking that floor to see you in the halls. Once we leave the office I'll take the back stairs to the security office on the third floor and you take the emergency stairs down to the yard. Got it?"

She nodded, looking straight ahead at the looming factory so he wouldn't see how frightened she was becoming with every passing second. "Should I have a gun?"

"No," Royd said. "You might be tempted to use it and we want you avoiding confrontation. It's safer for Kelly and it's safer for you."

"And you don't want to blow Kelly's cover."

"Absolutely," Royd said coolly. "I'm glad you realize the priorities of the situation."

"I had no doubt about that." They were almost to the gate and she could feel the perspiration dampen her palms. "And you'll be here at the door when I make it back here?"

"Or I'll go after you if you screw up." He

smiled faintly. "As you said, I can't have you blowing Kelly's cover."

"I won't screw up." God, she hoped she was telling the truth. She hadn't expected to be this frightened.

"Wait here." Kelly was opening the gate and slipping inside. Two minutes later he was back. "The guard's at the corner watching the loading. You stay here and keep an eye on him, Royd. I'll get her inside." He grabbed Sophie's hand. "Keep low and run!"

She ran.

Ten yards to the basement door.

Jesus, the lights were so brilliant, if that guard even casually glanced back he couldn't help but see them.

One yard more.

Inside.

She felt a rush of relief but Kelly didn't give her a chance to catch her breath. He was pulling her toward the door of the emergency stairs. "Hurry. We have three minutes before the power goes down."

They made it up the six flights of stairs in two minutes. Kelly took a quick glance around at the darkness of the glass-enclosed offices. "Empty. Step on it. With any luck we'll get into the office before the circuit—"

Darkness.

Total darkness.

"No luck," Kelly said as he put on his glasses and ran down the hall. "Stay with me. We may not have as much time as I thought. The timer might be a little off. We should have had another minute. . . ."

Shit.

Royd rolled beneath one of the cars in the parking lot as he heard the shouts and saw the security guards running in confusion. He glanced at his watch.

The timer had to be off.

And if the timer wasn't reliable, it could mean that the entire plan could go awry.

Should he go in after them?

No, there always had to be a backup man in a job this risky.

And he'd told Sophie she was on her own.

Face it, because he'd hoped she'd back out.

Not entirely. She had to know that if she committed herself then she was the one at risk.

Okay, don't go in. Scout around. Find a way to get her away from the facility if she did make it out that door before the plant lit up like a Christmas tree. Kelly had done the best he could, but his responsibility ended when Sophie walked out that basement door.

And Royd's responsibility began where Kelly's ended.

He glanced at his watch again. Two minutes had gone by. Ten to go.

He started to crawl from beneath the car.

"Ten minutes to go," Sophie murmured as she leveled the flashlight on the safe combination.

"Shh." Kelly's ear was pressed on the steel of the safe. His hands moved delicately, precisely on the lock.

Beautiful hands, graceful fingers, she thought absently. Weird to admire the hands of a safecracker. No more weird than being here and risking her neck with him.

For God's sake, get it open.

Seven minutes.

That last minute had seemed to last an hour.

Six minutes.

She could feel her heartbeat racing in the hollow of her throat. Come on. Come on.

The door of the safe swung open!

Kelly moved to one side. "I cut it a little close. You only have a couple minutes to go through it if you're going to have plenty of time to get out of here."

"Thanks a lot." Her hands were rifling, flying through the box of disks at the front of the safe. "It's not here." She reached for the second box of disks. "It's not here either, dammit."

"Time's almost up."

"It's not—" Then she saw it at the back of the box. Sanborne's encoding, which had been on the REM-4 disks.

"Did you find it?"

"It's not the same one. I don't know if—" She jumped to her feet, her glance moving frantically around the office. She had to find a laptop with battery power. She saw one in the corner and ran across the room. "I'm going to copy it."

Kelly cursed. "You don't have time."

She looked through the desk to get a blank disk while the laptop powered up. She'd have to save it to the hard drive and then make a copy. . . . "I didn't come here to go away empty-handed."

"Then take the damn disk."

"I will," she said fiercely. "I don't believe it's the right one, but it's Sanborne's private stock. We may be able to use it." She glanced over her shoulder. "Get out of here. You need the extra time to get back and remove that timer. I'll erase the record from the laptop, put the original back in the safe, and spin the combination. I'll be right behind you."

He glanced at his watch and then ran to-

ward the door. "Three minutes tops, Sophie.
Otherwise you won't have time to get out."

He was gone.

Power up. Power up, dammit.

The screen suddenly lit up!

It took another three minutes to finish the
copy process. She jabbed the button to erase
the copy from the hard drive, replaced the
original in the safe, and spun the combination.
Then she was running down the corridor
toward the emergency stairs.

Less than two minutes.

She was taking the stairs two at a time.

One flight.

Two.

Four.

Six.

She burst out of the emergency stairwell.

She still had a minute. She streaked toward
the basement door and jerked it open.

The lights went on!

"Come on!" Royd grabbed her wrist and
jerked her out of the facility toward the parking lot. He pushed her down and underneath
the first car he came to. "You're an idiot. Why
did you cut it so damn short?"

"Shut up. I had to do it." She couldn't
breathe. "And I sent Kelly ahead. He had
enough time to disconnect the timer."

"It's not going to do any good if they catch us. We've just got to hope everyone is going to stream inside to check the facility out."

"Can we get out the gate?"

"Can't chance any of the gates. I watched them send security out to the perimeter to make sure there were no signs of intruders."

"Won't it help when they find the power outage was accidental?"

"It will take time to determine that it was." He started wriggling from underneath the car. "Until then we're going to have to hang tight and hope for the best."

"In this parking lot?"

"No, too open. Keep low. I'll go ahead to make sure the way's clear. We're going to let them drive us out of here in one of the moving vans."

"What?"

"Do you have a better idea?"

"No." But she remembered how many people had been buzzing around those vans earlier in the evening. "I'm not sure it will work."

"Neither am I. It's our best bet. We can't go back in the facility and we'd get our asses shot if we tried to go out the gates. We have to hope that Kelly set up the power outage so that there's no suspicion, and that you didn't leave any evidence of tampering."

Had she? She'd been in a hurry but she'd tried to be careful.

"I don't like that silence."

"I don't think there should be a problem."

"There'd better not be," he said grimly as he crawled on ahead. "I don't like the idea of being caught like a mouse in a trap."

So far, so good, Sophie thought.

The area around the trucks appeared to be deserted. Well, why not? Supposedly there was nothing of importance in the vans and everyone was inside the facility trying to find out what the hell had happened.

"Up." Royd gave her boost into the van and quickly followed. He glanced around at the pieces of furniture. "The metal cabinet." He strode over to the six-foot metal cabinet and opened the doors. "Shelves, dammit," he muttered. He reached in his pocket and pulled out a key chain with a number of tools hanging from it. "Keep an eye out the back of the van while I get rid of them."

She crouched at the open door of the van. "What's that? A Swiss Army knife?"

"A good deal more sophisticated but the same basic idea. What's happening inside?"

"A lot of activity. Guards moving around. . . ."

And one was opening the front door of the factory!

"Hurry!"

"I am hurrying. One shelf to go. We can leave the top one."

"There's a guard coming— No, he's stopped and is talking to someone inside."

"Got it." He jumped to his feet and carried the shelves over to the leather couch in the corner. "Get in." He put the shelves behind the couch. "No room to stand, but enough for both of us to crouch inside."

"Not much room," she said as she ducked inside the cabinet. She could still hear the guard talking. Keep talking. Keep talking. "And you're no midget."

"That's an understatement." He crawled into the cabinet and shut one door. Then he grabbed the hinges of the other door and swung it shut. "It's a good thing you're skinny enough to make up for it. Now be quiet until they start the engine."

Pitch darkness.

Overwhelming closeness.

Helpless fear.

Her heart was beating so hard she was sure Royd could hear it.

"It's okay," he whispered. "These aren't rocket scientists or they would have never left the truck unguarded. Chances are they won't search."

She nodded jerkily but didn't reply. She didn't want to do anything to lower those chances.

Time crawled by at an excruciatingly slow pace.

Five minutes.

Ten minutes.

Twenty minutes.

Thirty minutes.

Forty minutes.

The van door slammed with such force that their metal cabinet rattled.

Relief surged through her.

The next moment the engine roared to life.

Would they stop at the front gate?

No, evidently they'd been waved through.

She collapsed back against the cool metal of the cabinet.

"I told you it would be okay," Royd said over the roar of the truck's engine. "Kelly is an expert. The power-outage check probably came out without a hint of suspicion."

"I hate people who say 'I told you so.'"

"I admit it's a fault of mine. I'm right so often that it can become really annoying to others."

He was joking. They were confined in this tight metal coffin and he wasn't bothered at all. She wanted to kill him.

"Actually, we should be grateful that they're not following usual procedure in transferring these loads to the ship."

"What?"

"Most of the time they just have sealed containers that they transfer to the ship by crane. In which case we would have been shit out of luck."

"Why aren't they doing that now?"

"You'd have to ask Sanborne. He must have told them he had to have very special hand handling."

"And how are we supposed to get out of this van when we reach the destination?" she asked through her teeth.

"Play it by ear."

"I don't operate that way. You play it by ear. I need a plan."

"Very well. Let's plan. You, first."

"They'll find us when they start to unload. We'll have to get out before that."

"Good plan. And my plan is to wait until they open the door and either kill them when they jump up to start unloading or wait until they unload one of the other pieces of office furniture and then take the opportunity to get the hell out. In short, play it by ear."

"I don't have to ask which option you'd prefer."

"Yeah, I'm such a bloodthirsty bastard that I can't wait for the next kill."

"No, I didn't mean— You made me angry. I have no right to blame you for—"

"Oh, for God's sake, shut up," he said roughly. "You have the right to say anything you want to say to me without going into a guilt spiral." He changed the subject. "Did you find the disk?"

"No, not exactly."

"Either you did or you didn't."

"I didn't find the REM-4 disk but I found another one with Sanborne's special encoding labels and made a copy of it."

"Why?"

"I wanted to see what it was." She paused. "And it made me angry that I hadn't found REM-4. Dammit, I **wanted** to find it."

"That was pretty obvious. It could have been a disaster."

"But you let me go for it."

"And that should scare you. If there's a chance of even a partial success, I'm going to let you try. In spite of the promise I made to you and to Jock. I'll always worry about getting you out alive after the fact."

"I never asked anything else. No, that's not true. If you ever put my son in danger, I'll kill you myself."

"That goes without saying. We all have an infinity button that can be pushed."

"Infinity button?"

"The one trigger that can release every evil and every good within ourselves. The Pandora's box. An act or a person that can cause you to do anything you have to do."

"And Michael is my infinity button?"

"Isn't he?"

Every good or evil . . .

"I suppose he is. But I was willing to kill Sanborne in revenge for what he did to my family. So there must be other buttons."

"In your case, they're all connected with people you love."

That was true enough. "And what are your buttons, Royd?"

"Pure hate."

She felt a little ripple of shock. She was

tempted to drop the subject yet was irresistibly drawn to probe further. "Hate is the product. What caused the hate? What was the trigger? Garwood?"

"Maybe."

"Royd."

He was silent a moment. "It took a long time for REM-4 to work on me. I fought it, and that frustrated Sanborne and Boch. They looked for all kinds of methods to enhance it as Thomas Reilly was doing with Jock. Boch came up with a great idea. They'd drawn me there by luring in my younger brother, Todd. They chained him to a wall at Garwood and every time I didn't obey instructions they beat him and refused him water. It had a satisfactory psychological effect on me when paired with REM-4. In no time at all I was the zombie they wanted. But Todd was no use to them after that because he was on his way to dying of abuse and malnutrition. So they killed him before my eyes. It was supposed to be a final test. They were pretty confident of me by that time. God, they were stupid. It just goes to show you how little Sanborne knows about human nature. Todd's murder was the first brick that toppled in the wall they'd built around me. It took another two months for the rest to fall, but it happened."

"Christ."

"I assure you that Christ had nothing to do with it. Neither Boch nor Sanborne is on speaking terms with any deity."

"I meant . . ." She had to stop as her voice broke.

He was silent a moment. "Are you crying?"

She didn't answer.

He reached forward and gently touched her cheek. "You are crying. I guess I should have expected it, but somehow I didn't."

"Why not?" She tried to steady her voice. "You're always telling me how soft I am."

He didn't answer for a moment. "I didn't want to play on your sympathies. You asked and I answered. What happened at Garwood happened and now it's over."

But he still had nightmares that he refused to give up because it kept the hatred white-hot. "It's not over." She wiped her eyes with the back of her hand. "That's a stupid thing to say. You're still living it."

"No, it's a new page, with me in control." He paused. "And you're in control too. As long as your mind and will are your own, they can't beat you down."

"I know that," she said wearily. "You don't have to tell me. Or maybe you did. I seem to be having— I guess I wanted to find that disk more than I knew."

"We'll find it. We'll just turn to the next page." His tone was absolutely confident. "In fact, we may do that when we manage to get out of this van. I want you to take cover and let me scout around. Kelly said that the vans were unloading at a dock. I want to know the name of the ship the contents are being put on. That way we can track the ship to its destination when it sets out to sea."

"Providing we can get out of here without setting off any red flags by your killing the drivers," she said dryly. "What would you do then?"

"Why, Sophie." She could hear the smile in his voice. "Then I'd just have to turn another page."

"Everything seems to be in order," Gerald Kennett said when Sanborne picked up the phone. "The blackout appears to have been caused by a power overload. It spiked and caused the main board to go down."

"And the emergency generator?"

"It blew the main distributor at the transfer junction. Everything went down within a fifty-mile radius."

"I still don't like it."

"Security has been over the entire facility with a fine-tooth comb. No intruders and nothing apparently out of order."

"Apparently isn't good enough. I'm leaving my house now to check for myself."

"Suit yourself. I'm just trying to save you a needless inconvenience."

"Didn't it occur to you that this blackout was too much of a coincidence when that Dunston woman is running around loose?"

"The power outage was an accident. And even if it weren't, it would have had to be done by an insider with the technical skill Sophie Dunston obviously doesn't possess."

"I don't like coincidences." Sanborne hung up the phone.

10

The van had stopped.

She could feel the sudden tension in Royd's body. "Be quiet," he whispered as he carefully opened the cabinet door. "And stay here until I motion you to come. Then follow me and move fast."

Did he think she was going to move in slow motion once she got out of here? she wondered in annoyance. Keep calm. It was panic that was causing her to be this on edge. She could see Royd ahead of her at the doors, crouched behind a pile of rolled-up carpets. There was a gun in his hand.

And someone was opening the doors of the van, talking to someone behind him. "Go get help from those Portuguese bastards on the ship. We only have orders to unload the vats personally ourselves and there's nothing but furniture on this trip. I'm not about to unload all this crap myself."

Laughter and then the doors slid open.

One short, stocky man stood there, looking over his shoulder and still talking. Then he turned and moved out of her line of vision.

Royd was rising, motioning to her.

Jesus, that driver couldn't be more than a few yards away.

What the hell? She could only hope Royd knew what he was doing. She scrambled out of the cabinet and ran toward the back of the van.

Wet, salt-laden air assaulted her as she let Royd lift her from the truck. She received a lightning impression of warehouses lining the wharf where a cargo ship was docked.

The ship . . .

No driver. Where was he?

Then she heard the slide of metal on metal as the truck driver opened the door of the other van parked directly behind the one from which they'd just jumped.

She dove after Royd, who was rolling beneath the van and crawling toward the driver's cab. Dear heaven, it seemed she'd been doing nothing but crawling underneath vehicles tonight. First the cars at the facility parking lot and now this truck. But the huge tires of the eighteen-wheeler formed a much safer barrier than the passenger cars'.

It was a good thing, because she heard the Portuguese seamen talking as she caught up with Royd. He motioned her to stop as he flattened himself next to one of the wheels, his gaze on the far side of the truck.

She held her breath.

Five men.

They were strolling leisurely, evidently in no hurry to start unloading. And they passed the back of their truck and went toward the one parked behind it.

"There's a warehouse twenty yards ahead," Royd whispered. "We can't count on it being unlocked and vacant. So we hide behind the oil drums in front and make our way around the back."

She nodded curtly. "Get going, dammit. Once they start unloading, they'll be all over the place."

He glanced at her and then smiled. "Right. I'm on my way. And you're on your own."

And the next moment he was crawling from

beneath the truck and running toward the warehouse.

She took a quick glance at the other truck, then followed him.

Twenty yards? It seemed more like a hundred yards. Every moment she expected to hear a shout behind her. Then she was diving behind the oil drums. Royd was already at the corner of the warehouse. The next moment he disappeared from view. He'd obviously meant it when he'd said she was on her own, she thought as she bent low and raced toward the corner.

"Very good." He was waiting for her as she reached the corner. "Now wait here while I get closer to that ship." He turned to go back on the dock. "As soon as I come back, we'll get out of here."

She felt a surge of panic. "Why go back to the ship?"

"I was in a bit of a rush and didn't get the name of the ship."

"I did. **Constanza.**"

He gazed at her in surprise. "You're sure?"

"Of course I'm sure. It was the first thing I looked at after I jumped out of the van. Now, how the hell do we get out of here?"

He turned back and started at a trot toward

the rear of the warehouse. "With extreme speed and infinite care."

It took Sophie and Royd four hours to get back to their motel. First, traveling by taxi to the airport to rent a car and then the two-hour journey back to the motel.

Sophie was almost numb with exhaustion as she watched Royd unlock the door. "**Constanza**. I have to check **Constanza** on my computer. It has to be a Portuguese registration and that should—"

"Give yourself a few hours' sleep first." Royd threw open the door. "It won't hurt and you won't be in danger of falling asleep at the keyboard."

"I won't fall asleep. And that truck driver mentioned something about vats. What the devil did he mean?" She headed for the adjoining door. "I'll take a shower to wake up. I need to—" She stopped as she caught sight of herself in the mirror over the desk. "Good God, I look like I've been through a tornado." She touched the oil on her cheek that must have come from the oil drums. "Why didn't you tell me? And why didn't you get this filthy?"

"I did. But you weren't noticing much after we got away from the docks. I believe you were a little tense. I cleaned up in the airport before

I went to the rental agency and picked you up outside."

"Tense" was an understatement. It had been an exhausting and frightening night. She probably wouldn't have noticed if he'd shed his clothes in the airport and picked her up naked. She shook her head. "I'm surprised the taxi driver let us in his cab."

"Most cab drivers aren't that picky about fares at that hour of the night, and I tipped him well. Actually, it was good that you were so dirty you were practically unrecognizable. Suppose I sit down with your computer and start a search on the **Constanza** while you're in the shower. That should save a little time."

She nodded. That made sense and Lord knows she wanted to get the information as soon as possible. "The computer's in my duffel. I won't be long."

"Take your time." He went to the duffel sitting against the wall and unzipped it. "Like I said, the **Constanza**'s not going to sail off into the sunset or sunrise today. The facility isn't ready to be shut down yet."

"I want to know." She grabbed her nightshirt and terry robe from the duffel and headed for the shower. "I want to know everything I can find out about what Sanborne is up to."

"You think I don't?" He flipped open the laptop. "And I'm not known for my patience."

"Really? I would never have guessed." She shut the bathroom door and started stripping. Keep going. She'd feel better after she washed some of the dirt and weariness away. It hadn't been a total washout of a night. She hadn't found the REM-4 disk but she had a copy of one that Sanborne might have valued. They hadn't been caught or hurt or killed and that didn't suck. And they knew the name of the ship that was transporting all the equipment.

She stepped beneath the shower and let the warm water flow over her for a few minutes before reaching for the shampoo. What was Michael doing now? It was almost 4:00 A.M. here and that meant it was 9:00 A.M. at Mac-Duff's Run. She had called him yesterday as she'd promised and he'd sounded happy, even excited. He'd said he had a night terror the night before but MacDuff took care of him. God, she hoped he was happy. At least he was safe, and that was what was important.

Keep well, keep happy, Michael. I'm working hard to bring you home.

Royd glanced up as she walked out of the bathroom ten minutes later. "Come over here. There's something you should see."

"The **Constanza**?" She moved quickly over to the desk. "You found out something?"

He shook his head. "I decided to check the local news first." He swiveled the computer around. "The police announced that there were no bodies in the fire at your house and that you were officially listed as a missing person."

She frowned. "But that's old news. You told me the fire department had already made that finding. Why are you acting as if it's—"

"We didn't expect what they reported in the second paragraph. Keep reading."

"What are you talking about? I don't see— Oh, my God." Her gaze flew to his face. "Dave?" she whispered. "Dave's dead?"

"So it would seem. I checked the related story in the newspaper. His body was found yesterday afternoon in a ditch outside the city."

Her gaze returned to the article. "Shot to death. Killer unknown."

"Except that the police are making a few guesses."

She shook her head to clear it of the shock. "Me? They're looking for me. They think I did it." She dropped down on the bed. "My God."

"It makes sense to them. You blow your

house up and hope that everyone thinks you're dead. Then you kill your ex-husband."

"But eventually they'd discover I didn't die in the explosion."

"Remember, the police believe you're a little unbalanced and not thinking straight."

"But why would I kill Dave?"

"There are usually disputes after a divorce. Are you saying that you didn't have any?"

"Of course we did. But I wouldn't—" Her body was starting to shake. "For Christ's sake, he was my lover. I had his child."

"And he married another woman after he divorced you when you went around the bend."

"I didn't go around the bend," she said through her teeth. "They would never have released me if I wasn't stable."

"No? There are all kinds of stories about premature releases that result in killing."

"Shut up."

"Just playing devil's advocate. It said in the story that Edmunds's wife said he left immediately after he got a call. He seemed very excited but he wouldn't tell her where he was going. It would be natural that he wouldn't be eager to tell his wife that his ex-wife was wanting to see him."

"Jean wasn't jealous of me."

"Why not? You're beautiful, you're smart, and you're Michael's mother."

"She just— She was the woman Dave should have married and she knew it. Her only aim was to be a stay-at-home housewife and help Dave in any way she could. She realized I wasn't a threat and only wanted what was best for Michael."

"But I bet she's thinking twice now. A grieving widow always wants revenge."

"Will you be quiet?" She lifted her trembling hand to her head. "I have to think."

"I'm trying to help you think. You're shaken and—" He stopped. "You're probably grieving over that bastard yourself. That's getting in the way."

Shock surged through her. "He wasn't a bastard. He had faults like anyone else but he—"

"Okay, okay." Royd closed the laptop with barely contained violence. "What do I know? But I wouldn't abandon a partner if he got into hot water. From what I hear, the marriage bonds are supposed to be a hell of a lot stronger. He should have been there for you."

"You don't realize how difficult it was living with Michael."

"You were living with him too. You didn't leave." He went on before she could answer.

"Grieve all you please if you're that stupid. But don't let it get in the way of self-preservation. This is bad stuff and we've got to cope with it."

"You know I didn't kill him." She rubbed her temple. "I wasn't near that ditch. The police will find that out if they investigate."

"Will they? Not if the person who killed him knew what he was doing. I don't believe Sanborne would send another Caprio this time. He'd use a top gun."

"What are you saying?"

"That he will have cleaned up any of the forensic evidence that would lead the police to him and planted a few items that would link you to the killing."

"How?"

"DNA. It's an assassin's best friend these days. Providing he can dodge the bullet himself."

"As I'm sure you could," she said bitterly.

"Yes, I'm damn good at dodging bullets. But you don't have to worry about me, you have to worry about the envelope or bits of hair that the cops are going to find."

"Envelope?"

"That was one of the objects that our teachers at Garwood suggested. You lick an envelope and the DNA is identifiable for years. You get a bit of hair from a brush in the subject's locker and it's another clincher. Did Sanborne have access to any of your correspondence when you were with him?"

"Of course he did."

"And do you keep personal grooming items in your locker at the hospital?"

She nodded.

"Then I'd bet the police will be taking a bundle to the DNA lab and your goose is cooked. Understand?"

She did understand and it terrified her. "He killed him just to frame me?"

"Good chance. You're proving to be a problem and there would be no better way to discredit you."

She shook her head dazedly. "It seems impossible. No, it doesn't. I just can't take it in."

"Then you'd better start." His tone was as hard as his face. "Because we've got to begin planning a countermove."

"Just go away, Royd. I need some time to myself."

"Later. You can mourn Edmunds after you realize the implications." He crossed his arms over his chest and leaned back in the chair. "The most important one for you is that you're going to be hunted. And that hunt will include Michael."

"Michael's safe in Scotland."

"Will MacDuff be willing to hide him if it means tangling with U.S. law enforcement?"

"I don't know. But Jock wouldn't let anything happen to him." Yet would Jock be able to offer him shelter if MacDuff refused him sanctuary? She just didn't know. "They may not be able to trace him." She had a thought. "Or maybe they will. Dave may have told Jean about Jock. Jesus, I don't know."

"We have to assume the worst to be safe. One, you're a suspect and it may take some fancy dancing to get you out of this. Two, as long as you're a suspect, you have no credibility and Sanborne is sitting pretty. Three, Michael will be vulnerable from both Sanborne and Boch and the police. Agreed?"

"Of course I agree."

"Good, then I'll leave you to get some sleep." He stood up. "I had to make sure it would sink in before I left you. It's more important that you consider your position than Edmunds's demise."

"No, it's not." She could feel the tears stinging her eyes. "I have to think about both of them. I was married to him, for God's sake. You may be able to compartmentalize, but I can't do it. I don't have that degree of coldness."

"Cold? I wish I were cold. It would make things a hell of a lot easier for me." He fell to his knees in front of her. "You want comfort? I'll give you comfort. Even though I don't think he deserves you blubbering about him."

She stiffened. "I'm not blubbering. And I don't want your—" She stopped as he pulled her into his arms. "Let me go. What do you think you're—"

"Shut up," he said roughly, his hand on the back of her head, pressing her face into his shirt. "Cry if you feel like it. I can't give you understanding, but I've got a handy shoulder and I respect your right to your opinion." His hand was stroking her hair. "I respect **you.**"

His big hand in her hair felt like a bear's paw, she thought. There was a clumsiness that should have been irritating but instead was oddly comforting. "Let me go. This is . . . weird."

"Tell me about it. But I'm all you've got right now. I'm better than a soggy pillow, aren't I?"

"Marginally," she whispered. Her arms instinctively tightened around him. It wasn't the truth. She could feel the pain and shock easing as if it were ebbing into him, as if he were willing it to leave her. "You don't have to do this, you know. I'd never expect it of you."

"It's a surprise to me too. I don't know how to do this and it makes me mad. I'm not good at all this sensitive stuff. Sex is easy, but I can't—" He drew a deep breath. "I didn't mean to mention sex right now. It just came out. Well, what the hell do you expect? I'm a man."

"And you respect me so deeply."

He pushed her back to look down into her face. "I meant that. You're smart and you're kind and you're a good mother. And I'm a good judge of maternal skills because I've had some foster stand-ins that were real doozies. It's not your fault your head's all messed up."

"My head's not messed up. You have to be the most tactless man on the face of the earth and I can't deal with you right—"

"Shh." He pulled her back into his arms. "I'll keep my mouth closed. At least, I'll try. If you start praising Edmunds, I don't promise anything. He didn't deserve you."

"He was a decent man. It wasn't his fault he married the wrong—" She broke off. She wasn't going to convince him and it was kind of nice having someone who was entirely in her corner. At least in this moment of hurt and despair. Tomorrow he'd probably turn away, but now he was here and offering help she desperately needed. "And he'd be alive if it weren't for me."

"Great. Another victim at your door. Don't you ever get tired of carrying around that load of guilt?" He stood up, bringing her with him. "If he'd been with you, you'd have been fighting Sanborne together. His death might never have happened." He pushed her down on the bed and lay down beside her. "Don't stiffen up on me. I'm not going to jump you. I just can't keep that position all night without getting a charley horse." He gathered her close again. "This okay? If it's not, I'll leave you. I promise."

"Are you telling the truth?" she asked unevenly.

"Probably not. Like I said, I'm not very sensitive. I have a tendency to try to bulldoze when I believe I'm right. I'd probably do my best to talk you out of it."

He was like a battering ram, and she didn't want to do battle. She believed he was honestly attempting to help her and was no threat tonight. She was glad, because he was someone to hold on to in the darkness that was beginning to come too near. "Too much talk . . ." She closed her eyes. "Just let me go to sleep, Royd."

"Sure." He pulled up the sheet and tucked it

around them. "Sleep well. I'll keep you safe, Sophie."

He'd keep her safe. . . . Strange, Dave had never said those words. Their marriage had never resounded with those basic primitive needs. He'd amused her, he'd filled her with admiration for his fine intellect, and she'd liked his body. In the beginning they'd had common goals and later they'd had Michael. He'd loved Michael. . . .

"Shit," Royd said roughly. "Stop crying. I don't like it."

"Tough." She opened her eyes to look up at his frowning face. "Didn't you cry when your brother died?"

He was silent a moment. "Yes. But that was me. I don't like you to do it. I didn't know I'd feel like this." His lips tightened. "But if you have to, go ahead."

"Thank you," she said with irony. "I'll do that."

He laid his head back on the pillow. "I'm saying all the wrong things. You probably wish Jock were here. He'd know how to handle this."

"No, I don't want Jock here. I want him with Michael." She closed her eyes again. "And, yes, he'd be much more sensitive than you. But I believe you're trying to help me and I appreciate it. Just give me a few hours and I won't need either one of you."

"Okay." His big hand was stroking her hair again. "I'll do whatever you want—for the next few hours, anyway."

She was aware of that endearing clumsiness again. Usually, he was one of the most graceful men she'd ever run across, but not now. He was obviously facing a new situation and it was bothering the hell out of him. And he was doing it for her. "Thank you." This time there was no sarcasm in her tone.

"You're welcome." He settled closer. He whispered, "And I'm glad Jock's not here either. . . ."

She was asleep.

He should let her go.

Not yet. Royd stared into the darkness, his arms tightening around Sophie. He didn't want her to wake and find herself alone. She was feeling too alone and vulnerable now anyway. His presence might not be the one she wanted, but that was too bad. He was a port in the storm that was engulfing her and it was an indication of how alone she felt that she had accepted him.

Why the devil had he fought so hard to make her let him stay? Her pain shouldn't matter to him as long as she could function.

Bull, it did matter.

She mattered. He was coming too close to her. He'd watched her, talked to her, seen her fear, seen her courage. He'd fought to let it mean nothing to him. It wasn't working. He had to force himself to keep his distance, to ignore the urge to touch her, stroke her, ease her.

Sex.

Oh yes, definitely sex. The arousal of his body right now was testament to that truth. It wasn't easy to lie here next to her and not move over her. Why not do it? he thought recklessly. He'd never been known for his restraint, and Sophie was very vulnerable at this moment. He could make her want it. What the hell was he doing trying to be some kind of noble schmuck? He'd always taken sex where he found it, as long as it didn't hurt the woman. Sophie was tough and she didn't give a damn about him. She wouldn't be hurt by a one-night stand.

If it was a one-night stand. He wasn't sure if that would be enough for him.

Stop thinking about it. He'd given her his promise and it was just making him more—

She stirred against him with a whimper.

Shit.

Her face was a pale blur in the darkness but he could see the dark spread of her lashes on her cheeks. She looked as helpless as a child.

Dammit, she wasn't a child. She was a woman who'd had a child and gone through hell for the last years. Sex could be comfort. It didn't have to be—

But there wouldn't be any comfort connected with any sex between them, so stop making excuses for taking what he wanted. It wasn't going to happen because he'd made that damn promise.

She smelled of lemon shampoo and clean soap.

Keep it burning low. Think of something else. He wasn't a kid. He might not be used to restraint, but he could do anything he had to do.

He hoped.

She cuddled closer to him.

It was going to be a long night.

11

Midmorning sunlight was streaming into the hotel room when Sophie opened her eyes the next day.

Royd was no longer beside her. Loneliness surged through her.

Stupid. Of course she was alone. She'd drifted in and out of sleep during the night and he'd been there but that didn't mean he—

"Good morning." Royd stood in the doorway. "How are you doing?"

"Better." Her lips twisted. "Or maybe not. Maybe I'm just numb. But, at least, I can think now."

"Then you'd better grab a shower and get dressed. We've got to get out of here."

"Now?" She sat up in bed. "Right away?"

"The sooner the better." He tossed her the newspaper. "You're on the front page again. Rehash of the same story but it's a good picture and we don't want anyone recognizing you." He paused. "There's a picture of Michael too. The police are concerned about his safety."

"So am I." She looked down at the photo of Michael. "They think I'd kill my son? They think I'm that nuts?"

"Your father killed your mother."

"And insanity runs in the family?" She swung her feet to the floor. "I'll be ready to leave in thirty minutes. Is that good enough?"

He shook his head. "I'll start packing for you."

She got out of bed and headed for the bathroom. "I can do it."

"I'm spinning my wheels waiting for you." He went to the desk and unplugged her laptop. "I need something to do."

She could see that. He looked restless and on edge. "Then look up the **Constanza**. I didn't do it last night."

"You were a little preoccupied," he said. "But I checked on it when I got up this morning. It's a Portuguese vessel but flies under a Liberian flag. Forty-two years old and can be leased to the highest bidder." He paused. "It's interesting that the last person who leased it was Said Ben Kaffir."

She stopped at the door. "And who is he?"

"A weapons dealer who supplies every religious fanatic and scumbag in Europe and the Middle East."

"Weapons dealer," she repeated. "And REM-4 creates a hell of a powerful weapon."

"Everything from suicide bombers to skilled assassins willing to risk their lives without question."

"And you think Ben Kaffir is involved in Sanborne's plans?"

He shrugged. "Who knows? But it's an interesting coincidence." He slipped the laptop in its case. "I'll have to explore it further as soon as I get the chance. Snap to it. Fifteen minutes, Sophie. I'll meet you at the car."

"Ten minutes," she said. He was curt and businesslike and completely different from the man who had held her through the night, she thought as she closed the bathroom door. No, that wasn't true. Royd may have been different last night, but this was no Jekyll and Hyde transformation. He had held her, helped her, but his gentleness had been awkward, and he was the first to admit that he had said all the wrong things.

But he had been honest, and that frankness

had been devoid of any hint of phoniness. Perhaps that was why she had been able to accept
his sympathy. What he said was what he
meant. That was a comfort in itself.

But she couldn't accept it again, she thought
wearily. She had already taken too much from
Royd when he'd been sent to Garwood. They
had to work together because it could be the
only way they could beat Sanborne and Boch,
but she had to be careful not to let him give her
any more than absolutely necessary.

Royd glanced at his watch when she got into
the car. "Ten minutes. You're a woman of
your word." He started the engine. "I checked
out and called Kelly. No undue activity at the
facility. Sanborne showed up and was questioning everyone, but Kelly's not under suspicion." He paused. "He went first to the
human resources office and checked the safe.
And that means the disk you took may be
valuable. Pop it into the computer and let's
check it out."

"Not now. We can do it later."

He glanced at her. "Later?"

"When we get to Scotland."

He smiled. "We're going to Mac
Duff's Run?"

"Of course. I have to be the one to tell Michael his father's dead. And Michael may be tracked down by either the police or Sanborne. I don't even know MacDuff. I've been taking Jock's word about him. I can't be sure that he'll protect Michael and keep him away from both of them. It's time I met him so that I can judge for myself. I have to be sure."

"I can see that." His smile faded. "But he'd be safer with almost anyone than you, Sophie."

"I know." Her hands clenched nervously together. God, she felt helpless. "And Jock trusts MacDuff. But **I** have to trust him."

He nodded. "Then we go to Scotland."

Relief surged through her. "You don't have to go with me. I wouldn't put you in that kind of jeopardy. I just have to have some way of getting the right documents to get me out of the country. Like MacDuff managed for Michael. You can do that, can't you?"

"Probably." He backed out of the parking lot. "But I'm not going to do it. It would be too dangerous and we have to work fast. We'll have to do without documents."

"What?"

"I can fly a plane and I learned a lot about smuggling when I was in Asia. I imagine I can smuggle you out of here and into Scotland."

"What about Homeland Security?"

"What about it? What do you have to lose?" His brows rose. "Other than your life if they shoot us down."

"Is that likely?"

"If it were, I wouldn't do it." His smile faded. "Trust me, Sophie."

"I have a problem with trust."

"That's pretty obvious. But this won't be a first for me, Sophie."

She studied his face. No, there probably weren't too many firsts left for him. "Okay, let's do it. When can you arrange for this plane?"

"It's already done." He checked his watch. "It should be ready at Montkeyes Airport by the time we get there in about an hour."

She stared at him in bewilderment. "What? Montkeyes?"

"It's a private airport between here and Richmond, Virginia. Very private. Very discreet."

"And you already arranged for it?"

"I've come to know you pretty well. I knew what would be first on the agenda. I even called Jock and told him to make sure that Michael didn't hear about Edmunds's death from anyone else." He made a face. "I was only hoping that you wouldn't insist on us jerking Michael away from MacDuff's Run."

"I still may do it."

"Then that's the breaks of the game. I'll have to deal with it."

"No, I'll have to deal with it. Michael's my responsibility." She looked away. "I wish I could do without your help. I've just been telling myself how I can't lean on you any longer and then I ask you to do this."

"Don't worry about it. I always get my own back."

There was something in his tone that caused her gaze to fly back to his face. His expression was totally unreadable.

He glanced sideways and smiled. "You're doubting me. Good God, I'm no knight in shining armor. You're confusing me with Jock. After last night you should realize that I'm no fount of human kindness."

"Last night was a surprise to me," she said slowly.

"It was a surprise to me too." His hands tightened on the steering wheel. "In more ways than one. I'm not what you call a restrained or tolerant man."

She stiffened. "I don't ask for your tolerance. I don't need it. What I felt for Dave was my own business."

"I wasn't talking about Edmunds." He punched the button for the radio. "I'm over it. I can deal with that too. If you'd really still cared about him, you'd have hit me over the head with a lamp. You didn't do it, so I figure you're far enough away from the relationship to see what I was saying had a kernel of truth."

She wanted to deny it, but he was right. Why had she wanted to blind herself after Dave's death to the truth she'd admitted in life?

"It's okay." He was studying her expression. "When anyone dies, it's normal to think they deserved better than they got. Unless it's someone like me, who gets jealous as hell and reacts like the savage I am."

Jealous?

"Yes, I said it," he said curtly. "I did it on purpose because I want you to start thinking about it. I want to go to bed with you. I've wanted it almost from the day I met you."

She felt a surge of heat go through her. Push it back. Crazy. "You said, you've been in the jungle too long," she said unevenly.

"Not just any woman. You. It has to be you."

"Yeah, sure."

"But I'm not pushing right now. So forget it, lean back, and listen to the music."

"Forget it?" She gazed at him incredulously. "You don't want me to forget it."

"Hell, no. I want you to store it away and bring it out and stroke it occasionally until you get used to the idea."

She moistened her lips. "That's not going to happen."

He ignored her words. "I think you'd like me. I'm not smooth and glib. I won't breathe sweet nothings in your ear. I don't belong to the world you shared with Edmunds. The only education I had past high school was what I taught myself. What you see is what you get. I'm not afraid that I can't meet the competition. I can do whatever I have to do. And I'll bet I want you more than any man you've ever had and I'll take the time to make sure you want me that much too."

She stared at him, trying to think of something to say.

"You'll like me," he repeated softly.

"I don't want to—"

"Like I said, no pressure." He stepped on the accelerator. "I know where your priorities lie. We have a job to do." He smiled. "Just think about it."

How could she help it? Dammit.

His big body was only inches away from her and she could feel her heart beating faster.

She leaned back and closed her eyes.

Listen to the music, she told herself.
Listen to the music.

"What's the story?" Boch demanded when
Sanborne picked up the phone. "Have the police found her?"

"Not as far as I'm aware. My contact in the
police department says they're still searching."

Boch cursed. "I need her out of the picture.
As long as she's running around loose, she's a
threat to negotiations. You said the frame
would do it."

"It will do it. The minute she's picked up,
she'll be on her way to jail. The DNA evidence
is solid."

"If your man didn't make a mistake."

"He didn't make a mistake. I supplied him
with her hair and an excellently forged note
with her saliva on the seal inviting Edmunds
to meet her. I told him to clean up the crime
scene."

"And the car?"

"Is now at the bottom of the bay." He
added, "It's now only a matter of waiting until
the police pick her up. Be patient."

"Screw patience. She'll start yelling about
you and REM-4 the minute she's given a
chance to talk to reporters."

"She won't talk to reporters for a while. She'll get legal assistance first. That will give me the chance I need for my man in the police department to get to her."

"What's he using?"

"Cyanide." He smiled. "Isn't that the traditional suicide pill? What a shame the police matrons won't find it when they search her. But after all, she is a doctor and has access to all kinds of deadly pills."

"What about the boy? We need him dead, dammit. There's no sympathy for a mother killing her child. We have to get to them before the police."

"My guess is that she'll have stashed the boy away when she realized he was in danger."

Boch was silent a moment. "Jock Gavin?"

"That's logical. And Gavin was under the wing of a Scottish Lord named MacDuff. I've sent the same man who put down Edmunds to snoop around the castle and see what he could come up with."

"Gavin is an expert. It won't be easy to take the boy away from him."

"Nothing worthwhile is easy. But the man I sent has orders to report before taking action. We don't want an international incident to stir up any more mud."

"Who did you send? Do I know him?"

"Oh, yes. You know him." He paused. "Sol Devlin."

"Holy shit!"

"I hope you'll agree he's efficient enough. After all, he's one of yours. You were very proud of him when he finished at Garwood." He added slyly, "Or perhaps it was just that you needed a success after Royd bolted."

"Devlin was a success. He's almost perfect, everything that Royd should have been."

"I agree. Lethal and obedient. That's why I've been saving him for a special job like this."

"I wanted to use him as an example for Ben Kaffir."

"That's down the road. This is more important."

Boch was silent. "Okay, I suppose you're right."

Of course he was right, Sanborne thought sourly. Grudging bastard.

"How are you going to kill the boy?"

"With the same gun that killed Edmunds. But if that bitch is on her way to him it will be better to wait until she's close enough to him to be suspicious. That's why I told Devlin to watch and wait."

"And if she's not? What if the police pick her up?"

"Then we kill the boy and toss him into the sea so no one will know when it was done. And Devlin didn't use all the DNA evidence at the Edmunds crime scene. It will all work out." He was tired of defending himself to Boch. "I have to hang up now."

"Wait. Have you received the analysis of the latest results Gorshank sent us?"

"No. It should be coming in any time."

"But no matter how it comes back, it still shouldn't stop us from moving."

Gorshank's results had everything to do with how they proceeded, Sanborne thought impatiently. Why couldn't he see that? Boch was using his usual steamroller tactics and he wasn't about to argue with him right now. "We'll talk about it later. I have to check in with Devlin." He pressed the disconnect and then dialed Devlin's cell phone. "Where are you?" he asked when Devlin answered.

"In the hills above the castle. I haven't seen anyone come in or out. I have to get closer."

"Then what's stopping you?"

"There's a shepherd's croft near here. I've had to keep dodging to avoid being seen."

"You're making excuses. If you have to get nearer, do it."

"If that's what you want me to do." There

was no meekness in his tone. It was quiet and without expression but Sanborne didn't feel he was dealing with a zombie. It had been part of the Garwood program to have the subjects behave perfectly normally in every other aspect but obedience. Yes, Devlin was almost perfect. Sanborne could envision him standing on the hill, compact, muscular, with sandy hair in a crew cut. A magnificent machine totally at Sanborne's command. It was quite heady to have that much power over a human being. He could feel the flush of exhilaration surging through him. Money was all very well, but dollars couldn't equal the charge that total domination could bring him. He'd had power at his fingertips for most of his adult life but this was different, this was excitement. "Make no mistakes, but do what you were sent to do." He hung up.

Sol Devlin hung up his phone.

Do what you were sent to do.

He could feel the pleasure begin to kindle within him. He hated to have Sanborne put restraints on him and sometimes he deliberately tried to avoid it by saying or doing something that would force him to release him. Most of the time Sanborne didn't even realize that the slave was controlling him.

He smiled at the thought. He didn't know if he could break free of Sanborne if he tried. He'd made an attempt once and it had been painful. Too painful when he didn't even know if he wanted life without the purpose Sanborne had given him. He was well fed; he was provided women and drugs.

And he enjoyed what he did.

How much was conditioning? He didn't care. The pleasure was there and that was what mattered. Like this moment, when anticipation was beginning to tingle through him at the thought of what was to come.

Soon. Within a few hours.

Devlin turned to stare at the croft several hundred yards below him.

"My mother is coming." Michael slowly hung up the phone. "She said she'd be here in a few hours."

MacDuff had been expecting that ever since last night, when Jock had told him about the death of Edmunds. "And how do you feel about that?" MacDuff asked quietly.

"Okay, I guess. She didn't want to talk. She sounded . . . worried."

"She has a right to be worried, from what you and Jock have told me."

Michael's gaze lifted. "But is there something else? Something you know but aren't telling me?"

Should he lie to him? No, the boy had been through too much without adding deceit to the mix. "Yes, and I have no intention of telling you. It's your mother who has that right."

Michael frowned. "I don't want to wait."

"Too bad." MacDuff smiled. "We don't always get what we want." He stood up. "But I'll volunteer to take your mind off it. Want to come down to the Run and practice a little soccer?"

"It won't take my mind off it."

"Want to make a wager? I'll work your ass so hard you won't be able to think." He turned to the door. "Come on, we'll pick up Jock on the way down to the Run and make him play goalie."

Michael hesitated. "You said you wanted me to go through these drawers and to see if I could find any old-looking papers."

"You're excused for today." MacDuff was going out the door. "I need a little exercise. . . ."

"What are those damn sheep doing in the middle of the road?" Sophie's hands clenched on her lap. "Someone should be taking care of them."

"The shepherd's probably nearby. You have to make allowances in Scotland." Royd carefully negotiated the sedan through the herd of sheep. "No big deal."

"I know it's not." Sophie moistened her lips. "I guess I'm nervous. For God's sake, don't hit them."

"Really? I'd never guess you were the least upset." Royd hit the bright headlights. "There's MacDuff's Run up ahead."

The castle was huge and intimidating and loomed over the countryside. It reminded Sophie of something out of **Ivanhoe.** "Then step on it. I have to see Michael."

"You're going to tell him tonight?"

"There's no use putting it off. He has to hear about Dave from me." She frowned. "I can't be sure that someone won't come bursting in and try to arrest me."

"I think you can be sure that won't happen," Royd said. "From what Jock told me about MacDuff, he's not one to be surprised."

"I'm not sure about anything— Stop!" They'd almost hit one of the sheep that had run back into the road. She jumped out and shooed the animal to the side of the road and then got back into the car. "This is going to take us all night just to get to the gates."

"I think we're clear now." Royd cautiously pressed the accelerator and the car moved down the road. "I'll be careful of the livestock."

"It's not your fault. This place is in the back of beyond and I'm surprised MacDuff doesn't have better—"

"Halt." A guard had come out of the shadows at the gate of the castle. He was carrying an M-16, and as the car stopped he shone a flashlight into their faces. "Ms. Dunston?"

"Yes." She shaded her eyes against the glare. "Turn that thing off."

"In a moment." He was checking a photograph in his hand. "Sorry." He turned the flashlight aside. "I had to be sure. The Laird doesn't suffer fools gladly. I'm James Campbell."

"Where did you get the photo?"

"Jock." He glanced at Royd. "Mr. Royd?"

Royd nodded. "Now will you step aside so that we can go inside?"

He shook his head. "The Laird said to send you to the Run when you got here. He and the boy are there." He pointed to the right. "Get out and go around the castle toward the cliff."

"I don't like this." Royd opened the door. "I'll go, Sophie. You drive on inside the gates.

I can't see MacDuff risking letting Michael run around outside the gates."

"Risk?" James Campbell's tone was indignant. "No risk. The Laird is there."

He might as well have said "Superman is there," Sophie thought. Evidently the man had the same respect for the Laird that Jock did. The similarity was reassuring. "I'm going with you." She got out of the car and joined Royd. "Is Jock with them?"

Campbell nodded.

"Then call him and tell him we're coming," Sophie said as she fell into step with Royd.

"You could let me handle this," Royd said quietly.

"I could." Her pace quickened. "But I doubt if there's anything to handle. I don't think any of Sanborne's men would be camped right outside the gates."

"And you want to see Michael as soon as possible."

"Oh, yes," she whispered. "I'm not looking forward to this and I want to get it over."

He was silent. "Will you let me go ahead and check it out?"

"We're in this together. I made the decision. If it's some kind of trap, then—"

"Michael."

She was Michael's mother. She had to be alive to protect him. She drew a deep breath and stopped. "Okay. You do it. If you're not back in five minutes, I'll go back to the castle and dodge Campbell at the gate."

"He's not easy to dodge," Jock said as he appeared on the path ahead of them. He was bare-chested and beaded with sweat, but he was smiling. "And if you succeeded, I'd have to dispose of the poor man." He held up his hand and wrinkled his nose. "Hello, Sophie. I'd give you a hug but I'm fairly disgusting at present. MacDuff and Michael are running me ragged."

"What?"

"Come ahead." He turned and disappeared into the darkness.

She was frowning as she followed him. Running him ragged? What the devil was he talking about?

Then she came around the corner of the castle and saw the Run. It was a level stretch of ground bordered on either side by huge, smooth rocks.

And racing across it were Michael and a tall, dark-haired man as bare-chested and perspiration-coated as Jock. His hair was tied back by a kerchief. Both were panting, laughing, and looking as if they hadn't a care in the world.

Sophie stared at them in shock. It wasn't the Michael she had been picturing during this journey. He looked . . . free. She felt a rush of happiness and then a surge of dread as she realized that she was going to destroy that joy.

"Mom!" Michael had looked up and seen her. Then he was running toward her.

She fell to her knees as he launched himself at her. Her arms closed around him and held him tight. He smelled of salt and sweat and soap. God, she loved him. She cleared her throat. "What are you doing out here? Playing? Shouldn't you be in bed?"

"I was waiting for you." He took a step back. "And the Laird doesn't mind. He says football is good for the soul any time of the day or night."

"I'm afraid I don't agree." She pushed his hair back from his forehead. "But you don't look any the worse for wear."

"I'm fine." He glanced over his shoulder. "This is my mother. This is the Earl of Connaught, Lord of MacDuff's Run. He has all kinds of other names but I can't remember all of them. I guess we'll have to stop now, sir."

"Too bad." The Laird was strolling toward them. "Delighted to meet you, Ms. Dunston. I hope you had an uneventful trip."

"Yes. Until we ran into your herd of sheep wandering all over the road."

He frowned. "Really?"

"Really." She forced herself to release Michael. "I need to talk to my son alone. Will you leave us?"

"No." MacDuff turned to Royd and offered his hand. "You're Royd?"

"Yes." He slowly reached out and shook MacDuff's hand.

"Will you take Michael and Ms. Dunston back to the castle? I need to have a word with Jock. I'll have him call James and tell him to show you your rooms."

"Michael and I can talk here," Sophie said.

MacDuff shook his head. "This place is special to him now. I won't have it tainted. Talk to him somewhere else." He turned away and moved toward Jock.

Arrogant bastard.

"Tainted?" Michael's anxious gaze was fixed on her face.

Her arm went around his shoulder. "We'll go back to the castle."

"I knew something was wrong," he whispered. "Tell me."

"I'm not trying to keep anything from you," she said gently. "But it seems I can't talk to you here. Let's go to your room." She nudged him toward the path. "Royd?"

"I'll be right behind you until you reach the castle and I know you're safe. After that, you won't want or need me, will you?"

She wanted to tell him she did need him. She'd grown accustomed to the companionship and strength she'd unconsciously leaned upon during these last days. But this had nothing to do with the tie that bound them together. This was between her and her son. She nodded as she moved up the path. "No, I won't need you."

Royd watched Sophie and Michael cross the courtyard toward the front door of the castle. Sophie's shoulders were very straight, as if she were bracing herself for a blow. He had seen that stance before. It seemed she had taken nothing but bruising hits since the moment he had met her and accepted them with that same enduring strength.

As the door shut behind them, his hands clenched at his sides. God, he felt helpless. She was hurting and she was going to hurt more as she told Michael about his father.

Well, he could do nothing about it. He was the outsider. So smother this impulse to run after them, and do something useful. He turned and went back through the gates to where Jock, MacDuff, and Campbell, the guard, were talking.

He broke into the conversation. "Okay, what's the problem?"

MacDuff raised his brows. "Problem?"

"The damn sheep. When Sophie told you about the sheep in the road, you reacted . . . It made you wary. And then you wanted to talk to Jock. What's happening?"

"It could be coincidence, you know," Mac-Duff said. "Perhaps I wanted to tell Jock to comfort Ms. Dunston in her time of need."

"Bullshit."

Campbell took a step forward. "You don't talk to the Laird that way," he said softly. "Do you want him gone, sir?"

"Easy, James. It's all right," MacDuff said. "Go and round up a few men and get back here in ten minutes."

"You're sure?" Campbell asked. "He'd be no trouble for me."

Jock chuckled. "Don't be so certain. He'd even be a bit of trouble for me, James." He jerked his thumb at the castle. "Ten minutes."

Campbell turned and strode through the gates.

"The sheep," Royd repeated.

"Tell him," Jock said to MacDuff. "We can use him if it's what we think."

MacDuff was silent a moment and then shrugged. "You're right." He glanced up the hill. "The sheep should never have been in the road. Those hills are my property, but I let Steven Dermot and his son run a small herd on it. His family has been permitted the right for generations. But Steven is very careful to respect my rights. I've never known him to let any of his herd wander onto my roads."

Royd's gaze followed his to the hill. "You check on Dermot." He started to turn away. "And I'll do some scouting."

"No questions? No arguments about coincidences?" MacDuff asked.

"One of the first rules of my training was that anything out of the ordinary was suspect." He glanced over his shoulder at Jock. "You coming with me?"

"I believe you can handle it." He added quietly, "I grew up playing on those hills with Steven's son, Mark. I'm going to the croft with MacDuff."

Royd nodded. "If I don't spot anyone, I'll come back and cover you."

"We'll have James and several more to do

that," MacDuff said. "I could spare some men to go with you."

"No, they'd get in my way."

"They know the land."

"They'd get in my way," Royd repeated. "I don't want to have to take care of anyone but myself."

"Campbell and the others aren't helpless," MacDuff said. "They served with me in the Marines."

"Good. You take them." He took off down the road.

Was he being watched? Probably. But he'd be out of rifle range for several hundred more yards. Then he'd fade into the trees at the base of the hill. . . .

"Crusty bastard," MacDuff murmured as he turned back to Jock. "I believe I'm a bit pissed. He'd better be good. Is he always like that?"

"He's good," Jock said. "And, yes, he's rude as hell. Maybe he's a little more abrasive than usual. I think I detected a trace of frustration. Things aren't going as he'd like them to go."

"When do they ever?"

"But Royd is having to deal with Sophie Dunston and he doesn't know what to make of her." He shrugged. "Or maybe how to handle her. It offends his bulldozer ethics to have to stop and consider someone else when he only wants to get at Boch and Sanborne." He glanced over MacDuff's shoulder. "Here are James and the lads. Let's get up to the croft."

12

He was being watched.

Royd stopped in the shadow of a tree, listening.

The wind rustling the branches. The sound of the sheep baaing in the distance.

He glanced up the hill to the stand of trees at the top. If anyone was up there, then he'd be a target if he moved out of the cover of these pines and started to climb.

If anyone was up there. It wouldn't be a position he would have chosen. It would give him a clear shot, but then there was a problem of getting down a hill almost clear of vegetation you could use for cover. Much better to stay here near the bottom of the hill, where cover was plentiful and the road close if you needed a quick getaway.

Besides, he could **feel** the bastard in the darkness.

Close. Damn close.

Did he have a rifle or a gun? He doubted it. If he did, he didn't want to use them or he would have tried to take his shot before this. Royd had been moving fast, zigzagging through the trees, but a bullet was the fastest way to eliminate an enemy. He took a step to the side and then another into the moonlight before ducking back.

No fire. Nothing. Maybe he didn't want the noise of gunfire.

But he was still there, waiting.

So Royd would wait too.

He drew closer to the tree. Three minutes. Four minutes.

Come on. Move. I'll stay here all night, if I have to, bastard.

No sound but the wind . . . the sheep . . .

Another six minutes passed.

The slightest whisper of sound several yards from where he stood. A sort of slither . . .

Pythons slithered. But so did men when they were brushing against the branches of a tree.

Or were coming down from that tree.

He waited. Come to me.

How many minutes had passed since that silky slither of sound? Two? Three?

Time enough for that snake to make his way to where Royd stood.

Don't move. Don't let him know that you're aware he's coming for you.

No sound of footsteps. The bastard was good.

He could feel the back of his neck tense.

Behind him. Every nerve, every instinct was screaming at him. He slowly turned his head.

Closer.

He caught a glimpse of movement out of the corner of his eye.

Now!

He fell to the ground and brought his legs around in a sweeping kick at the legs of the man a yard away.

He brought him down.

He got an impression of a short, compact man before the son of a bitch rolled away and threw the knife in his hand.

Royd instinctively lifted his arm.

Pain.

Royd could feel the blade slice into the muscle in his forearm. He pulled the blade out and threw it back. He saw the blade enter the man's shoulder.

"Royd?" My God, the bastard was laughing. "Sanborne didn't tell me. What a pleasure."

Jesus, Devlin.

Devlin tilted his head, listening. "Oh my, but I may have to cut this short. We're being interrupted. What a pity." He rolled over and scooted behind a tree.

Royd drew his gun and moved after him.

Christ, he was bleeding like a stuck pig. No time to bind the wound.

He caught a glimpse of Devlin zigzagging down the hill. He aimed and fired.

Missed. Devlin had dodged behind another tree.

The sounds of movement on the hill that had spooked Devlin were closer. Jock and MacDuff?

Devlin was moving through the trees at an incredibly fast pace for a wounded man.

Too fast.

The blood was pouring out of Royd's arm. He could end up dead if he didn't stop it.

Shit.

Try another shot at the bastard?

Out of range.

He stopped and cursed with frustration. Okay,

give it up. There would be another time. With Devlin there was always another time.

Get Jock and MacDuff up here and get the wound patched fast. Maybe they could go after Devlin.

Not that they'd catch him if he had this much of a head start. Devlin was too good.

Worry about that later.

He raised the gun in his hand and shot into the air. Then he pressured the pulse point above the wound and waited for Jock.

"It's not good. You should see a doctor." Jock finished wrapping the makeshift bandage around Royd's arm. "You've lost some blood."

"Later. I've had worse." He got to his feet. "I just had to get the damn blood stopped." He reached for his phone. "And I've got to call Sophie and make sure she's okay."

"She and Michael will be fine," Jock said. "The castle is guarded like a fortress. And only a madman would go after them right after you flushed him out of hiding."

"Exactly." He dialed Sophie's number. She answered on the third ring. He felt a rush of relief.

"How's Michael?"

"What do you think?" She paused. "And you didn't call me to ask how my son was doing. Where are you?"

He didn't answer. "I'll be back soon. There was a problem."

"What kind of problem?"

"It's over now. I'll talk to you later. Go back to Michael." He hung up.

She was angry and frustrated and that disconnect would be the last straw. Tough. He didn't have time for explanations.

"I told you she'd be fine," Jock said. "MacDuff wouldn't have left her if he weren't sure of that."

"Okay, okay. You'll forgive me if I don't have the faith in MacDuff that you do. I had to be sure."

"You actually thought there was a chance Devlin would go after her tonight?"

"If he thought he had even a tiny chance of getting to Sophie and Michael, he'd take it. He likes to walk on the edge." He watched MacDuff and five of his men coming out of the woods. "You didn't get him," he called to MacDuff. "I told you it was a waste of time. He probably had a car parked close by and is halfway to Aberdeen by now."

"I called ahead to the magistrate and gave him the description you gave me," MacDuff said. "They'll be on the lookout for him. We have a chance."

Royd shook his head. "Not much of one. He knows his business."

"Garwood?" Jock asked.

Royd nodded. "One of the best. Or worst, depending on how you look at it." He was silent a moment. "Have you gone to the croft yet?"

MacDuff shook his head. "We were on our way when we heard the shot." He motioned to Campbell and the men behind him. "Go back to the castle. We'll take care of it."

"There may not be anything to take care of," Royd said. "I don't think Devlin would have anyone with him. He likes to work alone. But I'll go with you."

MacDuff shrugged. "Suit yourself." He turned and started back up the hill with his men following.

Jock didn't move, his gaze narrowed on Royd's face. "Nothing to take care of?" he repeated.

"I misspoke," Royd said. "With Devlin there's always something to take care of."

"What?"

God, he was dizzy, Royd thought as he moved after MacDuff. "The cleanup."

Sophie hung up the phone. Damn Royd. She didn't need this. Something was happening and she was being left—

"Mom."

She turned back to the bed. Forget Royd. This was her job tonight.

"Coming." She put the phone back on the table and crossed the room to him. "It was nothing. Just Royd checking on us." She slipped into bed and pulled him close. "He asked about you."

"I'm okay."

He wasn't okay. He had taken the news with the shock she had known he would. "That's what I told him."

He was silent a moment. "Why?" Michael whispered. The tears were running down his cheeks. "Why Dad, Mom?"

"I told you." Sophie tried to keep her voice steady. "I'm not sure. But I think it has to do with what I'm doing, Michael. I never dreamed it would impact your father. But if you want to blame me, I won't argue with you."

"Blame you?" He buried his face in her

shoulder. "You're only trying to make sure those bad guys get stopped. It was them." His hands clenched on her shirt. "I . . . loved him, Mom."

"I know you did."

"I feel . . . ashamed. Sometimes I got mad at him."

"Did you?" She stroked his hair. "Why?"

"He made me feel . . . He didn't want me around. Not really."

"Of course he did."

He shook his head. "I was in the way. And I was a bother to him. I think he thought I was . . . crazy."

"That's not true." But a boy as sensitive as Michael would have picked up on those vibes Dave had sent. "And it wasn't your fault."

"I was a bother to him," he repeated.

"Listen to me, Michael. When a man and woman have a child, it's their duty to stand by him no matter how difficult it becomes. It's their job. That's what a family is all about. You did everything you could to cope with the problem you have and he should have been there for you. He was the one at fault, not you." She hugged him closer. "So stop thinking about blame. Think about the good times with him. I remember when he got you that toy Hummer when you were five and the two of you played with it all day. Do you remember that day, Michael?"

"Yes." The tears were falling heavier. "Are you sure I didn't make him unhappy?"

"No, you didn't. When someone dies, the first thing anyone does is wonder if they'd been good enough to him." Those were almost the words Royd had said to her this morning, she realized. "Well, you were good enough. You have my word on it."

"Sure?"

"Sure." It was a strange world, she thought sadly. Last night she had lain in Royd's arms and taken comfort from him. Tonight she was lying here in bed and giving that comfort to her son. It was like a circle that never stopped. Jesus, she wanted the need for that comfort to stop. "Will you try to sleep? I'm not going to leave you, I promise."

"You don't have to stay." But his arms tightened around her. "I'm not a baby. And I never want to be a duty to you. Not like I was to Daddy."

Damn it. She had said it all wrong. "Duty isn't a bad thing. When it's to someone you love, it can be a joy." She kissed his cheek. "You're a joy, Michael. My joy. Never doubt it. . . ."

* * *

There was blood everywhere. On the floor, on the table, a rivulet running from beneath the closed door across the room.

MacDuff stood in the doorway of the small croft and began to curse.

"Cleanup," Royd murmured as he gazed over MacDuff's shoulder at the blood-smeared chaos.

"Shut up," MacDuff said roughly. "James, how many people are living here now?"

"Old Dermot, his wife, his son. His son brought his little girl back from Glasgow when he got his divorce." James moistened his lips. "That blood . . . Do you want me to go check the rooms?"

"No, I'll do it." He strode across the room and threw open the door. He froze. "Oh, Christ."

Jock and Royd followed him.

"Sweet Jesus," Jock said, his gaze on the carnage. "Dermot?"

"It's hard to tell." MacDuff's voice was hoarse. "Someone almost cut off his face." He moved into the room. "And they didn't stop with Dermot."

A woman lay on the floor. Gray-haired,

thin, brown eyes staring sightlessly up at them. Blood was trickling from the corner of her mouth.

"Margaret, Dermot's wife." Jock's lips tightened. "Son of a bitch." His glance roamed the room. "Where's Dermot's son, Mark, and the child?"

"Maybe they got away." James Campbell's face was white. "God, I hope they got away."

"Look for them," Royd said. "Search the rest of the croft and the grounds. I hope you're right, but Devlin rarely lets a target slip out of reach."

"A child?" Campbell asked. "A child wouldn't be a—"

"Look for them," Jock said.

Campbell nodded jerkily and strode out of the room.

Jock dropped to his knees beside Dermot, gazing down at the ruin of the old man's face. "This is over the top. He took some time. An example or does he just like it, Royd?"

"He likes it," Royd said. "Even before he went through REM-4, he was a killer. Sanborne chose him because he thought he would take to the training better." He turned to MacDuff who was standing looking down at Dermot. "I'll get him for you." His lips twisted.

"No, I'll get him for myself. I stuck a knife in him and he's not going to forget it. The crazy bastard has a long memory."

"So do I." MacDuff's lips were tight. "And I'm the one who's going to cut the nuts off this son of a bitch. Dermot was one of mine." He whirled on his heel. "Let's go and find Dermot's son."

They met Campbell coming toward the house.

"The well." He swallowed as he nodded to the stone well some distance away. "He's on the other side of the well."

"Dead?" MacDuff asked.

Campbell nodded. "There must be fifty stab wounds in his body."

MacDuff was silent for a moment. "The little girl?"

"We think she's in the well. We shone a light down there." He swallowed again. "Or parts of her are in the well. He must have . . . butchered her."

MacDuff muttered a curse beneath his breath and started toward the well.

"You don't have to check it, sir. He's Dermot's son." Campbell was on his heels. "I know him. I couldn't make a mistake."

"I don't doubt you," MacDuff said. "I just have to see them."

"Why?" Royd asked as he and Jock caught up with him. "Dead is dead, MacDuff."

"I need to remember." MacDuff had reached the well and was gazing down at the man lying on the ground. "Time tricks us. Hatred can fade unless it's fanned, and memory is the best fuel. You may not understand, but I don't want to ever forget what Devlin did, even if years pass before I get my hands on him."

"Oh, I understand," Royd said.

MacDuff looked at him. "I believe you do." He braced himself and then shone his flashlight down into the well. He turned off the flashlight. "You're right, James." His voice was husky. "He butchered her." He reached for his telephone. "I'm calling the magistrates. Leave a man up here to meet them, Jock. The rest of us are going back to the castle."

"I'll stay," Jock said. "I don't want to leave him just now. He was my friend. What do I tell the magistrates?"

"Nothing. A random psychopath." Mac-Duff turned away from the well. "I don't want them to get in my way." He started back toward the cottage.

Royd watched him as he motioned for Campbell and the men to follow him. "He's pretty impressive," he said. "He really means to go after Devlin."

"Of course," Jock said. "And I wouldn't want to be Devlin if he catches up with him."

Royd frowned. "I'm not sure I like him stepping into the picture."

"Too late. MacDuff is involved. He might have stayed in the background if it were only a question of protecting Michael. There's no chance now that Devlin has killed his people." Jock followed MacDuff toward the cottage. "You'd better get back to the castle and get that arm tended. Do you need me to call for a car?"

Royd shook his head. "I'll make it okay." He turned and started down the path after MacDuff.

Devlin.

Why had Sanborne sent that crazy bastard to the castle? He must have known that there could be a bloodbath.

Or maybe not. Devlin had always been smart enough to make Sanborne believe he was fully in control. During those last weeks after Royd had managed to shake off the effects of REM-4, he had grown to suspect that Devlin was not so much manipulated as manipulating. He liked what he did. He loved the blood and the power of the kill. He could indulge that passion under the protection of Sanborne. REM-4 might have had a minimal effect, but he was a killer by nature.

And now Devlin had been given the chance he needed to free that lust for violence. Michael and Sophie had been the targets, but that hadn't been enough for him. That family he'd butchered would only whet his appetite. He'd go after the prime objective and never stop.

Damn you, Sanborne.

Voices.

Sophie lifted her head. She had left the casement windows open and the voices were coming from the courtyard below.

She carefully slipped out of bed and went to the window. Below were MacDuff and several men, and trailing behind them was Royd. She felt a rush of relief. She'd been lying here after Michael finally went to sleep worrying and cursing him for not calling back.

She glanced at Michael. He was sound asleep and she'd attached the monitor. She could spare a few moments. She glided toward the door.

A moment later she was running down the staircase and throwing open the front door. "Damn you, Royd. Why the hell did you—" She stopped as she saw the bandage. "What happened?"

"He's a bit damaged." It was MacDuff who answered. "You have a medical degree, don't you? Fix him." He went past her into the castle.

Royd grimaced. "MacDuff is in an autocratic mood tonight. He's upset. I may need a few stitches but I can call the local doctor."

She went down the steps. "How did you get damaged?" Christ, her voice was shaking. "And the local doctor may be better able to help you. This isn't my specialty."

"No problem." He started to pass her. "I'll take care of it."

"How did you get wounded?" she repeated.

"Knife."

"You're white as a sheet. How much blood did you lose?"

"Not too much."

She couldn't take any more. "Christ, I hate macho men who are afraid to admit to a little weakness." She pushed him toward the steps. "Get inside and let me take a look at it."

"Right." He swayed as he mounted the steps. "I never argue with a woman who's stronger than I am. And at the moment you're definitely stronger than me. Does that exempt me from the macho label?"

"Maybe." She followed him and took his elbow. "We'll have to see how sensibly you—"

He swayed and stumbled against the side of the doorjamb. "Oops."

"Oh, for heaven's sake." She put his good arm around her shoulders and glanced around for help. MacDuff and his men had all disappeared. "I can't stay down here. I have to get back to Michael. Are you able to make the stairs if I help you?"

"No problem."

"There is a problem." She started up the steps. "Admit it."

"Okay, there's a problem." He took the steps slowly. "But nothing I can't work through."

"You'd better warn me if you're going to faint. I don't want both of us toppling down the stairs."

"I'll go by myself. Just drop—"

"I didn't say I wanted to drop your ass. I said warn me so that I can keep us from falling. I'm not leaving you on your own."

"That's not very bright. There's no use you falling too."

"Neither of us is going to—" She drew a deep breath. "Though if you insult my intelligence again, I'll be tempted to dump you and let you bleed to death."

"I'm not bleeding any longer."

"Just shut up." They had reached the landing and she adjusted her grip and started up the second flight of stairs. "There's such a thing as accepting help gracefully."

He was silent. Then as they reached the top of the stairs he said, "I never learned how to do that. When I was a kid, I knew that I had to get by on my own. I can't remember anyone offering help. Then when I joined the service, it was different. I had to be the best."

"And anyone at the top of the heap couldn't ask for help?"

"I couldn't," he said simply.

Yes, she could see that he wouldn't be able to lower his guard to that extent. He was too scarred, and that bold, brash demeanor would have repelled anyone who tried to get beyond that tough exterior.

Jesus, she was actually feeling sorry for him. No one could want sympathy less than

Royd, but she could empathize with that kid who must have felt terribly alone. No, perhaps not empathize. Her parents had been everything that was loving and understanding when she was growing up. It was only after that terrible day at the lake that she had felt bewildered and alone. Even then she'd had Michael and Dave to ward off that sense of isolation. Yes, it was sympathy she was feeling. But it didn't lessen the urge to touch him, give him comfort.

"Stop it." He was glaring at her. "I can see you brewing that maudlin syrup you spread around. I don't want it. Dish it out somewhere else."

She gazed at him in exasperation. He was hurt and weak and that didn't stop him from being as rough and objectionable as usual. "I will. And I don't blame all your foster parents for not cuddling you. You would probably have bitten them."

"Probably." He was smiling. "That's better. That's the way I like to see you. But I wouldn't bite you." He added, "Unless you want me to."

Sensuality. One moment she'd wanted to comfort him and the next he'd made her feel that tingling awareness again. With everything that had been going on, she'd thought that her response to him had lessened.

She quickly looked away from him. "You're incorrigible." She pushed him down on a velvet-cushioned bench across the hall from Michael's room. "Stay here. I have to check on Michael. Or you can go next door to my room and wait."

"I think I'll stay here." He leaned his head back against the wall and closed his eyes. "Take your time."

With his eyes closed he appeared more vulnerable and she could almost forget those rough words. But she mustn't forget them. Royd was not vulnerable and she must not continue to feel this increasing softness toward him. "Don't fall asleep and tumble off that bench. I don't know if I could pick you up."

He smiled without opening his eyes. "I'd trust you. You'd manage."

She quietly opened Michael's door and slipped inside. He was still asleep. She crossed the room to look down at him. He seemed undisturbed, but that could change in a heartbeat. He looked so young and help-less. Vulnerable. Only minutes before she had thought that about Royd and he had sensed and rudely rejected it. Michael was beginning to reject any hint of pity too. He would never be rude to her, but his response had been the same as Royd's. He was growing up and wanting to shoulder his own burdens.

But he couldn't do that yet. Not yet. She still had him to love and protect for a little while.

She tucked the blanket over him and moved back to the door and left it cracked open.

Royd's eyes flicked open. "Okay?"

She nodded.

He struggled to his feet and started down the hall. "Then let's get this over. I know you want to get back to him."

"Yes, I do."

He was unsteady on his feet but she didn't try to help him. He'd make it and she didn't want to touch him right now. She followed him and opened the door. "But I'll leave my door open. I'll be able to hear him." She turned on the overhead light and nodded at the chair across the room. "Sit down. I'll have to run down the stairs and get a first-aid kit, if I can find MacDuff or one of his men."

"I don't think you'll have any trouble finding MacDuff. He won't have gone to bed."

He sank down into the chair. "He had a few matters to take care of."

"What matters is—" She broke off and headed for the door. "Be ready to talk to me as soon as I get you stitched. Or so help me, I'll—"

"Unstitch me?"

"I wouldn't ruin my own work. I'd find another way."

"Heaven help me," he murmured.

"Listen for Michael." She strode out of the room.

"Done." She stepped back as she finished bandaging Royd's arm. "It's nasty. You should probably go in and get a transfusion and have my sutures checked."

He shook his head.

She shrugged. "It's your choice."

"Yes, it is. I heal fast." He paused. "And I think that things are going to be moving very fast from now on."

"Why? Talk to me. What happened tonight?"

"Those sheep we almost ran into on the road. It sent up a red flag to Jock and Mac-Duff. It seems the herdsman who owned the sheep was very reliable and would never have let those sheep wander off. Considering the situation, it bore looking into."

"And what did you find?"

"One of Sanborne's men, Devlin." He nodded at his arm. "In the woods. He took a knife in the shoulder but got away. I still decided to call you and check."

"And not tell me a damn thing," she said through her teeth.

"There wasn't time, and you were comforting your son."

"Why wasn't there time?"

He was silent a moment. "We had to go check on the shepherd and his family."

Sophie studied him. He'd had no problem telling her about the encounter with Devlin, but he didn't want to discuss this shepherd.

"And?"

"Dead. Ugly dead. The shepherd, his wife, son, and the grandchild, a little girl about seven."

Shock rippled through her. "What?"

"You heard me. Do you want me to repeat it?"

"Why?" she whispered.

He shrugged. "There's a possibility the shepherd might have stumbled over Devlin and he killed him to avoid having his cover blown." His lips tightened. "No, I think Devlin had the opportunity and took it. He's a bloodthirsty son of a bitch. One little boy wouldn't have been enough for him. He took the bigger target."

"And you thought he might have come straight to the castle?"

"Not really. But Devlin has an amazing pain tolerance and I just had to be sure," he said jerkily. "I had to hear your voice. I had an idea what I was going to find at that croft. I didn't want to have to think about you when I was looking at Devlin's work. I knew it was going to bother me."

Her eyes widened. "Of course it would bother you."

He shook his head. "It wouldn't have had any real effect in the months after I left Garwood. It was as if I had calluses instead of emotions. I couldn't feel anything." He grimaced. "One of the side effects of REM-4. It lasted a long time."

"My God."

He shook his head. "Now you're all dripping with guilt again. I should have known. To someone like you, that would be almost as terrible as the mind control. If it makes you feel any better, what I saw at that croft tore me up. The little girl . . ." He stopped and swallowed. "Yeah, I felt a hell of a lot up at that croft."

"It doesn't make me feel better." Her voice was uneven. "I don't want you to hurt. I didn't want anyone to hurt. Those poor people . . ." She drew a deep breath. "No wonder MacDuff was so curt with me. He must be holding me responsible."

"Maybe. You'll have to ask him in the morning. I do know that he's mad as hell and going after Devlin. If I don't get him first." He saw her expression and added, "I'm not being sidetracked. I'm not going to have to hunt him down. He'll be after me. Devlin doesn't like to be hurt and I buried a knife in his hide. Even if Sanborne pulls him from the job, he'll be on my tail."

"Comforting."

"Yes, it is. It will make it easier." He struggled to his feet. "Do you know where I'm supposed to sleep in this museum?"

"The room two doors down. I'll help—" She broke off. "I forgot. Go on by yourself. If you faint in the hall, I'll step over you when I go down to breakfast in the morning."

"Just so you don't step on me." He moved

toward the door. "If you and Michael need me, call."

"Do you mean if we need 'help'?"

"Touché." He stopped at the door. "Do you want to undress me and put me to bed? I'll let you."

"No, I do not. You had your chance."

"Chicken. It's just as well. I'm not quite myself tonight."

She watched him slowly leave the room. She was tempted to go after him. He had to be in pain and more defenseless than he pretended. He had been more open to her than ever before, and that had no doubt been instigated by pain and shock. He'd probably been wishing for that deadness of feeling brought on by REM-4 at the croft tonight.

A little side effect, he'd said. Another horror she had to face. How many other side effects had REM-4 visited on those people at Garwood?

One thing at a time. She couldn't function if she had to tear herself apart worrying about Garwood. She had to go on. She had to protect her son and destroy Sanborne and Boch.

And she had to face MacDuff in the morning and listen to him tell her to take her son and get the hell out of his castle and his life. After this horror to people he cared about, there could be no other outcome. Royd had said he'd been angry and she was the one who'd brought these murderers down on this peaceful countryside.

Confront that tomorrow, she thought wearily, as she headed for the door. For now she'd stay with Michael and make sure his own personal horror didn't come visiting him again tonight.

13

"May I speak to you?"

MacDuff looked up from his desk and rose to his feet. "I don't have too much time, Ms. Dunston. The magistrate is bringing some men from Scotland Yard here within the hour."

"I won't take long." She came into the library. "We need to talk."

"Absolutely. I was going to get to you later. How is the boy?"

"Not great. I couldn't expect that. I only saw him for a few moments before he hit the shower, but he seems a little better than last night. And he didn't have a night terror last night. I was expecting it."

"He's only had one since he's been here. Maybe he's outgrowing them."

She shook her head. "But they're getting better."

"Sit down and stop hovering," MacDuff said. "I'm dead tired, I've had a hell of a night, and my blasted politeness will keep me standing until you put me out of my misery. It's the cross I bear for being raised to rule this heap of stone."

She dropped into the chair he'd indicated. "It's a magnificent heap and surprisingly comfortable."

"I agree. That's why I'm still fighting to keep it from the National Trust. Coffee?" He didn't wait for her to answer but poured a cup from the carafe on the desk and handed it to her. "Cream?"

She shook her head. "You're being very kind to me. I expected you to be angry."

"I am angry. I'm killing mad." He leaned back in his chair. "But not at you. I accepted Michael and I'm the one who's responsible for any consequences. But I expected any flak to be directed at me, not my people. That butchery last night was senseless."

She shivered. "Yes, it was. Royd said it was terrible. I expected you to hand Michael and me our walking papers."

"And let that son of a bitch Sanborne think he's won even the smallest battle? That he can throw his murderers at us and frighten me into sending Michael back for him to use against you?" MacDuff's eyes were glittering with anger. "I'd keep the two of you safe just to spite him."

"We may have to leave anyway. The police might pay you a visit if they figure out that I've sent Michael here." Her lips twisted. "They may think I'm crazy enough to harm my own son."

"I'll try to stave off Scotland Yard." He frowned. "But I'm a bit uneasy. I won't feel comfortable leaving Michael once I've left the Run."

She stiffened. "You're leaving?"

"Why are you surprised? Devlin killed my people. I can't let him get away with that." He frowned. "Don't worry, I'll see that the boy is safe."

"You just said you didn't feel that you could do that."

"I said he might not be safe here unless there's the right person in charge. I'm working on it."

"You don't have to work on it. He's my responsibility. I'm the one who has to make

sure no one hurts him." She got to her feet.
"You do what you have to do. I'll take care of
my son."

"No, you won't."

She stared at him in disbelief. "I beg your
pardon."

"I may need you and Royd. You're neck
deep in this mess and you have information
and insight that I don't. I can't have you worrying about your son and not able to function."

"Sweet Jesus." She shook her head. "You're
as bad as Royd."

"You mean self-serving? Hell, yes. I'd protect
the boy anyway, but if keeping you from making a mistake will get me what I want, you can
bet I'll do it." He waved his hand. "Run along
and find Michael and Royd. I have work to do
with the magistrate and the inspector from
Scotland Yard investigating Dermot's death.
Try to keep out of sight. I don't want him to
know there are strangers here at the Run."

"Neither do I," she said dryly. "They'd probably suspect me of those murders too." She
closed the door and moved down the hall. She
didn't know what she had expected of Mac-
Duff, but he had kept surprising her. Arrogant
and forceful one moment, charismatic the
next. The only thing that she had really learned

about him was that he was a man to be reckoned with and she would have to keep on her guard not to be swept away in his wake.

"You're frowning."

She looked up to see Jock standing by the front door. He was smiling faintly but the smile didn't reach his eyes. He looked strained and sad. Why shouldn't he? she thought with compassion. He'd been up all night keeping vigil with the dead. "Did you just come back?"

He nodded. "I had to stay until the inspector from Scotland Yard came. The local magistrate wasn't about to let me go." He made a face. "Even though he was on the phone with MacDuff half the night making him swear to my alibi."

"You shouldn't have been the one to stay. With your background, it was logical for—"

"I know. MacDuff didn't like it either. But Mark Dermot was my friend." He changed the subject. "Why were you frowning? I saw you coming out of the library."

"Then you know why I'm upset. Your Mac-Duff is arrogant as hell. I told him that he was just like Royd."

"There are certain similarities. They're both relentless and single-minded. How did Mac-Duff step on your toes?"

"He as much as told me that he was going to take care of Michael whether I liked it or not because I was too useful to act like a mother."

He chuckled. "He must have been tired. He's usually more diplomatic. MacDuff can charm the birds from the trees if he puts his mind to it."

"Well, he didn't put his mind to it this morning. He told me to run along and keep out of sight and he'd talk to me later."

"And are you going to do it?"

"Hell, no." She sighed wearily. "Yes, I'm going to keep out of sight. I'd be stupid not to do that. I don't want Scotland Yard breathing down my neck. But I'm not going to let him tell me what to do. I have to make the decisions." She shook her head. "Though heaven knows I've been tossed around like a drunken sailor in a hurricane lately."

"MacDuff has been very good to Michael, Sophie," he said quietly.

"I can see that. It's not every boy who has a Laird to play soccer with. And Michael mentioned something about treasure hunting? Did MacDuff make that up to keep him amused?"

He shrugged. "There are stories. At any rate it kept Michael from being bored. He was a little boy far from home."

"And I'm grateful. But not enough to let MacDuff run over me."

"I'll have a word with him."

"Do what you like." She turned and started to climb the stairs. "I've got to go check on Royd. He was pretty weak. He shouldn't have walked back to the castle last night."

"I offered to call for a car."

"I'm not blaming anyone. It's nobody's fault but his." She said over her shoulder, "The idiot thinks he should be Superman."

"You weren't very tactful," Jock said to Mac-Duff as he came into the library. "And Sophie doesn't take to being told what to do. You'll be lucky if she doesn't grab Michael and bolt."

MacDuff looked up. "I was too upset to be tactful. I had to speak my piece and tell her to make herself scarce until Scotland Yard leaves. Are they on their way?"

"Fifteen minutes behind me. He's Inspector Mactavish and he's pleasant enough." His smile faded. "When he's not accusing me of butchery. He made me watch when they pulled up the little girl out of the well. I think he wanted to see my reaction."

MacDuff muttered a curse. "I told you when

you said Scotland Yard was on its way that you shouldn't be the one to stay."

"Mark was my friend." He was silent for a moment. "When do we go after Devlin?"

"Soon. I have to clear the decks here." He added grimly, "And convince Scotland Yard that you haven't reverted and gone bonkers."

"She's not going to wait for you," Jock said. "Unless you can get Royd to intercede. She's accepted him."

"Then I'll talk to Royd." He got to his feet. "I'm going out and meet this inspector in the courtyard. I need some air." He frowned. "And you stay out of his way too. I don't want him to see any more of you than he already has."

"Out of sight, out of mind?"

"Whatever." He strode toward the door. "I just don't want you in his face."

"Then I'll obediently run along and hide with your other fugitives from justice. Any other orders?"

"Obedient? You don't know the meaning of the word." He stopped at the door. "Yes, you can do one thing for me."

"I'm at your service."

"Call Jane MacGuire and find out where she is and if she'll be available for a call from me this afternoon."

"Why not do it yourself?"

"It won't hurt for you to smooth the way. She's always liked you and knows you're no threat to her."

"No, she never considered me a threat even when I could have been to her. Incredible." He tilted his head. "And you think she considers you a threat?"

"Possibly. Just call her."

Michael wasn't in his room.

What the devil? She'd told him to wait for her.

"He's okay."

She turned to see Royd standing in the doorway. "Michael's waiting for you in my room. I came to check on him and I thought you'd rather he had company. So I had him help me change my bandage. Keeping busy helps."

"Yes, it does. Thank you." She studied him. "You look a little pale but better than you did. Did you sleep well?"

"Good enough. Why don't we go down and try to rustle up some food."

"Not yet. MacDuff is being paid a visit by an inspector from Scotland Yard. He wants us to keep out of sight until he leaves."

"Since the alternative spells disaster, we'll go

along with him, won't we? You've already talked to MacDuff?"

She nodded. "You were right. He intends to go after Devlin and he wants to use us to find him. No, that's not strong enough. He fully intends to use us. And he thinks Michael may not be safe here if he leaves. He's trying to work out another plan."

"And that's upsetting you? Why?"

"I wouldn't mind anyone trying to keep Michael safe. But yes, it bothers me that Mac-Duff doesn't give a damn about how I want that done."

"I'm sure you'll change his attitude." He grimaced. "Just as you changed mine."

"There's not much time. I was hoping that I could count on MacDuff for a little longer." She paused. "Do you think Devlin's original job was to kill Michael or was it a trap for me?"

"It could have been either or both."

"Dammit, then how the devil am I going to—"

"There's something you should know. I got a call from Kelly this morning."

She tensed. "And?"

"I told him to keep an eye on the ship. It sailed last night."

"What? But you said they hadn't stripped the facility yet."

"Evidently they took everything they needed and left the rest."

"Blast it, then how—"

"Take it easy. Kelly is on it. He rented a launch and caught up with the ship before it was out of the channel. He's trying to keep it in sight and his launch out of sight. It's heading south."

"And Sanborne?"

He shrugged. "Kelly can only be in one place at a time. But if we can track the ship, the odds are that Sanborne and Boch will rendezvous with it when it arrives at its destination."

"And if they don't?"

"Then we'll worry about going after them then. Or I will. I'm leaving right away to join Kelly, but you don't have to go along. If you'd rather stay with Michael and—"

"Be quiet. You know I have to go." And yet she had to protect Michael. "And you told me that you might need me. Why have you suddenly decided that I'm expendable?"

"No one is expendable. I've gotten along without you all my life. You could have proved helpful, but you'll be of no use to me if you're fretting about your son. So stay away from me."

"That's pleasant. You must be the most—"
She stopped and stared at his scowling face.
"My God, I believe you're trying to protect me.
How bizarre."

"It's not bizarre. I said I'd protect you if I
could."

"And then threw me into the fire at every
opportunity."

"I didn't have to throw you. I only gave you
the opportunity. You did it yourself." He
shrugged. "And now it's no longer an option.
You have to do what you have to do."

"And I will. So just shut up. You don't do
soft and noble well. You're much more convincing when you're rude and ruthless." She
went to the window and looked down into the
courtyard. "There's a car parked down there. It
must be the inspector. We can't go down yet."
She turned and rifled through her purse. "So I
might as well check the copy of that disk we
found at the facility. I'll play it on my computer. Will you stay with Michael while I'm
doing it?"

"I want to see it."

"I'll tell you about it. It may be nothing."

"If it was in that safe, it had to have some
value."

"May I be of some help?" They turned to see

Jock standing in the doorway. He glanced from Sophie to Royd. "Do I detect a little friction in the air?"

"Yes, you can help," Royd said. "Will you go to my room and distract Michael while we do a little research?"

"Sure." Jock started to turn. "It won't be long until I can take him down to the Run. He likes it there. The inspector should be almost finished with the Laird. MacDuff is a very important man and even Scotland Yard treats him with a bit of deference."

"Wait," Sophie said. "Why did you come?"

"To spread oil on troubled waters. Though not between you and Royd. I talked to Mac-Duff and he realizes he wasn't tactful. He does want the best for you and the boy, Sophie. He's doing everything he can to work something out."

"So that he'll be free to go off and kill Devlin."

He smiled. "Oh, I hope not," he said gently. "I hope he'll leave it to me. I have some wonderfully detailed ideas on that score." He left the room.

She shivered as she stared after him. Beautiful as the dawn and deadly as a pit viper. She wasn't used to this side of Jock. "Jesus."

"You didn't see that little girl in the well," Royd said quietly.

She nodded jerkily. "It just . . . surprised me." She turned and went to her duffel and drew out her computer. "I've got to get to work. I can't leave Michael alone for long when he's this upset." She sat down on the bed, flipped open the laptop, and inserted the disk. "Now let's see what we've got."

"Numbers," Royd murmured.

"Formulas," she corrected absently. She stiffened. "REM-4."

"What?"

"It's not my formula, but it's been used as a base."

"You knew that had happened."

"But not like this." Her gaze was fixed on the screen. "This is different."

"How different?"

"I don't know yet." She arrowed down to the next page. "But I don't like it. Go away. This is going to take some time."

"Anything I can do?"

"Go away," she repeated. She arrowed down again. Nothing but formulas. Intricate, complex formulas. Whoever had done this work was brilliant.

"How long will it take you?"

She shook her head.

"Okay, I'll come back in a couple hours."

He said something else but she didn't hear him. She was too absorbed in the equations. She was beginning to see a pattern. . . .

MacDuff called Jane MacGuire late in the afternoon.

She picked up the phone on the second ring. "What are you up to, MacDuff? It's not like you to have Jock call me and run interference."

"I had to make sure that you'd be available. I have something to discuss."

She was silent a moment. "Bull. My guess is that you wanted me to talk to Jock and reminisce a bit about old times."

"I could do that with you," he said softly. "We share those memories."

"But there's no edge in my relationship with Jock."

"I've given you more than a long time to dull that edge. I've only called you twice during that entire time. And I was sore tempted, Jane."

"What do you want, MacDuff?"

"How is your wonderful Eve Duncan?"

"No sarcasm. She **is** wonderful."

"I wasn't being sarcastic. I admire her. How is she?"

"Working herself to exhaustion, as usual. She was called to Washington to teach a class at a medical school."

"And Joe? Is Joe with her?"

"No, he's here." She paused and then repeated, "What do you want, MacDuff?"

"A wee favor. A bit of your time."

"I'm very busy. I have an art show in a month."

"Ah, but I'm sure you have time for kin."

"I'm not your kin."

"We won't argue about it. Kin or not, I know you have a great heart and won't want anything to happen to an innocent child."

"MacDuff."

"I need you, Jane. Will you listen?"

"I won't be used by you."

"A child, Jane."

Silence. "Damn you." She sighed resignedly. "Talk to me."

Sophie's palms were sweating. Take deep breaths. It was the third time she'd gone over the formulas to make sure she was correct.

She'd hoped against hope that she was wrong. She wasn't wrong. The few terse lines at the end of the disk spelled it out, but she hadn't wanted to believe it.

She took the disk out of the computer and put it back in its case. It was growing dim in the room. It was almost sundown.

Get up. Go tell Royd. He'd come back three times during the day and she'd ignored him. Now she wanted to share this nightmare with someone.

She went to the bathroom and splashed water in her face. That was better.

"Towel?" Royd was standing in the open doorway, holding a towel out to her.

"Thanks." She dabbed at her face.

He handed her a steaming cup of coffee. "You let the carafe I brought you get cold. I think you're ready for this now."

"Yes." The coffee was hot and strong going down her throat. "Where's Michael?"

"I just left him. Jock and I have taken turns keeping him company. They're at the Run now."

"I've got to go explain why I couldn't be with him."

"After you explain a few things to me," Royd said. "And the first thing is why you're pale and shaking like a malaria victim."

"I'm not shaking." Yes, she was, she found.

She couldn't go to Michael like this. And she wanted to talk to Royd. "I'm upset." She went into the bedroom and dropped down on the bed. "I checked it three times, Royd. It's true."

"What's true?"

"Sanborne went a step farther after Garwood. He hired a scientist to expand REM-4 capabilities."

"Expand?"

"REM-4 could only be created in small amounts. That was one of the problems I was working on. It was going to be very expensive to mass-produce for the general public."

"And Sanborne's scientist managed to solve the problem?"

"He increased the potency tremendously so that it could be dissolved in water and still retain its properties."

"Water?" His gaze was fastened on her face. "A glass of water?"

She shook her head. "Or a vat. Remember that truck driver mentioning that vats were being loaded on the ship?"

He nodded. "Go on."

"There were a few lines at the end of the formula. Though there were serious problems, the initial tests are promising. Gorshank promises that the island experiment will prove a success."

"Island? We're looking for an island."

"Presumably."

"Do we have a first name for Gorshank?"

She shook her head. "He must be one of Sanborne's scientists, but I've never heard of him."

"And the experiment?"

"Why would Sanborne need all those vats of REM-4?" She moistened her lips. "We're not talking about a controlled, limited experiment."

"And you're guessing?"

"He's going to dump those vats in some water source on the island and watch what happens."

He nodded. "Makes sense."

"How can you be so calm? He wants to see if he can make zombies of those people."

"And then sell the new formula to the highest bidder to drop in our water-processing plants," Royd said. "Very ugly."

"I hadn't gotten that far," Sophie said. "I didn't want to get past the disaster on the island." But the thought had been in the back of her mind, she realized. "It's experimental. It could kill people."

"Or make them docile to the point of letting any terrorist group run over them."

"We've got to stop it."

"Yes." Royd started for the door. "But we have a start. Gorshank. We'll find it hard to get Boch and Sanborne, but we might get to Gorshank."

"If we knew who or where he is." She followed him as he went out into the hall. "You have contacts. Can't you find out?"

"I can try. But we need to move fast. We have to have all the help we can get." He glanced over his shoulder at her. "I'm bringing in MacDuff. I can't help it if you're still on the fence about him. I talked to Jock and he says MacDuff is able to tap sources that I can't. He has contacts everywhere from the British Parliament to U.S. police."

"I'm not arguing." She grimaced. "Though I don't believe the police are going to listen to anyone if it concerns me. I'll let MacDuff do whatever he can to stop Sanborne. It's Michael that we may disagree about."

"That's between the two of you." He started down the stairs. "I'll let you battle it out."

"Thank you," she said with irony. "You're too kind."

"That's what you want from me, isn't it?" he said roughly. "You don't want me to step in and get in your way. You preach a lot about the good of people helping each other but you're as bad as I am. You've been hurt so much that you're afraid I'll do it too. Well, I might hurt you. But not if I can help it. And I'll kill anyone else who tries to do it. Hell, yes, I'd kill for you. Whether you like it or not."

She stopped to stare at him, shocked at the outburst.

"Too harsh for you?" He looked away from her and continued down the stairs. "Too bad. Suck it up. I had to say it. I've been damn diplomatic for me, and it was sticking in my throat."

"Diplomatic? You?"

"Hell, yes." He scowled. "Now, if you're going to go and see MacDuff with me, I suggest you get your ass down here." He started down the hall toward the library.

She slowly continued down the steps. Bossy roughneck. She should be angry. He'd been rude and judgmental and even threatening.

But the threat hadn't been to her. My God, he'd offered to kill for her.

And he'd meant it.

"Hurry up," he tossed over his shoulder.

Her pace instinctively quickened. He was right. They had to lay this latest disaster before MacDuff and see if he could help them. This was not the time to start puzzling out the enigma that was Matt Royd.

* * *

"Gorshank," MacDuff repeated. "No initials? No first name?"

"Only the last name," Sophie said. "This afternoon I tried to access a Gorshank on the Internet at various universities and scientific organizations. Nothing."

"Possibly not an American scientist?"

She nodded. "Possibly. But I checked the international organizations too. No Gorshank."

"There are a good many East European scientists who worked in the Soviet Bloc on some very nasty projects. They weren't encouraged to make themselves or their work known," Royd said. "After the collapse they drifted to all parts of the world."

"If he's part of that group, he'll be on somebody's list," MacDuff said. "Probably the State Department or CIA. I know a few people. I'll see what I can do."

"How long will it take?"

He shrugged. "I wish I knew. Even if they identify him, they may not be able to find him. He may have already gone to this island."

"We've got to hope that Sanborne won't want him there before they arrive," Sophie said. "They're very careful about the REM-4 formula and they won't want to take a chance

with a scientist who knows that formula being picked up by any of their clients."

"'Hope' is the word," MacDuff said. "I'll
get on it right away. I don't—"

Royd's telephone rang. "Excuse me." He
punched the button. "Royd." He listened.
"Shit. No, I know you couldn't help it.
You're breaking up. Call me back when you
reach port." He hung up. "Kelly lost the
Constanza."

"No," Sophie whispered.

"He was caught in a squall. He's lucky to
have made it out alive. But there was no way he
could keep sight of the **Constanza**. By the
time he fought his way through it, they were
gone."

She sank back in her chair. "Isn't there some
way he can track them?"

"If he had all the latest radar equipment he
might have a chance. But when he hired the
launch there wasn't time to specify anything
but fast. He had to move or lose them." He
turned to MacDuff. "So you'd better get hopping and find us another lead." He got to his
feet. "And I'm out of here. I'm not going to be
on the wrong side of the Atlantic if you call me
and tell me where I can find either Gorshank
or this island." He strode out of the library.

"You want to go with him." MacDuff was studying her face.

"I have to go with him." Sophie's hands clenched. "I opened this can of worms. I have to close it."

MacDuff nodded slowly. "Michael?"

"Of course it's Michael. I won't leave him without you and Jock being here. Unless you've changed your mind?"

"No, I'm on my way as soon as I finish the work you've assigned me." He paused. "But I may have a solution."

"Solution?"

"I have a friend who's on her way here. She should be arriving within the next few hours."

"She?"

"Jane MacGuire. She's bringing her adoptive father and they'll stay as long as necessary."

"Why should I trust her?"

"Because I do." He smiled. "And because her father is a detective with the Atlanta Police Department and one of the smartest and toughest men you could wish for."

"The police? Are you crazy? They'll take Michael into custody. They think I'm a homicidal maniac."

"I've explained the situation. Joe Quinn thinks outside the box and recognizes that things aren't always as they appear. He also loves and trusts Jane. If he commits, he'll stay to the end. I'll leave Campbell and several of the men here with instructions to obey Quinn implicitly. There won't be a problem."

She was still uncertain. A policeman whom MacDuff trusted. It sounded safe for Michael. "I don't know. . . ."

"Jane MacGuire is very strong, very smart, and has a good heart," MacDuff said. "She reminds me a little of you. That's why I thought of her. Besides being a tough cookie, she grew up in a dozen foster homes before she was adopted. She knows what it's like to be alone and abused. She also knows how to fight back. Michael will like her, and I can't think of anyone who could deal with his psychological problems better than Jane." He smiled. "Though I don't know if she plays soccer. That might be a deal breaker."

"You're sure that Michael will—"

"He'll be safe," MacDuff said. "I swear it. He'll be safe and cared for. Jane will see to that. It's the right thing to do. You can leave with a clear conscience. I mean it."

She believed him. "I want to talk to her and her father."

"It had better be by phone," MacDuff said. "I don't think that Royd is going to wait."

"He'll wait," she said grimly. "If I have to lasso and tie him up. I have to talk to Michael and then phone your Jane MacGuire. I may want to talk to Joe Quinn too. I'm not letting him run off without me."

"You have your work cut out for you. I believe he's looking for an excuse to cut you out of the picture."

"Why do you think that?"

He shrugged. "Intuition? Royd may be finding himself in the peculiar position of being between a rock and a hard place. It must be very disconcerting for one as single-minded as he apparently is. He doesn't want you hurt, but there's a possibility you could help get him Sanborne."

"Believe me, Royd's not soft enough to let emotion sway logic."

I'd kill for you.

"You've thought of something." MacDuff was studying her expression. "I'm not intimating that Royd is soft. But I'd judge he's responding to a stimulus not connected with the revenge that's been driving him. It might tend to make him unpredictable."

"He's been unpredictable from the moment I met him." She started for the door. "Will you arrange a phone call to Jane MacGuire for me? I'll be back within the hour."

He nodded. "I'll do my best. She's over the Atlantic now. It may take a little time."

She had a sudden thought. "She came without even checking with me? You must be very close."

He smiled. "You might say we're soul mates. But she didn't come for me. When I told her about your boy, she couldn't resist." He picked up the phone. "Now you'd best get to tracking down Royd and let me track down Jane. You didn't give me much time."

She hurried out of the room and ran down the hall. Royd had said Michael was at the Run with Jock but she had to see Royd first. She had told MacDuff he was always unpredictable, but something had changed. She sensed it even more strongly than MacDuff.

She would **not** let him leave her because he was developing a conscience about putting her at risk.

She tore up the stairs. Check his room first. Then go and make sure that he wasn't at the stable, where they'd parked the rental car.

He was sitting on the bed talking on the phone, his duffel open beside him. He hung up as she came into the room. "Did you come to say good-bye?"

"No, I came to tell you that I'm going with you. MacDuff's arranged for a satisfactory replacement to care for Michael."

"Really?" He stood up and zipped his duffel closed. "Are you sure of that?"

"Yes, and stop trying to shake my confidence." Her hands clenched. "This is the right thing to do. I know it."

"Tell me that when you're a thousand miles away from your son."

"Damn you." Her voice was unsteady. "You had no problem with using me when we started. What the devil is different?"

He met her gaze across the room. "The difference is how I want to use you."

She couldn't breathe. She could feel the heat tingling through her.

"You knew it," he said harshly. "It's been coming. I'm not a man who hides what he's feeling."

She moistened her lips. "But I didn't think sex would interfere with what was important to both of us."

"Neither did I. So maybe it's not sex." His lips twisted. "That shook you. If it's only sex, then it's strong enough to blow me out of the water. And if it's that strong, you're going to have trouble with me. I'm not cool and civilized like your ex. So think twice before you come anywhere with me."

"Are you trying to make me afraid of you?" She shook her head. "You won't rape me."

"No, but I might try anything else in my bag of tricks."

"I'm going with you."

"Fine. Good. Why should I worry? All I want is to screw the hell out of you before you get yourself killed." He grabbed his duffel. "I arranged for the plane. I want to leave here in thirty minutes."

"Then you'll have to wait. I have to talk to Michael. Is he still at the Run with Jock?"

"As far as I know."

"I'll meet you at the car as soon as I finish."

"I need to see Jock. Send him to the courtyard." He strode out of the room.

She drew a deep breath. Jesus, she was shaking. Yet she could still feel the heat spiraling through her. It bewildered her. She had been overflowing with fear and horror and worry about Michael and then suddenly had come this overwhelming need. The response had been intense and mindless as an animal in heat.

But she wasn't an animal in heat aching to couple with Royd just because his sexual appeal was raw and bold and . . .

Stop it. Get back on track.

Find Michael. Try to make him understand why his mother was going away again when he'd just learned his father had been murdered.

How the devil was she going to do that?

14

Michael and Jock were not playing ball. They were sitting on one of the huge boulders that bordered the Run.

"Hello, Sophie." Jock rose to his feet. "Everything okay?"

She nodded jerkily. "I need to talk to Michael. Will you leave us?"

"Of course." He studied her face and then turned to Michael. "I think your mother needs a little help, Michael. You take care of it. Okay?"

Michael nodded. "I'll see you later, Jock."

He smiled. "You bet you will."

"Royd wants you to meet him in the courtyard, Jock," Sophie said.

He nodded and strolled toward the path.

She turned back to Michael. How to begin?

"You're going away, aren't you?" Michael asked quietly.

She stiffened in shock.

Michael gazed out at the sea basked in sunset glow. "It's okay, Mom."

She was silent a moment. "It's not okay. I don't want to do this. I don't want to leave you. If you resent it and me, I'd understand."

He shook his head. "How can I be mad at you? You're my mom. Things are bad for you right now. You're trying to do what's best for all of us. Jock says I have to do my part."

"Jock?"

"But even if he hadn't told me that, I wouldn't be mad." His hand reached out and grasped her own on the rock. "Remember, last night when you told me about duty and that sometimes it was a joy and sometimes a kind of burden? You were talking about me. But I've got a duty to do too. You're in trouble and I've got to make it easier for you. That's my job." His lips tightened to keep from trembling. "I'm gonna be scared. I'm gonna worry about you. You've got to promise me you won't get hurt or anything."

"I'll try not—" Oh, what the hell. "I promise."

"Jock said that someone would be here to take care of me while he and MacDuff took care of you. I won't cause them any trouble, Mom."

Her throat was tight with tears. "I know you won't." She slid her arm around his shoulders and pulled him closer. "I'm very proud of you, Michael. Did Jock tell you who was coming?"

He shook his head.

"Well, I'll tell you what I know."

"I don't want to think about it. Jock will tell me later." He leaned back against her. "Do you think maybe we could just sit here together for a while? You don't have much time, do you?"

Thirty minutes. She could mentally see Royd pacing the courtyard. Too bad.

Her arm tightened around Michael. "Enough time. No hurry."

It was fully dark when she reached the courtyard. Royd had drawn the rental car out before the front door. She instinctively tensed as she saw him leaning on the passenger door. "I had to spend a little time with him."

"For God's sake, I know that. Do you expect a tongue-lashing?" He opened the passenger door. "That's why I waited over an hour before

I sent Jock back to break it up. Get in. I told Jock to delay him fifteen minutes so that we could be out of here when Michael got back. You don't want him to see you go, do you?"

"My duffel."

"In the trunk."

"I have to talk to MacDuff. I'll only be a moment."

"I've already talked to him. Jane MacGuire is going to call you back on your cell phone. Will you get in the car? You don't want this any worse for Michael than it already is."

She got into the car. "No, I don't want that." She leaned back and closed her eyes. "Get me out of here."

"That's what I'm trying to do."

She heard the driver's door slam and the engine spark to life. Royd didn't speak until they'd driven for a few moments. "Pretty rough?"

Her eyes opened. "Do you mean, did he have hysterics or shout at me? No, he was understanding and loving and he didn't do anything but break my heart. He's such a good kid, Royd."

He nodded. "I know. I wasn't around him much but I could see that." He paused. "But Jock said that he's certain Michael is going to be safe. He knows these people and he trusts them. That should make you feel better."

"It means everything." She glanced at him. "You're being suspiciously sympathetic."

"Am I? I'll have to watch that." His foot pressed the accelerator. "You might get to thinking I'm a decent human being."

"I never said I didn't believe you were—"

"Come on. You never think of me in connection with Garwood? You never remember what I was?" He lifted one shoulder in a half shrug. "What I am?"

"That doesn't mean you're not decent. If I believed that to be true, then I'd have to question my own decency." She changed the subject. "Jock told Michael that he and MacDuff were going away to help protect me. As far as I knew, MacDuff was going after Devlin."

"His horizons expanded after I told him that Devlin would be under Sanborne's protection. If he has to topple Sanborne and Boch to get at Devlin, he'll do it."

"And it's better if we have a common plan and aren't stumbling over each other."

"Exactly." His phone rang. "Royd."

"Kelly?" Sophie murmured.

He nodded. "Stay where you are, Kelly.

We're on our way to Miami. I'll let you know whether to come back to the States." He hung up. "He's in Barbados. It was the closest port when he lost the **Constanza**."

"Miami? Why Miami?"

"It's a good jumping-off place. We don't know where Gorshank is located. He may be in the islands or still in the U.S. . . ."

"Or anywhere else in the world."

"From what you've told me, my bet is that Sanborne would want him and his work close and under his thumb."

Yes, he would, Sophie thought. "When do you think we'll hear from MacDuff about Gorshank?"

"He's not going to drag his heels."

"I know. I just don't want— I'm scared. Before, the damage was limited. One on one. This is different."

"Gorshank's formula may be a bust. You said you didn't know how he came up with some of his results."

"And it may not be a bust." She straightened her shoulders. "I can't think about it now. I just have to take one minute at a time."

"Sound reasoning. It will be an hour until we get to the airport. You might try to relax."

"I can't relax." She gazed out the window

into the darkness. "Not until Jane MacGuire phones me."

"It didn't work out," Devlin said when Sanborne picked up the phone. "I did the best I could, but you didn't tell me Royd would be on the scene."

Sanborne cursed. "I wasn't certain that he was. You're sure it was Royd?"

"Oh, yes. I have a knife wound in the shoulder with his name on it. I know him well. We ran into each other frequently at Garwood."

"If you were that close, you should have taken him out. What good are you to me?"

Silence. "I'm sorry," Devlin said meekly. "What can I do to make amends?"

"Kill the child and the woman."

"It's too late. Royd identified me and will tip off MacDuff. If I get near the castle, they'll hunt me down. I obeyed your order and removed an encumbrance. Well, several encumbrances. The police will be all over the property."

"You careless idiot. You know that I didn't mean for you to compromise your mission."

"You told me to do what I had to do. I know

you don't want me to be caught when I can still be of use to you. Just let me go after Royd and he'll lead me to the woman."

"Then stay in Scotland and do the job."

"I don't believe they're still here. Royd knows me very well and he'll think he can track me down."

"And you think you can track him. Which one of you is right?"

"Me. Because he's burdened himself with the woman. That will drag him down."

"You said you shouldn't go back to the castle."

"If he's still there, he won't be long. He wants you and now he wants me. He can't get either sitting in that castle."

"And Sophie Dunston?"

"You gave me an order. Naturally, I'll get the job done. It just may take a little longer."

Sanborne thought about it. The priority had definitely changed now that he knew that Royd had linked himself with Sophie. He was a danger that must be removed quickly and efficiently. "The woman may be picked up by the police at any time. Royd won't stay with her if it puts him in danger. He wants me too badly to risk being picked up as an accessory."

"Then I can go after Royd?"

"When he surfaces. You'll stay with me until he does."

"To protect you?" Devlin added quickly, "That's smart. You mustn't be hurt."

"I'm glad you remember the prime directive," Sanborne said sarcastically. "Sometimes I wonder about you, Devlin."

"Why? I always do my job, don't I?"

"Always. But there's usually considerably more blood than I deem necessary."

"A means to an end."

"Perhaps." He looked down at the report on the desk in front of him. If the analysis of Gorshank's results was accurate, it could alter his focus. "Things are changing. Stay on the alert. I may have another job for you while we're waiting for Royd to pounce." He hung up. The blood that Devlin reveled in might not be so bad in this case. It might intimidate Sophie into coming into his camp. She must be feeling hunted, and having Devlin that close to her son could have been devastating to her confidence.

Go after the bitch and try to lure her again?

Maybe. He hadn't been pleased with Gorshank before and now he was becoming uneasier by the day. At first he had thought that he'd discovered the perfect replacement and that he could afford to rid himself of Sophie. But Gorshank wasn't as brilliant or innovative as Sophie, and the results of his last tests had been promising but tentative. Seven deaths and ten people who had shown only a small amount of the docility level he'd been striving to reach.

Wait until Devlin killed Royd and she felt more alone?

If the boy had not been behind stone walls, he could have taken him and let her son's pain persuade her. But Devlin had said the boy's security was very strong and now the countryside was crawling with police. Yet it might still be possible. . . .

He'd have to decide soon. Boch was urging him to proceed with the final tests and give him the go-ahead to start negotiating.

Come on, Royd. Devlin is waiting on you.

And this time I won't object to how much blood he spills.

Sophie's phone rang a few minutes before they were due to board the plane.

"Sophie Dunston? I'm Jane MacGuire." The woman's voice was throaty and young but vibrated with strength. "I'm sorry I didn't call you earlier, but I thought you'd rather I wait until I'd arrived at the Run and you could talk to your son."

"Yes, I would."

"He's in the next room. I'll call him when we're finished. You'll want to ask me questions. Go ahead."

"MacDuff has told you about my son's sleep disorder?"

"Yes, I'm sleeping in the room next to him. We'll get along." She paused. "He's a fine boy. I'm sure you're proud of him."

"Yes." She cleared her throat. "MacDuff said your father was a detective. I'm surprised you could persuade him to come with you."

"It wasn't easy," Jane said frankly. "Joe tries to go by the book. But not when a kid's life is at stake. Then he throws the book out the window. You can trust him. If I had a child, there's no one I'd rather have looking after him than Joe."

"You could get into trouble for doing this. Why are you willing to risk it? Are you that close to MacDuff?"

"Hell, no." She paused. "That wasn't a reassuring answer, was it? MacDuff and I have a history and we aren't always on the same page. But we agree in this case. The boy has to be kept safe and Joe and I can do it."

"Are you a policewoman?"

She chuckled. "Heavens, no. I'm an artist. But Joe has taught me to take care of myself and others. Any more questions?"

"Not that I can think of right now."

"Well, you can always call me back. I'll be here with your son, joined at the hip. I promise."

"Thank you." She cleared her throat. "I can't tell you how much I appreciate this. May I speak to Michael now?"

"Right away." Her voice rose. "Michael! Here he comes."

"Mom?" Michael came on the phone. "Are you okay?"

"Fine. I'm just about to get on a plane. Is everything good there?"

"Yeah, sure. Joe is a good guy but he doesn't play soccer. He said he'd teach me judo instead."

"That sounds . . . interesting. What about Jane?"

"She's nice. And pretty, real pretty. She reminds me of someone. . . ."

"Be sure and do what they say. They're only there to help you."

"You don't have to tell me that, Mom. I'm cool with it."

"Sorry, I guess I'm feeling a little out of the loop and trying to hold on to you. I know you'll be as smart and good as you always are with me." She drew a deep breath. "I love you. I'll call you whenever I can. Good-bye, Michael." She hung up.

"Satisfied?" Royd handed her a handkerchief.

"As much as I can be." She dabbed at her eyes. "Jane MacGuire seems honest and frank. I think she'll take care of Michael." She drew a shaky breath. "And he likes her. Even if neither she nor Joe Quinn can play soccer. He didn't seem to think it mattered. He says she's very pretty."

He smiled. "That could be trouble. Maybe Michael's testosterone levels are beginning to soar. You may come back to a boy with a king-size crush."

"I don't care. I'll handle that when I'm with him again." She handed him back his handkerchief. "Let's go." She started for the plane. "Where are we going to stay in Miami?"

"Well, not the Ritz. I rented a cottage on the beach up the coast. I've stayed there before. Private, isolated, and fairly comfortable. It should do until we know where we're going."

She nodded. "I want to go over that Gorshank disk again. As I told you, I thought I caught a few holes in those formulas. I need to work through them when I have time to concentrate."

"You spent an entire day concentrating on them."

"A day isn't much to spend on a work that probably took Gorshank at least a year to formulate." She paused. "And when I was studying that disk, I was shaken and scared and that doesn't make for clear and analytical thinking."

"Oh, I forgot." His smile faded as he followed her up the plane steps. "Your guilt complex had shifted into high gear by then. By all means, study those formulas. Maybe you'll find you're not really Hitler or Goering. That would be a pleasant surprise."

"Have you settled in comfortably?" MacDuff was standing at the bottom of the stairs as Jane MacGuire came down the steps. "Is the boy asleep?"

Jane nodded. "It took a while. He's pretty upset and trying not to let anyone see. He's quite a kid." She met his gaze. "And he likes you very much."

"What a surprise."

"Not really. You can be what you want to be. It pleased you to be kind to Michael." She came down the rest of the stairs. "Jock said there was a monitor in my bedroom and one in the library. Is that right?"

"Yes, but if you need any more, Campbell will set it up for you."

"When do you leave? I thought you were waiting for word on this Gorshank."

"I'll give it another night and then I'll hop a plane for the U.S." He added, "You're perfectly safe, Jane. I'm leaving most of my men here to ensure that you and Joe won't regret this. I wouldn't have brought you here if I'd believed any differently."

She shrugged. "What happens, happens. From now on it's up to Joe and me. Neither of us is a wimp. He's one of the toughest men I know and I grew up on the streets. Not in some fancy castle like you." She started down the hall. "Show me where the monitor is."

He chuckled. "I forgot how delightfully blunt you are." His smile faded. "No, that's a lie. I didn't forget. I haven't forgotten one single quality that makes you Jane MacGuire."

"I know." She opened the library door. "Or I wouldn't be here doing your job while you're off enjoying yourself making the world safe for democracy."

"Enjoying?"

"Most men enjoy hunting and gathering. It's the cave instinct. And if the hunting includes a little mayhem all the better." Her gaze searched the library and spotted the monitor on the sideboard. "Okay, I'll probably change the location. I can't see myself sketching in here. Maybe the hall."

"Who will you sketch? Michael?"

"Possibly. He has an interesting face for one so young. Maybe it's because he's had such a rough life. Much more intriguing than the usual child."

"And you like intriguing. I remember the trouble I had trying to keep you from sketching Jock."

"You didn't have a chance. Besides being the most beautiful human being I've ever met, Jock had all the torment of a Prometheus chained on a mountaintop. I couldn't resist." She gazed appraisingly at him. "I never sketched you. You wouldn't be a bad subject."

"I'm honored," he said dryly. "Even though I pale in comparison to Jock and Michael."

She shook her head. "I'd probably never even attempt you. You're too complicated. I wouldn't have the time."

"I'm just a simple landowner trying to keep his inheritance from falling apart around him."

She snorted. "Simple? You're half civilized aristocrat and half throwback to those robber barons that bred you."

"See? I must not be all that complicated. You have me figured out."

"I've scratched the surface." She turned and started back down the hall. "Keep in touch. I need to know what's going on."

"Oh, I will." He paused. "By the way, are you still seeing Mark Trevor?"

"Yes."

"Often?"

She glanced back over her shoulder. "That's none of your business, MacDuff."

"Aye, but on occasion I'm a nosy bastard. Chalk it up to those crude robber-baron ancestors. Often?"

"Good night, MacDuff."

He chuckled. "Good night, Jane. What a pity it's not working out between you and Trevor. But then I told you that it might be—"

She whirled on him. "Dammit, everything is fine with us. Why the devil don't you—" She stopped as she saw the devilish twinkle in his eyes. "I'm here to take care of the boy, not to listen to your goading. Take Jock and get out of my sight. You'd do better to try to help that poor woman who's bleeding inside because she doesn't know who to trust with her child."

His smile faded. "She knows who to trust now, Jane. She has good instincts and she'd be blind not to realize what kind of gem she has in you." He turned and started back inside the library. "Jock and I won't wake you to say good-bye. Thank Joe again for his help."

"Wait." He was probably playing her, she thought with frustration. He was a master at manipulating events to suit himself or she wouldn't be here. But she couldn't let him go into possible harm on that note of bitterness. "Keep safe, MacDuff."

A smile lit his face. "What a sweet, bonnie lass you are, Jane."

"Bull."

"It's true you keep it well hidden, but that makes it only the more challenging to search it out." He added, "I'll try to wind this mess up as quickly as possible. I've got too many goals to go after to waste any time."

The door of the library closed behind him.

Jane hesitated a moment before she started up the stairs. As usual, MacDuff had played on her emotions and made her run the gamut from frustration to anger to sympathy. Why the devil was she here?

She knew why she was here. The boy. It didn't matter that MacDuff was being annoying and trying to pry into her life. The strange bond forged between them still existed. She had tried to ignore it and put him out of her life. Obviously it wasn't meant to be, because she hadn't been able to refuse MacDuff when he'd told her about Sophie Dunston and her son.

It wasn't MacDuff, she thought crossly. She wouldn't have been able to refuse anyone who asked her help when it concerned a child. She had gone through too much hell herself in her early years. Eve and Joe had been there to help her, rescue her. Michael needed someone to stand by him in the same way. Even if it was on a short-term basis, she had to be here for him.

And MacDuff had nothing to do with that feeling of compulsion.

Except that he had read her character and used that knowledge to make her an offer she couldn't refuse. She couldn't deny that truth. Why should she? MacDuff was MacDuff and this encounter would be as brief as the last one. When Sophie Dunston was safe and came for her son, Jane would leave here with no regrets and the satisfaction of a job well done.

And thumb her nose at MacDuff.

* * *

The house north of Miami was a small, charming Spanish Mediterranean enclosed in high walls that hid a tiled courtyard. Royd parked the rental car at the street and unlocked the iron gates.

"Very nice," Sophie said as her gaze fell on a small fountain bubbling in the center of the courtyard. "You said you stayed here before?"

"A few times. It's comfortable." He locked the gates behind them. "And secure. I like walls around me."

"You have enough of them."

He looked at her. "I take it you're not referring to the house?"

"Sorry, it just tumbled out," she said wearily. "You have a right to ward off anyone you want."

"I'm not warding you off."

"Aren't you?" She looked away from the fountain to meet his eyes. She inhaled sharply. "That's not the way I meant it."

"Then watch what you say. Because I'm watching every expression, every intonation." He went ahead of her to unlock the French doors. "There are three bedrooms, an office, dining room, and kitchen." He gestured to the curving wrought-iron staircase. "Take any of the bedrooms. Grab a shower and meet me in the kitchen in an hour. I'll go out and pick up some take-out food. There's a Cuban restaurant a few miles from here. I know it's early but I'm guessing you could eat. Okay?"

"Okay." She started up the stairs. "Anything."

"Don't answer the door."

She stopped and looked at him. "I thought you said this place was so secure."

"It is secure. But only a fool takes safety for granted." He turned and went out the French doors.

And Royd wasn't a fool, she thought as she climbed the stairs. He'd lived with horror for years, the horror she had brought him, and he was still living on the edge. Every moment with him reinforced the regret she had felt when she had first heard about Garwood.

Forget it. He'd made it plain he didn't want her sympathy. She would take that shower and call Michael and make sure everything was still going well with him.

And hope that MacDuff had found out something about Gorshank.

* * *

Michael was sitting curled up in a chair by the window. The room was lit only by the moonlight pouring into the room.

"It's late. You should be in bed." Jane had merely meant to peek in Michael's room to check on him, but she could tell by the tension in his body that he was wound as tight as a wire. She came into the room and shut the door. "Can't sleep?"

He shook his head.

"Worried about your mom?"

He nodded. "I'm waiting for her to call. She said she'd call when she got to the U.S."

"She'll know it's late here."

"She'll call. She promised."

"She'd want you to stop worrying and go to sleep. I'll wake you if she calls." She made a face as she crossed the room to stand beside him. "That was kind of dumb of me. Wanting something doesn't always mean it's possible."

"The Laird said something like that." Michael's tone was halting. "You don't have to stay with me. I'm okay. And I don't want to bother you."

"You're not bothering me." She sat down on the floor and crossed her legs Indian fashion. "Are you afraid to go to sleep, Michael?"

"Sometimes. Not tonight. I'm just worried about Mom."

"You didn't let her see it. That was very brave of you. I could tell she's proud of you."

He shook his head. "I cause her lots of trouble."

It would be stupid to argue with him. He was an intelligent boy and he would recognize it as a lie. "That doesn't mean she doesn't have reason to be proud, and she thinks the trouble is worth it."

"Because she's my mom. No one else would think that." He stared her in the face. "You don't, do you?"

It was confrontation time. She had known it would be coming. He had accepted her because it was easier for his mother, but now they had to come to terms with each other. "I wouldn't be here if I didn't."

"You didn't even know me," he said curtly. "Why did you come? Because the Laird told you to do it?"

"The Laird doesn't tell me to do anything." Michael was still staring at her. He needed an answer. "I came because I thought you needed me. When I was a kid I didn't have a mom like yours and I was pretty lonely. Then a lady came along and took me in and changed everything for me. Her name is Eve Duncan. She and Joe gave me a home and drove the loneliness away. She taught me that people have to help people. I thought that maybe I could give back a little of what Eve and Joe gave to me."

"You felt sorry for me?" he asked defensively. "I don't need anyone feeling sorry for me."

"Of course I feel sorry for you. You have a problem that I want to help you heal. That doesn't mean I think you're pitiful. You're pretty tough, Michael. I don't know if I could go through what you've gone through."

He was silent, his gaze searching her face.

He needed something more and she had to give it to him even if it hurt. She tried to smile. "So tough that I almost turned MacDuff down until he told me your name."

He frowned. "What?"

"He said your name was Michael. I knew a little boy named Michael before Eve took me in. He was younger than me and we called him Mikey. I was like a big sister to him. We grew up together."

"Am I like him?"

"No, he was very sweet and I loved him, but you're braver and more independent." She cleared her throat. "But I can't help Mikey any longer and it seemed right that I help another Michael."

"Did your Mikey go away?"

"Yes." She looked away from him. "He went away." She rose to her feet. "Will you let me do it? It will make me feel better. Will you be my friend and let me help you and your mom?"

He didn't speak for a moment and then slowly nodded. "I'd like to be your friend."

"Then can I talk you into going to bed so that I can tell your mom I did my job?"

He smiled. "I guess so." He stood up and moved toward the bed. "I wouldn't want you to get into trouble. I'm not nearly as tough as Mom."

"I think you are." She watched him attach the monitors before she tucked him into bed. She whispered, "And I'm proud to be your friend, Michael. Thank you. . . ."

Sophie had just hung up from talking to Michael when Royd knocked on the bedroom door.

She shoved her phone in the pocket of her jeans and threw open the door. "Michael's fine. He was asleep. I'm sorry I woke him but it's a good sign. And MacDuff is still at the Run. He said he hadn't located Gorshank yet."

"Then he's probably champing at the bit,"

Royd said. "He's going to be pretty anxious to get on the road. Are you ready to eat?"

She thought about it and then nodded. "Starved. Did you find the Cuban restaurant?"

"Nope. I changed my mind." He nodded at the sack he was carrying. "I went to a deli instead. I thought we'd have supper on the beach. It sounded peaceful and I could use some fresh air."

So could Sophie. They'd been running at full speed since the moment Royd had appeared in her life and even a few hours of peace seemed alluring. "Let's get going." She passed him and started down the stairs. "But it surprises me you crave peace. You don't seem . . ." She stopped, trying to puzzle it out. "You're wired. I feel as if I'd get a shock if I brushed against you by accident."

"You didn't suffer any traumatic jolts when you spent the night in bed with me."

"No." She didn't look at him. "You were very kind that night."

"I'm not kind." He opened the door for her. "Almost everything I do is self-serving. Occasionally, I have a lapse, but don't count on it."

"I never would. I've learned never to count on anyone." She took off her tennis shoes as they reached the sand of the beach. "But I'd trust you more than most people."

"Why?"

"Because I know your motivations." The sun was going down, but the sand beneath her toes still felt warm from the afternoon heat. The breeze was blowing her hair back from her face and she suddenly felt lighter, free. . . . She lifted her face and drew a deep breath of the salt-laden air. "This was a good idea, Royd."

"I have them occasionally." He pointed at a cluster of boulders close to the sea. "There?"

She nodded. "Anywhere. As I said, I'm hungry."

"Starved," he corrected with a smile. "It's the first time I've heard you admit to a need that extreme. You appear to eat to stay alive." His gaze ran over her. "And it shows. You're too thin."

"I'm strong and healthy."

"You look as if you could be broken with one twist of my hand."

"Then my looks are deceiving." She stopped at the boulder. "You couldn't break me, Royd."

"Yes, I could." He dropped to the ground and began opening the sack. "I'm good at breaking things . . . and people." He looked up at her. "But I'd never do it. It would hurt me too much."

She couldn't breathe. She could feel the blood tingling in her palms and the sensitive inner flesh of her wrists. She couldn't look away from him.

His gaze finally shifted away from her. "Sit down and eat. Pastrami on rye. Dill pickles. And potato chips. The deli didn't sell wine, so you'll have to make do with a Coke."

"That's fine." She slowly sat down across from him. It wasn't fine. She felt weak and a little dizzy. Jesus, she hadn't felt like this since she was a teenager. "I like pastrami." She carefully took the sandwich he handed her. Don't touch him. Touching him would be a mistake. Hell, staring at him was a mistake, because it made her want to reach out and brush her fingers across his cheek. He was so hard, so taut and yet she knew that she could break that tension. It made her feel heady with power.

Cripes, Eve and Adam and the damn apple. What she was feeling was purely primitive.

Maybe not so pure.

"It's okay." He was studying her expression. "I'm not going to jump you just because you're feeling a little vulnerable. That's not why I brought you here."

She wanted to deny that she was vulnerable. She couldn't lie. She had never felt more vulnerable in her life. "Why did you bring me?"

He frowned. "You needed to relax. I wanted to see you without all the kinks." He bit into his sandwich. "And I wanted to tell you that . . . I was rough on you. I didn't want you to come with me, and I got ugly."

"Yes."

He shrugged. "I didn't mean it. I do care if you live or die."

He was like a churlish little boy reluctant to confess. Her brows lifted. "Oh, that's comforting. Then you lied about only wanting to screw me?"

"Well, I lied about it being the only reason." He smiled. "But it was definitely a prime motivation." His smile faded. "It still is. But I'm not pushing." He finished his sandwich and lay back in the sand and closed his eyes. "Yet."

She gazed at him with exasperation mixed with amusement. It was just like Royd to make a provocative statement like that and then ignore her.

"Finish your sandwich and stretch out." Royd didn't open his eyes. "You may not get the chance to relax after today. You should always take advantage of the good times when you can."

"I know that." She took the last bite of her sandwich and sat for a moment looking at him. Jesus, he appeared to be drifting off to sleep. Here she was, on edge, wary, and he was completely ignoring her. To hell with it.

She leaned back and propped herself against the boulder. "But if I go to sleep, you'd better give me a shake before the tide comes in. I don't like rude awakenings."

"And I sometimes enjoy them. A little shock and roughness stirs the blood. I'll show you sometime. . . ."

"I don't want you to—" Don't talk to him. Every word he said brought a picture to her mind. Royd naked in bed that first night. Royd gazing at her with that intensity that made her feel that queer breathless heat. "I can't relax if you keep talking to me."

"Good point. But then you're a very smart lady. That's one of my problems. You don't look like a doctor."

"What's a doctor supposed to look like?"

"Not like you. When you wash your hair, it's all curly and loose like a kid's. Most of the time you don't wear a lot of makeup and you look clean and smooth and glowing. . . ."

Dammit, she was beginning to feel that tingling heat again.

"You make me sound like Shirley Temple." She had to steady her voice. "I hope I'm clean, but there's nothing childlike about me." She closed her eyes. "I have a child of my own, remember."

"How could I forget? He dominates your life."

"That's right."

But Michael seemed far away in this moment. It had been a long time since she had felt this sense of being a woman instead of a mother. She was vividly aware of her body, her muscles, her chest rising and falling as she breathed. Though her eyes were closed, the memory of the sea and the sand and Royd was still with her.

"It's okay." Royd's voice was low. "That's how it should be. I didn't mean anything else. But you're human. If you need me, I'm here, Sophie."

She couldn't answer. Damn him. Gruff, bold, rude, and yet he had moments that made her want to hold him, comfort him. Just when she managed to harden herself against him, he said something that made her soften again. "Thank you." She cleared her throat. "I'll keep that in mind."

He didn't speak again. Was he asleep? She knew darned well she wouldn't be able to doze off.

Keep it in mind? How could she help doing anything else?

15

They didn't go back to the house until a few hours after dark.

"Are you all right?" Royd asked as he unlocked the gate. "You've been very quiet."

She forced a smile. "I'm fine. Why shouldn't I be? I've done nothing but loll on the beach for the last few hours." She went ahead of him into the courtyard. "You were right. I needed a few hours of peace and quiet." Though the peace had been ambivalent. Her body had been still but her mind and emotions had been vibrating.

And he had known it, sensed it.

She could tell by the alertness, the watchfulness in his expression. She gazed away from him and her pace quickened. "It was a good idea to skip the Cuban restaurant and go for the—"

"Am I going to get lucky?"

She stopped short. "What?"

"You heard me," he said roughly. "Maybe it's not the most diplomatic way to put it. But I have to know."

She turned to face him. "Are you going to get lucky?" she repeated. "For God's sake, you make me feel like a cheap pickup in a bar."

"It's not like that. I just have to— Oh, forget it." He passed her and took the stairs two at a time. "I should have known that I'd—"

She heard his bedroom door slam behind him. She stared at the door for a moment before she continued up the stairs. She felt stunned and indignant and confused.

And disappointed. She didn't know what she had expected, but it wasn't to be shut away from him like this.

So what did she want? She had told herself that no way should she become sexually involved with Royd. It would be a mistake. Their only joint interest was bringing down Sanborne and Boch, and they were as different from each other as night and day. You couldn't build a relationship with no common ground.

She'd had a hundred similar interests and goals with Dave and her marriage had still failed. It had been too weak to withstand tragedy. So how could she expect a relationship to work with a man who—

What was she thinking? Royd didn't want a relationship. He wanted sex.

And wasn't that what she also wanted? Why all this analyzing as if she were tiptoeing toward a commitment?

His door was opening.

Her heart jumped in her breast.

"I had to tell you." His voice was halting. "I said it wrong. I'm not stupid, but I'm damn inarticulate whenever I'm around you. I don't know why. Everything gets garbled."

Her hand clenched on the banister. "You seemed pretty clear to me."

He shook his head. "You think I insulted you. You used the word 'cheap.' That's the last thing I'd think about you."

She moistened her lips. "Really?"

"You don't believe me." His hands clenched into fists at his sides. "It just came out. Okay? I grew up rough and I've lived rough all my life. I said what I was thinking. It might be a catchphrase for the singles scene but that wasn't what I meant it to be."

She couldn't look away from him. "Then what did you mean?"

He was silent a moment. "That I'd consider myself the luckiest son of a bitch on the planet if you let me touch you. If you let me screw you, I'd feel as if I won the lottery." He grimaced. "That was crude too. I can't help it. It's me."

"It was crude." And even the crudeness excited her, she realized.

"But it was honest. I don't want to be anything but honest with you. I'm not trying to coax you into bed. I might have done that in the beginning, but it's too late now. You have to want it as much as I do."

"And if I don't?"

"It would be bad," he said simply. "I want it too much. I might hurt you trying to make you feel what I'm feeling. I can't do that. You have to want what I want. Otherwise, don't let me touch you." His gaze searched her face. "I'm scaring you."

"No, you're not." He had shaken her, stirred her, Christ, even touched her. But she was not frightened of him. "You've never frightened me since that first night when I thought you meant to cut my throat." She tried to smile. "And I don't think you'd hurt me. It's just . . .

not a good idea." She forced herself to release
the banister and started down the hall. "Good
night, Royd."

"Good night."

She could feel his gaze on her back. But he
didn't speak until she'd reached her door.

"You're wrong," he said quietly. "It's a damn
good idea. Think about it."

Her hand closed on the knob. Just turn the
knob, open the door, and close the door behind her. It was only sex. She didn't need him.
He didn't need her. "Ships that pass in the
night."

"Maybe. Maybe not. We'll never know,
will we?"

She was in the room. Now close the door
and don't look back at him.

She didn't want to shut the door.

All the more reason to do it.

She closed the door.

She would come.

No, she wouldn't. He was an arrogant fool
to think that she wouldn't fight the pull that
was drawing them together.

He walked naked across the room and
opened the window. He took a deep breath of

the warm salt air. Keep calm. Keep cool. She had to come to him. He hadn't lied when he'd told her he was afraid he'd hurt her. He usually had control but this was different. **She** was different.

His door was opening. He stiffened but didn't turn around.

"I changed my mind." Her voice was shaking.

He didn't move. "Thank God."

"Dammit, turn around. I want to see your face."

"If I turn around, it won't be my face you'll notice."

"Braggart."

He slowly turned to face her.

Her gaze searched his face and then moved down to his lower body. "Sweet Jesus."

"I told you."

Her gaze flew back to his face. "You were expecting me. You were waiting for me."

"I was hoping."

"I'll say you were." She pulled her sleep shirt over her head. "Okay, let's get to it." She threw the shirt on the floor and a moment later she was pulling the sheet on the bed over her naked body. "Come here."

"In a minute. I want to ask you something."

"No, you don't. You don't want to talk at all. Nothing could be clearer."

"All right, I need to ask you something."

"Come here."

"Not until you answer me. I can't come close to you or the answer won't matter a damn to me."

"I don't want to talk. Do you think this was easy for me?"

He shook his head. "I think it was very difficult. That's why I have to be sure it's for the right reason."

She raised her hand to her forehead. "Christ. Let me guess. You want me to promise that I won't believe this is a commitment on your part. Dammit, I don't want a commitment. I'd guess that you'd—"

"Screw commitment. I'd be an idiot to think that you'd consider any kind of tie with me now. I just want you to answer one question."

"What, blast it? Ask me!"

"Is this some kind of payback?"

She stared at him in bewilderment. "Payback?"

"Why are you surprised? You're soft as butter and every time you look at me I know you're remembering Garwood. You're so full of guilt that it's shaped and twisted these last years for you. I don't want you going to bed with me because you feel it's a way to make something up to me."

"My God, you're nuts." She swung her legs to the side of the bed and sat up. "And I'm not going to try to prove anything to you."

"Just answer me."

"No!" She glared at him. "Hell, yes, I feel sorry I was responsible for what happened to you."

"See? You weren't responsible, any more than a weapon in the hands of an assassin."

"I beg to differ." She got to her feet. "But that wouldn't make me offer myself on an altar like some stupid vestal virgin. I value myself too much. I made a king-size mistake, but that doesn't have anything to do with the fact that for some reason I found you— It was just sex." She started for the door. "But I'm not about to try to convince you. It's not worth—"

"I'll make it worth it." He was across the room in seconds, his hand grasping her arm. He fell to his knees in front of her. "Give me three minutes."

"Get up. I'm not giving you—" She shuddered as his lips moved across her belly. He could feel her muscles clench as his hands went around to cup her buttocks.

"Three minutes." His tongue moved against her skin. "You can always change your mind later."

"Can I?" Her hands clenched in his hair. "I'm not sure about that."

"Neither am I." He brushed his cheek back and forth against her. "I'm probably lying. So why not just come back to bed. Then there won't be any pressure. . . ."

"I'm feeling plenty of pressure right now." Her voice was uneven. "I think my knees are about to give way."

"Let them." He pulled her down to the floor and moved over her. "A rug is as good as a bed. . . ."

"Royd . . ."

"Shh, it's too late . . ." He parted her legs. Lord, she felt good around him. "We need it too much. You need it too much. I can **feel** it."

"Then give it to me." Her teeth clenched as her nails dug into his back. "And for heaven's sake, don't ask me any more dumb questions or I'll murder you. . . ."

"Okay?" Royd whispered as he eased off her. "I wasn't too rough?"

"Which time?" Her breath was coming easier but she was still shaking. He was only a few inches away but he wasn't touching her. She wanted that touch, the feel of him skin-to-skin. Cripes, she was acting like a nymphomaniac. They had come together several times, rolling around on the floor like animals, and she still wanted more. Then take it, dammit. She reached out her hand to stroke his chest. He felt warm, a little moist with perspiration. Her palm tingled as it brushed the wiry hair that arrowed down his chest. "Yes, you were rough. So was I. Now who's feeling guilty?"

"Just asking." He took her palm and raised it to his lips. "I'm taking a survey."

"What?"

"Could I ask you one more question?"

"Absolutely not." She gazed at him curiously. "What?"

He sucked at her forefinger. "Am I the best you ever had?"

She stared at him in disbelief. "You conceited bastard."

"Am I better than your husband was?"

"Royd, who asks questions like that?"

"I do." He lowered his head to brush her nipple with his mouth. "It's important."

"To flatter your ego?"

"No." He raised his head to look down at her. "If I did something wrong, I have to know about it. I have to be the best you've ever had. If I'm not, I have to work at it until I am."

She stared at him, stunned. "I knew you were competitive but this is carrying it too far."

He shook his head. "We're starting out with damn little in common. Maybe there are a few things we agree on, but we don't have time to explore them. Until we do, this is what we've got. I'm not letting it not be so good that you won't want to stick around."

"I have to stick around. There's REM-4."

His jaw set. "You have to want to stay with me."

"Why?"

He didn't answer for a moment. "Because I feel something for you. I'm not sure what it is but I can't let it go."

"What a precise declaration."

"You're the scientist, not me. The only thing I'm precise about is how to take down a man at a thousand yards." His lips twisted. "You're flinching. You didn't like that."

"Most people would flinch."

"Not necessarily. Some women like the idea of being that close to death. It gives them a thrill." He stood up. "Come on, let's go to bed."

"Maybe I'd better go to my room."

"Not yet." He pulled her to her feet. "I've said the wrong thing again. I've got to erase it."

"And prove you're some kind of sex king?"

"Hell, no." He pulled her closer. "I just want to be the best for you. What's wrong with that?"

He'd only touched her and she was beginning to tingle, ready. "I'm sure there's something. It's bound to be psychologically unsound. What if I asked you if I was the best you ever had?"

"I'd tell you that you're good but together we're great." He nibbled at her lower lip. "And that you shouldn't fool around with anyone else who might lower your standards."

She found herself smiling. "Royd. You're impossible."

He led her toward the bed. "But am I the best?"

"Maybe."

"That's not good enough. I guess I'll have to start to work." He pulled her down on top of him. "But you'll have to help. You'll have to tell me what you like, what turns you on. Will you do that?"

Her breath was coming fast, hard. "Probably not."

"Why not?"

"You idiot, because I can't think, much less speak, when you're doing this to me."

"Too bad." He grinned up at her. "We'll just have to analyze it later. In true precise, clinical fashion."

"We will not." She cupped his face in her two hands and stared down at him. "Shut up, Royd."

"Whatever you say." He was no longer smiling but she could detect a hint of latent humor in his eyes. "I thought you liked talk during sex. You were vocal enough before." He pretended to think. "But as I remember, it was mostly groans and shrieks and gasps. Oh, yes, there were a few 'mores' mixed in with— Ouch. That was wicked."

"You deserved it."

He rolled her over. "We'll have to discuss that too. You like inflicting pain on poor male partners. I don't know how much I can stomach, but anything for you, Sophie."

Eroticism, passion, and now humor. She hadn't expected the humor. "Bastard." She pulled him down and kissed him, hard. "Will you shut up now?"

"Oh, yes." His hands moved over her. "Like I said, anything for you, Sophie. . . ."

Her eyes opened sleepily. Sunlight streamed through the window into the room. Royd had been standing naked at the window last night when she'd come to him. His back had been to her and she'd seen the hard, lean buttocks and the powerful shoulders. She'd wanted to touch him then, and later her hands had learned him as if—

Royd was gone.

Her eyes flew to the indentation on the pillow next to her. No Royd.

She closed her eyes for a moment as disappointment surged through her. Stupid. What had she expected? They'd had sex and had a fantastic night. That didn't mean he had any obligation to stay with her.

"Ready?"

She opened her eyes to see Royd standing at the foot of the bed. His hair was wet and he smelled clean. "Ready for what?"

He smiled. "Sex? Shower? Breakfast? A morning swim? I listed your options in order of importance to me."

She felt a warm, comforting tide move

through her. Weird that those few words had banished the feeling of abandonment she'd been experiencing. "Your hair is wet. Shower or swim?"

"Shower. I thought I'd wait for you." He stood looking at her. "Either get out of bed or I'll come back in. Since it's almost noon I think we should wait until I feed you." He turned and headed for the door. "Hit the shower. I rifled through your stuff and put a change of clothes in the bathroom. I'll make coffee and an omelet. Twenty minutes?"

"I need thirty minutes." She sat up and threw back the sheet. "I have to wash my hair. I feel as if I've gone through a tornado."

"You did." He smiled at her over his shoulder. "We did."

He was gone before she could answer. She stood up and moved toward the bathroom door. Her body felt light, sleek, her muscles so relaxed and springy they were almost catlike. After a night of sex that intense she would have thought she'd be tired and drained. Instead, she felt glowing. She couldn't remember ever feeling like this with Dave. Sex had been satisfying, it had never been all-consuming.

Don't think about Dave. Don't make comparisons. What they had experienced last night had been unique. Sometimes it happened that two people were perfectly attuned to each other sexually. That didn't mean that they were attuned in any other way. Heaven knows she and Royd were miles apart on any other viewpoint.

She turned on the shower and stepped beneath it. The warmth of the water was another lazy, sensuous experience. Good. She didn't want to think right now. She wanted to be mindless and bask in the moment. She tilted back her head and let the water flow over her.

"You're five minutes late." Royd turned away from the stove when she walked into the kitchen. "But so am I. I had a telephone call."

She stiffened. "MacDuff?"

He shook his head. "Kelly. He wanted instructions."

"What did you tell him?"

"Find another boat with state-of-the-art equipment and wait for us." He scooped the omelets onto two plates. "Pour the coffee while I get the orange juice out of the fridge."

"Okay." She was still frowning as she picked up the carafe. "Why would we need a state-of-the-art launch?"

"Maybe we won't. I like to be prepared." He

put the plates on the table. "Stop worrying." He took the carafe from her and poured the coffee into two cups. "I don't like it."

She raised her brows. "Therefore I'm to cease and desist?"

"Until there's something to worry about. I knew I'd jar you when I told you about Kelly but I thought you'd resent it if I didn't keep you up to speed."

"Yes, I would."

"Sit down." He pushed her onto a chair. "And smile at me the way you were doing when you came into the kitchen."

"What way was that?"

He tilted his head as he gazed down at her. "Eager. Definitely eager. Do you know how that makes me feel?" His fingers touched her hair. "Silky. You're silky all over. Every place I touched."

She couldn't breathe. She could feel the heat scorching her cheeks.

He reached down and slowly rubbed her breast. "Beautiful and soft and silky," he said softly. "Want to try it on the kitchen floor?"

Yes, she did. She was trembling with the need to pull him down and—

"Come on," he said as his hand slipped inside her shirt. Skin-to-skin. The muscles of her stomach clenched. "We can eat later. It doesn't matter."

"No, it doesn't—" She drew a deep breath and reached up and took his hand from beneath her shirt. Jesus, it was hard to stop. "It doesn't matter when we eat. It does matter that you're using sex to distract me. I should be worrying about every single thing that's happening, and you're treating me like a doll you take out and play with and then put back in the box."

"Wrong tactics?" He shrugged and sat down in the chair opposite her. "Sorry, I'm feeling very protective of you. It's been sneaking up on me for some time and last night clinched it. It probably has something to do with the caveman instinct to preserve the family. I'm sure you know more about that than I do. You have all those degrees."

"You keep throwing my schooling in my face. Does it bother you?"

"No, not if it doesn't bother you." He lifted his cup to his lips. "I've learned I can learn anything I have to learn."

As he'd learned her body and every nuance of sensation he could bring to it last night, she thought. She veered away from that thought. Her body was still tingling, readying from his touch and she didn't need to remember how good he could make that joining for her. "You seem to be very talented in that direction."

He chuckled and her gaze flew to his face. He knew exactly what she had been thinking. She wouldn't look away. She picked up her fork and took a bite of omelet.

"I'm glad you think so." His lips twitched. "I can usually do what has to be done. If the incentive is tempting enough." His expression sobered. "We could talk around the subject for the next week, but I'll be damned if we'll do it. I'm walking on shaky ground and I have to firm it up."

"What do you mean?"

"Right now, I'm in pretty good shape. You had a good time last night and it's lingering nicely. You're feeling and not thinking. But I can't count on that as time passes. You'll get scared and you'll think about your son and your life and how different we are."

"We are different."

"Not in bed," he said roughly. "And the rest can be negotiated. I told you last night that I feel something for you. It's still there and stronger. Much stronger. I'm not sure where it's going but I can't let it go. I can't let you go, Sophie."

"I don't want to talk about this now."

"I do. I don't know how much time we have before everything blows up in our faces. I never expected this to happen but it did and we have to cope." His hand tightened on his cup. "I've been honest with you. Now level with me."

"What do you want me to say?" She moistened her lips. "Last night was better than good, it was fantastic. I've been something of a workaholic all my life and sex was never that important to me. It was just pleasant." Her lips twisted. "Sex is not pleasant with you, Royd. It blew my mind. You saw how I responded. I want to keep on going to bed with you. You thought that I might be going to bed with you because I was sorry for you. But it's myself I'm sorry for. Life hasn't been wonderful for me for the past years and I'm going to reach out and grab as much pleasure as I can. I think I deserve it. Is that what you want to know?"

"Partly. It's a start. No one-night stand?"

She hesitated. "I don't know how— Everything may change in a heartbeat. How can I be sure how I'll feel? There's Sanborne and I can't—"

"Okay. Okay. I'm better off than I thought I'd be. You're not having second thoughts about sex with me. You're just not sure about the future." He finished his coffee. "I can take care of that."

"You may not want to do it," she said quietly. "I'm no femme fatale. Whatever you're feeling may fade in a day or two."

"Maybe. Not likely. I'm pretty obsessive. Finish your breakfast and we'll go for a swim."

She leaned back in her chair and looked at him. Dear heavens, Royd was volatile. One moment he was intense and totally focused and the next he'd changed to an entirely new path.

"I'm just giving you breathing room." His gaze was on her face. "I pushed you hard. You need it."

"You're very sure of yourself." She stood up. "And me. A swim sounds good." She reached up and started to unbutton her shirt. "But not good enough. And it's not what I want right now. Take your clothes off, Royd."

"Sophie?"

"You promised me a romp on the kitchen floor." She finished unbuttoning her shirt. "Keep your promise, Royd."

"I will." He was behind her, his hands on her breasts. He whispered in her ear. "Always."

* * *

It was Sophie's phone that rang two hours later. She reached over Royd to pick it up on the nightstand.

"I've found out about Gorshank. Venable with the CIA came through," MacDuff said when she picked up the phone. "Anton Gorshank. Russian scientist who worked on some pretty nasty projects before the breakup of the Soviet Union."

"A chemist?"

"Right, and he was last heard from in Denmark. The CIA said he disappeared from their scope two years ago."

"They don't know where he is now?"

"They're working on it. They say they have a few leads. I asked Joe Quinn to put a little more pressure on them. He has a few friends in the Agency too. I expect word from them soon. I'll get back to you."

"Thank you. How's Michael?"

"Fine."

"May I talk to him?"

"You'll have to call Jane. Jock and I left the Run two hours ago."

"I . . . see."

"I told you that we'd be on the road as soon as we found out anything, Sophie," he said quietly.

"I know." But it still made her a little uneasy to realize that MacDuff and Jock were no longer with Michael. She had come to rely on them. "Where are you going?"

"We'll be heading your way. Good-bye, Sophie."

"Good-bye." She hung up the phone.

"Gorshank?" Royd asked.

She nodded. "We know who he is. Russian scientist who disappeared from Denmark two years ago. They don't know where he is. Mac-Duff is expecting word at any time."

"Good."

"And he and Jock are on the move. He evidently believes that there's going to be a breakthrough soon."

He raised himself on one elbow to look at her. "And you're uneasy about Michael."

"Of course I am. I'm always worried about him. It's been that way since the day my parents died." She rolled over in bed and sat up. "I'll call him and talk to Jane. That will make me feel better."

"Will it?"

"I've got to trust someone. I feel pretty alone right now."

"What am I? Chopped liver?"

"I didn't mean—"

"I know." He got out of bed. "You've just got a dose of cold water in the face and you don't see me in the role of helpmate and guardian. I thought I was doing pretty well in that department, but evidently not." He shrugged. "That's okay. I'll take what I can get. You told me you had problems with trust. How about that swim after you call Michael?"

"I guess so." She moved toward the bathroom. "If we don't hear from MacDuff by then."

"Naturally, that would come first. You've made me a little dizzy but not enough to forget the job I have to do."

"I'd be an idiot if I believed you to be the type of man who would be distracted to that extent. I've always known—"

"Sophie."

She looked back at him.

His lips were tight and his voice rough. "You're already distancing yourself from me. That's not going to happen. I'll take second place, but I'm not going to fade out of the picture."

"I don't know what you're talking about."

"You're probably telling the truth. You're so used to not thinking about anyone but Michael that you're trying to stuff the memory of what we've got in a little compartment and intend to ignore it. It's not going to be that easy. I'm going to make sure of that." His lips twisted. "The honeymoon is **not** over."

"Honeymoon? That implies a commitment that doesn't exist between us."

"Whatever you want to call it." He moved toward the door. "That's all I wanted to say. I just thought it fair to warn you."

"Good God, that sounds like a threat."

"What do you expect from someone like me?" He shook his head. "It's not a threat. I won't stalk you. If you walk away from me when this is over, good luck to you. I'll just do my damnedest to make it impossible for you to do it. And my damnedest is pretty good. Until then I'll be so civilized and agreeable it will make you happy as a clam and me want to throw up. I'll see you downstairs."

The door closed behind him.

Civilized and agreeable? The bastard didn't have any concept of the meaning of those words. He was rough and hard and being around him was like clinging to debris in the middle of a tornado.

Yet she hadn't wanted it any other way during the last twenty-four hours. If he was rough, there had been no pain, and he was an incredibly exciting lover. His unpredictability and hint of latent violence should have been intimidating, but she had found it addictive. At no time had she felt threatened by him. He was not smooth and easy but she had known he wouldn't hurt her. And even though she had accused him of threatening her a few minutes ago, it had been more of a defensive move.

Defensive. Why would she feel defensive when she had just admitted that she was not afraid of Royd?

Control.

The answer came zeroing in on her. All her adult life she'd had to be in control, in her marriage, her career, with Michael. When she was in bed with Royd, that control had vanished. She'd deliberately let go of the need for control because the pleasure was so intense. Cripes, she sounded like some dominatrix. She'd kept the reins with Dave because that's the way he liked it. As a doctor, she had to be disciplined and authoritative; with Michael, she was a mother and it went with the territory.

It would never go with the territory with Royd. He might compromise but that would be all. He said he respected her, but she'd have to earn that respect every minute of every day.

She closed the bathroom door and leaned

against it. Stop thinking about Royd. She had probably made a mistake in becoming intimate with him but it was done. She'd had a hell of a good time but that didn't mean she had to continue with it. She needn't cut it off abruptly but it was best if she concentrated on—

Jesus. The memory of Royd in that last minute before he had walked out of the bedroom came back to her. Naked, muscular, bold, and very erotic.

Yeah, stop thinking about him.

Not likely.

16

Her phone started ringing as she came down the stairs thirty minutes later.

MacDuff?

Royd came out into the hall and stood looking up at her.

Her hand was trembling as she punched the button.

"How are you, Sophie?" Sanborne asked. "Well, I trust."

She stopped in shock on the stairs. "What do you want, Sanborne?"

Royd stiffened, his gaze on her face.

"What I've always wanted," Sanborne said. "A partnership with someone I respect and trust. You must realize how futile this vendetta of yours is turning out. You can't win, and people you love may be hurt."

"Like Dave?"

"I don't know what you mean. The police are convinced that you're the one who killed Edmunds." He paused. "I was thinking of your son."

"You bastard."

"I hear that there was a horrible incident in Scotland. I'm so glad your son is still safe."

"And he'll stay safe," she said through her teeth. "You can't touch him, Sanborne."

"Because you've teamed up with Royd? That was a mistake. He's not stable. He'll drag you down with him."

"I'm not stable either. Not where you're concerned."

"Then it's time you got over it. I'm offering you a deal that you can't refuse."

"The hell I can't."

"You're in much worse trouble than you were when I last called. The police are after you. The DNA that linked you to the Edmunds crime scene has tested positive. You have no career and your son is in danger. Believe me, that last is certainly true. Come and join me, Sophie. You'll have money, power, and the boy will be safe."

"And I'd turn into a monster like you."

"Power, Sophie. It's the great equalizer between monsters and saints."

"You're sick."

He didn't answer. "You see how I'm keeping my temper? It should prove how much I want your cooperation."

"It proves that you're not as certain about REM-4 as you want to be."

"How clever you are. But you have an example of REM-4 with you now. Royd was one of my prime specimens. And it was all due to you."

"Shut up."

"Very well. I don't want to offend you when we have to work closely together. I'll be in touch." He hung up.

"Do I have to ask what he wanted?" Royd asked quietly.

"Me." She was shaking. "I didn't expect him to— It surprised me."

He was suddenly beside her, holding her. "Easy. He wants you weak and scared. Don't give it to him."

She clung to him. "He's such a bastard. He kept threatening Michael."

"It's his ace in the hole."

"And he talked about you. He said you were

a prime specimen and that I did it." She moistened her lips. "He's right. I did do it."

"And I am a prime specimen."

She stiffened in shock.

"At least you thought so last night. And you did do me. Any number of times."

"You know I meant—" She pushed back and looked at his face. "It's not funny."

"Yes, it is." He smiled. "It's funny to think he can hurt me or you with that garbage. We're way beyond him now." He turned her around and gave her a gentle swat. "Get upstairs and pack. We need to be out of here in the next five minutes."

"You think the call was traced?"

"It's possible. I'm using a satellite phone and the NSA can pick up signals on practically any phone service in the country. Boch has contacts with military-satellite departments that could zero in on us. I don't want to wait and see if the cops or some of Sanborne's men come down on us."

She hurried up the steps. "I don't think it will be the police. He was— I believe I caught a— He wants me, Royd. Not my head in a basket."

"Then we should ask ourselves why he's suddenly so urgent." He turned and headed for the front door. "But from a good distance from this place."

Sanborne turned to Boch. "Did you get the location?"

He looked up from his phone. "They're working on it. Somewhere in South Florida."

Sanborne cursed. "Where? Royd will have her out of there in minutes."

"Maybe they'll leave some clue to where they're—"

"I can't be chasing her all over the States. I need to get my hands on her now."

"Why don't we send Devlin to Florida? If he has a starting point, he should be able to track them. You've made sure he's an expert."

"No, I don't want to waste—" He stopped, thinking about it. Dammit, he'd wanted to lure the woman into his camp. It had been a slim chance but it was always better to have willing workers rather than forced. He had learned that through the experiments at Garwood. The possibility had existed that she might have felt trapped by having the police after her. Evidently she wasn't frightened enough. "Yes, we'll call Devlin. I need to talk to him."

* * *

"Talk to me," Royd said as soon as he got on the freeway. "What do you think Sanborne is up to? You said he didn't want your head in a basket."

"Oh, I'm sure he will eventually. Just not now." She frowned, trying to remember the words and nuances of that conversation. "He was actually trying to convince me to join his goon squad. Lord, can you imagine the ego of the man? I was supposed to just ignore everything he's done?"

"It's not ego. I've been studying him since before I broke away from Garwood. Sanborne has something missing in his psyche."

"Conscience?"

"Not even that. He doesn't have emotion as most people perceive it. He pretends but he doesn't get it. He's clever, he has an appreciation of beauty, and he enjoys the sense of power, but he doesn't really understand the pain and hatred he causes because he doesn't feel it himself. Since he does understand a thirst for power, he probably doesn't really see why you wouldn't put aside whatever he's done to hurt you if he offered you enough." He shrugged. "You're the doctor. You probably know the technical words for it."

"You did very well." It made sense. She had been so full of hatred and guilt that she had never tried to analyze Sanborne. She had just wanted to rid the world of him and REM-4. Yet when she thought about all her encounters with Sanborne she could see the signs. "And that's why he has no compunction about using REM-4 like this."

"My guess. Of course, he could just be a complete son of a bitch. It doesn't matter to me. I tried to learn what he was so I could have a better shot at destroying him. I don't care if he's a sicko. I'm not going to cure him. I'm going to take him down." He paused. "But why is he pushing you now? You told me he'd tried to persuade you before but after you turned him down, he set his dogs on you. Now all of a sudden he's backtracking. He could have been just trying to stall you while he tried to locate us. You're certain you read him right?"

"How can I be certain?" But she was almost sure, she realized. And there had to be a reason. "Gorshank."

"What?"

"I told you that the equations were brilliant

but I couldn't understand how he reached some of his results."

"You said you needed time to study them."

"But what if his work was faulty? What if it had a few giant holes in it?"

"Then they'd need to plug those holes and fast. By pulling in a scientist who knew the primary formula."

She nodded. "And they need that more than they need to get rid of me permanently. It's only a supposition but it makes—"

Her phone rang. "Shall I answer it?"

"If you get off quick."

She pressed the button.

"Gorshank is in Charlotte, North Carolina," MacDuff said. "Three twenty-one Ivy Street."

She put the phone on speaker so that Royd could hear. "How did they find him?"

"He transferred a large amount of money to a Russian bank to pay off a debt to the Mafia. Jock and I will make a connection at Kennedy and head directly to Charlotte."

"When will you get there?"

"Another seven hours."

Royd was shaking his head. "If Gorshank's on the hot seat that could be too long. There's not much difference, but maybe we can beat

that. We'll call you when we've made contact."
He hung up the phone before MacDuff could
argue. "We'll head for Daytona. We'll catch a
flight out of there for Charlotte."

"Hot seat?"

"If Sanborne believes Gorshank isn't per-
forming to his satisfaction, then he'll have no
more use for him."

"And he'll be a liability and a threat." Sophie took it a step farther. "Like all the other
scientists connected to the project that he
fired and then presumably sent hit men to finish off." Her gaze flew to Royd's face. "It may
be too late."

Royd nodded. "We've got to hope that Sanborne is keeping Gorshank alive until he finds
a way to get hold of you. He must have had
some confidence in him or he wouldn't have
put him on the payroll."

She shook her head skeptically. "I don't
know. Sanborne is totally ruthless. Everything
is black or white to him. If he thinks Gorshank
has been stringing him along, he's not going to
let him have a second chance."

"Then we may be going on a wild-goose
chase." Royd's foot pressed the accelerator.
"But I'm not going to miss a chance at gathering in Gorshank. He has to know where the is-

land is located and maybe about some of the defenses surrounding it." His lips tightened. "If he's alive, he'll talk."

Three twenty-one Ivy Street was set back from the road and surrounded by poplar trees that shaded the porch of the small gray clapboard building. The house was dark but there was a flickering light in the room left of the door that must have originated from a TV set. Gorshank had become an avid television fan since he'd arrived in the States. When he wasn't at his desk in the office, he was parked in front of the set, watching **The Simpsons** or **CSI** or any number of other programs.

Devlin had studied the surveillance reports on Gorshank that Sanborne had given him but it wasn't really necessary. The scientist was a man of ingrained habit and a multitude of self-indulgences that made him pitifully vulnerable. Too vulnerable. Devlin had been impatient when Sanborne had sent him here when he could have gone after Royd. Now that would have been a challenge.

But he had to keep a low profile after the feast at MacDuff's Run. No arguments or even attempts at manipulation for a little while. Besides, killing a fool like Gorshank would be a pleasure. Fools annoyed him.

He would check out the doors and find a way to enter the house. Gorshank would be sitting in his chair with his can of beer and Devlin would be on him before he realized what was happening. He'd decide once he had him helpless if he wanted to dispatch him quickly or take his time.

It was going to be a piece of cake.

"Stay here." Royd pulled the car to the curb. "Let me check the place out."

Sophie gazed at the flickering light coming through the front window of the house. It was a sight that was common to half the homes in this city. Nothing to fear.

Then why was she tensing as if that light from the TV were some kind of omen? "I'm coming with you." She held up her hand as he started to protest. "I'm not going to get in your way. Jock always told me that was a stupid thing to do. If you want me to wait outside, that's what I'll do. But I have the gun that Jock always had me carry and I know how to use it. I'm going to be within calling distance."

He didn't speak for a moment and then

shrugged. "Come, then." He opened the car door. "But wait until I scout around the grounds." He was gone only five minutes and was opening the car door for her. "It's clear, but you stay outside and you don't come in. Right?"

"Unless you call." She got out of the car. "And it could happen, Royd. You're not invulnerable."

"I try." He moved toward the side of the house. "The back door."

"We could just go up to the front door and knock. He doesn't know us. Is that too easy?"

"He might have been shown photos of you since he took over your work." He was moving quickly. "But you're right. I never think of the easy way. It wasn't the way I was taught." He stopped at the back door and listened, his gaze moving over the backyard. "And I don't think this is going to be a situation that's going to teach me to change my ways."

She could sense the tension that was electrifying him. "What's wrong?"

"Someone should be watching Gorshank if he's important to Sanborne and knows about REM-4. Where are they? I expected to be intercepted or at least spot someone." He paused. "Unless they've been pulled off because it's no longer necessary."

She shivered. "You mean if Gorshank's dead."

He didn't answer. "Stay out here. I'll leave the door cracked open." He bent over the lock and gave a low whistle. "Jesus." He straightened. "Draw that gun and keep it handy. This lock's already been jimmied." He opened the door and disappeared into the house.

Her hand closed on the gun in her handbag. Her heart was beating hard, fast. She found herself straining to hear something, anything from inside the house. Minutes passed, no, they crawled by. Dammit, she felt useless. If something happened to Royd, how would she be able to help him standing out here like a bump on a log?

Cool it. Jock had said that was how deadly mistakes were made. Too many cooks in the kitchen. What a trite, cozy expression for a situation so deadly.

She heard something.

A breath of sound, a footstep . . .

Where? In the kitchen?

No, not in the kitchen.

Behind her.

Thank God the house was small. It hadn't taken Royd long to go through it and make sure there was no one lying in wait. Now to check out the living room, where Gorshank was watching his TV. He moved silently down the stairs and across the hall. He had a clear view of both the TV and Gorshank from the doorway.

CSI was playing on the television.

But Gorshank was not watching it.

Royd paused in the doorway, his gaze on the chair facing the television set.

Ropes bound Gorshank to the chair and he was staring blindly at the flickering screen. He was gagged, his lids had been pinned open by staples and he had been castrated.

Christ. It had to be Devlin.

After checking the room, he glided toward the chair.

Dead. But it hadn't been long. The blood was still flowing from the final knife wound in his chest.

Okay, Gorshank was useless to them. But maybe he'd left some record, some clue that would help them. It wasn't likely. Devlin was usually very careful when it came to cleaning up a job.

But he had taken a long time with Gorshank and only finished him off a short while ago.

He stiffened. How short a time? Had he

been interrupted? Royd had checked out the rest of the house before he'd approached Gorshank and it had seemed neat and orderly. Not as if someone had gone through it searching for anything incriminating.

What if he'd heard Royd and Sophie on the porch, finished Gorshank, and then escaped through one of the windows? None of the front-facing windows was open.

The windows leading to the backyard? It was—

Then he heard the shot.

A gleam of metal in the hand of the man leaping toward her!

Sophie lifted her gun and fired it as she fell to the ground.

She heard the thunk of the bullet as it struck the man.

He stopped in his tracks, his face twisting with pain. "Bitch."

And then kept on coming.

She rolled to one side and shot again.

Missed.

Aim, Jock had told her. Don't get flustered. Make sure the shot counts.

How could she take time to aim when he

was coming toward her? It had to be Devlin. He was staggering, moving slowly, but the creepy bastard had a bullet in his chest and he didn't seem to feel it. And the look on his face . . .

"Bitch. Whore." His tone was dripping malevolence. "You can't hurt me. Your hand is shaking and you're scared silly. But I can hurt you in all kinds of ways. Do you think the kid is safe? Franks will be able to pluck the boy from the police easy as pie. Sanborne said I couldn't be the one to take the boy. I was too unstable. I might destroy his best card. He's right. But you've made me mad so I think I'll step in and see how the boy likes how I—"

She aimed. She wouldn't miss this time.

She didn't get the chance.

Royd's arm snaked around Devlin's neck from behind. "Go to hell, Devlin." He broke his neck.

Sophie heard the crack and then saw Devlin's eyes glaze over. Royd let him go and he fell in a lifeless heap on the steps.

Royd was beside her, falling to his knees. "Are you okay?"

No, she wasn't okay. She could still see the expression on Devlin's face and she probably would for the rest of her life. Evil . . .

She nodded jerkily. "I'm not hurt. But I shot him and he kept on coming. It was like something from a **Frankenstein** movie."

"You shouldn't be surprised. I told you Devlin had a high pain tolerance. And you knew what he did at the croft."

"Seeing him . . . was different." Stop shaking. She mustn't be this weak. Devlin was dead. She had to pull herself together.

"Let go." Royd's voice was rough but his grasp was blessedly gentle as he pulled her into his arms. "He's not going to hurt you. He's not going to hurt anyone again." His hand was pressing her head into the hollow of his shoulder. "And he was no mythical Frankenstein monster, so I don't want you letting him haunt you. I brought him down, and if I hadn't been here, you would have killed the son of a bitch yourself."

Her arms tightened around him. "Yes, I would. I had to do it. He was talking about Michael. . . ." She suddenly stiffened. "I think he was talking about Sanborne sending someone after Michael. Franks, he called him. He said that Michael could be plucked from the police with no trouble. Devlin was sent here instead."

"The police . . ." His tone was thoughtful.

"The only way the police could become in-volved is if they took Michael from the castle and held him for extradition to the States."

"But Scotland Yard didn't push for a search of the castle when we were there."

"MacDuff can be very persuasive. But San-borne must have found a way to bribe some-one pretty high up to make the move."

She pushed herself away from him. "I have to call Jane and warn them."

"They knew it was a possibility, Sophie. They're already prepared."

"Don't tell me that," she said fiercely. "They don't know that someone is on the way to get him."

"You're right." He pulled her to her feet. "Come into the kitchen and away from Devlin and make your call. I have to search through Gorshank's desk."

Gorshank. She'd almost forgotten him in the emotional turmoil of the past few minutes. "Is he dead?"

He nodded. "We must have almost caught Devlin in the act." He pushed her inside the door. "Make your call. We have to hurry. Someone might have heard those shots."

"Then the police will be on their way."

"Not necessarily. You'd be surprised how

many people choose to ignore neighborhood violence. They don't want to be involved. They prefer to think it's some kids setting off fire-crackers." He headed for the hall. "But just in case there's a conscientious soul out there, we'll hurry."

He disappeared from view.

She dropped down in the kitchen chair and drew a deep breath. Perhaps she should turn on a light. It was dark in the kitchen. But it had been darker outside facing Devlin. Twisted and ugly and dark. Death out there on the porch. Death in the next room. Don't think about it. Think about what she had to do.

No, it would be better not to turn on the lights. She could see well enough to speed-dial the number of MacDuff's Run. She pulled out her phone.

"Calm down. I know you're scared. You have a right to be." Jane had listened to Sophie with-out interrupting. "Bastards."

"Warn Campbell to be on the alert. I'll be there as soon as I can."

"Wait a minute. Let me think." Jane was silent a moment. "No, don't come. I'm bring-ing Michael back to the States."

"What?"

"If Sanborne manages to get the local police to come in and get Michael for extradition, the chances are that his men will be able to get their hands on him. We won't be able to protect him. Hell, we may not even be able to find out where he is." Her voice was filled with frustration. "Where the devil is MacDuff when we need him?"

"On the way here."

"Well, I'm not counting on him being able to pull strings from long distance. I'll take care of it myself."

"You can't leave the castle. You'll be seen."

"There's a way out. I've used it before."

"Jane, I don't like it."

"I know. The idea of stone walls around Michael is very comforting," Jane said gently. "But he'll be safe where we're going. Joe will have every cop on the force keeping an eye on him."

"Atlanta?"

"It will give him the greatest security. Trust me, Sophie. In this world, stone walls can be too easily breached by money and political pull. We need Michael out."

"Maybe if we call MacDuff, he can—" She was reaching for any way that wouldn't put

Michael into danger even for a moment. Jane was right. The image of stone walls was very comforting. "I have to think about it. I'll call you back."

"Not too long." Jane hung up.

"Come on." Royd was coming through the door. "We should get out of here."

She nodded and rose to her feet. "Did you find anything?"

"I think so." He was pulling her past Devlin's body sprawled on the steps. "And I called MacDuff and told him to get his friends with the CIA out here to get rid of Devlin. We may not want Sanborne to know he's dead yet." His gaze was on her face. "What's happening with Michael?"

"Jane wants to take Michael back to Atlanta. She says she can get him out of the castle without being noticed." She tried to keep her voice steady. "I'm scared."

"Did you give her the go-ahead?"

She shook her head. "I have to—"

"If you trust her, tell her to move." He opened the car door for her. "I don't like the idea of the government becoming mixed up with Michael. When there's red tape involved, it's too easy to get to someone being held supposedly for their own safety."

"You seem very sure. Have you done it?"

"Once. Syria." He got into the driver's seat. "But you don't want to hear about that." He started the car. "Any more than I want to tell you."

No, she didn't want to hear how easy it was to reach someone surrounded by police or military. And she didn't want to visualize Royd being the one to do it. Twice she had watched him kill men and there had been a frightening sleek efficiency about every action. Yet she had to ask. "Sanborne?"

"No, it was when I was in the SEALs. Call Jane back and tell her to get Michael out of there."

"Have you heard of this Franks?"

"Simon Franks. Not as good as Devlin, but he knows what he's doing." He paused. "And he'll do whatever Sanborne tells him. He's not like Devlin. He's a drone."

"Christ."

"That may not be a bad thing. He wouldn't cut Michael's throat unless he was ordered to do it. Devlin would do it for the pleasure and then worry about making it right with Sanborne later."

"I can't believe we're sitting here talking about those men killing my son." Her voice was shaking. "You may not have any feeling for Michael but it's a little more difficult for—"

"Who said I didn't have any feeling for the kid?" Royd asked roughly. "I like him. I don't love him. I haven't had the chance to get to know him that well and love doesn't come easy to me. I'd be lying if I told you anything different. But don't treat me as if I were still the numb retard I was when I left Garwood." His hands tightened on the steering wheel. "I'm feeling too damn much these days."

She had hurt him, she realized. She hadn't thought she had the ability to give Royd pain. He was too tough. The callousness had been ingrained over the years. Or had it? She was constantly discovering something new about Royd. "I didn't mean to imply that you—"

"Forget it," Royd said. "I just wanted you to know that the only reason I'm telling you about Franks is not to scare you but to let you know what you're up against." He pulled into the Wal-Mart parking lot. "I told MacDuff we'd meet him here. If you're going to make your call to Jane, you can do it while we're waiting."

"Bully."

His lips twisted. "It goes with the territory."

She hesitated. God, she didn't want to

make that call. Stop being a coward. Do what was best for Michael. She quickly dialed the number.

Ten rings. No answer.

Her heart was beating hard, her hand was shaking as she dialed again.

No answer.

17

The headlights of several vehicles speared the darkness as they approached Mac-Duff's Run. They were still far away but moving fast.

"Ten or fifteen minutes," Joe said as he turned away from the window back to Jane. "It looks as though Sophie was right about them trying for extradition."

"What else could they do with a defenseless child?" Jane asked. "And since the scumbag who told Sophie had a bullet in him I don't believe he'd have much reason to lie."

"No." He rose to his feet. "And that means that we move."

Jane felt a surge of relief. "You agree?"

"I've seen too many prisoners chopped by other prisoners not to know that no security house is entirely safe." He jerked on his jacket. "And Sanborne has enough money to play God." He started for the door. "We'll take over now. It will be a relief to be back on home turf."

"Thanks, Joe."

"Don't thank me. You know I didn't want you involved with MacDuff again. I had to come to make sure that nothing happened to you."

"Liar. You didn't want anything to happen to a child."

He shrugged. "That too. And Eve would never have forgiven me if I'd turned my back on either of you. I'll meet you downstairs in fifteen minutes. Go get Michael. I'll talk to Campbell and tell him to stall."

Jane flew up the stairs and threw open the door to Michael's room. "Michael, wake up." She gently shook him. "We have to go."

He opened sleepy eyes. "Mom?" He stiffened as he recognized Jane. "Is Mom okay?"

"She's fine. I just talked to her. But we've got to get out of here." She went to his closet and threw jeans and a shirt at him. "Hurry. Joe says we have to be out of here right away."

"Why?" But he was throwing on his clothes with the speed of light. "I thought we were going to stay for—"

"I did too." She was tossing clothes into his backpack. That would have to do. She glanced out the window. The headlights were closer. She hoped Joe's estimate was correct. "It didn't work out that way. If we want to keep your mom safe, we have to keep you safe. And that means doing what we have to do." She opened the door and jerked her head. "Come on. We've got to travel. Joe's waiting."

He was racing down the stairs. "In the car?"

She ran after him. It was difficult to keep up, she thought ruefully. She'd forgotten how fast a young boy could move. "No, we're not taking the car."

He glanced over his shoulder, puzzled. "No? How?"

She lowered her voice melodramatically. "You'll see. A secret passage. Isn't that exciting?"

His eyes widened. "Really?"

Michael might be old for his years but the lure of the mysterious obviously appealed to him. What boy wouldn't be intrigued?

"Really. But you've got to be quiet and do everything I say." At the landing, she glanced out the window. The lights were closer. Damn.

She passed Michael and grabbed his hand. She flung open the door. Joe was standing talking with Campbell in the courtyard.

"About time," Joe said grimly. "Get going, Campbell. Stall and give us at least five minutes. I hope to God that's enough time."

Sophie tried to call MacDuff four times after she failed to reach Jane.

He wasn't answering either, dammit.

"What the hell's happening?" She dialed Jock. He didn't pick up.

Panic was soaring through her. "What if they picked up Michael? I should have told Jane to get him out."

"Easy," Royd said. "MacDuff and Jock should be here any time now."

"Then why isn't someone answering? So much for technology." She dialed Jane again. Her hand clenched on the phone. "It's turned off. No voice mail. The damn thing's turned off."

"That doesn't mean that she didn't do it herself for a good reason."

"I know that."

MacDuff pulled into Wal-Mart twenty minutes later and Sophie was across the parking lot before Jock and he could get out of the car.

"Why didn't you answer your phone? Do you know what's happening at the castle?"

"The answer to the first question is that I was busy. I had some calls to make. The answer to the second question is there's nothing happening at the castle right now." MacDuff opened the car door and got out. "Except there are a number of very frustrated officials streaming over my property trying to find your son."

"They won't do it, Sophie," Jock said gently as he got out of the passenger seat. "Jane has him safely out of the castle and heading for the airfield outside Aberdeen."

Sophie felt dizzy with relief. "You talked to her?"

"We had no choice." MacDuff grimaced. "As soon as she got the boy a safe distance away she was on the phone blistering me for going off when she needed help to get away from my 'crumbling heap of a castle.' Then she ordered me to arrange transport to Atlanta and make sure the boy was properly guarded until he got on the plane."

"Could you do that?"

"That's why we were on the phone," Jock said. "It took a few calls and a little arranging but we set it up." He checked his watch. "They should be boarding a plane in about ninety minutes. I'll be called the minute the plane takes off."

"Good." Her knees felt weak and she leaned against the car. That ninety minutes would seem like forever. "Atlanta. That's so close to here. Do you suppose I could see him?"

"Maybe. Let's think about it," Royd said from behind her.

"I want to see him." Her gaze flew to his face. "You think he'll still be in danger?"

He didn't answer the question directly. "I believe Franks won't give up. Sanborne won't let him give up." He turned to MacDuff. "Did you get rid of Devlin's body?"

He nodded. "That was one of the calls I made. They're sending the local boys to take care of the cleanup."

"No problem?"

"Devlin had a long record even before Sanborne tapped him for Garwood. They're willing to cooperate for the present. The CIA is very leery of what happened to those men who'd been brainwashed at Thomas Reilly's compound, where Jock was kept before being sent to Garwood. They don't want a bunch of suicide bombers running all over the U.S. . . . ." He paused. "Why do you want Devlin to just disappear?"

"It may be better if Sanborne doesn't know that we found out about Gorshank."

"Why?"

"It could buy us time. If we don't know about Gorshank, we couldn't know about the papers I found in Gorshank's desk."

"Papers?"

"Diagrams of a water-purifying installation." He smiled. "On an island called San Torrano, off the coast of Venezuela."

"You did find it," Jock murmured. "Hot damn."

"Do you still want to go after Sanborne? Devlin was your target and he's dead."

"And I'm not pleased you cheated me out of killing the bastard," MacDuff said grimly. "And hell yes, I want to go after Sanborne. He sent Devlin to kill and maim and then managed to turn the police of my own country against me." His lips tightened. "And I don't like the idea of anyone trampling over my property. They can just stay away from Mac-Duff's Run."

"There's your answer." Jock's gaze was narrowed on Royd's face. "And I have a hunch that you already have an idea as to how you want to use us."

"I wouldn't presume."

"The hell you wouldn't."

He shrugged. "I do have a glimmer of an idea but I have to think about it for a while. There are a few factors that are turning me off."

"What factors?" When Royd didn't answer, Jock's gaze shifted to Sophie and rested there for a moment. He slowly nodded. "Okay. Let us know as soon as you decide."

"I will." He took Sophie's elbow and nudged her toward their car. "In the meantime, keep Sophie up to date on Michael."

"Absolutely."

"What factors?" Sophie asked. "Stop being so damn enigmatic. If you know a way to go after Sanborne, tell me."

"I intend to tell you." He grimaced. "Bastard that I am, there wasn't really any doubt about that." He opened the passenger door for her. "But not yet. I have to call Kelly and tell him to expect us down there right away. And then we wait until we know that Michael is safe."

She watched the glow of the red taillights of MacDuff and Jock's car disappear around the corner. "What are you up to, Royd?"

"What I've been up to since Garwood." He dialed Kelly on his phone. "Nothing new. Using everyone. Risking everyone. All for the sake of bringing down Sanborne and Boch." He spoke into the phone. "We're taking a flight out of Atlanta. Get the launch ready and find out everything you can about an island called San Torrano." He hung up.

"I've never heard of San Torrano," Sophie said.

"It's probably the size of a postage stamp. Boch and Sanborne wouldn't want to use an island that was well known." He started the car. "The smaller, the better."

"We're going to Atlanta? I can see Michael?"

"Why ask me? There's no way I could keep you away from him."

"I meant it's safe for me to see him?"

"God knows."

"Royd, what the devil is wrong with you? You're being an ass."

"What's wrong with me? I've been remembering you lying on the steps of that house with Devlin coming at you."

She frowned. "Why? It was horrible but it's over. I wouldn't think you'd be one to dwell on the past."

"Are you nuts?" he asked harshly. "What else are we doing? We can't move forward because we're stuck in the mire. Only this time you were almost sucked down in the quicksand. I should pull you out on safe ground and walk away from you."

She looked away from him. "You did pull me out. You might have saved my life. And if you want to walk away I can't stop you. But I'll follow you. We're coming too close."

He was silent a moment. "And I'd let you." He pressed on the accelerator. "Now be quiet and let me plan how I'm going to risk your neck this time."

"Did they get hold of the boy?" Boch asked.

"Not yet," Sanborne said. "They weren't at the castle. But Franks has questioned one of MacDuff's men and found out who was taking care of him. It won't be long."

"Stop fooling around and just have Franks kill her," Boch said harshly. "We can go with the REM-4 we have on hand."

"It's too chancy. Can't you see the situation has changed? I'm not going to risk my investment with an inferior product when I can solve the problem."

"I need a foolproof demonstration and we only have a week."

"It will be enough time. No one knows REM-4 like Sophie Dunston, and Gorshank's initial experiments were successful. He just couldn't follow through."

"And tried to cheat us."

"That's been taken care of. We should be hearing from Devlin at any time." He was tired of soothing Boch. "I have to go now. I have a few things to wrap up before I catch my flight for the island tomorrow. When will you be there?"

"Two days. Why are you going down so soon?"

"I have to be on site when we get the woman. I'll be in touch when Franks gets his hands on the boy." He hung up.

And they would get Sophie Dunston. She would come meekly when he had the boy. Women seemed to have a weakness where their children were concerned. It always filled him with wonder. Even his own mother had possessed that weakness. Until she had started to shy away from him when he was a teenager. Shortly after her desertion he had learned to pretend that warmth that was so important to everyone around him, but it was too late to bring her back under his power. She had avoided him until the day she died.

Not that it mattered. She had taught him a

lesson about human nature and women in particular.

And that would be very valuable in dealing with Sophie Dunston.

Royd's phone rang when he and Sophie had almost reached Joe Quinn's lake cottage outside Atlanta. It was MacDuff.

"Campbell just called." His voice was taut with anger. "Charlie Kedrick, one of his men, was picked up in the village. Presumably by Franks or one of his men. He's dead."

"Shit."

"And it wasn't an easy death. They tortured him. Whatever they wanted to know, he probably told them. It wasn't much but he knew Jane MacGuire's name and who she was. She'd been at the castle before. That means that they're probably tracking down Jane and the boy right now."

"How long do we have?"

"It depends how quick Franks moves."

"He's going to feel as if he has egg on his face, so he's going to try to make amends with Sanborne."

"Then you'll be lucky if you have more than a few hours. Where are you?"

"On the way to the lake cottage. You said that Michael should be here soon."

"And so should Franks. Stay where you are. Jock and I will be there in about forty minutes."

"No, I'm not going to risk Sophie that close to Franks and his men. It could be a bloodbath." He made a U-turn. "I'm turning around and heading for the airport."

"No!" Sophie grabbed his arm. "What's happening?"

He didn't answer her. "You go to the lake cottage, MacDuff. Tell Jock I'll call him right back." He hung up and told Sophie, "Franks has found out that Michael is with Jane and he knows who she is. That means that he may be on his way here soon."

"Then what the hell do you mean you're not risking me? I'm not going to go off and leave Michael now. Turn around and go back."

"After I talk to you." He pulled to the side of the road. "Then if you still want to go to the lake cottage, I'll take you. Will you listen?"

"I want to go to—" She stopped. "I'll listen. Hurry."

"We have an opportunity here." He looked straight ahead. "We need to get on San Torrano and find a way to destroy the installation and REM-4. Boch is no fool. He'll have security all over the island."

"So?"

"We need an inside man." His lips twisted. "Or should I say 'inside woman.'"

She went still. "What are you saying?"

"Sanborne wants to get his hands on you. That's why he's after Michael. I'm saying I want to hand you to those bastards on a silver platter." He closed his eyes. "May God forgive me."

Shock jolted through her. "I don't—" She stared at him in bewilderment.

He opened his eyes. "What do you expect of me? I've told you before I'm neither kind nor civilized. You practically offered yourself on the sacrificial altar." His knuckles turned white as his hands clenched on the steering wheel. "Why wouldn't I take you up on it?"

There was so much pain and bitterness in those words that they hurt her to hear them. "You make me sound as if I were a psycho. Stop beating yourself up and talk to me."

He was silent a moment and then the faintest smile touched his lips. "You may feel like beating me up yourself."

"I won't know until you stop mumbling and come out with it."

"Okay." His voice was brusque. "The bottom line is that we need you on the island. MacDuff and I can handle the destruction of the treatment plant, but we need information as to where the disks on REM-4 are kept. It's not going to do any good to get rid of those vats of REM-4 if Sanborne has the means to make more."

"I've always known that." She tried to smile. "You want me to be another Nate Kelly."

"Kelly can't do this. Neither can I."

"You want me to pretend to join Sanborne? He won't believe me. I've turned him down too many times. And even if he lets me go to the island, he won't trust me."

"He doesn't trust anyone. But under certain conditions he'd allow you a greater amount of freedom."

"What conditions?"

"If he thought he had power over you." He was silent a moment. "If he thought he could kill your son, if you didn't do what he wanted."

Her eyes widened in horror. "You want me to let him take Michael?"

"God, no," he said harshly. "I may be a son of a bitch but I wouldn't— I said if he **thought** he could kill Michael."

"And why would he think that?"

"Because I've worked out a way to make him believe it."

"How?"

"I'll go into the details later. What's important to you is that I'd make sure that Michael is safe. You have my word on it."

She felt sick and scared. "You've said that before."

"He's still alive, Sophie."

"I know. Tell me those details."

"I tell Jock to set a trap for Franks and his men. Jock captures Franks and then we make Sanborne think that Franks has Michael."

"It sounds very . . . simple. It's not simple."

"No, but we can do it."

Try to think clearly. Clearly? Her mind was a jumble of possibilities and none of them very optimistic. She gazed out into the darkness. "This could help end it, couldn't it? It could be over at last. It's the quickest way to get to them. It gives us our best shot."

"Yes," he said hoarsely. "The quickest and the best."

"And you can make it work, Royd?"

"I'll make it work."

She was silent again. "Then let's do it."

He started to curse.

Her gaze shifted to his face. "Isn't that what you wanted?"

"No." He pulled back out into the road. "I wanted you to tell me to go to hell. I wanted you to accuse me of trying to get you killed and tell me not to mention it again."

She was taken aback at the torment in his expression. "And let you off the hook? This is your idea. You can't have it all ways, Royd."

"I'm not shifting the responsibility. I knew exactly what I was doing. And I'm not off the hook. But it feels more like a crucifix." He stomped on the accelerator and reached for his phone. "I have to call Jock back."

What the hell?

Sanborne frowned as he tore open the Priority Mail envelope with Sol Devlin's name in the return-address box.

Sir,

You must realize by now how well I performed the task you set me. I've enclosed the San Torrano documents I retrieved from Gorshank's house that I knew would be important to you.

I'm sure you want me to get on with ridding you of Royd now. He's a danger to you and you have to be protected. I'll report as soon as the situation is resolved.

Devlin

Sanborne muttered a curse as he dropped the letter on the desk. It was just like Devlin to not phone him but go straight on the hunt so that he could not immediately object. It was yet another sign of a deplorable lack of true obedience. What if Sanborne had decided not to kill Royd? What if he'd wanted to send Devlin as backup for Franks in Atlanta? Franks had been staking out the lake cottage since yesterday evening, waiting for the opportunity to strike.

No, Devlin was too unstable to work with anyone. It was just as well he was busy tracking down Royd. It would be to his advantage to take out Sophie Dunston's protector.

But that didn't keep Sanborne from being annoyed with Devlin's independence. He'd have a stern word with him when he came running to him for praise after he'd accomplished his mission.

* * *

Barbados

"Is it done?" Sophie asked. "Is Michael safe?"

"Not quite," Royd said. "But soon. Everything is going well, Sophie. Sanborne left his office this morning for points unknown."

"I don't care about Sanborne right now. I want this done and Michael safe."

Royd's phone rang. "MacDuff." He answered the phone. "Good." He hung up and stood up. "It's a go. Let's get moving."

San Torrano

"I have the boy," Franks said when Sanborne picked up the receiver. "What do you want me to do with him?"

"Was he hurt?"

"Bruises."

"Good. Where are you?"

"Still at the lake cottage." He paused. "I had to kill the woman and her father and two other men who were with them. Is that all right?"

"If it was necessary. How safe are you at that cottage?"

"It's isolated. I can see anyone approaching from the road."

"Then stay there for a while. If the situation changes, let me know."

"How do I treat the boy?"

"No more bruises. I want you to make a DVD and I don't want the boy to be in too bad shape." He hung up the phone and went to stand at the end of the pier to gaze out at the **Constanza** anchored offshore. Everything was going splendidly. For a few days he'd been a little worried, but he should have known that Franks would persevere. After he got through with this business tonight he'd get great pleasure out of calling Sophie Dunston.

He waved at Captain Sonanz on the bridge. "Welcome to San Torrano," he shouted. "I hope you had a pleasant journey. If you'll start to unload, you can have it done by nightfall and we'll have dinner and drinks." He smiled. "Give your men shore leave and bring your officers with you."

Barbados

Sophie was on the launch Kelly had leased when the call came from Sanborne.

"You've survived much longer than I thought you could," Sanborne said. "How lucky that you joined forces with Royd. I'm sure he's been a great help to you." He paused. "But it's time you parted ways. You'll be much safer away from Royd now. Devlin is after him and he doesn't recognize the concept of innocent bystanders."

"Go to hell."

"Don't be disrespectful. It's not a fitting way for an employee to treat her boss."

"You're having a case of déjà vu."

"No, I thought it time I gathered you back in the fold. I've been a little impatient of your arrogance. I was kind enough to offer you a wonderful opportunity and you threw it back in my face. Now you have to be punished."

"What are you talking about, Sanborne?"

"Your son. I believe Michael is his name."

Her hand tightened on the phone. "I won't listen to threats. My son is safe."

"Your son is only as safe as I want him to be. Get on a plane and come to Caracas. I'll meet you there."

"I'm not going anywhere near you."

"I'll give you one day. I'm pressed for time. I'm sending a DVD to your name at a post-office box in Caracas. Don't be upset by the bruises on the poor boy." He hung up.

"He wants me to go to Caracas." She turned to Royd. "He says he's going to send me a DVD of Michael. He said that I mustn't be upset at the bruises." She shivered. "Bastard."

"But you are upset. Why? You know it's not true."

"He was so smug." She moistened her lips. "So certain. I almost believed him." She stood up and walked toward the rail. "It's starting, Royd."

"Yes." He moved forward to stand beside her. "You can back out."

"No, I can't." She gazed out at the sea. "Tell me about San Torrano. What did Kelly find out about it?"

"It's a tiny island off the coast of Venezuela. It used to be a possession of Venezuela, but it's now listed as privately owned by a Canadian corporation. You can bet if we sifted through the paperwork we'd find Sanborne as the bottom line. The population is less than five thousand, mostly of Indian descent, principal occupation fishing. The children rarely make it through more than a few years of elementary school before starting to work."

"The water-treatment plant?"

"It's sixty years old and was built by the Venezuelan government when there was a cholera epidemic. It almost wiped out the whole population. The treatment plant serves the entire island and the natives are very cautious about drinking any water other than what comes out of their taps."

"So if they drop REM-4 into that water they instantly have five thousand test subjects. Men, women, children . . ." She shook her head. "Charming."

"It won't happen."

"God, I hope not. Where is this treatment plant?"

"According to Gorshank's diagram and notes it's about two miles from the west coast of the island. I can scuba to the coast and get to the plant to set the explosives. But we have to make sure that all the vats are in the plant and destroyed." He paused. "You'll have to be the one to find that out for us. Along with finding out the location of the REM-4 disks. The moment you do, I'll come in and get you out of there."

"And if we destroy the plant, we risk exposing those people to cholera again."

"And if we don't they're going to drink REM-4 and we don't know what effect that

will have on them. It's virtually untested. I'm
sure Gorshank's orders didn't stress safety over
effectiveness."

"I'm sure of that too. Gorshank's formula
was very strong." She frowned. "I don't know.
It's a catch-22."

"Which risk would you rather run?"

"Cholera." The answer came instantly. "We
don't know what kind of mind damage REM-
4 might cause in this form. But maybe I can
find a way of destroying the vats without blowing the plant."

"Don't risk it. They'll be watching you. As
long as they think they have a hold on you,
they'll give you a certain amount of freedom.
But if you arouse suspicion, they'll put you
down."

Her lips tightened. "I have to see if there's
another way. Don't worry, I won't jeopardize
you or anyone else."

"That's almost funny. You're the one who'll
be walking the tightrope."

"Then let me do it my way. And I'm not the
one who'll get killed if they catch you on the
beach or during your trek those two miles to
the plant. You're much more vulnerable than I
am." She shrugged wearily. "It doesn't matter.
We'll get it done. One way or the other. I just

have to know that Michael is safe while we're doing it." Her gaze shifted to his face. "He is safe, right?"

He looked away from her. "I told you he was safe."

"Then why can't I talk to him?" She made an impatient gesture. "Yes, I know you told me that it wasn't safe to use the phones because they might be traced, but just one call for only a moment?"

He shook his head. "Don't blow it at this stage, Sophie."

She was silent. "It's hard for me, Royd."

"Obviously." He still wasn't looking at her. "Don't you trust me?"

"I wouldn't be here if I didn't trust you."

"It's a wonder. I told you once that I'd do anything to get Sanborne and Boch. I've risked you and the boy constantly since the day we met."

"I have free will. I'm the one who set the risks." She paused. "I do trust you. Just tell me one more time that Michael is safe."

"Your son won't be hurt." He turned. "I've got to go to the bridge and tell Kelly to head for Caracas."

She watched him walk away with a feeling of unease. Ever since they'd left the U.S. he'd been too quiet, almost curt. Perhaps it was to be expected under the circumstances. She was also tense and had to control the panic that lay in wait when she thought about what was ahead. But it wasn't panic she sensed in Royd. Every now and then she caught him looking at her, watching her.

Destroying Boch and Sanborne meant everything to him. It was the obsession that drove him. Did he think she would back out?

She didn't know. He was an enigma these days, and she didn't have the energy or concentration to spend trying to decipher him. Now wasn't the time to start analyzing his every mood and move. She had told him she trusted him. She did trust him. This nervousness she was feeling had nothing to do with Royd and everything to do with the confrontation looming in the next days.

She **had** to trust him.

Caracas

She took the portable DVD player out of the envelope and snapped the DVD into the slot.

"Mom?"

She heard Michael's voice before the picture zoomed to his face.

Christ.

There was a bruise on his left cheek and his upper lip was cut and swollen. He looked terrified.

He tried to smile. "I'm okay, Mom. Don't be scared. And don't let them talk you into doing anything you don't want to do."

She could feel the tears sting her eyes.

"I've got to go." Michael was looking at someone out of her vision. "He didn't like what I said. But I meant it. Don't let them—"

The video camera was turned off and the disk ended.

She leaned against the table as waves of panic washed over her. If Michael had been acting, he deserved an Academy Award. Those bruises . . .

Trust me, Royd had said.

Damn you, Royd.

Trust me.

Don't fall apart now. He'd told her the DVD would look authentic. It had to pass inspection by Sanborne.

Bruises . . .

Her cell phone rang.

"You've had time to watch our little home movie," Sanborne said. "How did you like it?"

"You son of a bitch." She couldn't keep her voice from shaking. "He's just a little boy."

"Obviously it didn't please you. I thought the boy displayed amazing courage. You should be proud of him."

"I am proud of him. I want you to let him go."

"In good time. When the first test of REM-4 proves successful."

"Now."

"No demands. It upsets me." He paused. "Every day that you refuse to help me is a day you'll receive a video from your son. I'll start off with bruises and then advance to body parts. Do you understand?"

She felt sick. "I understand."

"That's better. I'll have one of my men pick you up at Bolivar Square at six tonight and bring you to the island. Be prompt. I don't want to have to make a phone call that would make you unhappy." He hung up.

She pressed the disconnect.

She felt frozen in place. She had to move. She had to meet Royd on the side street beside the post office. She'd come to the post office alone in case she was watched, but he had to know about the DVD and the call from Sanborne.

But she couldn't face him until she had more control of herself. She was too panicky right now. She'd give herself a minute to pull herself together.

If she trusted Royd, why was she as terrified as if she believed that horrible DVD?

Trust him. Trust him. Trust him.

18

Try to get him to let you go to the treatment plant tomorrow." Royd slowed down the car as they approached the center of Caracas. "He may want you to work at a lab in the village, but make an excuse why you need to go to the treatment plant."

"Very well."

"I'll try to set up the operation for three days from now. I'll get MacDuff and his men down here and we'll be ready to move by then. We'll hit the island at sundown. Be sure you're down at the plant. I'll go in ahead of MacDuff and Kelly and get you out first. I can't give you a wire now because you're almost sure to be searched when you reach the island. Once you're established there it should be safe. You have to be able to contact us if everything blows up on you."

Her lips twisted. "If everything blows up on me, I'll probably be blown up too. I won't need that wire."

"That's not funny," he said sharply.

"Sorry. How are you going to get this wire to me?"

"I'll place it close to the front gate of the plant. Very close to the surface so that you can just brush the earth away."

She frowned. "What are you talking about?"

"I'll plant a couple of yellow flowers that are native to the island. They're really weeds but they're pretty. Pick a couple of flowers and palm the wire. The wire will be no bigger than your thumbnail. Keep it on you at all times. If we see the situation going downhill, I'll come for you."

"That would be stupid. You'll get yourself killed. Wait until I tell you to come."

"We'll see how it goes."

"No, you wait. I'm not risking my neck without being able to call the shots."

He was silent a moment. "I'll wait. Until I can't wait any longer."

"That's not much of a concession."

"It's a hell of a concession," he said roughly. "The biggest I've ever made to anyone." He pulled over to the side of the street. "Get out. I can't go any farther or I might be seen with you. Bolivar Square is two blocks down that street up ahead. You'll have to go it alone from here."

Alone. She tried not to show him how those last words shook her. She had been expecting it. She would have fought him if he'd told her he'd changed his mind about sending her. Yet now that she was facing the separation the reality was frightening.

"Right." She tried to smile as she reached for the door handle. "Well, I guess I'll be in touch, but not before you get that damn wire to me." She got out of the car and then hesitated. "Royd, I have something to ask you."

"Ask it."

"If anything happens to me, will you take care of my son? Will you make sure he's safe and happy?"

"Oh, shit."

"Will you promise me that?"

"Nothing is going to happen to you."

"Promise me."

He was silent. "I promise."

"Thank you." She closed the door.

"Wait."

She looked back at him.

He'd rolled down the window and was staring at her with a glittering intensity that held her motionless.

"Do you remember I once told you that I'd kill for you?"

She nodded.

"Well, I've been thinking about it. And it's changed, gotten bigger." His voice was uneven. "Now I believe I'd die for you."

Before she could answer he pulled away from the curb and was driving down the street away from her.

Royd watched Sophie in the rearview mirror as she stood looking after him for a moment before turning and hurrying down the side street.

Damn. Damn. Damn.

His hands clenched on the steering wheel until he forced himself to loosen them. All he needed was to have a car wreck right now because he couldn't control himself.

She had tried to keep him from seeing it but had felt very alone and uncertain in those last moments. Who could blame her? He had deliberately thrown her into the lion's mouth.

She wouldn't suffer for it. He would see to it that she'd come out of this safe and sound.

He reached for his phone and dialed Kelly. "I've dropped her off. Meet me at the dock."

"How is she?"

"How do you expect her to be?" he asked harshly. "Gutsy, scared, and wondering if she'll come out of this alive." He hung up.

Call MacDuff. Resist the temptation to go and snatch her away before she met with Sanborne's man. Even assuming she would have come with him now that she was committed to the plan. She hadn't done this only because he'd persuaded her it was the best way to end it. At least he hoped that wasn't the only reason. He'd accused her of obsessing with guilt, but the tables were truly turned now.

He dialed MacDuff.

San Torrano

The island looked lazy and tropical and completely normal in this warm early evening, Sophie thought, as the motorboat churned through the sea toward the long pier where Sanborne waited. It was a very long pier and she had a moment of déjà vu that sent a chill through her. It had been on a pier like this that her father and mother had died and the hideous nightmare had begun.

Sanborne was a handsome man in his early fifties, with graying hair and a deep tan that made him look perfectly at home in this setting. If anything, he looked younger and more debonair than when she had worked for him. He was smiling and waved casually at her.

She felt the muscles of her stomach tense. How could he appear this affable? And why hadn't she realized what a monster he was when she had been working for him? She had never found him unpleasant during those months. Perhaps because she had been so absorbed in the work that he had never really mattered to her.

But he had mattered later. He had twisted her life and destroyed people she loved.

He strolled toward her as the speedboat pulled alongside the pier. "Sophie, my dear, together again at last." He glanced at the man driving the boat. "Any problems, Monty?"

The man shook his head. "She came alone. We weren't followed."

"Well done." He extended his hand to her. "Let me help you."

She avoided contact and jumped out of the boat. "I can manage."

"Always independent." His smile didn't waver. "I'm not accustomed to that quality anymore. Thanks to you, most of the people I deal with are meek and very self-effacing."

"That must please you."

"Oh, it does. I can't tell you the rush I get from knowing that I'm the master of all I survey."

"Why? You have everything. Money, influence. Why do you have to crush down those around you?"

"If you don't understand, I can't explain it. Boch thinks it's money and the ability to move the world. That's the urge that drives him. With me, others' subservience gives me a thrill I don't get anywhere else. Come along." He started down the pier. "I'll get you settled. I want you to start work right away."

"Where am I supposed to work?"

"I have a lab at the house I had built on the island. I brought Gorshank here once and the equipment is still in place."

"The chance of me being able to continue this Gorshank's work with any degree of speed isn't likely. First, I'll have to study his formulas and then do some experiments to see where the fallacy lies. Or perhaps the formula itself was completely impractical. It might not work no matter what adjustments I make."

"Oh, it works on a limited basis. Gorshank assured me of that, and I made a few experiments of my own since we got here."

Her gaze flew to his face. "On the natives?"

"Not yet. The crew of the **Constanza**." He glanced at the ship lying at anchor. "They needed to be eliminated anyway. We couldn't chance letting them go free. They might have talked."

"And were they 'eliminated'?"

"We lost eight of the crew the first night after they drank the water we took from the vats. It seemed to be a painful demise. We gave the captain and first mate a double dose and they died screaming. The others have been quite mellow and receptive to suggestion. We have them working in the gardens in back of the house under guard until we can judge how long that state lasts. The ideal situation would be a permanent change to the brain patterns but that's probably too much to hope for. We'll have to continue giving them doses."

His tone had been casual and matter-of-fact. He wasn't feeling anything, she realized with a shudder. "It will take time," she repeated. "I'm not experimenting on innocent people unless I'm sure that it won't harm them."

"Very laudable. But the experiments must be done." He made a face. "Boch and I disagree on exactly how extreme. I believe Boch's customers will allow a small percentage of deaths, but they want followers, not corpses. And if they use it in U.S. water supplies, they don't want any obvious signs that the supply has been contaminated. They'll want—"

"Brainless zombies for them to pick up and use when needed."

"Or perhaps for them to continue drinking the water for a year or two until it also affects future progeny."

"Babies."

"Slave obedience that starts in the womb. What a concept."

"Hideous."

"But you'll do it." He smiled at her. "Because you don't really care for those strangers. You care about your son."

"I do care about those people." She swallowed. "But I'll do as you ask. However, I want my son brought here alive and well before I finish."

"We'll discuss it after the first test."

"I'll need to analyze the water in the vats. Where are they? The treatment plant?"

"About half of them are there. We allowed the crew to stop unloading after a few hours so that we could start the experiments on them. The other half of the vats are still on the **Constanza.** But you don't need to go to the plant, you'll be brought samples at the lab."

She opened her mouth to protest and then closed it without speaking. Don't push it. "That may not be what I need, but we'll try it."

"How very obliging you are. I may reward you and let you speak to your son on the phone tonight. Would you like that?"

"Yes," she said through clenched teeth. "You know I would."

He was studying her expression with a kind of malicious curiosity. "I'll think about it." His gaze shifted to a man striding toward them. "Ah, here's my friend Boch. I'm sure you're eager to meet him."

"No."

Boch was big, well built, with close-cut brown hair and a straight, military bearing. He was brusque, cold, and had none of the false charm that Sanborne exhibited. "You've got her? Stop this inane chatting and put her to work. We're running out of time."

"You see?" Sanborne said. "Boch is a little tense. He wasn't pleased with the fatality ratio from the **Constanza**. He knew it would make me more determined to slow down. But I know you can fix the formula."

"We should give her REM-4," Boch said curtly. "We could make her work harder."

"Nothing is going to make her work harder than the ace I have. And if she dies or her thinking is blurred, it would destroy everything." He nodded at the large, columned white house ahead. "Let's get you settled in the lab with Gorshank's notes and after a few hours, we'll see if you deserve to talk to your son."

She didn't come out of the lab until nine that night. Her eyes were stinging from deciphering Gorshank's closely written hand notes as well as the computer notes and her head was whirling from the horror that had unfolded before her eyes. A guard immediately stepped in front of her.

"I want to see Sanborne."

"It's not allowed. Go back."

"I'm not doing any more work until I talk to Sanborne."

"My dear Sophie." Sanborne had come out of an adjoining room. "You have to learn that you're not to initiate actions. Things aren't like they were when you were my employee."

"You said I could talk to my son."

"If I thought you worthy. What have you accomplished? What great discovery have you made?"

"I've discovered that you hired a man with as little conscience as you have. According to those notes he did as many experiments as the Nazis did in their concentration camps."

"He said it was slow work."

"Slow work? He killed people. He drove them mad. He was very clinical about documenting their reactions. Sickeningly clinical."

"They were only tramps and homeless people. But he eventually came up with a formula that was promising." He met her gaze. "Now can you clean it up without weakening it?"

"I don't know."

"That's not what I want to hear."

"I've tried to analyze the sample of water you brought me but it's not enough. I need to go to the vats and analyze both the water and container to make sure there are no contaminants leaking into the water."

He stared at her for a moment. "That makes sense."

"Of course it does. When can I go?"

"Tomorrow."

"Now may I talk to my son?"

"You've not given me anything deserving of a reward." He smiled. "But you may need an incentive." He took out his phone and dialed a number. "Franks, she's being permitted to talk to the boy." He handed her the phone. "Not long."

"Hello," she said into the phone.

"One minute. I get him for you." The man Sanborne had called Franks had a heavy New York accent.

"Mom?"

"Yes, baby, I just wanted to tell you that I'm doing everything I can to keep you safe."

"Are you safe?"

"Yes, and soon we'll be together. Are you okay? No one is hurting you?"

"I'm okay. Don't worry about me."

"That's difficult not to—"

Sanborne had taken the phone from her. "That's all you get." He hung up the phone.

"And more than you deserve considering your lack of progress. No other contact until you start producing."

"I understand." She looked away from him. "Your man Franks has some kind of accent. . . ."

"Brooklyn, to be exact. It's very distinctive, isn't it?"

"Very distinctive." And that hadn't been Jock on the phone. Even if he'd been faking the accent she would have recognized his voice.

"He was involved with one of the gangs there before I chose him for REM-4. Now get back to the lab."

"It's after nine. I have to sleep sometime."

"You may go to your room at midnight. But I want you up early to keep on working. Boch is a bit crude but he's right about the time factor. You have to get the job done."

"I'll get it done." There was an opening here. "But I'm going to need my original notes on REM-4 to make comparisons. Do you have them on hand?"

He smiled mockingly. "Do you mean you don't have the formula memorized?"

"You know how complicated it was. I

could reconstruct it, but that would take time you don't want to give me."

"Quite right." He hesitated and then turned and went back into the library. He came out a few minutes later with a computer disk. "I want it back at the end of every day. I keep it in the safe." He handed the disk to her. "Aren't you happy I take such great care of your work?"

"I should have burned it before I let you get your hands on it." She turned back to the lab. "But if I have to do this, you'll have to cooperate with me. I can't do it alone."

"Of course I'll help. We're just one happy family here on the island."

She didn't answer as she closed the door behind her. The moment she was alone the memory of that phone call that she'd tried desperately to block out came rushing back to her.

Brooklyn accent. A voice she didn't recognize. Bruises on Michael's face.

It couldn't be true. There had to be an explanation. Royd wouldn't have let Franks take Michael to make sure that Sanborne was convinced that his hold on her was real.

I'll use you or anyone else to get Sanborne and Boch.

Oh, God.

But that was when they'd barely met. They knew each other now, they'd slept together, in many ways she felt closer to him than she did to anyone else.

Yet he'd not hesitated to send her into danger here on San Torrano.

I'd die for you.

Those last words had struck her to the heart. They'd stunned her, but in that moment she'd believed he meant what he said.

But she'd also believed him when he said he'd use anyone. She had to stop this. She was being torn to pieces by the inner conflict. In either case she would still have to survive these days on the island. She would still have to keep Sanborne content enough to not make a move on Michael. She would still have to find a way to destroy Sanborne and Boch. She was in too deep to do anything else.

She pulled Gorshank's notes closer to her and tried to concentrate. She wouldn't have put it past Sanborne to have the lab bugged. Every move she made must seem legitimate. Study the notes. Process another water sample. Block out all thought of Royd.

I'd use you or anyone . . .

* * *

Stay quiet.

Don't move.

Royd lay in the brush waiting for the sentry to pass. It would have been quicker and safer to put the guard down but he couldn't do that. No one must die tonight. Sophie must have her chance to pick up the wire without suspicion.

The sentry moved around the edge of the fence.

Royd rose and ran toward the patch of grass a yard in front of the gate. He had the plant out of his waterproof pack within seconds and a minute later it was in the ground. He spread the dry, dusty dirt he'd brought with him over the fresh-dug earth. Then he was on his feet and running back toward the brush.

He'd made sure his wet suit was dry before he'd made his move, so there would be no water trail. It would take very close examination to tell the flowers had not been growing in that spot, and weeds popped up overnight sometimes.

So swim back to the launch.

And wait for Sophie to contact them.

* * *

"There's our treatment plant." Sanborne waved at the small stucco-tile-roofed building surrounded by chain-link fence. "Not very impressive, but it will do for our purpose."

"Killing thousands of people?" Sophie asked as she got out of the car. She tried to be casual as her gaze wandered over the area. A yellow flower. Dammit, where was it?

"I told you that wasn't our intention. And if you do your job properly, you can save all those people you're so concerned about. That should make you feel very important."

There it was! Tiny scrawny yellow flowers a yard from the gate. She quickly looked away from them. "I'll do my job. I have to do it." She walked toward the gate. "Though God knows how. I'm going to need all the luck I can beg, borrow, or steal to save my son from you. I'll have to—" She stopped. "Luck. Maybe luck will be on my side after all."

"What?"

"Michael loves yellow flowers. When he was very little, he'd pick me bouquets of dandelions." She moved toward the clump of yellow flowers. "Maybe it's a sign that everything is going to go right for him." She knelt and picked the flower closest to her, using her body to block Sanborne's vision. The wire. A tiny microphone the size of her thumbnail. She palmed it and let it slip down her sleeve. "I can use a little luck."

"Yes, you can. How perceptive of you. But a weed can't help you. I'm the only one who can do that. I'm surprised a scientist would be superstitious about such things."

"I'm also a mother." She tucked the flower into the buttonhole of her shirt. "And you may have realized how desperate a mother can be about her child. Of course you have. That's why I'm here. I'll take luck or anything else that will keep him safe."

He smiled. "Keep your sentimental little token." He opened the door for her. "It's rather pitiful but I like the idea of you being that desperate. It makes me feel quite heady with power. You know, I've always wanted to enjoy that master-slave relationship with you. When we were in Amsterdam and you were so full of exhilaration and confidence, I could see that you didn't care anything about me or my opinion. You knew you were right and you were only being polite to me. It was very irritating."

"Is that why you went after my family?"

"Partly. You needed taking down a notch or two."

Anger and pain surged through her in a hot tide. "My father and mother were innocent. They didn't deserve to die."

"It's done now. Forget it. You should concentrate on the matter at hand."

Forget it? It was unbelievable that he would think that she could forget that afternoon on the pier that had shattered her life. Yet she could see that it didn't seem strange to Sanborne. "Yes, it's done now." She looked away from him. "And I assure you that I'm definitely concentrating on the matter at hand."

"Good." He opened the door of the treatment plant. "The vats are in the back area of the plant." He nodded past the huge machines. "I have to go. Tell the guard when you're ready to come back to the lab." He started to turn and glanced back at her. "This installation is very well guarded. You may have noticed. No one could get near it or out of it without my permission. If you decide your son isn't worth the risk, you might think of yourself. You're very young to die."

She watched him walk out the door. Arrogant bastard. Royd had not only gotten near the installation, he'd managed to plant the wire. She felt a surge of fierce pleasure at the thought. For the first time since she'd arrived on San Torrano she was experiencing a tingle of hope mixed with determination. Royd had broken through Sanborne's defenses. He'd made contact with her.

They could do this!

"She's wearing the wire." Kelly looked up from the monitor as Royd came into the cabin. "She picked it up about ten minutes ago." He grinned. "Right in front of Sanborne. She handled it slick as glass. Bright girl."

"She's in the installation?"

"Checking out the vats now. Sanborne isn't with her. She hasn't tried to communicate with us yet."

"She's probably being closely watched. As you said, she's very bright." He dropped down in the chair beside the desk. "She'll talk when she believes it's safe."

"Have you heard from MacDuff?"

"They're on their way. They should be here within a few hours."

"Royd."

He jumped at Sophie's voice coming from the monitor.

"I feel like I'm talking to myself. I hope to hell someone's out there listening." She paused. "I checked out this place. No cameras and I don't think it's bugged. Gorshank did all his work at the lab at the house. There wouldn't be any reason to spy on him here. I'll keep it short in case one of the guards comes in and sees me talking to myself. The records on REM-4 are kept in the safe at Sanborne's library at the house. I'll try to find a way to destroy them. I hope you managed to plant those explosives. If you didn't, you might try to get to the vats on the **Constanza**. Half the vats are still on the ship. I'm going to work on Sanborne to move the rest of the vats from the ship to here. I'll need a gun. Plant it in one of the vats if you can." She paused. "We may not be able to wait until day after tomorrow. Boch keeps pushing to empty the vats and to hell with the consequences. It's Sanborne who's hesitating. But it's purely business with him, and if Boch convinces him that they can still make the deal with a big percentage of casualties, then he'll do it."

"Damn right," Royd murmured.

She didn't speak for another moment. "I spoke to Michael last night." Her words came haltingly. "And the man who came on the line wasn't Jock. I'd recognize his voice even if he was faking that Brooklyn accent. It . . . frightened me. I'm trying to work my way through it. That's all for now. I'll get back to you if anything happens."

Royd cursed softly and vehemently.

"She's going to destroy those records?" Kelly said. "I thought she was there just to locate them."

"That was my plan, it's evidently never been hers. I should have known that if she found the records she'd feel duty-bound to do the job herself. She'd reason it was her work that did the damage and it was her job to rid the world of it."

"And she's not trusting you to do it."

"No, she's not trusting me." He got up and headed for the door. "Not at all."

Boch was with Sanborne on the porch when Sophie came back that evening. There was evident tension between them in spite of Sanborne's clear attempt to hide it.

"Good evening, Sophie." Sanborne smiled.

"I hope you have good news for me. My friend here is being distinctly skeptical about your ability to pull our fat out of the proverbial fire."

"I'm not there yet. I want you to bring the other vats from the **Constanza** for me to examine."

"Why?" Boch asked coldly.

"I discovered traces of an unknown element in the vats in the treatment plant. I want to make sure that it comes from the vat itself and not some added ingredient Gorshank put in these particular containers."

"It's a waste of time," Boch said. "She's stalling, Sanborne."

"Perhaps." He studied Sophie's face. "It could be that I'm relying too much on the maternal instinct."

"I need those vats." She didn't have to fake the desperation in her voice. That subtle threat in Sanborne's words sent a ripple of panic through her. "You're tying my hands if you don't let me examine them."

"Heaven forbid." Sanborne hesitated. "Of course we'll bring you the vats." He turned to Boch. "We'll bring them to the plant tonight. It's what you wanted anyway, wasn't it?"

Boch's gaze flew to Sanborne's face. "You're going to do it?"

"I'm not a stubborn man. We'll compromise. We pour the vats into the water supply tonight after she takes her samples. Then we allow her a few more days to come up with a solution to Gorshank's blunders. If REM-4 causes a disturbing number of deaths during the next few days then we produce our Sophie as the answer to our client's problem."

"No," Sophie said sharply. "There's no need to empty those vats. Give me a little time and I'll make sure REM-4 is safe."

"Boch believes we've run out of time," Sanborne said. "He has no faith in you. Can you imagine that?"

"No." Her hands clenched into fists at her sides. "You have my son. I can't imagine anyone believing I wouldn't do everything in my power to give you whatever you want."

"Don't listen to her," Boch said. "It doesn't matter any longer. You agreed, Sanborne."

"So I did." He turned back to Sophie. "Go back to the treatment plant. You'll have your vats."

"No," she whispered. "Don't do it."

"But I didn't do it, you did. You didn't bring me the results I needed. I told you

Boch was in a hurry. It's your blame, not mine."

Her blame. For an instant she was stricken and then the rage burned it away. "The hell it is. You son of a bitch. What would it hurt you to wait?"

"Don't be nasty. I don't like it." He turned to Boch. "Send some men out to the ship to get the vats. How many are left on the **Constanza**?"

"Eight." Boch was hurrying down the path. "They'll be here within two hours."

"Excellent." He watched Boch for a moment before turning to Sophie. "You'd better hope that Boch's client objects to the potency of REM-4. Otherwise I'll have no use at all for your services. I'm becoming a trifle annoyed with your arrogance." He started into the house. "And I wouldn't talk to Boch as you have to me when he brings those vats to you. He's an emotional man and he might take measures that would prove unpleasantly fatal for you. After that of course I'd have to make a call to Franks and have him kill the boy. I'd have no need of him then."

She stared after him, filled with rage and frustration. Why couldn't the bastard have waited one more day before he caved to Boch? Two hours . . .

She wheeled and ran down the steps and strode along the path toward the treatment plant. Two hours. She couldn't let it happen. They had to stop it. She distanced herself from the guard by several yards and pressed the wire. She tried to keep her voice low.

"You can't wait. The vats are being emptied in two hours. We have to move tonight. I'll be at the treatment plant." The guard had almost caught up with her and she didn't dare say anything more.

Oh, my God. Two hours . . .

19

Get your samples." Boch was watching his men set the vats on the edge of the tank. "I'll give you twenty minutes."

"How generous." She grabbed the tray with the empty vials and moved toward the row of eight vats that had just been brought from the ship. Which one had the weapon she'd asked Royd to plant? And what if none of them did? What if Royd had not been able to get to the ship in the short time since she'd communicated with him this morning? How the hell did she even know if that damn wire had been functional?

Trust him. Royd had gotten the wire to her against all odds. He would have made sure the wire worked. And he wouldn't have taken a chance and waited to plant the weapon.

I'd die for you.

For God's sake, stop questioning every move Royd made. She would not have trusted her son to him if her instincts had not told her that Michael would be safe with him. Yet she had done nothing but worry and suspect him since she'd arrived on the island. Royd wouldn't leave her alone to stop this madness. Royd would be here because he'd said he'd be here.

Trust him.

She had reached the vats. She approached the first one and lifted the lid and filled the vial.

Nothing in the tank.

She placed the vial in the tray and moved to the next vat. Move slowly, take your time.

No weapon.

She went to the third vat. Filled the vial. No weapon.

At the fifth vat she caught sight of the weapon as soon as she lifted the lid. It was in a black waterproof bag fastened to the side of the tank. Relief poured through her.

She shifted a little so that she stood between the tank and Boch. Thank God, he was paying no attention to her. He was shouting orders to the workers about the positioning of the other vats. She filled the vial, then plucked out the weapon and dropped it on the concrete floor between the vats. She set her plastic container with the other vials beside it and moved down the row.

"Hurry," Boch called to her. "We're ready to go."

"Two more vats." She quickly filled the two vials and went back to the plastic tray. She knelt down, put the vials in the container, scooped up the weapon, and threw it beneath the vial tray. "Done." She stood up and headed for the door. "I'll take them back to the lab."

"Wait."

She stiffened and looked over her shoulder.

Boch was smiling maliciously. "Don't run away. I want you to watch me pour the REM-4 into the supply."

"Because you know I don't want you to do it?"

"Maybe. I think you've been stalling. You've caused us a great deal of trouble. Sanborne bungled your handling. He should have left it to me."

"Believe me, Sanborne was sufficiently sadistic to please even you."

"Stand there and watch." He turned back to

the men beside the vats. "One at a time. First vat."

"Don't do it," she whispered.

"First vat."

The men tipped the vat and the liquid poured into the holding tank.

Boch called, "Second vat."

She slipped her hand into the vial tray and took the pistol out of the plastic bag.

"Third vat."

She took the gun out of the tray.

"Boch."

He glanced at her.

She shot him between the eyes.

The look of surprise froze on his face as he crumpled to the floor.

She whirled and tore out of the installation.

There was an uproar behind her.

And there was a guard directly in front of her as she raced for the gate. He started running toward her.

She raised the gun again.

The guard fell to the ground.

Knife. There was a knife in his back.

"Come on." Royd was grabbing her arm. "They'll be pouring out of there any minute." He was half-carrying her out the gate. "Boch's men are going to be confused but that won't stop their training from kicking in."

"I killed him," she gasped as they ran up the hill. "Boch was pouring the vats into the water supply and I shot him. I shot him. . . ."

"I know. I saw it." He pulled her down the hill on the other side. "I took out the first guard and was able to get to the window on the far side. Why the hell couldn't you just walk out of there? He'd already contaminated the water supply after the first vat went in the water."

"Maybe not enough to hurt anyone. I couldn't be sure. I had to stop him."

"So you made sure all hell would break loose."

She could hear shouts behind her.

Panic swept through her.

"Move!" Royd jerked her toward a clump of trees a hundred yards away.

"I am moving. And we can't hide in that sparse bit of shrubbery. It's too—"

"Shut up." He pushed her to the ground as they reached the trees. He reached into his jacket pocket and was pulling out something. "We're about to have a distraction."

Distraction. What did he mean by—

The ground shook as an explosion rocked the earth!

Fire turned the night sky scarlet beyond the hill.

"The treatment plant," she whispered. "You blew up the treatment plant."

"It was the only way to make sure that no REM-4 remained. You knew it was probably going to happen." He stuffed the remote back in his pocket. "I told you I was going to wipe it from the face of the earth." He got to his feet. "Come on. I have to get you to the beach on the other side of the island. MacDuff's men should be at the plant doing a cleanup operation. Kelly is waiting to take you to the launch."

"No."

"Yes." He looked down at her. "You've done enough. Let us do the rest."

"Sanborne. He's at the house. He has my files in that safe. **My** files."

"I'll get them for you."

"My files, my work, my responsibility." She started at a trot in the direction of the house at the top of the hill. "And I have to move fast. He must have heard that explosion. He'll guess what's happening and he'll grab those files and get out. He probably has an escape route planned."

"Sophie, trust me."

"I do trust you. For a while, I didn't. You were right, I have a problem with trust. But I decided if I believed in myself and my own instincts, I had to believe in you." Her pace increased. "Trust has nothing to do with this."

He muttered a curse. "Okay. Then, dammit, we'll do it together. You don't have to try to take care of everything yourself. You've already cheated me of Boch. If you'll remember, I have a vested interest in ridding the world of Sanborne."

How could she forget? She nodded.

"And I call the shots. Or so help me you'll have to shoot me to keep me from decking you." He stared her directly in the eyes. "And you know I'll do it."

"Yes."

The house was only a few hundred yards away. No guards in view. That didn't mean there wouldn't be guards inside, she thought. "Sanborne has two bodyguards that are always with him. I don't see them."

"Can we get to the library from the back of the house?"

"Yes, there's a veranda that opens off the library." She headed around the corner of the house. "There aren't any guards. Where are they?"

"You said he only had two bodyguards?"

"He probably thought he didn't need any

more with all the potential slave labor here on the island." She nodded at the French doors. "That's the library."

"No lights. Will you stay here while I check it out?"

"No."

"Screw it." He glided toward the door. "Then keep in back of me." He kept to one side, reached over, and threw open the French door.

No shots.

He dove in and rolled to the side.

She followed.

No shots.

He lit a flashlight and shone the beam around the room. Vacant. No sound in the room. No sound in the entire house.

"He may have run down to the treatment plant when he heard the explosion," she said.

"I don't think he'd do that. He wouldn't take the chance with his valuable hide. He'd run away to fight another day." He got to his knees. "And that means you're right and he's probably taken off with the REM-4 disks."

"How?"

"Air or boat." He headed for the door. "No sound of a helicopter. I'd bet he headed for the pier and his launch." He was moving at a dead run by the time he reached the veranda.

* * *

Sanborne was getting in the launch at the end of the long pier when they reached the dock. One of his guards had just started the engine.

"Damn," Royd muttered, his hand tightening on the gun. "That pier's too long. We're still out of range. We've got to get closer." He put on speed.

"Dear Sophie," Sanborne called as the launch started to pull away. "I was hoping for a chance to see your face to tell you that your son is now suffering a slow, agonizing death. I made the call when I saw the treatment plant blow."

"He's not dead," Sophie said. "You've been had, Sanborne."

"I don't believe you."

Surely they were almost close enough.

"It's true."

"Then I'll have to make sure that you never see him again." Sanborne nodded at the guard beside him. "Shoot her, Kirk."

The man raised a rifle.

Oh, God, a rifle would have the range that their guns did not.

"No!" Royd moved in front of her and knocked her to the ground. He lifted his gun as he dove sideways and fired.

But the rifle fired at the same time.

The thunk of a bullet against flesh.

Royd's flesh, she realized in panic.

His knees buckled and he was falling.

Blood. Blood pouring out of his chest. His eyes were closing.

"Royd!"

Another shot. The bullet splintered the wood of the pier next to her. She instinctively threw herself on Royd, covering his body with her own. She lifted her gun and started to aim.

And then let it drop.

Sanborne was slumped forward in the boat. The top of his head was blown off. The man he'd called Kirk had dropped his rifle when he realized that Sanborne had been hit and was bending over him.

"Did I . . . get . . . him?" Royd's eyes were open and he was looking up at her.

"Yes." The tears were pouring down her cheeks. "Shut up. Don't talk." She was tearing his shirt open. "Why did you do it?" Her voice was unsteady. "You shouldn't have done it, dammit."

"Yes . . . I . . . should." His eyes were closing again. "Couldn't do anything . . . else. Told . . . you."

I'd die for you.

"Don't you dare die. I won't have it. Do you hear me? I didn't ask you to act like some damn hero." Jesus, the wound was in the upper chest. Don't panic. She was a doctor. Act like one and take care of him. "You hold on. I won't have it any other way. You've always told me that I was paranoid for heaping blame on myself. Do you want me to spend the rest of my life reliving this?"

"Wouldn't . . . think of it."

"Then be still while I stop this blood and get you stable."

"Never been stable. Not my modus . . . operandi."

"You're about to change." She took out her phone and dialed MacDuff. "We're at the pier. Royd's been shot."

"I'll get help to you right away."

"Good." She hung up. "Now I'm going to check to see if that bullet's still in you or if it passed through. It's going to hurt."

He didn't answer.

He was unconscious.

"Sophie."

She looked up to see MacDuff and Campbell standing over her. "You took too long."

Her arms tightened around Royd. "He could have died."

"Ten minutes." MacDuff knelt beside her. "We came as quick as we could. How is he?"

"Shock. Loss of blood." She shook her head. "I don't know what else. I've done all I can. We need to get him to a hospital." She carefully took her arms from around Royd and sat up. God, she didn't want to let him go. She had the totally unreasonable feeling that as long as she was holding him he wouldn't slip away from her. "He's been unconscious since I phoned you."

"I called for a helicopter right away. They should be here soon." He said to Campbell, "Go watch for it. I told them to land at the house."

"Right." Campbell turned and trotted down the pier.

MacDuff turned back to Sophie. "Are you okay? Is that his blood on you?"

"Yes." She looked dully down at her blood-stained shirt. "I'm not hurt. He took the bullet for me."

"Sanborne?"

"Dead. Royd shot him. I don't know where he is. He was on a launch with two of his body-guards. . . ." Her voice was trembling and she tried to steady it. "You've got to find him. He had the REM-4 disks with him. I have to have them. They'll always be a threat. . . ."

"We'll find him." He reached out and squeezed her shoulder. "It's going to be okay, Sophie."

She closed her eyes. Empty words when Royd lay here fighting for his life. No, they were both fighting. She wouldn't let him die. He had to live or she didn't know if she could survive.

Christ, how selfish could she be? He deserved to live long and happily and it didn't matter about her. The phrase repeated over and over in her mind like a mantra. He had to live. He had to live. He had to live.

"Sophie," MacDuff said gently. "I think I hear the helicopter."

Her eyes opened. She heard it too. Hope surged through her. Her hand tightened around Royd's. "Then let's get him out of here."

An hour later they arrived at Santo Domenico Hospital in Caracas. Only a minute later Royd was whisked away from Sophie and taken into surgery.

"Are you okay?" MacDuff studied her expression. "He's stayed alive this long, Sophie. That's a good sign."

"It could go either way," Sophie said. "I appreciate you trying to comfort me, but I know that. But at least he was able to get a transfusion on that helicopter. That ups the odds."

"Let me take you to the waiting room and get you a cup of coffee."

She didn't want to go to the waiting room. She wanted to barge into that operating room and watch what they were doing to Royd. She wanted to **help**, dammit.

She drew a deep breath. "In a minute. I have to go outside and use my cell phone." She headed toward the emergency-room doors. "I was going to call Michael anyway. I may as well keep busy." She glanced over her shoulder. "Royd told me he was with Jock. Is that still the case?"

He nodded. "At the lake cottage outside Atlanta."

Her lips twisted. "He must be a great actor. I didn't recognize his voice, but evidently Sanborne thought he was Franks. It scared me for a little while."

"Jock is very good at whatever he does." MacDuff opened the glass door for her. "But he wouldn't risk imitating Franks's voice without a little technical aid."

"What?"

"He played cat and mouse with Franks for a day and a half before he took him out. He let him get close and then scampered away."

She frowned. "I don't understand."

"Jock needed to get a good voice recording of Franks talking to his men, talking to Sanborne on the phone, just talking. Then he and Joe Quinn took the disk to an expert at the local field office of the FBI. Quinn used to be an FBI man and he still has contacts. They had a device made to attach to the phone Jock took from Franks." He smiled. "Voilà, Jock's voice became Franks's. He fooled Sanborne very neatly."

"And terrified me."

MacDuff's smile faded. "I'm surprised Royd didn't tell you what was happening."

"He told me. In broad strokes. No details. And when I heard what I thought was Franks's voice, I was already on the island." She shrugged. "It was too late to question him. I just had to decide if I really trusted him."

"And did you?"

"After a hell of a lot of soul-searching. It wasn't easy." She leaned wearily back against the wall. "Nothing about Royd is easy." But, dear God, she wanted that difficult, rough bastard to live. "I had to operate on instinct."

"And maybe something else?" MacDuff didn't wait for an answer. "Make your call. I'll go get you a cup of coffee. Black?"

She nodded and he disappeared back into the hospital.

Something else? Liking? Perhaps . . . love? Her hand tightened on the phone. Passion, closeness, admiration; she knew she felt all of those things for Royd. And now she had to accept this terrible emptiness and panic she felt when she had thought she'd lost him.

She might still lose him. The tears stung her eyes. She had to hold on. Keep busy. She dialed Jock's number.

Jock answered on the third ring. "I don't believe you want to talk to me, Sophie. I have a young man here who's about to snatch the phone away from me."

"Wasn't I good, Mom?" Michael came eagerly on the line. "Jock said I had to pretend so that you'd be safe."

"Very good, baby. How are you?"

"Fine. It's pretty here on the lake. Jane has a dog called Toby who's half wolf and he's really cool. And Jane's teaching me to play poker."

"Any episodes?"

"One." He rushed on. "Jock said that you're safe now because you beat the bad guys. When are you coming to get me?"

"As soon as I can. I have one more thing to do here. Let me talk to Jock again. I love you."

"Me, too."

"He's fine, Sophie," Jock said when he came on the line. "One episode and it was a mild one. He's been great."

"Where did he get the bruises?"

"Jane."

"What?"

"Eye shadow. She used it to make him look a bit abused." He paused. "How's Royd?"

"We don't know yet. We're at the hospital waiting to hear." She swallowed hard. "I'll be there to pick up Michael as soon as I can, but I don't want to leave Royd yet."

"No problem. Jane and he are getting along famously, and now that he knows you're okay he'll be happier."

"It sounds like he's pretty content right now. Poker?"

"Every lad should be adept at games of chance." Jock's tone became grave. "I wish I could have been with you on San Torrano.

Maybe things would have been different for Royd."

"Probably not."

"Now, you've hurt my feelings. You mean you don't believe I'm a man who can move mountains?"

"I believe you're my friend who kept my son safe when he could have been hurt or killed. That's a pretty big mountain right there."

"Worthwhile, but not dashing or exciting." He gave a mock sigh. "But I'll continue being steady and worthwhile until you relieve me. Call me when you have news. Good-bye, Sophie." He hung up.

She pressed the disconnect and drew a deep breath. At least everything was all right with Michael.

"How is your son?"

She turned to see MacDuff standing a short distance away. "He's fine. He's learning to play poker and Jane's dog is keeping him entertained."

"Toby?" He handed her the coffee. "I hear he's quite an animal. She's crazy about him."

"I'd think you'd know from firsthand experience. You're such good friends."

"Our relationship is a bit . . . difficult. I've never been invited to the lake cottage."

"I could wish that it hadn't been necessary for Michael to stay there." A sudden thought occurred to her. "I may have trouble getting to Michael. Just because Boch and Sanborne are dead doesn't mean that everything's okay. I'm still wanted by the police for Dave's death."

"Maybe not for long. I persuaded the CIA to send their own forensic team to investigate the crime scene. Even if Devlin planted your DNA there's a chance he left a bit of his own. It may take a while to do it but the CIA will persevere. They're very grateful that we managed to rid them of a potential headache in REM-4." He took her arm. "Let's get you inside. It's getting a little chilly."

The sharp, cold air, free of the smell of antiseptics, felt good to her. But she should go to the waiting room to be available when the doctors got through with surgery. Someone would come and tell her—

She stopped as panic knifed through her. He wasn't going to die. He'd make it through the surgery. When the doctors came to the waiting room, they would tell her Royd was going to get well.

She nodded jerkily and started for the glass doors. "You're right. We'll go inside. We should be hearing soon. . . ."

* * *

"Are . . . you waiting . . . for my last words?" Royd asked hoarsely.

He was stirring!

Sophie tensed and sat bolt upright in the chair beside the bed. "You shouldn't talk. Do you want anything?"

"Oh, yes. I have an entire list." He closed his eyes. "But if I'm dying I'll . . . have to get my . . . priorities in order."

"You're not dying. Not now." She held a glass of crushed ice to his lips. "Take a little and let it melt in your mouth."

He obeyed. "REM-4. Did you get . . . the files back?"

She nodded. "MacDuff managed to locate the launch by helicopter. Sanborne's briefcase held all the REM-4 material."

"What did you do with them?"

"Burned them. Every single document."

"Good. When can I get out . . . of here?"

"A month, maybe longer."

"How long have I been here?"

"Two days." Two long, terrible days when she had watched him lie here and doubted every minute that he'd wake out of that drugged sleep. "But last night you took a turn for the better and I knew you'd live."

"Michael?"

"He's fine. He's still in Atlanta."

His eyes opened. "Then why . . . are you here?"

Because during those hideous hours she hadn't known if she could survive if Royd died. Because doubt about her feelings for him had become agonized certainty. "I told you, he's fine. He didn't need me."

His lips twisted. "And you had to do your duty."

"Shut up." Her voice was shaking. "I'm trying to be compassionate and I can't slug you in your condition. But I'll store it all up for the time when you walk out of this hospital."

"Tell me, why are you gentle with everyone but me?"

"I was gentle . . . when you were unconscious."

"And you thought I was dying. Next time you might let me appreciate that side of you when I'm awake." He closed his eyes. "I'm going to sleep now. I need to get well damn quick. We have a hell of a lot to settle between us and I'm going . . . to need all the strength . . . I can get."

"Yes, go to sleep. You need it."

He was silent a moment. "Why did you stay with me instead of going to Michael?"

"You needed me."

"And?"

"You saved my life."

"And?"

"Go to sleep," she said unsteadily. "You're not getting anything else from me."

"Yes, I will. You just wait. . . ."

His breathing was slowing as he drifted off to sleep.

A hell of a lot to settle, he'd said. Royd had been pushing, exploring, even as he fought for strength. How could they settle anything? They were both casualties, survivors, of the horror visited on them by Sanborne and Boch. She couldn't think logically or clearly. She was so tired that she could barely think at all.

But she could feel. Oh, yes, she could feel.

She reached out and gently stroked the hair back from his face. It felt good to touch him and feel the life and vitality that was returning. He'd come so close. . . .

He opened his eyes. "Caught you," he whispered.

She blinked back the tears. "You were playing possum."

"A man has to do what a man has to do." He turned his face to touch his cheek to her hand. He closed his eyes again. "Don't stop. . . ."

"I won't." Her palm stroked the hard plane of his cheek. "You couldn't make me stop. . . ."

EPILOGUE

MacDuff's Run
Six months later

S ophie."
He was coming!

She turned away from the sea to watch Royd striding down the path. He was moving fast, impatiently, his expression intent. Her heart was beating so hard that she couldn't speak for a moment. "You're looking very well." She had to steady her voice. "How do you feel?"

"Mad as hell. I woke up the next morning in that damn hospital and they told me you'd left the country. Why?"

"I realized I couldn't stay."

"Michael."

"That was one reason. He needed me more than you did."

"The devil he did." He paused. "How is he?"

"Doing well. He's only had two episodes in the past month. I think he's turned a corner."

"Great. Now, what was the other reason you left me?"

"The other reason was more personal. I was confused and I needed time to sort myself out."

"Without me."

"Without you. I have trouble thinking clearly when you're around."

"Good."

She met his gaze. "You needed the time too. You deserved a breathing space. You deserved the chance to walk away from me and forget I existed. Forget every bad thing I brought on you existed."

"You brought a hell of a lot of good things into my life too. How long is it going to take me to convince you we're even?" He didn't wait for an answer. "So you got MacDuff to bring you and Michael here and tell me to stay away from you."

"Until I was ready for you." She smiled. "I had a few other things to do after I was cleared. Jane MacGuire and I managed to raise a good portion of the money needed to rebuild that water-treatment plant at San Torrano. She's quite a woman."

"So I hear." He was silent. "You know, I almost organized a commando raid to bombard this place."

"But you didn't."

"I was going to give you another month to issue an invitation." He grimaced. "Maybe I'm getting civilized after all."

"No way. But you're smart and you know that I was right to do this."

"Right for you. I didn't need the time. I knew what I wanted." He took at step closer. "Am I going to get it?"

"And what do you want? Sex?"

"Yes. And you talking to me and letting me get to know you. And the two of us living together and doing stuff like going to the movies and grocery shopping and to Michael's soccer games."

"Michael. You do realize it would be a package deal?"

"I'm not an idiot. We'll work it out. He's part of you." He was only a foot away from her. "Just like I'm going to be part of you. With every breath you take, everything you do. Does that scare you?"

"Does it scare you?"

"It did when I first realized what I was feeling for you. Now I'm used to it." He drew a deep breath. "I . . . love . . . you." He shook his head. "God, that was hard to say. I hope it was worth it."

Joy soared through her. "Oh, it was worth it."

"You don't have to say it back. Love means different things to different people. You have to get used to me. After our first year together, we'll talk about it."

"How generous of you." She cupped her hands lovingly around his face and smiled up at him luminously. "But I believe we'll talk about it right now."

LIKE WHAT YOU'VE SEEN?

If you enjoyed this large print edition of **Killer Dreams**, here are a few of Iris Johansen's latest bestsellers available from Random House Large Print.

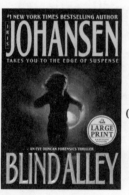